D1174495

Gillian

FRANK YERBY

Gillian

The Dial Press • 1960 • New York

DESIGNED BY WILLIAM R. MEINHARDT

MANUFACTURED IN THE UNITED STATES OF AMERICA

BY THE HADDON CRAFTSMEN, SCRANTON, PENNA.

CAST OF CHARACTERS

GILLIAN MACALLISTER: The lovely blonde who causes everything in this book to move.

MICHAEL AMES: Her husband.

HERO FARNSWORTH: An exotically beautiful young widow who did not know how exciting she was.

GREGORY LYNNE: A young man in trouble, the brother of

GEOFFRY LYNNE: The narrator of this story, which includes:

HEDDY MACALLISTER: Gillian's mother.

HENRY MACALLISTER: Gillian's father.

BARTON and DOROTHY BYRCE: A young couple whose domestic felicity left something to be desired.

WILLIAM RIKER: An old Iron and Steel man.

FRED KLOVAC: A private detective.

BIG JOHN KLOVAC: His brother

and

A girl named Hilda, a girl named Anna, a prince called Cesari, a steel-mill owner named Franz Schuler, a black woman called Buleah, a chauffeur called Tim, and others of lesser consequence.

Gillian

PROLOGUE

The Moving Finger writes; and, having writ,
Moves on: nor all your Piety nor Wit
    Shall lure it back to cancel half a Line,
Nor all your Tears wash out a Word of it. . . .

So wrote Omar, called the Tentmaker. Or at least so Fitzgerald said he did; having no Persian, I cannot know. There
is some dispute among scholars as to how much of The
Rubáiyát, as we know it, is translation, and how much par-
aphrase. Some cynics insist it is much Fitzgerald and little
Omar. Which does not matter. Those words are true.

But when the finger does not write? When what remains is silence? Should I break that stillness? Fix in time,
in space, a tale that even I know is better far forgot? Expose
to the eyes of strangers that death in life the three I loved
best of all the world suffered because of Gillian?

What excuse have I to reveal it now, after so many,
many years? Certainly not to take vengeance upon Gillian
MacAllister. She is beyond the reach of any man's vengeance.
So are all the others, except Hero Ames—and she has urged
me to set it down. Nor even to vindicate my brother's memory. To do that I should have—at least in part—to lie. And
the only justification a tale like this can have is to catch the
mortal agony of truth.

So, no excuses, then—not even the petty one of vanity. For I am very old, and death is already in me. I shall never see what success or failure this shall have; and I care not a jot for either. I have had both with my own works, and survived both.

My reasons are—a writer's reasons: That life and tragedy are sufficient unto themselves; that though there is no answer to the question of evil, the question must be forever put, the answer forever sought. That a history so charged with the bitter wine of truth should not be allowed to die with its authors.

That plural is correct, for it will not be I who pens this strange, eventful history. It was told to me. I took it down —all but the few parts in which I played a distinctly minor role. What I do now is but to recopy it from the pages of a notebook nearly thirty years old, adding nothing, shaping letter by letter this tale of a modern Electra more cruel than the one that old Euripides dreamt, this ancient theme, complete with chorus, strophe and antistrophe, lacking only the god from the machine.

Absent, despite our bitter need, from life, as the savior gods forever are. No deity took pity upon my brother's anguish, upon Michael's, Hero's—or on mine. We suffered and endured, fought the fight, perhaps even won. But not without scars. And the cruelest of those scars is memory.

So now, if you like, let us begin.

Geoffry Lynne
Birmingham, Alabama
April 2, 1932

1

GEOFFRY LYNNE

My Homecoming

Birmingham, Alabama, October, 1908

To come home again is strange. And the truth of the matter is—you can't. Not really, not after eighteen years. Because, if you are at all like me, you have given yourself away bit by bit in a hundred cities, worn away your illusions in many a casual bed, played the prodigal, sold your youth, your talent over half the world—and for what? A mess of pottage, a handful of gold, a little uneasy fame. . . .

I was thinking like that on the last leg of my homeward journey from London to Birmingham, Alabama. Wondering why, though I was now quite successful, even moderately rich, I was still afraid to come home. Which made no sense, but there it was. I remembered how it all started, eighteen years ago, seeing it as I see everything, a scene. Myself, the fledgling Raphael—for I hadn't even sense enough to realize that my true talents lay in the scribbler's pen rather than in the dauber's brush—shakily trying to get up nerve enough to tell my bearded patriarch of a father that I wanted to go abroad. That I was determined to leave the city and the

5

region whose crudity, violence, and cultural barrenness I detested. That I wanted to wear a flowing tie and cape, and stride the narrow streets of Montmartre, brush and pallet in hand. That—but I was not fool enough to tell my father the dreams I had of amorous adventures with lovely models content to shiver and starve in garrets with me, warmed only by my great genius. . . .

I could picture beforehand the stormy scene when I presented my demand to be freed from a future of molten iron, sulphurous smells, sweaty workers, intolerable heat, and people whose vocabularies consisted entirely of such terms as ingots, pigs, heats, puddling, open hearths, bessemers, blasts, and slag. It is a measure of my temperament that I, having spent the first twenty years of my life in a city where the making of iron and steel is a religion, and whose god is truly that iron Vulcan who lies rusting now in the city park, cannot, with any degree of accuracy, tell you what those terms mean.

It took me several days to get up my courage; but, finally, I went. My father listened to me gravely, then turned to my brother, Greg, with a quizzical smile.

"Shall we let him go, boy?" he said. "God knows he's not worth a tinker's damn around here. . . ."

"Sure," Greg laughed; "maybe he can paint pictures. There must be *something* he can do. . . ."

So ended my stormy scene. And so, curiously, ended one of my identities; for we grow year by year into vastly different beings, as time wears our bodies down into trembling wreckage and erodes our egos into that painful humility that men call the wisdom of age. What they mean is the defeat of age; but calling things by their right names is deuced bad form. Jeff Lynne, student, young man about town, ended then and there.

Nor did G. Lynne, painter, last very long. Oh, I worked at painting for a year, dabbled and played at it for four more; but I had already begun to write. And, by 1896, with Hero Farnsworth's involuntary aid, because of her gallant living of the plot of my *Episode in Florence*, I was already famous—or perhaps infamous would be the better word.

I wondered what she was like now. And if I dared face her. For I still had her letter tucked away among my notebooks. And a phrase from it was branded upon my brain:

"You swine. Didn't you know, or care, that it is precisely the truth which is unpardonable?"

For I had told the truth in that one. The naked, bitter truth. And, by so doing, lifted myself from the hack—who slaved away winters in London, turning out penny dreadfuls and shilling shockers by the ream so that he could afford some rare, glorious summers in Paris and Rome—into a writer. There are worse professions. And having carved myself a small but distinctly respectable niche in the world of letters, I could not slip back again.

The closer I got to Birmingham, the deeper my mood of near terror became. I don't know why I was afraid. Call it a premonition. Call it superstition. But I had a sudden, completely irrational impulse to take the very next train out of Birmingham as soon as I should get there. And, I thought, if Greg isn't there to meet me, I'll do just that!

But he was there, as I had known he would be. I've lived all my life in the tranquil assurance of knowing what Greg would do next: the right, the decent, the steady thing. And he, in his turn, has always known that I would pile one unconventional, outrageous, scandalous action upon the next. That kind of knowledge is a comfortable thing.

Yes—Greg met me at the station.

And knocked my comfortable belief that I knew him, that he had no hidden depths, finally and completely to hell.

His behavior was so radically different from anything I had expected that it shocked me to the core. I had expected him to be overjoyed at my coming; from the moment that the train rolled into the smoke-filled hollow of Jones Valley and I saw the angry glow of the Sloss—Sheffield furnaces turning the eternal, man-made clouds above Birmingham a dirty orange, I had played over in my mind a thousand variations upon the theme of how, upon my long-delayed homecoming after eighteen years of literary vagabondage in Europe, my brother would receive me.

I hurled my valise to a grinning redcap before the train stopped moving; leaped down, went rushing toward Greg with my arms outstretched. But a yard away from him, I stopped. His face stopped me. His eyes.

He came toward me like a marionette, the strings controlling that jerky stride almost visible in the smoky air above him. Took my hand in a hand that felt like ice, shook it limply. Said, in a voice as colorless as his face:

" 'Lo, Jeff, boy; glad you're back."

That was all. I'll be damned if I can understand it. All day, I've had the uneasy feeling that something is radically, terribly wrong. I haven't seen Greg since he left for the office. I've told you he is dark, but there is a ruddy glow under his tan—usually. This morning, his face was slate gray, except. . . .

That was the strangest thing of all. Coming from the station this morning in a hack, an idiot in another of those diabolical evidences of hideous modernity, an automobile, frightened even our poor nag into fits by squeezing remorselessly upon the rubber bulb of his horn. I put my head out to give him a choice example of the vocabulary I had acquired while wandering among London's underworld in pursuit of material for a series of detective tales I was doing, when something about the man, himself, stopped me. I realized, in that precise instant, that I knew him; that I was looking into a face I had seen before, perhaps half a world away. But his name, the place, and the circumstances under which I had met him, would not come back to me. It was a maddening thing: My certainty that I knew this individual was absolute; equally so my conviction that his presence here in Birmingham, Alabama, his being clad in a chauffeur's uniform, and driving a snorting monstrosity of gleaming brass rods, polished black tonneau, and blinding acetylene lamps, were abnormalities; more, that his present occupation and its livery were the *reasons* I could not call his name and former habitat to mind.

When I mentioned my puzzlement to Greg, even the gray left his face, leaving him white as death. But he recovered admirably.

"He's Gillian's chauffeur," he said. "Name's Nelson—Tim Nelson. When she and Michael came back from their honeymoon abroad, she brought with her a full staff of British and European servants for the house, most of them ex-jailbirds from their looks. . . ."

I considered that. The name, Tim Nelson, evoked no memory. In an Englishman, it was very nearly as meaningless as "John Smith" would have been. But the word "ex-jailbirds" registered. Was this Nelson—probably an alias anyhow—one of the spivs, thugs, pimps, blackmailers, and thieves to whom I'd talked in London while doing that research for my *Black Cat* series of mysteries?

No. Because then I should have surely remembered him. I had never talked to Gillian's new chauffeur before. And yet—and yet. . . .

"Must have shocked the old burg no end," I ventured.

"Did. Especially since she turned the colored help out

with no provisions whatsoever made to compensate them for losing their jobs. . . ."

"That's Gilly," I said. "By the way, Greg, how is she?"

He turned away from me abruptly without answering my question.

"Be seeing you," he said. "Lynne Steel still has an office, you know. . . ."

And with those words he left me, striding from the room without even saying good-by.

I have just had a terrible shock. While I was consigning the above few lines to my journal, the telephone had been ringing for some minutes. I ignored it, rightly considering that ignoble clangor to be the concern of the servants. But no one came, and finally, my protesting nerves forced me to answer it.

Hero Farnsworth's voice came over the wire, shrill and edged with something like—terror.

"Greg!" she gasped. "You must come! You must! They— They've arrested Michael!"

"Arrested Michael?" I said, not troubling to identify myself, knowing that neither Hero nor anyone else could distinguish me from Greg by my voice. "Good Lord! What on earth for, Hero?"

Her voice came from a thousand miles away, quiet and still, miraculously controlled once more.

"They found Gillian dead this morning," she said flatly. "Murdered, Greg. Naturally, under the circumstances, they think Michael did it."

I hadn't the faintest idea what the circumstances were; so I said, realizing a heartbeat after I had spoken that my Briticisms had given me away.

"Hold on, old dear. I'll pop right over. By the way, where are you?"

There was a silence; then Hero said:

"You're not Greg. Jeff! Of course, you're Jeff! When did you come back?"

"This morning. I must say I didn't know what I was getting into. Rum show, eh, old girl? Where are you, and what do you want me to do?"

"I'm at home," Hero whispered. "I want you to call Greg. Then come over, both of you. And"—there was a flash of bitter fire in her voice—"I want your promise that you won't write about *this*, too. . . ."

I knew she was thinking of my *Episode in Florence*, for I had changed even the locale in order to disguise things better. I was aware that I had wronged her cruelly by writing that story at all; so I said gently:

"Forgive me for that, won't you? Of course I promise. Now ring off like a good girl so I can call Greg. . . ."

I had some difficulty getting through to my brother's office. The telephone is still a long way short of perfection. But I reached him finally, having gotten three wrong numbers and worn my arm out cranking that balky device; and never in my life have I heard a silence as blank and utter as that which greeted my announcement of poor Gilly's death.

"Greg!" I said. "Are you there, old boy? Hero wants us to—"

"I know," he said; and his voice was but a variation of that silence. "Wait where you are, Jeff. I'll be home at once."

He must have borrowed the flying machine of those Dayton bicycle makers—when will people let well enough alone? Nothing else could have brought him home with such dispatch. The gray was gone from his face, and his natural color had returned. But his eyes—

I once wrote a murder tale in which the victim, a mute, died with his eyes screaming. This, I was sure, was but an extreme example of my unfortunate weakness for the purple phrase. But that was exactly what Greg's eyes were doing now: screaming silently in intolerable agony.

"Greg—" I whispered.

"Come," he said, "I've ordered the fly brought around. You drive. I'm not up to it. And Jeff—"

"Yes, Greg?"

"Drop me off at the police station. Then go to Hero and tell her not to worry."

"The police station?" I got out.

"Yes, boy," my brother said. "To give myself up. You see, Jeff—I killed her."

2

GEOFFRY LYNNE

Pages from my 1908 Notebooks

I have just returned from visiting Greg again. The trial is set for two weeks from today. This is unusual; I am sure that Judge Rollins is holding it back in order to find some way to escape the melancholy duty of sentencing the son of an old, old friend to hang. For, as it stands, there can be no other outcome. Knowing Greg, the Judge, like everyone else in our circle, is convinced that the provocation on Gillian's part must have been gross. But Greg alone knows the facts, and he refuses to reveal them—even to me.

I have existed these last weeks in a state of mortal terror. I have lost seven pounds, and aged visibly by more than ten years. Against this thing, nothing serves. In vain have I quoted the Bard's immortal lines: "Cowards die many times before their deaths;/The valiant never taste of death but once." Because I taste of it nightly now. I am sure that I could face my own necessary end with greater equanimity; but Greg—God in heaven, Greg!—with half his life still before him, to be faced with this ugly, terrible way of dying! For

13

it does make a difference. Since it comes to us all, the "how" of it is the only variant; the sole aspect that has importance. And such a man as my brother should be allowed to sink into eternal slumber peacefully upon his honored bed, surrounded by his children and grandchildren; and not have that immense and tender vitality of his jerked out of him at the end of a rope. So—whatever must be done to save him, I shall do.

I have told Greg of my plan. He tried to dissuade me; but seeing my determination, he shrugged.

"Go ahead," he said. "None of them knows anything that would help. I'm the only person who does know. And I can't tell it, Jeff, I quite literally can't. . . ."

"Why?" I said.

His eyes, turned upon my face, held all there ever is of death and hell.

"Get out of here, Jeff," he said. "You heard me—go!"

It has been two weeks since that last lamentable interview with my brother that you have read upon the preceding page. The trial is over. The result was exactly what I had feared: Some ninety days from this date, Gregory Lynne is to be taken from the prison and hanged by the neck until he is dead, with the usual prayer that God have mercy upon his soul.

Judge Rollins could hardly pronounce sentence. I pitied him. It is a hard thing to condemn to death a boy you held upon your knee and fed candy to as a child, the son of a man with whom you had shared a relationship as close as that between brothers. But Greg gave him and the jury no alternative.

"Yes, I killed her. I struck her down in a fit of rage."

"Why?"

"I prefer not to say. It concerns only Mrs. Ames and

myself. After I am dead, it will concern no one at all. That is the way I want it. . . ."

So, my brother is to die—unless I can prevent it. Unless something in this tremendous mass of notes I have made from my interviews with Michael Ames, Hero Farnsworth, Joseph Riker, Barton and Dorothy Byrce, Grace Rollins, Big John Klovac, and his brother, Fred, Heddy MacAllister, Buleah Land, Red Waters, and Gillian's servants contains something I have overlooked or badly interpreted.

I am faced with an embarrassment of riches. I know more about Gillian MacAllister Ames than any man living. I could weave a web of circumstantial evidence that could send Bart Byrce, Michael Ames, Fred Klovac—or for that matter, even Hero Farnsworth, herself—to the gallows in Greg's place. But they did not kill Gillian; Greg did. I have blasted my own hopes that he might be sacrificing himself to protect a beloved friend. His recital of the crime fits all the known facts: the struggle, the blow, his presence in the house at the hour fixed by the coroner as the time of death —everything. I am sure that the others, if it were necessary, could furnish proofs of their whereabouts at the time that Gillian died. But it is not necessary; there is no doubt that Greg killed her.

Yet—and herein lies the mystery—each of the persons above, with the exception of Buleah Land, Gillian's old nurse, and her present corps of servants, had a strong, even compelling reason for murdering Gillian. But none of them did; while in all this pile of foolscap there lies not one word, not even a hint that would indicate Greg had any reason for killing her at all. From what I have been told, one might assume that Greg could not tell his motives for the crime for the simple reason that he hadn't any. He has been seen with Gillian, of course; but only at functions whose very public nature rendered them innocent. According to the servants, he had never, before that fatal night, remained at the Mac-Allister mansion longer than the time required for her to appear, dressed for one of the social events he took her to. His friendship with Michael was well known and remarked upon; people interpreted his silence upon the subject of Gillian as evidence of a true gentleman's fair-minded dislike of gossip and criticism. And everyone knew why, in the absence of her husband, Gilly chose Greg to be her escort: His reputation was so spotless as to make him, under the circumstances, the obvious choice. But despite all this, he stands convicted of what has every indication of being a *crime passionnel*. Was my brother in love with Gillian? To this question, every one of the people to whom I have talked answered with a prompt and unconditional "No."

Yet, if my researches into the life and times of Gillian MacAllister have led me into a dead-end street as far as Greg is concerned, I at least know one thing: where to begin this—where and how. Every person to whom I spoke kept returning again and again to that fateful garden party that Henry MacAllister gave in the spring of 1894, with the double purpose of introducing his nineteen-year-old daughter to society and announcing her engagement to Barton, heir apparent to the steelmaking clan of Byrce.

So, let us begin with that. It will serve, as nothing else could, to set the stage for all that follows. I shall let Hero begin it, because I was in Paris at the time and did not witness it. Besides, she is truly a better writer than I ever was. So, I give you Hero Ames—or Hero Farnsworth, as she was then.

3

HERO FARNSWORTH

Birmingham, May, 1894

When I came up to the MacAllister mansion in the surrey, I could see the Japanese lanterns bobbing among the trees in the garden. I had thought that I was going to be early; but there were already crowds of people drifting in and out of the pools of lantern light and shadow; and, as Anxious drew up the horses, I could hear the tinkling of glasses and the sound of laughter.

I got down from the surrey, telling Anxious to come for me at midnight, for I didn't think it proper for a widow of only six months to stay later than that at a party—if, indeed, she should have come at all—and walked up the flagstone path, feeling for all the world like a somber raven in my mourning garb, set down by mistake amid a flock of birds of paradise.

Gillian, herself, greeted me. She came drifting down the walk in a silvery cloud of organdy and tulle, with a spray of diamonds like droplets of frozen fire at her ears and throat, and the blinding blaze of a tiara lighting her pale blond hair. She was so lovely—so achingly, exquisitely lovely—that I stopped and stared at her. And waiting there for her to come to me, I hated her with all my heart.

"Hero!" she laughed. "So glad you could come!" Then she kissed my cheek, her perfume enveloping me like a cloud, mingled, I noticed, with the smell of champagne on her breath.

I fought the impulse to raise my hand and scrub away the spot her lips had touched. Instead, I said: "Every happiness, Gilly. Where's Bart? I want to congratulate him. . . ."

A momentary frown clouded her eyes.

"The beast!" she said gaily. "He's late. Isn't that just like a man? Do come have some champagne and mingle with the others. You've been a recluse long enough. Of course, it's right to show respect for poor, dear Rod; but a girl as young and pretty as you are shouldn't overdo things. . . ."

"I hardly think six months' mourning is overdoing things," I said.

"Oh, I don't know. You should be thinking about marrying again. All that money Rod left you—think what a wonderful honeymoon you could have! Paris, Rome, Venice—"

"Gilly, please," I said.

"I'm sorry," she laughed; "it's the champagne, Hero darling; and the excitement of it all. . . . It's wonderful, wonderful, wonderful! Bart and I. . . . Don't you think we'll make a divine couple?"

"Perfectly divine," I said. "Gilly—"

"Yes, dear?"

"I—I don't see Michael. Didn't you invite him?"

"Oh, yes. He's here—shut up in the study with Father. I've persuaded Father to hire him as chief of the testing lab. Michael's the only trained industrial chemist-physicist in town. Father's so old-fashioned! 'We got by without that scientific folderol in my day,' he says. But this is 1894, and times change, don't you think? Besides, Michael is the sweetest thing! But you know that. Anyhow, he should be out in a little while, as soon as they finish talking about new ways of making all that old hot, smelly iron. You want me to send a note in to him by one of the servants?"

"No," I said; "I'll see him when he comes out. . . ."

She stopped and stared at me, swaying a little.

"Why," she said, opening her blue eyes very wide, "that would be just perfect! You and Michael! You're both so—so gentle. . . . I'll have to work on that—"

"Please, Gilly, no," I said. "Besides, you mustn't take up so much time with me. Go attend to your other guests. . . ."

"Right, my sweet," Gillian said. "I'll tell William to bring you some champagne. Just wait right here, love. . . ."

Then she was off in her cloud of organdy, tulle, perfume and champagne, piercing the night with the icy blaze of her diamonds. I stood in the dark under a tree and gave way to the illness Gillian MacAllister always awoke in me.

I mustn't be jealous, I told myself; I mustn't! After all, she is marrying Bart Byrce, and Michael will be free. . . .

But that wasn't very much reassurance. I looked down at my thin hatrack of a figure and thought about how my face, which has the appearence of an oriental mask—an ugly oriental mask, must look above my drab mourning dress. I could see Gillian drifting in and out among her guests. From a distance, she seemed to be floating, a wisp of luminosity, entirely etherial, lacking either solidity or weight.

And constrasting this mist-light creature of magic and enchantment with the Gillian I knew, was too much. I bent my head and wept.

"Don't," a voice said from a spot a little way above my head. "You must stop crying now, Hero. Life goes on, you know."

I looked up into Greg Lynne's face, grave and concerned in the light of the lanterns.

"If," he went on kindly, "you were an old woman who had lost a husband of many years' standing, there'd be more excuse for this. But you were—let me see, nineteen when you married Rod Farnsworth. That makes you twenty-one, or less, now. . . ."

"Less," I said. "my birthday isn't until September."

"And you must have known that Rod was dying when you married him. He was a perfect gentleman. I can't believe he would have lied to you about his condition. . . ."

"No," I whispered; "I knew. That was one of the reasons I accepted him. I thought I could bring him a little happiness before he died. He—he had a right to that, Greg."

"You're sweet," Greg said. "What I'm getting at, little Hero, is that his death could not have been such a shock to you. You must stop this—this moping in corners and shedding lonely tears. For your own sake. You're young; you're quite attractive; and all that money that Rod—"

I must have become a little hysterical then.

"Oh!" I wept. "All that money! I hate it! Do you hear me, Gregory Lynne? I hate it! Everybody keeps talking about it as though it changes everything. Don't they realize I know how I look? Look at me, Greg! Just look! I'm as thin as a rail—and this face! Attractive? It looks like something carved on a totem pole! My eyes slant like a Chinese's; my mouth's too big, and my bones stick out all over. I'm dark—there are mulatto girls working in my house who are fairer than I. People don't just look at me, Greg; they stare!"

He was staring at me now, his face the picture of pained astonishment. But I couldn't stop; I had held it all in too long; I had to let it out now.

"All that money! Tell me, Greg Lynne, if I gave it

away—every penny of it, would that make me as beautiful as Gillian is? Would it?"

"You—you disappoint me, Hero," he said. "I'd thought you were—well—above petty jealousy. . . ."

"Sorry, but I'm not. I'm jealous of Gillian, like any other ugly, unattractive female would be. I'm the richest young widow in the whole state of Alabama, and I'm jealous of her. I've all that money. I have a lot of suitors, too, now, Greg. Funny, isn't it? Screamingly funny, what a magical transformation a fortune makes in a woman's looks—at least in the eyes of a certain kind of a man. . . ."

"Don't be bitter, Hero," Greg said. "What you should do is get away from here. Travel—forget. I know those miserable fortune-hunting bastards are a nuisance; but all men aren't like that. Go abroad—to Paris, say. I'll give you Jeff's address there. He'll be delighted to squire you about. Take off this black which doesn't become you, and buy yourself some pretty Parisian gowns. They'll work wonders for you."

"Nothing," I said bitterly, "could work wonders for me, Greg. Oh, why the dickens did my grandfather have to marry that Cherokee woman? If it weren't for her, I'd at least look like a human being!"

"I've heard my father say," Greg said gravely, "that your grandmother was one of the most beautiful women he ever saw—and that you look like her. Tastes differ. I, for instance, find your appearence oddly attractive. And Jeff swears you're the most exciting creature in the whole blamed state."

"Thanks," I said; "but it's no good, Greg. I have to stare at this face every morning in the mirror while Eliza combs my hair. You should hear her grumble; 'I just can't git no curl in this here horsehair you got nohow, Miz Hero.' She's so right. It's exactly like a horse's tail."

"You are in a mood, aren't you?" Greg said.

I put my hand on his arm.

"I'm sorry," I said. "That was unfair of me. I shouldn't have inflicted my troubles upon you, Greg. You know, I think I talked like that because I feel so close to you. I've always made substitute brothers of you and Jeff."

"Yes." He smiled. "Maybe, one of these days, I'll get around to changing your mind about that brother-sister business."

"Oh, no," I said; "don't try to cheer me up with flattery, Greg. You are very, very handsome. So is Jeff, because the two of you are more alike than any two people, even brothers, have any right to be. But I could never feel romantic about either of you. I know you much too well. . . . Let's walk a bit, shall we? I'd like a glass of champagne. Apparently Gilly has forgotten she promised to send me one. . . ."

"Good," Greg said, and took my arm. "You look a lot better now. Did you good to get that out of your system, didn't it? Tell you what, little Hero: Any time you need someone to throw your tantrums at, I'll rally round and listen."

"It's not all out of my system," I said; "I doubt it will ever be. You're a dear to endure me, Greg, but I won't trouble you like that ever again. My situation isn't going to change. I'll go on being me, with all that money, which can buy anything in the world except the things I need: good looks, and happiness, and—"

"Yes?" he said, "and what, Hero?"

"And the man I love," I whispered.

He stopped, and turned to me, taking both my hands in his. He stared at me, somberly.

"Sometimes," he said, and his voice was almost savage, "sometimes I think Michael Ames is the biggest fool who ever drew breath!"

We were standing there like that, facing each other, when Dorothy Rollins came upon us. She takes after her mother. Certainly so fine a Christian gentleman as Judge Martin Rollins should not be blamed for Dorothy. She smiled maliciously. The word describes her; everything Dot does is malicious.

"How sweet!" she cooed. "I knew that business of mourning wouldn't last too long. Especially not with all that money to emphasize your natural charms, Hero, love. May I be the first to congratulate you?"

I looked at her in purest astonishment. She was over-dressed, as usual. She had on a princess evening gown of white satin, cut in extreme *décolletage* to display as shame-lessly as possible those elements of her figure that men tell me are her most attractive features. Her enormous puff sleeves were of pale blue lace over white satin; and gigantic dark blue bows of the same material caught the corners of her lace bib, dividing it from the sleeves. The streamers of the bows came down to the hem of her dress. Around her throat she had a ruff of ostrich plumes dyed to match the lace; full-length gloves of the finest suede covered her arms, while the diamond bracelets without which, I swear, any Birmingham débutante of the nineties would have felt positively nude, encircled her wrists over the gloves. She, I must admit, looked lovely. The Rollinses are a handsome clan. She is blond, too—a darker shade of blond than Gillian —and extremely good-looking. Her figure is rather on the plump side. I could guess that the corsets which maintained that hand span of a waist were costing her agonies with every breath.

But it was not her appearance which held me staring at her in astonishment, but the incredible fact that she should be here at all. Not that Gillian should have invited her. I expected that. It probably delighted Gilly's vicious

soul to send Dot the   invitation. But that Dorothy should
have accepted it! It had been a settled matter for years
that Dorothy Rollins was to marry Barton Byrce; and
Gillian had broken them up, for her own purposes.

Yet Dorothy certainly did not look crestfallen at the
prospect of losing her beau to a younger girl. Quite the
contrary. I thought I could detect, even in the flickering
light of the lanterns, an expression of smug satisfaction upon
her face.

"You're wrong," I said calmly enough; "Greg is holding
my hands because I felt so low in spirits. You look lovely,
Dot. I must say, though, that I'm downright surprised to
see you here. . . ."

Dorothy laughed.

"Sorry my congratulations were—premature," she said.
"But as far as your surprise is concerned, Hero, dear; I'm
going to let you in on a secret: The surprises of *this* evening
haven't even begun yet!"

With that she tripped on down the path. I looked at
Greg. Wonderingly, he shook his head.

We made our way to the refreshment tables. A little
to the left of them, I saw Heddy MacAllister, Gillian's
mother, chatting gaily with Grace Rollins, Dorothy's aunt.
Heddy was, as usual, something to see. There was a look
of grim disapproval on Grace's face. I like Heddy. But I can
understand why the matrons of Birmingham can neither
fully accept nor forgive her. When one spends fortunes, as
they do, to hide or repair—never quite successfully—the
ravages of time, a woman who is *always* mistaken for the
slightly older sister of her own-nineteen-year-old daughter
is hard to bear. Actually, Heddy must not be much more
than thirty-eight or nine; for Mr. MacAllister is years older
than she. But, if you will accept the word of an extremely
truthful woman, she doesn't even look twenty-five. She is,

actually, far more childish than Gillian. It is this, I think,
that has preserved her looks. She thinks and acts like a child.
She is as gay and playful as a kitten. Every older man in
town, married or single, is in love with her.

To make matters worse, Heddy will neither confirm nor
deny the rumor that she is General Stuart Varden's daughter.
In Birmingham, the point is important. Our town is a
matriarchy. Almost every family I know of—Michael's, Dot's,
Gillian's, Bart's—are the descendants of Yankee adventurers,
who, seeing Jones Valley during Union General Wilson's
raids, decided to come back and exploit its great wealth.
Poverty forced the daughters of the former planter aris-
tocracy to marry them. So, when you hear a Birminghamer
saying, "My family—" it is nearly always his mother's family
he is talking about.

As the daughter of Alabama's almost legendary Confederate hero, Heddy could have taken her place at the
very head of the raw, young city's society; but she flouted
every convention, and outraged the Quality by saying:

"I don't know. I'm a Varden, all right. Maybe I'm General Stuart's daughter; but I don't remember him. I was too
little when he died. . . ."

I mentioned this to Greg as we sipped the pale champagne.

"Makes sense," he said. "General Varden was killed by
bushwhackers in sixty-five, after he had been invalided out
of the Confederate Army. The state was going to hell, then
—and those upstate counties had always been sympathetic
toward the North. What with the reverses of the last year
of the War, pro-Union sentiment got to be mighty damned
strong. Anyhow, a crowd of those blackguards killed General Varden—and his wife, after—well—subjecting her to
repeated personal indignities, to put it in a way fit for a
lady's ears. Heddy—if she is his child—couldn't have been

more than eight or nine years old at the time. How could she be expected to remember?"

"I remember things that happened when I was eight," I said stubbornly. "Besides, the people who brought her up must have told her something about her parents. . . ."

"Matter of fact," Greg drawled, "it isn't very likely that they knew anything about General Varden. They lived in Selma, where Varden's Irregulars never operated, and were known, if at all, only by hearsay. Remember we know a mighty heap more about that War, thanks to history books, than any eye-witnesses possibly could have. Bill Riker tells me that he and Henry MacAllister, who were with General Wilson, found the child crying beside the half-burnt bodies of her folks. They took her South with them and turned her over to the first family who would take her, after they captured Selma. And Heddy does come from Selma, and her name is Varden. Besides, when he came South again in seventy-two and met Heddy during the epidemic of the next year, Henry was convinced she was that child grown up. He still is. You should talk to him—"

"Doesn't interest me that much," I said. "Oh, Greg, I do wish Michael would come out and join the party so I could talk to him!"

Mr. MacAllister had hired a band of colored musicians. At that moment, they began to play. I felt Greg's hand close convulsively over my arm, and, turning, I saw Bart Byrce coming up the path.

He was quite obviously drunk. And he didn't have on his evening clothes. He wore, instead, a checkered riding habit that he probably had put on that morning. Everybody turned and stared at him. All over the garden the talk and the clatter of the glasses died. The Negroes stopped playing. I could feel the silence crawling along my nerves like a living thing.

Gillian, who had been talking to one of the Sloss boys, turned and stared with the rest. I could see pure disbelief in her eyes. Then it changed into that anger of hers which is more akin to earthquakes, tornadoes, and other catastrophes of nature than anything human.

I instinctively glanced at Dorothy and Grace Rollins. They knew. Their faces were wreathed with the cruelest smiles I had ever, up to that moment, beheld upon human countenances.

Gilly walked over to Bart. Her self-control was absolutely superb. She took his hand, and led him aside. I am sure that no one breathed during all that time. I saw Heddy MacAllister make a frantic gesture toward the musicians. They started to play again, much too loud. Or perhaps it was the contrast with all that silence.

I could see Gilly talking to Bart. Then, suddenly, she whirled and mounted the platform in front of the musicians. She silenced them with an imperious wave of her hand. Then she spoke.

"You can all go home now," she said, without even the trace of a tremor in her voice. "The party is over. For his own most excellent reasons, Mr. Barton Byrce has chosen to break our engagement. Good night!"

Then she leaped down from the platform and fled into the house. A moment later, Heddy followed her.

I turned to Greg. He shrugged, eloquently.

"When did you tell Anxious to come for you?" he said.

"At midnight," I whispered. But I wasn't even thinking about the fact that it was not even ten o'clock yet. Inside I was crying: "Oh, Michael, Michael, Michael!" For knowing Gillian, I knew with a certainty that brooked no contradiction my poor heart could offer, exactly what she would do next. Michael Ames might be poor; but he was brilliant and talented and acceptable socially, and wonderfully, wonderfully handsome. . . .

I think Greg must have divined my thought, for he patted my hand clumsily.

"Come, little Hero, I'll take you home now," he said.

4

MICHAEL AMES

Birmingham, May, 1894

Henry MacAllister stroked his muttonchop whiskers and
stared at me.

"In effect," he said, "what you're actually getting at,
son, is that I ought to quit trying to make more steel than
anybody else, and make the best. That's it, isn't it?"

"That's it," I said. "Look, sir; you can't compete with
Sloss or De Bardeleben. They're too big. And you know
what's been happening the last few years to small foundries. . . ."

I could see him stiffen.

"MacAllister Steel isn't exactly small!" he growled.

I wanted that job. God in heaven knows how much I
wanted it. It would mean everything to me: a chance to
vindicate my ideas; a good deal more money and comfort,
though that wasn't important to me, then; a chance to be
near Gilly, even if I had finally and irrevocably lost her to
Bart Byrce. But I wasn't going to lie to get it. To knuckle
under to Henry MacAllister now would defeat the very

thing I was trying to introduce into the industry. Quality
control is funny. All right, the laboratory head is an em-
ployee, but he cannot take orders from the boss. Especially
not when the boss is an old rule-of-thumb ironmaker like
MacAllister. I had to be hired to tell Mr. MacAllister how
to make steel, good pig, good cast; which, with all humility
possible, were things that not he nor anybody else in
Birmingham knew how to do. Which is not to say that they
never made good heats. They did, or certainly they wouldn't
have been in business this panic year of 1894. But the best
heat they ever made was never as good as it could have
been, while the waste from heats gone sour, the utter lack
of consistency from one day to the next, were, knowing
how easily good iron and steel can be made, holding it to
the same impeccable quality day in and day out, to me
absolutely appalling.

I considered my answer carefully. After all, I was no
longer in a hurry. The sound of music and laughter coming
through the window of Henry MacAllister's study from the
garden party outside reminded me of that. Because the
reason for, the source of all my ambitions was ending with
appropriate ceremony, with oblations and sacrifices before
the high gods—of vanity, pomp, and circumstance—the only
ones we truly worship in our hearts. Still, I had gone too
far to let the whole thing drop now. And life must go on—
without Gillian. God, how dreadful that seemed to me, then!

"That depends upon what you measure it by, sir," I
said firmly. "If you want to be swallowed up by Tennessee
Coal and Iron like eight or ten smaller companies already
have been, the only thing I can say is, Please excuse me.
I would like to wish Gilly happiness, and congratulate Bart
some time tonight. I don't mean to be rude, Mr. MacAllister; but do you think you can really compete with them?
All right, they'll make you a vice-president, maybe. They've

got thirteen vice-presidents now. And you'll be taking orders instead of giving them. I don't think you'd like it."

"Damn it, son," he roared; "the way you've explained things, I'll be taking orders from you!"

"Yes, sir," I said; "in a way. But you'll be hiring me to give those orders—which, I promise you, sir, will make you more money than you've ever seen in your life. And you'll still be boss, really. If you don't like a method I suggest, you can always countermand it. There wouldn't be a blessed thing I could do about that except to quit; and that, I warn you from the outset, is exactly what I'd do. . . ."

Slowly Henry MacAllister relaxed. I could see the twinkle in the corner of his eyes. I'd won. I didn't even dare change the set of my face, but I knew I'd won.

He smiled.

"Michael," he said, "I talked to you tonight because that perfect little holy terror of a daughter of mine wouldn't have given me any peace if I hadn't. I thought that she was so insistent because you're an extremely presentable young fellow—hell, you're damned good-looking, let's face it. But I like your guts. Nobody has stood up to me like this in years. Besides, if you're right, you'll enable me to compete with those damned hogs—"

"Not compete, sir," I said; "enter a market where they can't even compete with you. Armor steel for the Army and Navy; steel that can take the millions of pounds per square inch pressure that a coastal defense gun must every time it's fired. Tool and die steel. And the best cast, pig, and plate that Alabama's ever seen."

He took a fragrant Havana out of the rosewood box on the table. He offered the box to me.

"I don't smoke, sir," I said.

"Good. Filthy habit. Wish I didn't, myself. All right, explain it to me again. Not like before. Remember I never

even finished high school. Use words I can understand.
What do you mean when you say quantitative analysis?
Torsion testing? Tensile strength? What the devil are impact
and fracture tests anyhow? And why do we have to do
them?"

I had not realized how much my scientific vocabulary
was a part of me until I sought for words—ordinary words—
to explain the chemical analysis by which you found out
exactly how much carbon, nickel, manganese, vanadium, or
chromium there were in any given heat of steel; and the
destructive methods by which you pulled, hammered,
twisted, pressed, and otherwise tortured the metal to death
to determine the minimum standards of strength it ought
to have. The two things go together. Once you know what
any of the various kinds of steel should be able to take
before it shatters into a thousand pieces with a crash like
thunder, you can easily find out what to put into it to reach
and maintain that strength.

It was hard going, but he got it. I could see comprehen-
sion, then wonder, then excitement in his eyes. He leaped
up from his chair with his hand outstretched.

"You're hired!" he growled. "Now, about your salary—"

"No salary at all, Mr. MacAllister," I said. "I'm going
to work for you for three months free of charge. After that,
you look at your earning charts and balance sheets, and pay
me what you decide I'm worth. If you're not satisfied, we
can part company at that time, with no hard feelings on
my part, or on yours. . . ."

He peered at me, cocking his head to one side.

"You're smart," he said. "But actually, that's not fair.
I'll give you two hundred a month living expenses during
those three months. You've got to eat, and dress decently.
And a young fellow your age must have a girl. . . ."

Sadly I shook my head.

"Gilly, eh?" he said. "Take it from me, son—you're lucky. I feel sorry for that Byrce boy. I love my daughter, but I'll be happy to have her off my hands."

I could see that his words had escaped him without his intending them to.

"Oh, she isn't that bad, sir," I said. "I know she has a temper; but I've always been able to get along with her."

He turned toward the window. His voice, speaking now, was low and troubled.

"You don't have to live with her," he said. "I sometimes wonder where I got her from. She's nothing like me or her mother. I remember once, when she was a child—"

"Yes, sir?" I said.

"Don't know why I'm talking to you like this even if I have known you all your life. I shouldn't, really. To talk this way about my daughter grieves me to my soul. But there's something about you—a man feels you can be trusted, somehow. And, damn it, son, I've got to talk to somebody! I've held it in until it's choking me. Anyhow, she'd done something particularly horrid—I don't remember what it was, which is hardly strange, considering that not a day passed that Gilly didn't do something or another no other human child would have even thought of—"

"Human, sir?" I said; for I had caught the emphasis, slight as it was, that he had placed upon the word.

He looked me straight in the eye.

"There have been times I've doubted it," he said dryly. "In the Pennsylvania Dutch country I came from, people still believe in witchcraft, and that devils walk the earth in the shape of men and women. Anyhow, I whipped her. That," he whispered, "was the last time I've raised a hand against Gillian. . . ."

I stood there, waiting.

"She—she didn't move. She didn't flinch, or even

whimper. She just stood there, staring at me, and her eyes were cold as ice. I think I must have gone a little crazy. Anyhow, I beat her until I drew blood from her legs with that green peachwood switch. She didn't shed a tear. She just stood there, looking at me. I stopped beating her, and she turned and marched away into the house without a word. She went to bed. She stayed in that bed one full year, alternately screaming gibberish, or just lying there, staring at the ceiling. The doctors agreed there was absolutely nothing wrong with her. Buleah took care of her all that time. Gradually brought her back to her senses, for which I was profoundly grateful. But one day Heddy went in to sit with her, and without a word, Gillian attacked her mother, tried, actually, to kill her. Without provocation, Michael! And that"—his voice was lower still, so that I had to lean forward to hear him—"was the first time I realized that I had sired—a monster."

"Now really, sir!" I said.

"You think I exaggerate?" he said, turning to me. "Why, I could tell you—but no matter. It doesn't concern you, and you wouldn't believe it, anyhow. Let's have a snort of bourbon to celebrate your joining MacAllister Steel. Don't tell me you don't drink, either?"

I didn't; but I didn't think it wise to tell him so.

"Well," I said, "a light one, then—" I stood there watching him while he poured enough bourbon in the glasses to floor a medium-sized ox.

"Sit down," he said. "This shindig will go on all night, and it's just a quarter to ten. Besides, I've a powerful lot of questions to ask you."

I dropped into the comfortable leather-covered chair.

"First of all," he began, "how much is this scientific business going to—"

That was as far as he got. The door flew open with a

crash that shook the chandelier. Gillian came hurtling through it and threw herself into my lap. Her father had said she hadn't cried when he had whipped her; but she was crying now. Never in my whole life, before or since, have I heard anyone cry like it. I swear you could hear the tissues inside her throat tearing as the sobs came through. She wrapped both arms around my neck so tight, I literally couldn't breathe. I put up my hands and loosened her grip; but she lay there, soaking the stiff bosom of my dress shirt with her tears.

At any other time, and under any other set of circumstances, I should have thoroughly enjoyed holding Gillian MacAllister in my arms. Not that this was the first time. But to hold her like that, in her father's study, under his own outraged eyes, was something else again. I was as thoroughly uncomfortable a young man as it is possible to imagine.

"Gilly!" he thundered; but she ignored him.

"Michael!" she sobbed. "Oh, Michael, darling, take me away from here! Far, far away! Oh, my dearest, I can't, I won't—"

She must have felt me stiffen; for she turned in my arms, and stared into her mother's eyes.

Heddy stood in the doorway. Her face was white and working.

"Gilly," she whispered, "I must say that your father and I have put up with an awful lot from you. But this takes the cake! Would you mind explaining what happened between you and Bart? And why in the name of high heaven you decided to insult two hundred of the best people in Birmingham?"

Gilly stood up, slowly. Have you ever seen a cat flatten itself along a path as it creeps to attack a bird? That is exactly the way Gilly walked toward her mother. I could see Heddy's cheeks getting paler and paler, her blue eyes wider and more frightened. A yard away from her, Gilly stopped. When she spoke, finally, her voice wasn't even loud.

"You whore!" she said. "You filthy, unspeakable whore!"

I have always felt that the word, whore, is the ugliest single word in the English language. Not only because of its connotation, but because of the sound of it. But I had never felt the full impact of its ugliness until I heard Gilly drag it up out of her throat, grating the "r" round into long-drawn-out hideousness before hurling it into her mother's teeth.

"Gillian!" Henry MacAllister roared. "I'll not have this—"

She spun in a blur of organdy and faced him.

"Oh yes, you will, Father!" she spat. "In fact, you already have! General Stuart Varden's daughter, ha! This —this thing! Funny, isn't it? Hilarious! And people believed it! Let me tell you, Father—"

The "Gilly!" he got out was weaker, now.

"Let me introduce you to your wife—and my mother! Heddy Varden MacAllister. Oh, that Varden's correct, all right. Your angelic wife is really a Varden—drunken Ned Varden's daughter from Shantytown on the edge of Selma. The mistress, the kept woman of every rich man in the county! Like it, Father? Wait—there's more. I've been made sick to my stomach often enough by that story of how she nursed you through the cholera epidemic. Want to know why she came to Birmingham in seventy-three, Father dear?"

"Gillian!" Henry MacAllister's voice was that of a man dying under torture. I did not know then that my thought was quite literally true.

"My mother—my beautiful, childlike mother—was driven out of Selma by an outraged wife armed with a buggy whip!

You doubt me? Ask Grace Rollins! She can furnish you with names, addresses, dates. . . ."

She turned upon her mother once more.

"You wonder, Mother dear—dear, dear Mother—that Bart broke our engagement? How long did you think you'd be able to get away with it? Tell me, how long?"

She stood there, breathing like a beautiful, savage animal; then her lovely face twisted into a mask of absolutely venomous hatred.

"Whore!" she screamed. "Whore! Whore! Whore!"

I came up behind her, caught her by the shoulder and whirled her around.

"Gilly," I said quietly. "Are you going to shut up, or do I have to slap you?"

She stared at me, her eyes glittering with insane mockery.

"You, slap me?" she laughed. "You! Oh my God! What on earth ever made you think you were that much of a man, Michael Ames?"

It was then that I struck her, bringing my open palm across her face so hard that her head jerked sideways on the slim,· swanlike column of her neck. She hung there, staring at me, while the white imprint of my fingers on her cheek turned red.

Then, whimpering like a child, she came to my arms.

"Forgive me, love," she whispered. "I—I needed that, I guess. . . ."

I could see her father's face. He looked at us a long moment before he turned to his wife. He didn't need to ask. Just looking at Heddy anyone could see that Gillian hadn't lied.

5

GRACE ROLLINS

Birmingham, May, 1894

I

My sister-in-law is a fool. Never could understand how a man intelligent enough to be the fine judge my brother Martin is could have ever married a simpering idiot like Mathilda Hines. And the daughter she gave him is not much better. I'm fond of my niece, Dorothy, but I must admit she's not too bright either. Well, Mathilda would have sat right there moaning and wringing her hands, while that horribly impertinent snip of a girl walked off with the best catch, matrimonially speaking, in all Alabama. Not that the Byrce boy is any great shakes; but you have to respect that much money. People nowadays have got into the habit of sneering at money, making silly remarks about how it can't buy anything important like health, happiness, or peace of mind.

What rubbish! In all my years—don't you look at me like that, Jeff Lynne! I'm not that old. I've never seen anything it couldn't buy yet, not a blessed, living thing. Health? Who commands the services of the best doctors? The poor?

Happiness? Which girl is likely to have her choice of beaux?
The heiress in the velvet gown, or the salesgirl in the five
and dime? Peace?—I ask you: How are you going to be
peaceful worrying about unpaid bills and not knowing
where your next meal's coming from?

All right—I'll get to the point. Those MacAllisters are
too pushy. Oh, Henry's a decent enough sort—but that
Heddy! The flightiest, giddiest young-old fool I ever did see.
As for Gillian, the least said about her, the better. I've
always suspected that she had the morals of a she-cat in a
back alley, and now—

Look here, young man! I know she's dead; but I can't
speak kindly of her, for all that. Seems to me that with your
own brother about to hang because of her, you'd— All right,
all right! How did I find out about Heddy MacAllister?
I really don't see how going that far back will help you save
Greg; but if you think so, I'll tell you. 'Cause nobody should
swing for killing Gillian Ames. If it were left to me, I'd vote
Greg a medal for public service!

What made me try to find about Heddy in the first
place? Why, that's as clear as daylight. Seems to me you
ought to be able to figure it out yourself. Plain stood to
reason if there were any chink in that family's armor, it had
to be Heddy.

Why? Look at the facts. If you were a woman, I
wouldn't have to explain it to you; but men are positively
dense. Even my brother, for all that he's a judge. Heddy
MacAllister rode along for years, letting people think she
was General Stuart Varden's daughter. Only she was too
clever, for all her flighty ways, to come right out and claim
she was the General's child. Too risky. Somebody from
Selma just might pass through Birmingham long enough to
recognize her.

So, when my idiotic niece came home bowed down in

tears because that fool boy had broken off with her to marry
Gillian, I didn't join in the hand-wringing and crying. Somebody in a family has to have some get up and get about
her. I marched off to the railroad station and bought myself
a round-trip ticket to Selma without saying anything to
anybody.

Even before I went, I was sure I was going to find out
something useful. Why was I sure? Now look here, boy;
use your brains, if you have any. Any woman who was
General Varden's daughter would have shouted that fact
from the housetops. What if she really didn't know whether
she was or not? Lord God, Jeff, how little you know about
women! Most females part company with the truth from
the moment they first see the light of day. It purely stands
to reason she would have claimed the honor whether she
was sure of it or not. Even if she knew she wasn't, she
would have claimed it just the same, unless there was some
reason she didn't dare. And that was what I was betting on.

So I called on my old friend, Mildred Sims. That
woman's nose has got a permanent crook in it from being
poked into other people's business. I figured that if anybody
would know, it would be Milly.

I had to beat about the bush awhile, because I most
certainly didn't want Milly Sims to find out why I needed
that information. But you should have seen her eyes pop
out when I asked her.

"Gen'l Stuart Varden's daughter?" she said. "Of course
I knew that poor child! Randy Sturgis and his wife brought
her up. Delicate, sickly little thing—always grieving for her
real folks. No wonder she didn't live long. . . ."

"You mean she's dead?" I said.

"Why sure. Let me see—she died of the cholera in
seventy-three, when she was around sixteen years old. . . ."

I must say my head was working that day. I put on a long face and said:

"Some friends of General Varden's were trying to trace her. She's buried here?"

"Right here in Live Oak Cemetery," Milly said. "Everybody chipped in and bought her the finest marble headstone you ever did see."

"Milly, do me a favor," I said. "You got a pretty fair photographer here in town, haven't you? Well, I want you to call him up and have him meet us at that poor child's grave this afternoon—"

"Name of God, Grace, why?" Milly said.

"For these people who're trying to locate the girl. If I bring them back a nice clear photograph of that tombstone, they can quit spending their time and money on a wild goose chase; 'cause they'll have absolute proof to send back to those Yankee relatives of the General's."

Milly is sharp.

"Relatives?" she said; "I thought you said friends, before. . . ."

"Did I?" I said calmly; "well, it's both. The folks who are stopping in Birmingham, asking about the child, are the General's friends, or so they claim. But some cousins of his up North asked them to find out. I think there was money in it for the girl—poor thing. By the way, her name was Heddy, wasn't it?"

"Lord, no! You're getting her mixed up with those lowdown, no account Shantytown Vardens—no kin to the General, though they like to claim they are. They had a girl named Heddy; the wildest, flightiest, wickedest little bit of fluff you ever did see. Gen'l Stuart's daughter's name was Grace, same as yours. But that Heddy—"

I had all I could do to keep from hugging her.

"Tell me about her," I said, offhandedly, as though I really wasn't much interested.

And she did: names, dates, places. Milly has a memory like a steel trap. She told me everything right down to the minute that Mary Ann Trevor chased Heddy out of town with a buggy whip, slashing at her 'til she jumped aboard the Birmingham train. I came home loaded for bear, as my father used to say. I had it all: the names and addresses of the men who had kept little Heddy—because she was never anything so crude as a streetwalker. In fact, she was so high-class, they used to say in Selma that no man could claim to be a success until he'd kept Heddy Varden for a few months or a year. And I brought back a great big enlarged photograph of poor Grace Varden's headstone with the words showing up real clear:

"Sacred to the memory of Grace Varden, only child of General Stuart Varden, Legendary Hero of the Confederacy. Bowed down with grief for her martyred Sire, she went willingly to join him in the fullness of her youth." And under that, the dates: 1856-1873.

Even then, I had to manage things. I kept tight reins on Mathilda and Dot. They were all for calling up Barbara Byrce at once. But I put my foot down. Let that get out too long ahead of the party, and that Gillian, who, unlike her mother, was nobody's fool, would have found some way to twist Bart Byrce around. No—it had to be timed. I figured that if we told Barbara the morning of the party, she'd make Bart break with Gilly that same night. In fact, I suggested the idea to her.

The scandal had to be big; the ground had to be cut so far from under Gillian MacAllister that she wouldn't have a chance to recover. Because, unlike a lot of other folks, I never underestimated her. It's like that old saying: When you strike at a queen, strike to kill!

BARTON BYRCE

Birmingham, May, 1894

II

I know what you're thinking, Jeff. All right, I'm a weakling and a coward. Yep, I'm drunk, too; else I wouldn't be talking like this. I'm drunk pretty damned often. Only way I can face the life I've got to live now.

Of course I didn't want to give Gilly up! No man in his right mind who'd ever really known her would have wanted to. What's that? You knew her, and you couldn't stand her? Rot. You didn't know her. Nobody else knew her but me. She was—strange. I sometimes think she was two people in one. Like that Jekyll-and-Hyde business Stevenson wrote about. And whichever one of the two she was at the moment, she was more intensely than anybody ever is anything in this world. You didn't like her. All right. You never knew the angel out of God's own glory she could be. I tell you, Jeff, there never was a girl sweeter, nicer, gentler, more tender. . . .

Then why didn't I marry her? My family. My blessed, pompous, insufferable family! I should have stood up to my mother; told her it wasn't Heddy I'd be marrying, but Gillian. But you don't stand up to women like my mother. It's my father's fault. If he'd let her feel the weight of his hand or his cane when they first married. . . . Funny. He couldn't, either. You've heard him roar in directors' meetings? You should hear him at home: 'Yes, dear. No, dear. You're perfectly right, dear. . . .' "

Hadn't I any doubts, personally, about the matter?

Frankly, yes. I've told you Gilly was an angel. Don't reckon I have to tell you she was a devil, too. She could change from one to the other in the blink of an eye. Yet, that side of her—that pure, undiluted hell—wasn't repulsive either, Jeff. Not enough, anyhow, especially not to a man like me. Something in my nature it appealed to. Something rotten in me that she reached without even half trying—that way. And five will get you ten that same rottenness exists in damned near every man. Because—ah, God—even that way she was worth it! If you'd ever been seared by that fire, you'd count the world well lost to keep her; you'd accept anything: abuse, insult, infidelity, spiritual and moral degradation until even a pig wouldn't puke on you—just to stay by her side. . . .

How many times have I crept home in the dark with my legs like rubber under me, my mouth so bruised and torn I couldn't bear to close my lips together, my shirt sticking to the ribbons she'd clawed my back into. Lord God, Jeff! That girl got into your blood like a fever, so coming home all but dead, you still couldn't sleep. You'd lie there hurting all over, and crying inside your guts from the pure damned agony of wanting her, wanting her, that never stopped, not one instant of the day or night. That hasn't stopped even now—and she—dead. Lord, Jesus! Gilly, dead!

Why, she used to— Very well, I'll stop it. You're damned right, Jeff Lynne; there are some things even a man as drunk as I am shouldn't say.

But one thing more: I hope they hang that murdering bastard of a brother of yours! I want to see that. I want to see him kick and choke! Because, while she lived, I had hope. Not much, but some. Now—nothing. Drunk myself to death, 'cause I haven't the guts to do it with a gun. When I go, that'll be on his head, too. When he killed her he killed me, too. It'll take a little longer for that wound to drain the

blood and breath and life out of me. But it was mortal;
boy—mortal as all hell. . . .

I'm sorry I said that. He's your brother. But I don't
take it back. I can't, Jeff. I can't—

WILLIAM JOSEPH RIKER

Round Mountain, Alabama, April, 1865

III

You want me to tell you about General Stuart Varden and
the child? How we came to find her and all that? You're
damned right, boy; I'm the only man living who knows that
story. But you're wrong about one thing: Henry MacAllister
would have married Heddy Varden anyhow, even if he had
known she wasn't General Varden's daughter.

Mind you, Heddy never claimed she was. That was just
an idea Henry had. Of course, she never admitted she wasn't,
either, though she must have known the truth. Reckon she
figured the social standing it would give her in Birmingham
would help matters. Can't blame her for taking that little
advantage; that was just good poker. She figured right. But
Henry wasn't even slightly concerned about that angle; he
married her because he loved her. Why, before that, he'd
never even thought about looking for the child. He didn't
care about all that society folderol anyhow. Well, it was
like this. . . .

[Here I have cut several pages from the narrative. Bill Riker
is an old man and tends towards verbosity.—Geoffry Lynne.]

We got out of there, and when we came to the top of

the rise, we pulled up the horses and looked back. The furnaces and rolling mills at Oxmoor were burning like a torch.

Henry MacAllister looked at me.

"Hell of a thing," he said.

"They're Reb foundaries, captain," I pointed out.

"I know; I know. Tell me something, lieutenant: How long did you puddle iron in Pittsburgh?"

"Damned near all my life, sir," I said.

"And you like doing this sort of thing?"

"No sir," I said. "For an old iron-and-steel man to wreck a foundry is a hard thing."

He didn't answer me. He sat there on the piebald stallion and watched the foundries burn. When he spoke, I knew he wasn't talking to me, so I didn't try to say anything.

"A hard thing," he said. "It's more than wrecking; it's murder. It's killing a part of yourself." Then he looked at me and grinned.

"But we'll build them back, eh, lieutenant?" he said. "Just you and me. After the fighting's over, we're going to save every penny we can get our hands on and come back here. You ever see better iron country than this? Coal right at hand, and the best damned hematite I've ever laid eyes on. Hell, Bill, even the dogwoods are red."

"Yes, sir," I said.

He gave one more look at the fire, and his face changed.

"Let's get on with it, lieutenant," he said.

We moved off in the jingle and clatter of cavalry, heading toward Round Mountain. We'd been riding about an hour, when one of the horses lifted his head and neighed. And then we heard the shots.

We went up the next rise at a gallop, breaking through the dogwood trees with those blossoms that were like masses of spring snow, with now and then a pink one between. Henry said it was the iron ore that caused them to turn that color. Lord, it was pretty! I remember thinking: It's a hell of a thing to have to die and leave all this. . . .

Henry lifted his hand, and we reined in. I rode up beside him. Down below, in the hollow, I could see the big white plantation house; and all around it, in the woods, the puffs of smoke. Funny. You'd see the smoke puffs first, then a half second later you'd hear the crash of those Enfields.

The people in that house were shooting back real slowly as though they were trying to make their ammunition last. It was a creepy feeling, watching it: That big house, whiter than milk in the sunlight, and all around it the darkness of pine trees, with dogwoods scattered amongst 'em—white with a whiteness that hurt you inside looking at it, with a feeling that was like somebody had cried out real suddenly in the dark. It didn't look real. You couldn't believe people were killing each other down there. While I was watching, a minnie ball broke a dogwood branch, and the blossoms showered down so slow, so slow, that I lifted my glasses to watch 'em. They fell into the face of a dead man lying under that tree, and some of 'em got into the mess of blood and brains he was lying in. I put the glasses down.

"Whackers!" Henry said.

Maybe God hates sin and the devil as much as a regular army man hates bushwhackers, but I doubt it. Here in northern Alabama, those skulking bastards were supposed to be on our side. But they'd bushwhack a lone Union soldier as quick as they would a Reb. Quicker. We had more stuff worth stealing. And by April of sixty-five, even our superior officers had seen enough of our boys lying with their throats slit from ear to ear where those fine "Unionist Irregulars" had come upon them after they'd been wounded, and finished them off for their boots, not to interfere with us

when we ran across a gang of 'whackers. Our tactics were real
nice and simple: We shot them on sight, low, aiming for
the big gut. Then we asked them very politely whether they
were Unionist or not. Of course, by then, they mostly couldn't
answer; but that made things simpler still.

"Bill," Henry said to me; "take half the men around to
the other side and flank 'em. Don't wait for a signal. Soon
as you're ready, go for 'em. I'll be ahead of you, anyhow."

He was. We couldn't have taken five minutes to get in
position. But it was over when we got down there. I counted
eight of the bushwhackers lying under the trees. I could
hear the rest of them crashing through the pine saplings and
the dogwoods as they got the hell out of there. Which, as
it turned out, was the biggest mistake Henry MacAllister
made in all his life. For, if he had waited on me, we'd have
got them all. And General Varden would have lived. And
the question of who his daughter really was would never
have come up at all. Everything would have been changed.
You can see that, can't you, boy?

I looked at the dead 'whackers. Some of 'em had on
blue uniforms, and some butternut brown. They'd got both
kinds of uniforms the same way: stripping them off dead and
near dead Rebel and Union soldiers after a battle, without
showing partiality. I spat.

Captain MacAllister got down off the piebald stallion.
"Come with me, lieutenant," he said.

We walked up to the front door. I kept my hand on
my sidearm; because, after all, more than half of those rat
bastards had had on blue. Couldn't blame those folks in that
house a lick if they'd started shooting at us. But they didn't.

A tall, blond lady opened the door.

"Thank you, captain," she said; "and you, too, lieutenant. Thank you mighty kindly. . . ."

ROUND MOUNTAIN, ALABAMA, APRIL, 1865   **49**

I knew right then she was Army, because she'd recognized our insignia with half a glance.

"Please come in," she said; "the General wants to thank
you in person—"

"The General, ma'am?" Henry said.

"General Varden," she said; "General Stuart Varden,
C. S. A., and—my husband."

We both stared. We'd generally just as soon not tangle
with Nat Forrest. We'd always given Jeb Stuart as wide a
berth as possible. But nobody ever said Stuart Varden's name
out loud. Even our mounts would panic when they heard it.

"We're highly honored, Mrs. Varden," Henry said—he
could be more courtly than any Reb planter you ever did
see when he wanted to. "The more so because we were
under the mistaken impression that General Varden was
killed last fall—"

"Only half killed," Mrs. Varden said. "His spine was
nicked by a spent ball. He—he's paralyzed from the waist
down. Please, gentlemen, don't show him any concern—or
pity. He's so dreadfully proud. . . ."

"Don't worry, ma'am," I said; "I'm just going to have
myself the pleasure of shaking the hand of the greatest
cavalry leader in the history of this country, so I can tell
my grandchildren about it. Then I'll go. . . ."

We went inside. General Varden was sitting in a big
chair by a window with an Enfield across his lap. He was
surrounded by five or six colored boys with guns in their
hands, too. Folks say the colored brother won't fight. But
they didn't know General Stuart Varden's people and the
way they loved him.

The bushwhackers' gunfire had messed things up right
smart; but I wasn't looking at that. I was looking at General
Stuart Varden, sitting in that chair, with his wasted legs
covered by a ragged blanket. Half a glance told me he'd

been starving for weeks. Then I saw the child. She wasn't anything but bones. Just looking at her, I wanted to cry. And a man who has spent his life puddling iron in an open-hearth furnace ain't given to easy tears.

But, even sitting there like that, half-paralyzed and half-starved, General Varden was something to see. Finest figure of a man I ever laid eyes on. Coal-black hair, turning gray at the temples; ice-blue eyes exactly like Gillian's, though I know now she really wasn't his granddaughter; a mustache and goatee that looked good on him. He had a face like what you'd imagine a king ought to look like, and a voice to match.

"Sorry I cannot offer you the hospitality of my house, gentlemen, along with my heartfelt thanks," he said; and his voice sounded like the pipes of the biggest organ, in the grandest church anybody ever heard tell of. "But, as you can see, we're fresh out of rations. . . ."

The child whimpered a little when he said that. He turned toward her and his face was kind of sad. "Hush, baby," he told her quiet-like.

I looked at the child once more, then I turned to Henry and saluted.

"Excuse me, captain," I said; "I'll be right back."

Henry nodded. He knew what I was going to do.

Field rations: hardtack and bacon and jerked beef and tinned beans aren't fancy grub; but when Mrs. Varden saw them, she cried and took my hand.

"My husband has always said," she said to me, "that you Yankees are mostly brave men and gentlemen; but I didn't believe him till now. Thank you, lieutenant; thank you mighty kindly. I'll be glad when this cruel war is over—so we can all be friends again. . . ."

"Ma'am," I said, bowing, "I haven't ever been anything but your friend. I'm just a soldier doing a job I was sent to do. I respect you folks and your opinions. And Lord knows, whatever Abe Lincoln sent me down here for, it sure didn't include making war on women and children. . . ."

"Wish your General felt the same way about it," General Varden said.

All I could do was to hang my head. Old J. H. Wilson was a disciple of Sherman, both of them holding that any means of getting the war over would be merciful in the long run. But I didn't like that scorched-earth policy—and I don't yet.

We spent the evening with the General and his lady before riding off to raid Round Mountain. Mrs. Varden played the piano, and we all sang "Lorena," which was the favorite song of both armies, then she taught us some funny Reb songs like "Goober Peas," and "Mister, Here's Your Mule." After that, she and the General sang that duet where the soldier tells the girl he's going away to fight for her and maybe even find a lonely grave, and she answers that it's harder to have to wait and be scared she was going to have to face the years all by herself. It was something. The General's bass was like summer thunder, real far off, and soft, mingling with Mrs. Varden's voice—the sweetest, prettiest soprano in the whole damn world. As I said, I ain't the sentimental type; but my throat felt like I'd swallowed a bullfrog before they got through. . . .

A week later, we came back there like we'd promised, to see how they were making out. We had left them both grub and pistol ammunition. But we were armed with Spencer repeating carbines by then, which fired cartridges like guns do now, so we hadn't any powder and ball to leave them for their Enfields. And they, goddamnit, were just about out of ammunition for their rifles.

When we got to the top of the rise, we thought we were at the wrong place. Then Henry pointed, and I saw the pile or burnt rafters still smoking in the middle, and how the trees for yards around were seared black.

We filed down that slope without saying anything. Henry and I got down from our mounts and walked real close. Then he turned to the men.

"Clear some of this stuff away," he said.

We were able to recognize the General by his twisted legs. The others must have been some of the colored boys. You couldn't tell. But none of the bodies was small enough to have been the child. And they were all male. They weren't too charred not to be able to make that out; you just couldn't tell whether they'd been white or colored before.

"Form details!" Henry said. "Search the woods!"

I found them. Without thinking, I fired a shot to bring the others. The child screamed and screamed until I had to put my hand over her mouth to stop her.

Henry came over to where Mrs. Varden lay. He took off his campaign hat and turned his back quickly, like the gentleman he was.

"Halt!" he roared at the men. "Right about face!"

They stood in the ranks with their backs turned toward us. Henry had one arm around the child's thin shoulders. She went on crying.

"Reed and Martin, fall out," Henry said. "Both of you get a blanket out of your saddle rolls. Then report back here."

They went away and came back with the blankets.

"Reed and Martin, halt," Henry said; "right about face! Now advance, backwards! Eyes front, damnit! Now pass those blankets to me and the lieutenant."

I took one side of the blankets and Henry took the other.

"Close your eyes," Henry said to me. "And that, lieutenant, is an order!"

We walked past the body on both sides with our eyes closed.

"Now," Henry said; and we dropped the blankets over her. It didn't cover her face. But that was one Southern gentlewoman who had her modesty respected even in death, by an outfit of Northern barbarians, as they still like to call us.

Henry stood there, looking at her. I looked too. Her face was bad, very bad, the worst. She hadn't been dead long enough for decomposition to set in; besides, it was still cool in those hills in April. The reason it was bad was all the things they had done to her were frozen upon it, mirrored in the glassy horror of her eyes. What brought the vomit to the back of my throat was the amount of invention those bastards had shown. They'd had a hell of a lot more imagination than I'd ever given 'em credit for.

Henry turned to the men. His voice was curiously soft.

"Fall out," he said quietly. "Now I want every man to walk by here single file and look at this woman's face. Forget she was a rebel general's wife. Forget everything but that she was a lady. And when we catch up with those blackguards, read yourselves your own orders!"

Not a man said a word, going past her. The child was off to one side, sobbing quietly in Sergeant Tucker's arms. He was trying to get her to eat. But she couldn't.

After we had buried the General and his lady side by side under a wooden cross, with full military honors, we left the sarge to take care of the child and went back to where the horses were. We mounted, still not uttering a mumbling word. We rode along in a jingle of spurs and stirrups, the slap of leather against a flank, the clang of a carbine striking metal. But nobody talked. Nobody even swore.

We caught up with them near Briarfield. They were

pitching camp for the night, making shebang lean-to's, or
spreading out the canvas flies they'd stolen from our camps.
Nobody gave any orders. We just came swarming down
upon them in a roan-colored and blue tide, not even shooting yet, just riding in, rising in the stirrups, leaning forward,
going on.

I don't remember hearing the gunfire. There was smoke
everywhere, and I could see men falling. I rode a big,
bearded fellow down. Funny. I never heard the shooting,
but I heard his ribs go, with a sound like sticks broken
inside of cotton; and, after that, the sound of him screaming. We swept through their camp, leaving it in tatters with
the first charge. Then we swept back again. Three times.
The last time, the seven or eight of them who were left
alive threw down their arms and raised their hands above
their heads. We rode up to them and formed a ring around
them, sitting on our horses. You could see their eyes shifting
from one of our faces to another. . . . Then the smallest of
them started screaming:

"No! 'Fore God, no! We's yore friends! We's Union men!
We done jes' kilt Gen'l Varden for you! 'Sides, we done
surrend—"

Then Billy Thomas, a straw-headed, freckle-faced kid
who looked like a choirboy, shot him. In the belly. I could
see Billy crying as he pulled the trigger. The tears kept
pouring down his face as he shot and shot again, the big
Colt jumping in his hand, the sound of it blending in with
the other Spencers and sidearms, 'cause all of us were shooting by then, until finally, in the oldest, tiredest voice in the
world, Henry MacAllister said:

"Quit wasting ammunition, boys. They're done. . . ."

We left those 'whackers to the crows and buzzards,
but we buried the colored boys in one big grave after we

got back to the General's place. They deserved that much consideration for their loyalty. It was scant enough, God knows. Then, with Henry carrying the sleeping child cradled in his arms, we rode off, heading south.

To Selma.

WILLIAM JOSEPH RIKER

Birmingham, May, 1873–May, 1874

IV

The thing that woke me up that morning was the death carts going past my window. From the sound of them, I knew what they were; but, all the same, I got up and went to the window to watch them. Cholera is an awful thing. They'd covered the bodies on the carts over with canvas, but they hadn't done such a good job. I could see arms and legs sticking out and dangling.

I counted the carts. When I got to twenty-five, I quit counting. Twenty-five was enough. Twenty-five carts filled with the corpses of the citizens of a city not yet two years old.

Good-by, Birmingham, I thought, as I got dressed to go see Henry. Good-by MacAllister Steel Company, I added as I came out in the street. I didn't know enough to run a steel mill, and I knew it. If Henry MacAllister was already in one of those carts, we were both done.

I was scared to enter that warehouse where they were nursing the ones who weren't dead yet. Of course, I hadn't any business going in there anyhow, because it was under quarantine. But in May, 1873, there were no law officers left either on their feet or still in town to enforce a quarantine. And the docs were too busy.

Yesterday, Henry had been damn near dead. I could see him lying on the bunk now, with his back toward me. He was still, too still. I found myself tiptoeing as I walked toward him.

But when I was still a good yard away from him, he turned over. He saw me and started grinning so that I thought if his mouth spread any further it'd cut the top of his head off.

"Bill!" he roared. "I've found her! Damn it all, man, I've found her!"

I stood there gaping at him. Then I said:

"Found who?"

"That kid! General Varden's daughter! You remember we brought her down to Selma and turned her over to a family named Sturgis? Well—"

"You really shouldn't talk so much, Henry," the sweetest, gayest, prettiest voice I ever did hear, said.

I stood there. Knock me over with a feather? Hell, all you'd have had to do was to wave one near me and the breeze would have floored me. I was too smitten to even think. Or even then I would have realized that she couldn't be. Why? Look, son; the kid we took to Selma wasn't any more than eight or nine. And that was in 1865. Say she was nine. That would make her only seventeen in seventy-three. And Heddy was older than that; I'd have given her twenty that day. Funny—she kept on growing up 'til she got to twenty-five. Then she quit. Damned if I know how she did; but she never aged a day since. . . . .

"This, Bill," Henry said, taking her hand, "is Heddy Varden, General Stuart Varden's daughter. . . ."

That was another thing. We never heard that child's name spoken that day we were on the General's place. The

General and his wife called her Baby. But Heddy was a cool one, I tell you.

"Oh," she laughed, "I don't know about that. I come from Selma, and my name is Varden; that much is sure. The rest I wouldn't swear to."

"Your name," I said, "is Angel-face as far as I'm concerned. Hank, you think if I touched you I could catch it? Sure Lord would be worth getting cholera to have a nurse this doggoned pretty!"

"Hold on there, lieutenant," Henry growled—he always called me lieutenant when he was getting mad, even if we were partners in Birmingham's newest, and smallest, steel mill—"none of your levity! You're speaking to the future Mrs. Henry MacAllister, and I'll have you treat her with respect!"

I could see from her expression that this was as much of a surprise to her as it was to me. She stood there, looking at him a long, long time. Then she said:

"Is—is this a proposal, Henry?"

"Yep!" Henry barked; "Sorry I can't get on my knees. Come on, don't just stand there! Answer me! Is it yes or no? For God's sake, Heddy, speak up!"

"If you don't want him, I'm available," I said; and I was only half-joking. Maybe not even half.

"Goddamnit, Bill, shut up!" Henry shouted. "Well, Heddy?"

"I—I'll have to think about it," Heddy Varden said.

They were married on New Year's Day, 1874. Right after Charlie Linn's Calico Ball. Charlie Linn was the only man, aside from Henry, who had any faith in Birmingham, then. Eighteen seventy-three was a real panic year; worse than ninety-four by far. But Charlie Linn built a three-story, spanking-new brick building for his bank right where First

Avenue and Twentieth Street are now. Folks called it Linn's folly, because he'd spent all of thirty-six thousand dollars on it, big money in those days.

Then he sent out five hundred invitations to a Calico Ball. It was his way of shaming folks into having some faith and courage. Everybody had to come dressed in calico; no other kind of cloth was allowed.

Birmingham people, once they'd thought about it, rose to the occasion. Men came in formal even attire of the finest cut, and every stitch of their outfits—tie, shirt, waistcoat, tailcoat, trousers—was made of calico. And I've seen the women hereabouts wear some fancy duds to balls, but I'll swear I've never seen women look so pretty as the belles of Birmingham looked that last night of December, 1873, in their calico evening gowns.

So, as I was saying, Henry MacAllister married Heddy Varden on January 1, 1874. They were happy, right from the start. A sweeter, nicer woman than Heddy Varden MacAllister never drew the breath of mortal life; and I don't give a tinker's damn what people say about her now! They stayed happy right along, though that child cost them a lot of grief.

She—Gillian, I mean—was born in the spring of 1875. I loved that baby girl like she was my own; but I never understood her. She was a—a changeling, like in the fairy tales. That's about all. . . .

What I will say, though, is it's a pity the General's real daughter died. Maybe things would have been different if it had been her, 'stead of poor Heddy, that Henry married.

You're going to see her? Ask that doc up there again for me, if there's any hope. . . .

6

GEOFFRY LYNNE

Tuscaloosa, Alabama, October, 1908

I

When I got off the train in Tuscaloosa, I had the feeling I was going to be lucky. I distrusted that feeling profoundly. When I told the cabby to drive me to Byrce Hospital, he eyed me suspiciously. Probably wondering what the hell I was doing out. Then he grinned.

"Visiting a relative, mister?" he said.

"No," I said, "it's just that I keep getting these strange impulses."

His jaw dropped a little at that one.

"What kind of impulses?" he said.

"For instance, I have the strong desire to strangle cab drivers," I said peacefully, "especially when they talk too much. So be a good chap and drive me over there quietly, friend."

Old and tired as that nag was, he whipped it up into a gallop in less than a half a block. I tipped him handsomely. He needed the money to buy himself a new horse, maybe, because that fugitive from the glue factory was completely blown.

The nurse on the reception desk also looked at me with suspicion. I fought back the impulse to announce grandly: "Go tell Josephine that Napoleon is here!" but I realized that taking care of Alabama's only truly imaginative and talented citizens was hardly conducive to the development of a sense of humor. So I said:

"I'd like to see Dr. Brandt, if I may."

"He's on vacation," old vinegar puss snapped; "whattaya wanta see him about?"

None of your ruddy business, I thought; but I kept my temper. Certain jobs attract certain people, and the types who want to be policemen, soldiers, priests, and keepers of the insane have my rather weary pity.

"Isn't there anyone I could see instead?" I said politely; "the nature of my visit is both delicate and private."

"Everybody's visit is delicate and private," she said wearily, "that is, when they walk in here of their own free will." Dr. Conner is in charge. First door to the left. . . ."

I knocked and a great, booming voice sang out cheerfully:

"Come in!"

I pushed open the door. And saw this boy sitting behind the desk. He was busily pushing tobacco into a battered corncob pipe. His deep-blue eyes twinkled merrily as he performed that monumental task. He was immensely tall— all of six feet four, I guessed; but he didn't look a day over nineteen years old.

"What may I do for you?" he said in that astonishingly deep voice.

"You—you *are* Dr. Conner?" I said.

"Guilty as charged," he grinned; "and I'm thirty-one years old—which will save you from wasting both your time

and mine trying delicately to find out how the hell a young-
ster can be in charge of the local bedlam. Sit down. What
can I do for you? Been having any strange impulses lately?"

"Doctor," I said solemnly, "if you knew me, you
wouldn't ask that question. You'd try to find out if I'd had
any sensible ones. The answer is, I have, and it worries me.
Permit me to introduce myself. My name is Geoffry Lynne."

He looked at me, and I knew instantly that he was
good at his chosen profession. Damned good. That look
penetrated to the bone.

"Gregory Lynne's brother?" he said quietly.

"Yes," I said; "that's why I'm here. . . ."

"I see," he smiled as he spoke. "You want my professional opinion as to your brother's mental state when he
committed that crime—as a possible insanity plea? I couldn't
answer that offhand, not being a charlatan. I should have to
examine him rather carefully, and over a long period of
time. I'd guess that he was sane, which wouldn't help your
case at all. . . ."

"It certainly wouldn't," I said.

He lit that noisome pipe of his. Studied me through
the smoke screen he made. I had a feeling he often did
things like this: tricks of the trade, perhaps, delaying actions, giving him time to pry up what he wanted to know.
But he smiled again; and his face was once more frank and
open. Maybe he'd decided I was a good sort. I didn't
know. . . .

"But there are other approaches, you know," he said.
"I assume you came here for help. Frankly, that pleases me.
You may even have come to the right place, since your only
chance of saving your brother is to establish a motivation
so strong, a provocation on Mrs. Ames' part so gross, that
an appeal might win him a retrial, and a prison sentence instead of death. An acquittal is too much to hope for."

"Is it?" I said. "Ever consider the possibility that he didn't do it? That he's sacrificing himself to save someone? Someone whom he loves?"

"Yes," Dr. Conner said. "I have considered that possibility, and discarded it. For that would involve only one circumstance: that your brother knows Hero Farnsworth killed her. He wouldn't die for anyone else. He simply isn't that big a fool."

"Good lord!" I said; "you do know an awful lot about this case!"

"Because I'm involved in it," he said simply. "Thirteen years ago, they brought a woman to this place—a woman whom Gillian MacAllister wrecked. Even, I'd venture to suggest, the woman you came here to see: Mrs. MacAllister, Gillian's mother. She'd spent ten years of hopeless misery here until, three years ago, I joined the staff. Since then, she has improved tremendously—but we'll go into that, later. You're probably pressed for time. What would you like to do?"

"Doctor," I said, "is there any reason I shouldn't talk to Heddy MacAllister?"

He looked at me, and his candid eyes clouded with real pain. Then they cleared. I could see speculation in them, feel his thought: Can I trust this oddball? Dare I?

"I mean," I added quickly, "that I shouldn't like to say anything that might get her excited or upset. From what you've said, she's recovering; and a shock might—"

"Cure her completely," he said crisply. "It often does when the patient is sunk in lethargy and melancholic depression. It is only when the sick person is overexcited already that one has to avoid—shocking—him or her. . . ."

There was, I realized, an awful lot he was leaving unsaid.

"You're saying, Doctor," I said, "that Mrs. MacAllister is one of those who *needs* to be shocked?"

"I didn't say that," he said softly. "My field is too new for us to be certain of anything, yet. But, if you want my *opinion*, an opinion to which strong opposition exists, even among my colleagues, I'd say—yes. Furthermore, I'd say that if certain information now being withheld from Mrs. MacAllister were made available to her, she'd make a start-lingly swift recovery—"

"And that information is?" I said.

"Professional and classified," he said dryly. "Come, I'll take you to her, now."

HEDDY MACALLISTER
and
GEOFFRY LYNNE
Tuscaloosa, 1908

II

[I was surprised at the change in Heddy. For the first time in her life, she looked her actual age. She had surrendered now, gone plump and gray-haired, soft and matronly. Even like that, I liked her very much.—J. L.]

"Don't you think my doctor's awfully nice, Geoffry?" she said gaily. "He's taught me so many things! I'm just a bundle of complexes; but then, so are you, so's everybody else. . . ."

"Even Gilly?" I said.

"Gillian? More than anybody else, the poor, poor thing! You're surprised that I pity her? Why? She's my daughter, you know; and she really isn't responsible for her actions. . . ."

"If *she* isn't, who is?" I said.

Heddy hesitated.

"Jeff—you—you won't laugh at me or think I'm—crazy, if I tell you what I really think?"

"No," I said stoutly; "of course not, Heddy—"

She leaned forward, staring at my face a long, long time. Dropped her voice to a whisper; said:

"Buleah. Buleah Land. . . ."

"You mean that Buleah—?"

"Made Gillian what she is today?" she said. "Yes, Jeff; I do think that. Only don't ask me why I think it. I—I don't know. It—it's just a feeling I have."

"Oh, come now, Heddy," I said; "it must be more than merely a feeling. . . ."

She held me with her eyes.

"No, Jeff. No more than a feeling," she said; "but feelings are—sometimes—quite enough. . . ."

Again I saw how hopeless my efforts were. I hadn't come here to talk about feelings. What I needed were facts, concrete evidence, clues that would lead to—

But then, at that moment, I looked into Heddy's eyes. Saw, for the first time, what lurked below their bright blue candor. Saw what it was that had held her in Byrce Hospital all these years: not madness—terror.

And Dr. Conner's cryptic remarks came blindingly clear. Heddy didn't know that Gillian was dead! I was, in the long moment that I went on staring at her, prepared to stake my life upon the accuracy of that guess.

Further, the doctor, being a kindly man, had willed that I reach precisely this conclusion; moreover, had desired me to act upon it; had skirted the edges of professional ethics as closely as he dared to put into my hands the key of Heddy's deliverance.

I opened my mouth. Closed it again. Because even Dr.

Conner wasn't that sure. He believed that the shock of this news would free Heddy of the fear she'd lived with for thirteen years. On the surface, it was logical enough; say: "You've nothing more to fear, Heddy; for your oppressor, your nemesis, is—dead. . . ."

Only the human spirit is a tender thing, as nebulous, as tenuous as air. How could I know, be sure—

Then, abruptly, savagely, I decided. It was damned well worth the chance. If Dr. Conner's belief was correct, I'd free Heddy. If not, she couldn't be much worse off than she was now. So I said:

"Don't you ever think about coming home again, Heddy?"

She stared at me, those blue eyes opened wide. Then she whispered:

"What home, Jeff, dear? You don't imagine that I could live in the same house with Gillian, do you? I'm not a very strong person, you know. She would put me back here forever—and not like I am now, a little too nervous—but really insane."

I blurted it out then, my voice tight and harsh, doing nothing to soften the blow, nothing to shield her.

"Gillian can't harm you," I said flatly; "she can't hurt anyone any more now, Heddy. You see—she's—dead."

She sat there frozen, her very flesh, it seemed to me, turned to stone. Then those matchless eyes of hers clouded, filled, brimmed, spilled.

"Heddy!" I got out.

"Oh, Jeff!" she whispered. "Yes, yes, I'm crying! She was my baby, don't you understand? I held her in my arms, nursed her at my breast. . . . And she was what she was, because I—I failed her, wasn't a good mother, didn't know, couldn't understand—"

"Gilly," I said, a little angrily, thinking how wasted

was this tender grief, "would have been the same had you been an angel out of glory. And you damned well ought be glad she's dead!"

"No, no!" she wept; "don't say those things! I'm not glad she's dead! I wish it were me, Jeff! I wish it were me! I'm all alone now, so alone. Henry—gone, hating me before he died; and now—Gillian. . . ."

I didn't say anything. The required words were beyond my talents. They required genius—or saintliness, both of which I lacked.

"Please, Jeff," Heddy whispered, "go away now. I need to be alone. And don't look so worried. I'm going to be all right. I'm not really sick, you know. I—I'll get over this, too. I've had to get over so many things. . . ."

GEOFFRY LYNNE

Tuscaloosa, 1908

III

I went to look for Dr. Conner. I was badly frightened. Heddy's reaction had been a bit too intense for my liking. But when I found him, I was unable to tell him my fears. You see, he was not alone. He was talking to, of all people, Gillian's chauffeur, Tim Nelson.

"How do you do, Mr. Lynne," Tim said respectfully. "Sorry I was unable to say anything at Mr. Gregory's trial that would have helped. But—honor bright, what, sir? I only told the truth. . . ."

I stared at that oily, unctuous bastard. And, as always, those aching questions: Where the devil have I seen this

mug before? and, What damned crooked thing was he up
to then? clawed deep into my mind. I said:

"What are *you* doing up here, Tim?"

He flushed.

"Paying a call on the good doctor, y'might say, sir. He's
been jolly decent to me, y'know. I used to bring things up
here to Mrs. MacAllister on Mrs. Ames' behalf—that's how
I had the honor of making his acquaintance. . . ."

"I might say you're calling on the doctor, all right," I
said grimly; "but I happen to prefer the truth. Why are you
up here, Tim?"

"It's—it's private, sir," Tim said slowly; "and personal,
quite. But if you insist—"

"I insist," I snapped.

"You're barking up the wrong tree, Mr. Lynne," Dr.
Conner said pleasantly. "There's nothing mysterious about
Tim's visits. Chalk them up to that old biological urge—or,
if you prefer, Dan Cupid's marksmanship."

Tim Nelson blushed. He actually did.

"Nurse Meadows," he said. "Nurse Tilly Meadows, on
reception, you know, sir—has consented to make me the
happiest of men. . . ." (Don't blame that beaut of a phrase
on me! Tim actually talked like that. His idea of gentility
seemed to have come straight out of the very worst mid-
century novels.)

"How charming," I sneered. "When's the happy event
to take place, Tim?"

His face lengthened into a caricature of a beagle's.

"That's just it, sir," he said lugubriously; "I don't know.
Tilly hasn't come back from her vacation. Fact is, the doctor
here tells me she's long overdue. . . ."

"Meadows took a fall vacation," Dr. Conner said, "together with accumulated sick leave. But she should have

been back a month ago. Strange. . . . Tim, I'd suggest you drive down to Mobile and look her up—"

"Righto, Doctor!" Tim said. "I'll do just that. Tilly's far too sweet a girl for a chap to let go without a struggle, what? You'll excuse me, Doctor; Mr. Lynne? Gentlemen, your servant! And a very good day to you both!"

After he had gone, I told Dr. Conner the effect my brutal announcement of Gillian's death had had on Heddy. He smiled.

"Good!" he said. "Very healthy! I thank you, Mr. Lynne. You've done nobly. I'll drop in to see her in a little while."

"Doctor," I said, "doesn't that chauffeur strike you as—odd?"

"No," he laughed. "Tim's rather a bit too normal. Great eye for the ladies. Only his mannerisms might be all right on the other side of the Atlantic; but I'm afraid they're a handicap here. I'm sure Tilly didn't come back because she's changed her mind about marrying him. . . ."

"All right," I said; "let's drop the subject of Tim Nelson. Doctor, is it possible for a child's nurse—even an ignorant colored woman—to so warp that child's personality as to make her into what Gillian was?"

"Definitely," he said without hesitation. "And neither the color nor the ignorance would have much to do with it, except, perhaps, to make it worse. A child's mind is a very plastic thing, easily shaped or distorted. And in our society, unfortunately, the child usually comes more directly under the nurse's influence than under the mother's. But why do you ask this?"

I told him what Heddy had said about Buleah Land.

"Hmmmn," he mused; "I most certainly would talk to this Buleah Land if I were you, Mr. Lynne. . . ."

"Why?" I said acidly.

"Why?" he echoed. "Because most things go much further back than we know. Even murder. We may know what hand struck the blow; but do we realize how far back in childhood the festering seed of hate may have been planted?"

"So, not knowing which hand—" I suggested.

"We look for that seed," Dr. Conner said.

BULEAH LAND

Gillian's Childhood

IV

My baby were th' sweetest lil thing, Mister Jeff! 'N anybody what says she been wild 'n wicked all her life purely ain't telling the truth! She changed after she was so awful sick that time. 'Twas after that that Miz Heddy caught her under th' front porch steps with that there po' mill-trash boy, 'n packed her off to Canada. . . .

That ain't what you wants to know? How come she changed? Lawd, Mister Jeff, honey, I dunno! 'Cause when she was little, she was a angel. Putting her soft lil arms 'round my neck 'n a-whispering: "I loves 'oo, Booley, 'n not nobody else!" Why I used to take her for walks in the woods, clean outa town, packing a lunch so's I could keep her to myself long as I could. Lawd Gawd I loved that baby child so! Used to make like she was my po' Lillian I'd done lost. Wasn't hard. My Lilly was damn near white, herself. Even had yaller hair. Only 'twas kind o' kinky. Lawd, Lawd, I was crazy 'bout that pretty child! When that no-good tomcatting black bastid she'd took up with cut her throat, I plumb nigh lost my mind! Fact is, I did lose it for

a spell, Mister Jeff. Reckon if I hadn't gone to work for Miz
Heddy a-taking care o' my little angel baby they'd of had
to lock me up. But that was what saved me, taking care of
Miss Gilly—made up to me for losing my Lillian; gave me
packed her off to Canada. . . .

What did I do after Miss Gilly come back from her
honeymoon 'n put all us niggers out? Oh, I worked here 'n
there for different folks. But mostly I didn't have to work,
'cause I'd finally married my Rad, after his old woman died.
Hard-working man, my Rad, always made good money.
Nawsuh—'course that boy o' his'n ain't mine—the no'count
scamp! He was Rad 'n Rachie's child. Never could stand
him myself—always a-gittin into trouble. Still, it was a pity
he got killed down there in that mine. . . .

Yep, I worked for Miz Hero for a spell. Mighty sweet
lil girl, Miz Hero. Reckon she'n Mister Michael'll get married, now; a heap sooner than is decent, considering my
poor baby ain't even cold under ground.

What's that? Do I know who killed her? Why sho',
Mister Jeff! It were—your brother, Mister Greg. . . .

Mister Jeff! What ails you, suh? Leggo o' my arm!
What's all these heah scars on the inside o' it? Well, like I
done tol' you, when I lost my Lillian, I was right pert bad
off, suh; 'n Dr. Forbes had to give me a mighty heap o'
injections to keep me from harming myself. . . .

What's that? I ain't tellin' th' truth? Mister Jeff, Mister
Jeff! What a suspicious mind you's got! Sho Lawd feels
sorry for you, suh, spending all your time thinking bad o'
folks 'n talking ugly 'bout 'em. That's why you couldn't
understand my baby nohow. . . .

All right, I'm a-going. But you ain't got no call to git
riled at me, suh. Ain't I told you ever thing you wants to
know?

GEOFFRY LYNNE

Pages from My 1908 Notebooks

V

Useless. The whole thing's a pack of lies. I honestly don't believe that Buleah answered truthfully a single question that I asked her. I had gotten nothing of value from her. Nothing at all. But I had enlisted a valuable ally: Dr. Conner. I wrote him constantly, asking advice. And as hard as it was to follow, one thing he told me stuck in my brain.

"Go very far back, Jeff. The motivation for this dates back to her childhood. I've studied your brother rather carefully, now, although he is very difficult to work with since he will not talk. But I am convinced you're right. If Greg killed Gillian Ames, it was by purest accident. He is not at all the type who kills. There exists the possibility that he is protecting someone for reasons of his own—even *mistaken* reasons. Have you talked to Hero Farnsworth? Does there exist any reason for Greg's believing—rightly or wrongly—that *she* could have killed Gillian?

"If not, explore the past in depth. Because, if the killer were someone besides your brother, he had to be someone Gillian had known a long, long time. Almost surely a lover. One whom she was accustomed to admitting to her bedroom without question."

Hell, Doc, I thought wearily, you'll have me investigating half the male population of Birmingham.

Then, because I couldn't think of what else to do, I again talked with Michael Ames.

MICHAEL AMES

My Childhood

VI

Frankly, I don't see how talking about my childhood could
possibly help save Greg, no matter what that booby-hatch
keeper says. The motive for the crime goes back to Gillian's
childhood and that of the murderer? Jeff, I ask you! That's
just about the most arrant piece of nonsense I have ever
heard.

All right. My background was much the same as yours
or Greg's, or almost anyone else's that we know. Except
that your father and the father of our friends lived long
enough to make it. Mine didn't. So, I had a rough childhood.
I remained socially acceptable, but poor. Which is one bad
combination, Jeff. People felt sorry for me; and there is
nothing harder to endure than that. I was invited right along
to all the birthday parties, picnics, and, later on, to the
dances and balls. But my clothes were shabby. I had to
wear a suit long after it had really ceased to fit.

Come to think of it, perhaps your doctor friend is right.
A childhood like mine can damned well warp a man.

The worst of it was that I was twelve years old when my
dad died. Old enough to remember him, old enough to recall the good life I'd had before. You see, Jeff, he was a
prince. And twelve years was long enough. What he'd done
for me by then, not even my mother could destroy.

Though, God knows, she tried. I wonder why some
women are like that. What instinct is it that makes them
want to wreck their sons?

Mind you, it's not cruelty—not conscious cruelty, at any rate. It's that cloying, prehensile side of femininity gone absolutely off the deep end. Yet the effects of it are often cruel: up until the day she died, my mother never stopped trying to convince me that I killed my father!

How? You know that he died of burns he got while saving Mother and me from our house the night it burned to the ground. He saved me first, then went back for her. I think she never ceased to resent that fact. The trouble was that even then I was interested in science. I'd bought a set of chemicals out of my pocket money; set up a childish laboratory in our basement. And—Mother may have been right, Jeff. That fire did start in the basement. Started there, and was completely beyond control before any of us woke up.

But even if I did—which remains unproved—because too little was left to really prove anything; my dad's death remains a tragic accident, and not a crime. Yet, day after day, I had to hear: "Oh, if your poor dear father had only lived! Oh, why did I ever let you buy those horrible chemicals!"

I was feeling like a monster, beginning to loathe myself. What saved me, I think, was her death. When I was a junior in college. And yet, she was a good woman, Jeff. She loved me wholeheartedly, sacrificed her life for my sake. She could have married again, you know; she was only in her early thirties when my father died.

Go a bit more into detail? All right. No, I wasn't too friendly with Gillian as a child. Just about like the rest of you. I was invited to her parties, that was all. I don't think I even liked her; she was such a wicked little minx! For one thing, she was cruel to animals, which is a thing I cannot abide.

I was rather fonder of Hero, who has been an angel all her life. As a child, she was so sweet and shy. Guess I've always been in love with her without realizing it. I cannot imagine what satanic impulse made me turn to Gilly after I'd grown up.

Strange, because although I was unaffected by my mother's attempts at psychological gelding, I seemed to have no defenses against the kind of knife that Gillian swung. You might ask your friend Conner what he thinks of all that.

GEOFFRY LYNNE

Page from my 1908 Notebooks
A Letter from Dr. Conner

VII

I did ask him. Here is his reply:

"Men always marry the kind of woman that something in them craves. When that craving is healthy and normal, the marriage is apt to be a success. When it is not, the results are apt to be disastrous. It seems abundantly clear that despite Michael Ames' rationalizations, his mother did succeed in instilling a deep-seated sense of guilt in him over his father's death. And guilt feelings are one of the bases for masochism. I think it could be demonstrated that it was precisely her cruelty, which he knew, that attracted Michael Ames to Gillian MacAllister. You see, Jeff, sub-consciously, he wanted to suffer; he was fairly begging to be punished for murdering his father, which was what his mother had convinced him he had done. For some women are worse than black-widow spiders or praying mantises; not only do they devour their mates but finish off their sons for dessert, as well!"

Which, as you can see, was no help at all. I decided to

ignore the good doctor's advice and come closer to the present. So I asked Michael to tell me more of his courtship, more of how he came to marry Gillian, to see if in *that* there were some kind of clue.

MICHAEL AMES

Birmingham, June, 1894

VIII

"Michael," Mr. MacAllister said to me, "will you have supper with us tonight?"

I didn't want to. Those suppers at the MacAllisters were pure torture. We sat around the big table and nobody said anything. Gillian picked at her food. When she looked at her mother, Heddy jumped as though someone had struck her. Both Heddy and Gillian looked terrible. Neither of them had eaten enough, since that catastrophic garden party, to keep a bird alive. I knew Henry MacAllister invited me so often because things were even worse when I wasn't there. I didn't know how really bad they were, during my absence; but, just looking at Henry, I could see they were bad enough.

He was gazing at me now with the eyes of a dog imploring his master not to beat him. As much as I hated those suppers, I couldn't refuse.

"Very well, sir," I said. "Thank you very much."

He put his big hand on my shoulder.

"No, Michael," he said gravely; "Thank *you* very much. You're doing me a favor. A very great favor."

"Hardly that, sir," I began; but he went on, stubbornly:

"She respects you. Strange. I think it's because you

had the guts to slap her when she damned well deserved it—"

"I'm sorry I did that, sir," I said.

"I'm not! I'll tell you one thing, son. Any man who'd let that little witch get the better of him, just once, would see hell from her the rest of his life. Well, shall we go?"

In the carriage, riding toward Birmingham—for Mac-Allister Steel is a good long way out of town—I could feel his eyes upon me in the darkness. Finally, when we were almost to the house, he said:

"Tell me, Michael, are you in love with my daughter?"

I didn't hesitate.

"Yes, sir," I said. "I guess I always been. But considering the fact that my father left my mother very little money, I've never had much hope."

He stared out of the window a few seconds.

"Your mother was a wonderful woman," he said. "A pity she didn't live to see you now. But, as far as your lack of money is concerned, that's no real objection. This is America, son. People don't have to stay poor. You won't. With your training, you're sure to reach the top of the ladder —and soon. You've been working for me a month, and already you've cut my losses from bad heats more than seventy-five per cent. I've investigated and found out that every heat we've had to scrap was due to some stubborn old jackass, like Bill Riker, for instance, changing your orders. I've had it out with Bill. He'll cooperate in the future. And I've made the rest understand that the next man who deliberately refuses to do exactly what you've told him gets his walking papers. Mind you, I'm leaving them leeway for honest mistakes; but this damned insubordination has to go!"

"Thanks, sir," I said.

"I haven't a son," he said slowly, shyly. "Only—Gillian.

You say you love her. How can you? You were there when it happened. You've seen Gilly as she really is. Name of God, Michael, how can you?"

"Gillian," I said, "is the most beautiful girl I've ever known. But let's skip the obvious. I've always had a partiality for the weak and the helpless, for small animals and people who needed me—"

"Gillian—weak and helpless? Michael, you're crazy!"

"Undoubtably," I said; "but I think you're the one who is mistaken, sir. You believe that Gillian's rages and her fiendish temper are signs of strength. That just isn't so. Anything a person can't keep a checkrein on is a weakness. Maybe I'm wrong, but I think I can bring out the real Gillian—the goodness and sweetness I know are there. . . ."

"Goodness and sweetness," he muttered; "Michael, you're wrong. I wish to God Almighty on His throne on high that you weren't, but you are!"

"I don't think so," I said easily. "Mr. MacAllister, may I ask you something?"

"Why sure, son," he said.

"Would you have any serious objections to my courting Gillian? Beyond that, would you consider me an acceptable son-in-law?"

The carriage had drawn up before the mansion as I spoke. Henry MacAllister made no move to get out. He sat there, looking straight ahead. Finally he turned to me.

"Those are hard questions, Michael," he said gravely; "but I'll try to answer them. First of all, I do object to your courting my daughter; but only for your own sake. You're young, well-educated, brilliant. You've a right to a happy married life. With Gillian, you wouldn't have it. Wait—don't interrupt me—

"I've studied you carefully, son. All right, that once she pushed you into slapping her—mostly, I'm sure, in defense of her mother and me. But you weren't yourself, then. You don't have a mean streak anywhere in your make-up. And anybody who hasn't is lost with Gillian. The second question is easier: I'd be delighted to have you for a son-in-law. When I die, I should like to leave MacAllister Steel in capable hands. And you're extremely capable. Besides, son, I like you. So—court Gilly if you must—with my permission. But remember that I warned you what you're getting into. Come on now, we'd better go in. . . ."

That night, the atmosphere around the supper table was even worse than usual. I tried to ease things by talking casually about business, plans for the future, new techniques I'd read about, to Mr. MacAllister. He answered me slowly and absently, his mind obviously a thousand miles away.

Abruptly, Gillian stood up.

"Oh, for God's sake, Michael!" she said. "If you think I'm going to sit here and listen to you and Father talk shop, you're wrong. I've never understood why he couldn't have made his money in something less vulgar—like breeding race horses, or working a great plantation. Those are gracious occupations. But this smoky, smelly business of iron-making, ugh!"

"It—it has kept you clothed, fed, and given you an education!" Heddy MacAllister flared suddenly. Heddy, too, had her limits, and they had been reached and passed.

"You—you spoke to me!" Gillian whispered. "You dared! You! Excuse me, one and all! I've taken my last meal in this company. Surely I can be spared the presence of street-walkers—"

"Gilly!" Henry's roar was that of a wounded lion.

"During mealtimes as well. From now on, Father, I shall eat in my room—if you care to send me up something. If not, I'll do without. I'd rather be dead anyhow than to—"

I was on my feet, too, by then.

"You'll apologize for that, Gilly," I said.

She turned and stared at me, her blue eyes widening in her face. Then, suddenly, startlingly, she began to laugh.

"Oh, Michael!" she gasped. "You are so funny! Especially when you're trying to act like a man! But you can't, darling. Don't you know that? You're awfully sweet. I mean that, really. I even think I'm going to marry you—"

"Gilly!" I whispered.

"But you're a boy. You'll always be a boy—a very pretty pink and blond boy whom some woman will have to take care of. Don't look so hurt, darling. You're in good company. Father's a boy, too. All American men are. I don't know about foreigners—those Canuck lads I met when I went to French School in Canada did seem different—but our men can't or won't grow up. The great American boy-man! It's a good thing we women were born with a lot of patience. . . ."

She seemed to have forgotten her mother's presence, or what had started the whole thing. She was smiling at me with that enchanting expression I'd always loved. But, for the first time, I was beginning to fathom what lay behind and beneath that angelic smile; and there was a coldness at my heart's core, making it hard for me to breathe. She kept on smiling. Her expression did not change. Her voice continued bright, well-modulated, pleasant, as she said:

"Oh, yes, I rather think I shall marry you, Michael. You should be easy to manage. But let us set matters straight right now, my beloved. I don't take orders. I never have. I never will. If you don't believe me, ask Father—"

I flashed a glance toward him. What I saw sickened me with pity; but Gillian was talking still.

"There isn't any way, Michael, that you'll ever be able to force me to do the slightest thing I don't want to do. A moment ago, you were insisting that I apologize to this— this creature who unfortunately happens to be my mother.

Well, I won't. Not now. Not ever. I'll see her dead and in
hell first. And you, Michael dearest, cannot make me. Say
you were to revert to your bully's tactics and slap me. I
assure you that you'd give the whole thing up from sheer
physical fatigue long before I'd even be tempted to budge
an inch. You could slap me and slap me and slap me all day
and all night and all the next day and the next night for as
long as you could keep it up, and I still wouldn't apologize.
And the price you'd have to pay for having hit me would
convince you that no matter what I did, however provoking
I should be in the future, you'd never dream of striking me
again. . . ."

"'I'm not so sure of that," I said grimly.

"Oh, don't be unnecessarily stupid!" she said, with only
the barest hint of the clangor of steel in her voice. "I am,
actually, being very fair to you, Michael. I'm giving you
every chance to run. You know what I'm like. If we should
be married—and Father will consent to it gladly for the pure
relief of being rid of me—you can never say I deceived you.
I don't love you. I don't love any man. I've never seen a man
yet who was worth it. But I am fond of you. You are a very
pretty little boy, with an odd, appealing sweetness about
you. I shall be very kind to you—so long as you never attempt
to give me orders, or question my coming and going, or
object to anything, no matter how strange it may seem, that
I choose to do. And what's more, quite frankly, I don't know
whether I shall have more contempt for you if you're fool
enough to stay—or coward enough to go. . . ."

She turned slightly toward her parents.

"Good night, all," she said pleasantly; "even to you,
Mother—dear. . . ."

Then she walked out of the dining room like—no, not
like a queen, like a goddess. And the silence after her going
was absolute. The clock on the mantel ticked on. Each

pendulum stroke was the blow of a drop forge crashing against white-hot metal. I could feel the jar of it in the very tissues of my brain.

"Michael," Heddy whispered; "I—I wish you'd stay the night. I'd feel safer with you in the house. . . ."

I wanted to say to her, to shout: You're wrong! She is not mad. This is not insanity; but something else—something worse. . . . But I could not tell them what it was, because I did not know, myself. So I said, very gently:

"Very well—that is, if Mr. MacAllister hasn't any objections—"

"No," he said wearily. "No, Michael—please stay. . . ."

That night, for the first time, Gillian MacAllister came to my bed. I do not know how she knew or found out I had stayed. But at two o'clock in the morning, she pushed open the door and stood there silhouetted against the gaslight in the hall, and I saw that she was as naked as the day her mother gave her birth. No—nakeder. For the developments of pubescence had taken place early in her. Gillian had been all woman since she was thirteen years old. And the round, pink, soft dimpled nudity of babies is one thing, while that of a woman—but that is wrong, too. Gillian didn't look like a woman, that night. She looked—female. There is a difference, you know.

My friends insist I am not a sensual man. Some of them, extremists by nature, declare, especially when they're in their cups, that in another, younger, purer age, I might even have become a saint. Beyond the fact that a man without sensuality does not exist, they forget the hair shirts and the knotted whips that the saints, themselves, have flayed their own bodies with, to tame the beast that howls unchained in the cavern of every human heart.

She left me in the morning, when the first light was

fading the stars out, graying the dark. And I, lying there, staring at the ceiling, feeling the knot of terror tangling up my guts, examined the shape and the dimensions of my new slavery. For it was that, Jeff. No lesser word would do.

7

HERO AMES

June, 1894

Eliza came into my room with the black dress over her arm.

"No," I said; "I'm not going to wear black any more, Eliza. Look in the closet and you'll find a white one. Handle it carefully; it's new. And bring those boxes off the top shelf."

Eliza stared at me. My father, Professor Giles, used to frequently say before the war that it was distinctly debatable whether he owned Negroes or the Negroes owned him. I'm inclined toward the latter view. And I don't think the war changed matters. Nowadays, we pay them, but they still own us. Colored people, by and large, make the most exasperatingly inefficient servants the world has ever seen. Only they manage, with ludicrous ease, to make you love them. Then they've got you. And they know it. Eliza stood there glaring at me, exactly as though she were my mother and I were an exceedingly naughty child. I haven't the faintest doubt that that was precisely the way she felt about it; which, come to think of it, was hardly strange, since my mother died giving birth to me, and Eliza nursed me at her own voluminous breasts.

"Lord God, Miz Hero," she said; "it ain't decent! Poor Mr. Rodney ain't been under ground seven whole months, yet, and—"

"Eliza!" I snapped. "You go get me my white dress, right now!"

"Yes'm," she grumbled; "but if you ain't the beatingest chile I ever did see! Folks going to talk about you real scandalous. All right, all right, I'm going!"

She came back the precise instant before I had finally made up my mind to go look for her. Eliza's sense of timing borders on the miraculous: she knows to the last grim second how long she can balk before I will explode.

Without a word, I held up my arms, and she slipped the dress over my head. I sat very still while she fastened the twenty-odd buttons that ran up the back. When she had finished, I turned to her.

"Open the boxes, Eliza," I said. "The smaller one first."

She had already stopped grumbling. She took the white kid shoes out of the box and handed them to me. I slipped them on, and watched her out of the corner of my eye as she opened the big hat box. I could see her eyes light up when she saw the hat. She took it out and stood there holding it in her fat, black hands with actual reverence. Then she came up behind me and put it on my head, managing, as usual, to set it at an angle that was horrible.

I adjusted the hat. It was made of white satin, like a turban, except the ends of it flared upward into wire-stiffened points. And, on the crown of it, one above the other, three stuffed white birds nestled. I hated the cruel fashion that took the lives of harmless creatures to adorn a woman's silly head; but I wasn't going to let Gillian MacAllister outdo me. She was far too pretty for me to compete with

her in that regard; but I thought I could show her a thing
or two when it came to style.

The hat was fastened about my neck with two bands
which tied into a huge bow of satin. I can wear white. It
does things for my dark complexion.

Eliza stood there with her arms folded, beaming at me.

"I do declare!" she said; "I just nacherly do declare!"

"You do declare what?" I teased. I looked nice, and I
knew it.

"You just nacherly looks good enough to eat, Miz Hero!"
Eliza laughed. "I 'pologizes right now. You was right. Time
you took off that ugly black. Lord, Lord! Bet my bottom
dollar you comes back from that there wedding with a
brand-new beau. . . ."

"No, thank you, Eliza," I said sadly.

"Now, don't you worry your pretty head none a-tall,"
Eliza said. "Mr. Michael ain't nobody's fool. He got too
much sense to git hisself mixed up too much with that there
awful MacAllister gal. . . ."

Negroes, I swear, have second sight. I hadn't even
mentioned Michael's name to Eliza in over three years.

"Oh, you make me tired, Eliza!" I said.

"No, I don't. Knows my baby better'n she know herself.
I'm glad to see you showing some spunk at last, Miz Hero.
You go right out there and fight for your man. . . ."

I stood up.

"Eliza," I said, "go tell Anxious to bring the surrey
around."

"Yes'm, Miz Hero," Eliza grinned. She knew as well as
I did that this was just an excuse to get rid of her. It was
far too early to go to Dorothy Rollins' wedding. She ambled
toward the door. In it, she paused long enough to fire a
parting shot:

"Reckon them Rollinses is scairt. They sure Lord rush-

ing things afore Miss Gilly takes herself a notion to grab
that Byrce boy back. She could, too. All she got to do is to
crook her little finger an'—"

I'd had enough. "Eliza!" I screamed. "You get out of
here!"

There was nothing for me to do but to leave the house.
I wouldn't have had a moment's peace from Eliza if I hadn't.
There have been many times I've wished I could fire her and
hire a younger woman. But I couldn't. It would have been
like trying to fire my own mother.

So I told Anxious—he's Eliza's husband and he's called
Anxious because he's always saying "I'm just plumb anxious
over it."—to take me for a drive. And then I realized that he
and Eliza were engineering a conspiracy. Negro house servants just love to arrange the lives of their white folks. And
the surprising thing is how often they succeed. Nobody will
ever know how many marriages got started when some
family's Eliza or Rachel or Buleah said to her mistress:

"You know, Miz Jane, I been thinking. That there
Thomas boy would make Miss Sue a mighty fine husband.
Them Thomases is real quality, and 'sides they got a awful
heap o' money. . . ."

Anyhow, the first thing I knew, we had turned into the
block where Michael lived. I couldn't tell Anxious to turn
the horses around in the middle of the block without giving
myself away. The necessity for preserving our dignity is our
greatest weakness as far as our colored people are concerned.
They are forever backing us up into corners we'd have to
make utter fools of ourselves to get out of. I still wonder
whether or not Michael's Ernest weren't in on the plot.
When I saw Michael coming out of the house, I could hear
with furious certainty Anxious whispering into the mouth-
piece of the telephone, which, in my house, unfortunately,
is located downstairs in the hall:

"You git Mr. Michael to come outside long 'bout ten. 'Liza's going to git Miz Hero ready real early. . . ."

Michael saw me, and smiled. Anxious pulled the horses up at once, without a word from me. I could see Michael walking toward me; and my heart climbed into my throat, then dived into the pit of my stomach. I was quite sure I wasn't going to be able to talk to him at all.

He came up to the surrey and took my hand. I gave his hand a polite squeeze, then opened my fingers to let go, because just the touch of his fingers was enough to send the shivers racing up and down my spine. But he stood there smiling at me, with my hand imprisoned in his grip; and his eyes had a strange, puzzled look in them. It was as though he were seeing me, really seeing me, for the first time in his life.

"My God, but you're lovely, Hero," he said.

I was as flustered as a schoolgirl at her first dance.

"It's—it's the dress," I stammered idiotically; "I've been in black so long—"

"It's not the dress," Michael said in that solemn tone he always used when he was going to tease me; yet I had the feeling, somehow, that he was not entirely teasing; "It's you. You look like a pagan princess—a very lovely princess come by caravan from far Cathay. You should be surrounded by beturbaned slaves with scimitars in their hands; and you should be wearing a wisp of veil to hide your mouth, and add to the mystery of your eyes. . . ."

Michael was like that. Even as a child, he used to talk poetic nonsense by the hour. I started to tell him rather sharply that I knew only too well how I looked; when I saw he meant it. Every woman on earth is entitled to a moment of perfect happiness at least once in her life; and I had mine now. I felt warm, suddenly—warm and good. The sunlight slanting along that street took on a richer golden tone; in the trees, a million invisible birds that had not been there a second ago began to sing, trilling their notes up to the very sky. There was music everywhere: in the little talking wind that rippled the trees, in the soft clipclopping of passing horses, in the swift and secret beating of my heart. I felt Michael's hand tighten over my fingers; and he leaned forward suddenly, peering into my face.

"Why," he whispered, "why, Hero, you're crying!"

I hadn't been aware of it; but now I felt the scalding rush of tears flooding my eyes. That made it worse; they rained down all the faster.

"Why are you crying, little Hero?" Michael said.

"Because—because you said I was p-p-pretty!" I sobbed. "Oh, Michael, I—I've n-n-n-never been called pretty, before! I—"

"To be called pretty makes you cry?" he said. "That's odd. Why does it?"

I wanted to tell him the truth; that it was because it was he who had said the magic words; but I didn't dare. So I said:

"I'm sorry, Michael. I guess I am odd. You see, when you have been the ugly duckling all your life—"

"Ugly?" Michael said. "You?"

His voice was genuinely surprised. And I knew Michael Ames. He was the most utterly truthful person I've ever known. It simply never occurred to him to lie, not even for form's sake.

"But I am ugly, Michael," I said; "I'm all bones, and I have eyes like a Chinese, and horrid cheekbones and a big mouth and—"

"You," Michael said, his voice very soft and deep, "are willow slender, and you have the eyes of a startled faun. Didn't you know that, little Hero? They're wonderful eyes, really, and that tiny slant they have makes them more

exciting. They're so big. Sometimes I think they're going to
eclipse your whole face. And they're always changing—one
minute warm and glowing, the next, frightened and shy. . . ."

I squeezed his hand shamelessly.

"Michael," I whispered, "do you really see all that when
you look at me?"

"Of course. All that and more: a nose that's small and
straight, a mouth that's full-lipped and generous. I've a
feeling that the man who earns the right to kiss that mouth
will be transformed into a new being, exalted, somehow, into
a person finer than he ever thought to be."

My heart was crying, You've that, Michael; you've
always had it— But I was a coward and a fool, so I sat there,
trembling, and stared at him.

"But best of all," he went on gravely, "are those very
bones you complain of. The structure of your face is ex-
quisite. You've an arrangement of planes, angles, and masses
that would delight a sculptor—or drive him mad trying to
copy them. No, it's exactly as I said: You're an oriental
princess come from Xanadu, from the storied palace of Kubla
Khan. And now, what can her most devoted admirer do for
Her Highness?"

"You," I said breathlessly, amazed at my own boldness,
"can take me to Dorothy's wedding. . . ."

I saw his face change.

"Oh, I am sorry, Hero," he said, "but I've already promised to take Gillian. . . ."

The golden tone fled abruptly from that wash of sun,
leaving the street oddly gray; the million, million birds took
flight; and the whirring of their wings was a cold wind
blowing through the darkness of my heart. There was no
music anywhere, in a world gone discordant, harsh, and
out of tune; and I, having used my tears for joy, had none
left for grief.

I am entirely without guile; my face mirrored how I felt.

"But," he said quickly, "if you're free, I'll call for you this evening after the reception. We can go for a nice long ride and talk and talk and talk. What do you say, Hero?"

I felt a savage female impulse to tell him I had another engagement; but trying to hurt Michael Ames was for me a bootless game that served for nothing at all. So I said, humbly:

"I'm always free, Michael—you know that."

"Good," he said; "I'll call for you at nine. And Hero—"

"Yes, Michael?" I said.

"Wear this same dress, won't you?" Michael said.

The wedding of Dorothy Rollins to Barton Byrce was as beautiful and splendid as money could make it. But, Grace Rollins to the contrary, there are some things that money cannot buy. All the treasure in the world could not have wiped that expression of acute misery from Barton Byrce's face, nor hid the worried look in Dorothy's eyes. But it went off well; better, in fact, than I had expected it to. There was just one bad moment, and it, I am sure, was planned. For as the rector said, "If there is one among those present who knows of any reason why this man and this woman should not be joined in the bonds of holy wedlock, let him speak now, or henceforth forever hold his peace. . . ." Gillian MacAllister slipped into the church on Michael's arm.

The timing was perfect. She had been—I'd stake my life upon it—waiting just outside the door for the Reverend Mr. Steidler to say those words. She did not sit down, but stood there lingeringly, deliberately prolonging the frozen hush of expectant horror with which every person in the church stared at her. A slow smile played across her face. Idiotically, I found myself whispering, just below the level

of audible sound, a quotation from Hamlet: "That one may
smile, and smile, and be a villain. . . ."

Then, at the last possible instant before the breaking
point; the precise second before someone would have had
to say something, do something, however ridiculous or
wrong, Gillian slid noiselessly into the pew, without having
said anything at all. The sound of the congregation letting
out their collective breath was like the noise of a rising wind.

What the rest of the wedding was like, I do not know.
I was not there; at least my mind was not. From where I
sat, I could see Michael Ames and Gillian MacAllister
clearly; but around them and behind them, the rector, the
bride, the groom, their attendants, the spectators, the flowers,
the decorations, the church itself, faded out of time and
mind into a meaningless jumble of blurred lights and colors,
into a babble of sounds without significance or sense.

Only the faces of Gillian and Michael were clear to me;
terribly, poignantly clear. I could see Michael looking at her
with eyes filled with troubled questioning; while she—

I could not define that look. All I knew was that I had
seen it before. And then, quite suddenly, with a stab of
abject terror, I remembered just when, in time long past, I
had seen Gillian MacAllister look that selfsame way. . . .

There was a morning—I was twelve years old, I think—
that I came running over to Michael's house to give him
something—a toy, a picture I had painted, some cookies
Eliza had made—I do not remember now, and it does not
matter; I was forever laying my small offerings upon the
altar of my private idolatry—and I found Gillian there. She
was all of nine years old, and as beautiful as a cherub by
Raphael; but even then, she was—Gillian.

She was standing on a chair on the veranda with her
hand inside the cage where Michael kept his canary. I
stopped dead. I could not have moved or spoken for the

life of me. As I watched, she drew the bird out, deftly wrung
its neck, and, climbing down from the chair, stuffed the
dead bird into the mouth of Michael's cocker spaniel, Tommy. Tommy let the canary drop at once, and stood there
looking at Gillian with the same expression with which I've
seen many people regard her since. Then she called out,
with that perfect mastery of deceit that made her the
greatest actress I've ever known:

"Oh, Michael! Tommy's got your canary!"

I can still see the tears on Michael's face when he
picked up the broken, bloody bundle of feathers from between Tommy's feet. I can see the look of horror with which
he stared at Gillian when she said:

"Why don't you kill that filthy, horrid beast!"

Perhaps he should have, I thought now, sitting in the
church at Dorothy Rollins' wedding; the real one, I mean.
Some one will, one day. Perhaps even I—

I sat there feeling the sickness inside me. In all my
life I have never voluntarily harmed a living creature; but
I knew now I was capable of murder. Seeing Gillian with
Michael had brought me to that. Even to that.

I decided then that I wouldn't go to the reception. I
would not risk once more encountering Gillian at Michael's
side. Then the stubborn streak so characteristic of the
Gileses took over; I'd be blessed if I'd let Gillian MacAllister
control my life.

So—I went. From the expression on Dorothy's face, it
would have been difficult to determine whether she were
celebrating what is traditionally supposed to be the happiest
day in a girl's life, or the funeral of a beloved relative. As
for Bart, he was already embarked upon the pursuit that
was to occupy the rest of his life. That is, he was drunk. Not
offensively so; but gravely, sadly drunk, with that serious

preoccupation with drinking that is the mark of a man who seeks in whisky a refuge.

I went up to Dot and took her hand.

"I wish you every happiness, Dorothy," I said.

"Thank you," she whispered. "Right now, Hero, I'm beginning to doubt I'll ever have it. . . ."

And, looking at her, I could see she had been crying. She was not crying now; when you come from a family like the Rollinses you learn well the social graces, including self-control. But I knew then that Dot, too, had found her lifelong occupation, which was to run concurrently with her husband's drinking: the daily, nightly necessity of shedding lonely tears.

Then, because I knew not what else to do, I moved over to where Bart stood, or rather swayed, with the intention of congratulating him. But I never did; for that was the moment that Gillian chose to sweep—uninvited, I later learned, as she had also been uninvited to the wedding—into the reception on Michael's arm. She came directly up to Dorothy. I, standing a scant yard away, had a wild impulse to flee. But I could not. My limbs would not obey my mind's command.

She took Dorothy's hand and stood there smiling that smile of perfect, angelic innocence, which is, after you get to know Gillian, absolutely the most terrible thing about her. Then in a soprano as clear as a silver bell, that carried without effort, without even being raised, to every corner of the room, she said:

"I'd wish you happiness, Dot, if I were a hypocrite. But I'm not; and you'll never have it, anyway. You see, you chose to interfere with my life. And that, Dorothy darling, was, coming from you, lèse-majesté. It simply isn't intelligent to strike at your superiors or enter a battle you cannot win—"

"Gillian!" Michael said; but she ignored him. Across the

room I could see Judge Rollins and his wife frozen into the poses they had held when Gillian began to speak. She went on blandly:

"I don't want that drunken sot you've married. I don't suppose I ever did. He once seemed suitable for my purposes, that's all. But I'm going to make him leave you, Dot —just to show you, your precious aunt, and all the world I can. Then I'll probably toss him into the gutter he belongs in. So now, Dorothy dear, for form's sake, I will wish you all the happiness you can find. I think you know by now how much that will be. . . ."

It was then that I surrendered to the disgust within me. Seeing Dot standing there, helpless to reply, I said, quietly:

"I think, Gilly, that you're the wickedest, cruelest creature on earth!"

She turned to me with a gay, carefree laugh.

"I know I am," she said; "but what you can't even imagine, you dear little mouse, is how much fun it is!"

It was then that I fled ignominiously. It was no good to stay. For I would have been defeated utterly, and I knew it. You cannot fight with puny human weapons a creature whose membership in the race of man is, I think I knew even then, questionable.

I did not even get dressed that night; I was so sure that Michael would not come. But, to my consternation, come he did. From the head of the stairs, peeping down at him as he handed his stiff straw boater to Eliza, I realized once more that he was the most beautiful male creature I had ever seen.

Michael was tall and blond. He had the kind of skin that tans with difficulty if at all. His eyebrows, which are heavy and much darker than his hair, served to emphasize the soft blue of his eyes. His face—how can I say it?—was the face of a saint, so wonderfully, terribly sensitive that it

would have been painful to look at were it not for that
mysterious reserve of inner strength he seems to call up at
will. And, strangely enough, considering his complete lack
of vanity, he was always beautifully dressed. I think his
impeccable clothes were due to his veritable passion for
beautiful, well-made things. In any case, just looking at him
now made me literally weak.

"Make yourself at home, Michael," I called down to
him; "I'll be down in a minute." I was furiously aware that
there was a noticeable tremolo in my voice. Even today
there is a certain lingering prejudice against a girl who too
obviously shows her fondness for a man who does not return
her affection. In my time, it was one of the cardinal social
sins. But I couldn't help it. I loved Michael Ames beyond
all sense or reason.

I don't think I ever dressed faster in my whole life. I
knew that there was a popular feminine school of thought
which held it smart to keep a suitor cooling his heels for an
hour or more. But Michael was not a suitor; and I, given a
chance to be with him, counted every second lost a crime.
He stood up as I entered the room. Michael's manners were
as beautiful as his person.

"You're lovely," he said; "but your eyes are sad. Why?
Was it because Gilly—"

I stiffened.

"Do me a favor, Michael," I said; "unless I ask you to,
please don't mention that creature's name to me ever again!"

He looked at me a long, long time. I believe that at
that moment he had an aching, terrible need to confide
in me; but I faced him, rigid in my pride. I have regretted
it ever since. Perhaps my stubbornness that night was the
thing that cost me fourteen lost and lonely years.

"Well," he said, "shall we go?"

I nodded dumbly, angry at him, but angrier at myself.

He took my arm and led me outside. Before the door, was the smartest rig I'd ever seen, drawn by a horse whose coat shone like satin. I was not surprised. Birmingham is a small town. I already knew that Henry MacAllister had put aside the trial period that Michael had offered him, and was paying Michael exceedingly well. He had to. The miracles Michael was performing daily at MacAllister Steel were the talk of the industry. It was not rumored, but positively stated that both Sloss and De Bardeleben had approached Michael at the Manufacturers' Club to ask him to come to work for them, stating he could name his own salary. Neither of these men, our town's premier coal and iron barons, had denied the report. I wondered, in a perfect agony of jealousy, if Michael had chosen to stay at the smaller, less important MacAllister Foundries because of Gillian.

We rode for a long time, without speaking. I could see that Michael was casting about desparately for a subject for conversation; but I sat there stubbornly, and would not help him. Finally he said:

"Tell me, Hero, where did you get such an odd name? You're the only person, man or woman, whom I've ever heard called that. Was it because your father wanted you to be brave?"

"No," I laughed. It was nervous laughter, arising from relief. "You didn't know my father, did you?"

"Not very well," he said. "We were too poor to dream of employing a tutor. And certainly not a scholar as eminent as Professor Aldious Giles. Only the rich hereabouts employed your father to prepare their sons for college. . . ."

"Father," I said, "was an old darling. He was my grandfather's oldest son; but he gave up the plantation to his younger brothers in order to follow the life he loved. I'm sure he counted the whole of human history since the fall of Rome a total loss, and all the modern tongues so much barbaric babble. I'd swear, Michael, that he thought in Attic Greek!"

"Greek—" Michael mused. "Of course! Hero and Leander—the Hellespont. That's it, isn't it, Hero?"

"That's it. One of these days, I want to make a pilgrimage to Sestos, where my namesake flung herself into the sea; and visit Abydos, the spot Leander swam from to visit her, until the night he drowned. You know, Michael, I've often wondered—but that's too silly!"

"Go on," he said gravely; "tell me what you've wondered, Hero."

"Whether," I whispered, "my father knew or suspected I was born for sadness. I want to go to Greece; but I've a fear of going. I wonder, if I saw the spot where the first Hero plunged into the sea, I might not be tempted to—"

"Good Lord, Hero!" Michael said. "What on earth makes you have thoughts like that?"

I looked him straight in the face.

"I think you know, Michael," I said.

Then I saw the honest bewilderment in his eyes. For the first time in my life, I agreed with Grace Rollins' often repeated statement that men are positively dense. How Michael could have passed a considerable portion of his life in my company without realizing that I loved him, was beyond me. But now, I clearly saw he had.

Life has progressed since then. Today, I'm sure, a girl would have frankly confessed her feelings. But in 1894, you didn't tell a man you loved him, not until he had declared himself first. Such a thing was not only unthinkable; it was unimaginable.

"No, I don't, Hero," he said; "honestly—"

I patted his forearm.

"It doesn't matter," I said. "You will, one day. I'll

probably tell you. But not now. Tell me something, Michael: Are you in love with Gillian?"

He stared at me, and I could see the pain moving in his eyes.

"I thought you didn't want to talk about her," he said.

"I didn't then; but now I do. Woman's prerogative, Michael. Tell me—are you?"

He bent his head, and stared at his own strong, well-kept hands.

"Yes," he said, his voice slow and still and sad; "yes, Hero, God help me; but I am. . . ."

I started to cry out, to say: "Michael, you can't! You mustn't!" but one of those curious coincidences that so much influence human affairs, and which are, I believe, designed by fate to show us our helplessness, stopped me.

We were passing the railroad station at the time. As I sat there, trying to find words to warn him, a fast-driven hack cut in front of us and stopped so sharply that Michael had to haul back on the reins to avoid a collision. It was night, but the gaslights before the station made the street as bright as day. I saw the driver of the hack climb down from his seat, open the door, and help a woman down. Then he plunged his hands into the carriage and began hauling out valises. The woman stood there waiting. I could see her face quite clearly.

It was Heddy MacAllister.

I turned to Michael, my eyes wide with questioning.

Sadly he shook his head.

"I've been expecting that for weeks," he said.

8

MICHAEL AMES

Birmingham, July, 1894

I

I waited outside the bedroom. I took the papers out of the brief case and tried to read them. But I couldn't. Nurse O'Rourke was busy with her knitting, and even the clicking of the needles distracted me. Besides, I didn't need to read the papers anyway; I knew their contents by heart.

I wasn't worried about getting Henry MacAllister's consent to purchase that coal mine in the Warrior Field. By now, he'd agree to anything I suggested; partially through a touchingly complete faith in my judgment; but even more because his indifference to business, the world, and to life itself, had become complete. I was running Mac-Allister Steel, and all the world knew it. Our clients no longer even went through the motions of consulting Bill Riker. They knew he'd only growl: "See the boy!" That was the way I wanted it; for the first time in Alabama's history, a steel mill was being operated on a completely scientific basis. But I owed Mr. MacAllister the respect of these pretended consultations. I knew he didn't want to be bothered with them; yet, in the final analysis, MacAllister Steel was his, not mine.

Nurse O'Rourke looked at me and smiled. She was a florid woman, with an open, honest face. In the short time I'd known her, in the three weeks since Henry MacAllister's nervous collapse because of the flight of his wife, I had begun to like her very much. She had competence written all over her. Yet, this morning, like every morning I had visited the sick man, she sat quietly knitting while Gillian took her father's breakfast in to him.

"Mr. Ames," she said suddenly, "if you don't marry that little girl, you ought to have your head examined!"

I stared at her. But I was already getting used to the blunt frankness of her speech.

"You think so?" I said.

"I'm sure of it," she said firmly. "A nurse gets to know people, Mr. Ames. Why do you think I sit here and knit and let that poor, sweet child do what I'm hired to do?"

"I haven't the faintest idea," I said.

"Because it's my job to get him well, not keep him sick. That child is doing wonders for him. I've seen some mighty nice people in my time; but Miss Gilly beats 'em all. She's a perfect angel for my money!"

I could feel a tiny warmth stirring at the core of my heart. It was pleasant to listen to what I wanted so desperately to believe. But all my scientific training was against it. Years of discipline had forced me to strongly suspect the preconceived notion, the experiment which gave the anticipated and desired results, anything at all that was too facile, that lacked the inevitable complications with which all of life is hedged about. I deliberately called to mind Gillian's face, twisted into a mask of hatred as she screamed at her mother; the chilling calm with which she had told me she meant to be her own mistress, married to me or not; the icy cruelty in her voice when she demolished Dorothy Byrce at the wedding reception. It required an effort, for already these memories were beginning to fade.

To fade, and to be replaced by newer, completely contradictory images: Her face, angelic in its sweetness, haloed by the lamplight as she sat by her father's bedside, reading to him; the soft music of her voice as she said: "Try to get better, Father. I'll find Mother for you. And I'll be ever so good to her when she comes back—I promise you. . . ."

That, and the way she treated me: hanging upon my every word as though it were a pearl of wisdom dropping from the lips of a sage; sending me delicacies, made with her own slim hands, to my lodgings; behaving in my company in a fashion so gently affectionate, and at the same time so girlish and shy, that I would have sworn she copied it down to the last gesture from Hero, who, I had already realized, was the nicest, sweetest girl I've ever known. Speaking of Hero, I had often thought that if it were not for Gillian, I'd—but that seemed to me nonsense then, for I had always been more of a brother to Hero than anything else.

Afterward, when I learned how long Hero had loved me, I felt both humbled and ashamed. But even if I had known then, Jeff, it would have changed nothing. I should have felt sorry for Hero; but Gillian was my very life. Nothing, or no one could have helped me escape her. There is a curious inevitability in a man's fate, isn't there? I was not intended to evade Gilly. She was part of my shaping. Remember Paris? I suppose I should be grateful to her, in some ways. For if it had not been for her, I should have remained the same placid fool you felt so much contempt for, then. No, don't protest; you were entirely justified.

Where was I? Oh, yes. The strangest part about it all was that Gilly seemed to have forgotten that night she came to my room. She never again mentioned it. Her behavior afterward was exactly as though it had never happened. But the thing that awoke something akin to terror in me was the fact that I was absolutely, unshakably certain that Gillian was not acting. So now, sitting there, facing Nurse O'Rourke, I kept thinking over and over again: It's all true. She's wild and cruel and savage and terrible. And it's also true that she's tender, and sweet, and gentle and kind. Two things, contradictory and apart. But which of these is Gillian? In God's name, which?

"Well—" I began doubtfully; but Gillian came out of the bedroom with the tray in her hands. She gave it to Nurse O'Rourke, and, bending over, kissed my mouth. It was the lightest, briefest kiss imaginable; but at the same time it was vibrant with tenderness. As she drew away smiling, the thunder of my heart drowned the cold, persistent questioning of my brain.

"You can see him now, darling," she said. "But try not to tire him. I'll be waiting for you. Oh, Michael, I have the most marvelous idea!"

"What is it?" I said; but she laughed and shook her head.

"Later," she said. "It's not important. It can most certainly wait while two great Steel Barons discuss weighty matters. . . ."

I looked at her. But there hadn't been even a hint of sarcasm in the way she had pronounced the words, "Steel Barons." Rather there had been something else: a note of fond pride, actually. I gave up. I would never understand Gilly. From now on, I resolved happily, I wasn't even going to try.

Henry MacAllister lay propped up in bed. He looked

much, much better. That is, until I saw his eyes. But even his eyes had changed. Before, they had held the expression of a beaten man, bowed down by intolerable anguish; but now there was a new look in them—a mingled aspect of fear and astonished puzzlement and a dawning hope that he did not dare accept. He beckoned me closer.

"You've seen her?" he whispered hoarsely. "Tell me, Michael, what do you think has got into her?"

"I think, sir," I said confidently, "that she has found herself at last."

He shook his big, lion-like head.

"Wish I could believe it," he said; "but I can't. Still— Name of God, Michael! I don't know her anymore! This —this is the daughter I've always dreamed of having. She's been a perfect angel out of God's own glory. If I groan or cough in the night, she's there as if by magic. When I was worse off than I am now, she'd be bending over me asking: "What's wrong, Father?" before O'Rourke even woke up— and O'Rourke was sitting right by my bed. It's—it's frightening, boy—"

"Hardly that, sir," I said.

"Yes, it is," he insisted. "It's the same thing, taking another form. Don't you see, Michael, she's as perfectly consistent this way as she was the other? Everything fits. Nothing breaks the pattern. Always smiling, always gentle, always sweet! God damn it, boy; human beings are never *always* anything!"

There wasn't any answer to that I could think of; so I didn't even try. Then he looked at me and smiled.

"Let's hope she stays the way she is now," he said. "By the way, boy, what was it you wanted to see me about?"

"That new coal seam in the Warrior field," I said with great relief, and opened my brief case.

When I came out of the bedroom with all the papers signed, Gilly was not waiting for me as she had promised. Nurse O'Rourke saw my worried look.

"She's in the study," she said, "talking to a strange young man. Good-looking young fellow, too. Maybe you'd better—"

"I'm not the jealous type, Mrs. O'Rourke," I said; "I'll wait—"

But I had scarcely finished speaking when Gillian came out. The man with her was slim, dark, somehow foreign.

"Michael," she said easily, "I want you to meet Mr. Klovac. He's a detective, and he's been telling me the most fabulous stories!"

I put out my hand.

"Klovac?" I said. "Now where have I heard that name before?"

I saw the quick flush cross his face. Then he smiled.

"My brother, perhaps," he said. "He works for you, Mr. Ames."

"Of course!" I said. "Big John. Good lord, but this is—" I stopped, embarrassed by the faux pas I had been about to commit.

"Astonishing, you were going to say?" Klovac smiled. "It is. I'm very grateful to my brother. You see, he paid for my education. Every time I got discouraged and wanted to quit, he'd swear he'd break my neck before he'd let me end up a 'working stiff' like himself."

"Big John," I said, "is one of nature's noblemen. He's big and rough, and he has a voice like a foghorn; but I've a sneaking suspicion that he has one of the kindest hearts imaginable."

"He has," Klovac said; "and the worst temper. I thought he really was going to break my neck when he found out

I'd stopped studying law. But I wasn't cut out to be a lawyer. Too dull. Detective work suits me better."

"You never did tell me how you became a detective, Fred," Gillian said.

"Just luck, Miss Gillian," Fred Klovac said. "I was out of work in Chicago, and I saw an advertisement that had been put in the paper by the Pinkerton people. I applied, and because I'd had two years of law, I got the job."

"That's strange," I said; "a worker's brother joining the Pinks—"

"Which is exactly why I quit them," Fred said, an edge of bitterness in his tone. "The first time they sent us out to break a strike, and I saw what they did to working stiffs like my brother, I turned in my badge. Then I set up my private agency—and starved, because I wouldn't take divorce cases. When John drifted south and began making good money down here, he sent for me. So, I set up an agency here, and starved some more, or I would have but for John. Then one set of scruples got in the way of another. I couldn't let John support me all my life, so I started taking domestic cases. Now, I specialize in them, and make more money in a month than John does a year."

"You mean," I said, "that there are enough cases of— of—"

"Marital misbehavior," he supplied, "to make a living from them? Mr. Ames, you're lucky. That you can even ask that question shows you've had a happy life." He looked at Gilly and smiled. "I hope you will continue to have one," he said. "In fact, I'm quite sure you will."

"I—I've hired Fred to find Mother, Michael," Gillian said. "It was my fault she left, and I want her back again. For my own sake, as well as Father's. . . ."

"I'll do my best," Fred Klovac said. "Now if you'll excuse me. . . ."

"Nice chap," I said, after he had gone.

"He is," Gilly said; "but let's not talk about him. Don't you want to hear my wonderful idea, Michael darling?"

"Of course," I said. "What is it, love?"

"Love!" she laughed gaily, clapping her hands like a child. "You called me 'love'! That's the first time you've ever said anything sweet to me. Oh, Michael, I'm going to kiss you!"

And she did. The kiss itself was gay, childlike, carefree. I stared at her, thinking: Perhaps I'm the one who's mad; perhaps I dreamed that night. . . .

"Tell me," I said, "about this wonderful idea."

"Tomorrow," she said, "is Sunday. And the weather has been delightful. And you've been working much too hard. And I don't want to become a widow before I've been a bride. And—"

"Who," I teased, "ever told you I was going to marry you, Gilly?"

"Well, you are," she went on in that same bright tone; "next April, after I'm twenty, and the dogwoods are in blossom. Stop interrupting me! We'll go out to the lake and have a picnic—"

"Good lord!" I said; "that's all of twenty miles!"

"We'll start early. I've already called up Greg and asked him to bring Hero. Dear little Hero. I am so fond of her!"

This, I reflected, was quite true. I've never heard Gillian say the slightest unkind thing about Hero, neither then, or even afterward, when she might have had some reason to. Including the times she was in one of those black and bitter moods, she was never mocking or cruel toward Hero. And yet, as I well knew, Hero hated Gillian. It would be many years before I found out why. . . .

"Think she'll come?" I said.

"I know she will—if only to sit and gaze at you. Poor little thing, she loves you so terribly."

"Hero?" I said; "Now, really, Gillian!"

"Oh, Michael, how can you men be so smart in some ways and so stupid in others? Hero worships the ground you walk on. And I'm just the tiniest bit jealous of her at that. You know why, Michael?"

"No. Why are you?" I said.

"Because she's ever so much better suited for you," Gillian said, her blue eyes wide and candid, searching my face. "She's much, much nicer than I am—kinder, sweeter, smarter. And she truly isn't too bad-looking, once you get used to her."

"I," I said solemnly, "think she's perfectly lovely."

"Oh!" Gillian said; "now I really am jealous! Tell me, darling, do you want me to give you up to her?"

"No," I said; "I'm in love with you, Gilly. Especially when you are the way you are now. . . ."

Her eyes clouded.

"I—I have been bad, haven't I?" she whispered. "I don't understand myself, Michael. Sometimes I'm frightened of —me. . . ."

"Don't be," I laughed. "I'm going to be around to keep you just as you are this minute. . . ."

"Thank you," she said softly, and going up on tiptoe, kissed my mouth. "I—I need you, Michael—"

I stood there, holding her. She swung back against the circle of my arms.

"Call for me at eight tomorrow," she said; "I want to have the whole day to spend with you. . . ."

Going back to my lodgings, I thought suddenly of Gillian's assertion that Hero loved me. Taken in conjunction with Hero's strange behavior the day of the Rollins-Byrce

wedding, it came to me for the first time that this could
well be true. But Hero had married Rodney Farnsworth
during a period when I was entirely free and unattached
—during which, moreover, I had given up all hope of win-
ning Gilly. If Hero had made the slightest gesture toward
me at that time, all my life thereafter would have been
completely saved. Later, of course, I realized that Hero was
absolutely incapable of such gestures, that her womanly
modesty was bone-deep. I have not changed that opinion,
not even in the light of subsequent events. But on that day,
I searched, I know now, with unconscious deliberation for
another explanation for that odd behavior, just as a dope
addict seeks for some justification, however illogical, for his
vice. For deep down, dimly, my mind told me there wasn't
any comparison possible between Hero and Gillian; my
scientifically trained intelligence insisted coldly that I was
making the poorer choice. So I had to deny that a choice
existed; I had to close my eyes to the abundant evidences
of how much Hero loved me—in order to follow, willy-nilly,
the path to moral degradation, to shameful servitude—that
I wanted, Jeff! That something in me craved like—to wear
out my simile—a narcotic.

I found my feeble explanations: Lingering grief on
Hero's part for poor Rod. Loneliness, responding unac-
customed to needed kindness; a shy girl's reaction to praise
of the looks she didn't even know she had. And all the time
I knew—I must have known!—that I was committing the
most contemptible of sins—lying to myself. So, I deserved
what happened to me. I made my destiny, shaped my ugly
fetish in the image of everything that was warped, weak,
unmanly in me. And paid the price. All of it. So now, what
we've got to do is see that Greg doesn't have to. That account's closed. My hopes, beliefs, joys, illusions were enough.
My years of slavery. My youth. His life shouldn't be piled

on top of them. And science be damned, a man should not
be hanged for killing—a witch.

You'll call me, Jeff, if you have some news?

HERO FARNSWORTH

Birmingham, July, 1894

II

"No!" I screamed at Greg Lynne; "I wouldn't walk across
the street with that creature!"

Greg sat there, smiling at me with that infuriating calm
of his. I've always adored you both, Jeff; but I confess I've
always found it easier to get along with you, than with poor
Greg. You are so—so human. You do silly, stupid things;
then win people over by laughing wholeheartedly at yourself. And you have a warm tenderness for human frailty
that is wonderfully appealing. You once said something I
have never forgotten. Mind if I quote?

"The good and the great can take care of themselves.
It's the little, muddle-headed people who never quite know
how to manage, the sinners of small sins, who need us. Not
even the great sinners. There's a glory in greatness, even
when it's evil; and the monsters of history either wreck half
the world and die in the ruins themselves; or end up enshrined in our chronicles under as thick a coating of white-
wash as their sycophants can apply. No—give me the little,
human people—like that raffish crowd Jesus of Nazareth
ran around with: thieving tax collectors, roistering fisher-
men, spiteful housewives like Mary—or was it Martha?—
warmhearted horizontalist like the woman at the well, even
a small-town demimondaine like Mary of Magdala. . . ."

[I was flattered that she remembered my idle, playful words. But she wasn't quoting. I didn't say it like that. She improved upon my poor style considerably.—Jeff Lynne.]

But your brother, even as a boy, was noted for his rectitude. He was not, and is not, a prig. He's wonderfully kind, just and forgiving. And that, I realize, is why I prefer you to him. You mingle with people, Jeff dear, and the idea of forgiveness simply never enters your head. You'd probably say, if anybody mentioned it to you: "Forgive them? For what? Lord God, Hero, they're human beings! Besides, I need an awful lot of forgiveness myself. . . ."

It's always seemed to me, however, that Greg looks down upon people from the lofty heights of his rectitude. He's sorry for them, and he forgives. He was only twenty-two years old back then in 1894, and, as you know perfectly well, Jeff, he hadn't ever been known to miss services on Sunday, take one drop too many of the cup that cheers, or indulge in an even slightly disreputable amatory episode. Which is why I don't believe he killed her. I know he's confessed; but why, Jeff? Why? To shield whom?

You're right. The only way we'll arrive at any clue is for me to stick to my subject. Anyhow, as he sat there that night, smiling at my hysterical response to his invitation that I join him, Michael, and Gillian on a picnic, I had the disturbing thought that perhaps I resented him because at heart I recognized that I had not a few of the qualities which people say go to make up an exceedingly sinful woman—and which I afterward proved to your satisfaction, if not to my own—that I was even equipped with all the necessary elements that you writers attribute to a successful courtesan—except the essential one: attractiveness.

"Now, Hero," he said mildly; "don't get upset. I think you should come along. In the first place, for Michael and Gillian to drive twenty miles out into the country alone, would certainly cause talk. Young as you are, you're still a widow, and—"

I stood up.

"Greg Lynne!" I spat. "I most certainly won't be Gilly's chaperone!"

"All right. Then come along for my sake. It's been months, Hero, since I've had a chance to talk to you. In fact, I have something quite serious to say—"

Oh, no! I thought; he's not going to propose! Not Greg! Then I realized what a foolish thing a woman's heart is. Your brother was very nearly the perfect suitor from anybody's point of view. He was young, very handsome, far too rich to be included among the fortune hunters who plagued my life; and he had a wonderful future in front of him.

Excuse me, Jeff, but I'm going to be indelicate now. I can with you. The way you proved you understood a woman's heart—my heart, to be precise, in *Episode in Florence,* gives me the right to, I think. You see, I had been married; and though my experience in those matters was somewhat limited due to poor Rod's ill health, I knew precisely what was expected of a wife. Oh, no, I thought suddenly, I couldn't sleep with a marble statue—not even a benign and smiling marble statue. And then, realizing what I had thought, my face turned fiery red.

Your brother, of course, being a man, misinterpreted my blushes.

"Little Hero," he began, "dear little Hero—"

But I cut him short.

"Please Greg," I said; "let me speak clearly. I don't want to go to your picnic for the best of all possible reasons. I love Michael Ames. I've been in love with him all my life—long before I even met Rodney. I entered into one loveless marriage, out of pity. But I wouldn't do it again. Since, from all I've heard, Michael's going to marry Gilly, in all probability I shall remain unmarried all the rest of my life."

He sighed. Then he looked me straight in the eye.

"You're wrong, you know," he said firmly. "You aren't being fair to Michael. All right, I've entertained some hopes —but no matter; I can lose like a gentleman. What I mean is, Hero, that Michael should be rescued from this—this infatuation. I know Gillian MacAllister. She'll make his life a perfect hell!"

"But, Greg," I whispered, "I—I couldn't—"

"Why couldn't you? Forget you're an interested party. If I were able to, *I'd* break up this match because I don't want to see my best friend slowly destroyed. You should look at it the same way. Put aside any self-interest you have in the matter and consider only the danger that Michael faces. If, afterward, he should turn to you—well and good. But do it *for* him, Hero."

"How could I?" I wailed. "Greg, don't you realize how pretty she is?"

"Yes," he said; "Gilly's pretty; but you—you're beautiful, Hero. Wait. Can't you see what a commonplace Gillian's cold Nordic beauty is? It's your self-depreciation and your shyness that hurt you, not your looks. If you should ever travel abroad take a look at the sculptured head of Queen Nefertiti—Jeff sent me a colored postcard once, which was a tinted photograph of it. It's in the British Museum, I think; or the one in Cairo. Then go look in a mirror. You look so much like her. I'm sure you could win Michael over if you really tried. Come, little Hero, what do you say?"

I thought about all that. I did so want to go on that picnic. My life, since Rodney's death, and even before, had been so deadly dull.

"Well," I faltered, "I still don't know, Greg. The last

time I saw Gilly, we exchanged words. I was frightfully rude to her."

He smiled.

"If so, she's forgotten it," he said. "You see, Hero, this invitation comes directly from Gillian, herself."

"That doesn't mean anything," I snapped. "You know Gilly as well as I do. She probably invited me to flaunt Michael before my face."

Slowly he shook his head. When he spoke again, his voice had a new quality in it. A tone of—wonder, it seemed to me.

"I don't think so," he said; "Gillian has changed, Hero."

Michael, himself, had spent the better part of an hour upon our last chance encounter explaining this miraculous change of heart in Gillian to me. Coming from a man in love, with all the traditional blindness that implied, I had dismissed the whole thing as one more proof of Gilly's matchless histrionic skill. But hearing it from Greg, spoken in that tone of voice, lent immense weight to it. Your brother was nobody's fool, even then. Young as he was, some of our sharpest-dealing industrialists, bested by him in a contest of wits, had already paid open if somewhat grudging tribute to his shrewdness.

"You think she's really changed?" I said.

"Yes," he said simply.

"And yet," I pointed out acidly, "you were, not two minutes ago, pleading with me to rescue Michael from her clutches. If she's become such an angel, why should I?"

"Because it makes her all the more dangerous," he said. "She won't stay like this, Hero. One day, a cog in her machinery will jar back into place, gears will mesh, and she'll turn back into the fiendish little witch we knew. But now, she's formidable. Before, her behavior would have

finally driven away a man even as patient as Michael is.
But now—"

"She's got him," I said bitterly; "because of this new
dramatic rôle she's written for herself. . . ."

The look in Greg's eyes silenced me.

"It's not an act, Hero," he said.

"Then what in the name of heaven is it?" I demanded.

He stood there gazing at me, a long, slow time. Finally
he sighed.

"I wish I knew," he said. "Why don't you come and
see?"

I heard my own words, far away and faint as though
they came from another person's mouth.

"All right, Greg," I said; "what time will you call for
me?"

"At eight tomorrow morning. I know that's terribly
early, but—"

"Don't worry about it," I said. "Eight will be just fine."

Eliza prepared the picnic basket for me. She made the
usual things: ham, cold chicken, potato salad, sandwiches,
cheese, fruit, cake, wine. I doubted that I should eat any
of it. Michael and Greg, I was sure, would have to consume
that lunch, and the one Gillian would bring; for Gilly, I
knew from past experience, had the appetite of a bird.

I dressed in my tennis suit. It was of white linen and
striped chambray, with huge leg-o'-mutton sleeves. It fitted
closely to my waist, which, thank goodness, was even smaller
than Gillian's, and flared out below my linen belt to my
ankles. I wore white low-heeled oxfords, and a red tam-o'-
shanter, which, I hoped, would emphasize the tint of rose
beneath my coppery skin. I also took along my bathing
dress, since we were going to the lake. I am one of the few
girls I know who can actually swim. I couldn't help regret-

ting the fact that modesty prevented the designing of a more practical bathing costume for women. Mine was very pretty, but it was hard to swim in. In the first place, it had leg-o'-mutton sleeves as big as those on the rest of my dresses, a flared skirt that came to my knees, under which I wore heavy bloomers, black cotton stockings, and canvas shoes. How I envied the boys their simple costume which resembled nothing in the world so much as my father's winter underwear, dyed black. Still I don't suppose it would do to expose the female figure *that* much. Especially not a figure as thin as mine.

As Greg and I came up to the MacAllister mansion that morning, Gilly and Michael were already outside, waiting for us in Michael's smart little rig. They waved to us gaily and started off at a fast trot, without waiting to even exchange greetings. We followed them. All the way out to the lake, neither Greg nor I spoke a word.

When we got there finally, Gillian leaped down from the buggy and came running over to us. She, too, was dressed all in white, with a straw sun bonnet tied under her chin with white veiling. She was perfectly stunning. Just looking at her, my heart sank to the tops of my oxfords. I climbed down, and she clasped me in her arms, kissing me as fervently as though I were a long-lost sister.

"Oh, Hero," she laughed; "I am so very glad you came!"

"Why?" I said stiffly.

She stared at me. Apparently she had forgotten our last encounter at the Rollins-Byrce nuptials.

"Because—because I'm so fond of you," she said simply. "You're the nicest girl I've ever known. I try so hard to be like you. I can't, of course; but even trying has made me better. . . ."

There was a splinter of ice moving up my veins toward my heart. It was mid-July in Alabama, but I felt cold all

over. Because I saw now exactly what Greg Lynne meant.
Gillian MacAllister was neither lying nor pretending. I know
sincerity when I see and hear it; and Gillian, so help me,
was utterly sincere.

I didn't know what to say. Fortunately for me, Michael
ended the impasse.

"Hello, Hero," he said; "what's that in that package?"

"My bathing dress," I said; "aren't we going to swim?"

"Oh!" Gillian wailed. "Oh, Michael! I forgot mine completely! Did you bring yours?"

"Of course," Michael said a little crossly. "You told me
we were coming to the lake, Gilly. Oh well, it's too late
now."

"I'll keep Gilly company," Greg said, "while you and
Hero have a bathe. Then, when you come back, I'll paddle
about a bit myself."

I could see Gillian looking at me speculatively. And
then, quite suddenly, I recognized the look in her eyes. It
was fear. Gillian MacAllister—lovely Gillian MacAllister was
afraid of me!

I felt a surge of dizzy, intoxicating joy. I don't suppose
there's a woman alive, no matter how gentle, who does not
have a streak of pure, feline cruelty somewhere in her
make-up.

"Why, thank you, Greg," I said sweetly; "it's been ever
so long since I went swimming with Michael."

I stood there, waiting for the explosion that all my past
experience with Gillian told me was sure to come.

Instead, she laid a gentle hand on my arm and said, a
little sadly:

"Run along and change, then, dear, while Greg and I
prepare the spread. And Hero—"

"Yes, Gilly?" I said. She leaned close to my ear.

"Don't steal him from me," she whispered. "You could, you know—and he's all I've got. . . ."

I stared at her. Then I said:

"I won't, but only because I can't. You underestimate your charms, Gilly—"

"There are more important things," she said; "especially to a man like Michael. And you've got them all!"

Michael and Greg had been taking the baskets out of the buggies during this exchange. But now, they were staring at us, looking as puzzled and foolish as men always do, when women do things they don't understand—which is to say, practically always.

"What are you two whispering about?" Michael demanded.

"You, of course, darling!" Gillian laughed. "I was begging Hero not to steal you from me. Oh, Michael, doesn't she look stunning in white? It sets off her lovely dark complexion so wonderfully!"

"Perfectly stunning," Michael agreed with a smile. "I'll go down there, Hero," he said, pointing, "and you can go up behind those trees. Unfortunately there aren't any bath houses here."

"All right," I said, blushing. I don't know why I blushed. Everybody knew you had to take off your clothes to get into a bathing dress.

I went up into the little pine grove. Slowly, I began to undress. There was a shaft of sunlight falling through those trees, and as I picked up my bathing dress to put it on, the light fell on my naked body. It felt wonderful. As my father's daughter, I am naturally something of a pagan. I straightened up, holding the bathing dress in one hand, and turning, raised my arms to the sun. How long I stood like that I will never know; but suddenly I heard the whisper of footsteps upon the pine needles. I whirled, scarlet from head to toe, covering myself with the bathing dress.

And Gillian MacAllister walked out of the woods toward me.

"Don't hide yourself," she said gravely; "it's only me. The boys are too gentlemanly to peep." She stood there looking at me; then she said, still with that utterly shocking sincerity:

"It's a pity they can't see you, though. Oh, Hero, you have the loveliest body in all the world!"

I was already struggling into my bathing dress, but I stopped at her words.

"Now, really, Gilly!" I said.

"Really, Hero," she whispered. "Such lovely, lovely golden skin. And you truly aren't thin at all, the way anybody seeing you dressed would think. You're a *fausse maigre* like they used to call me when I was in Canada. That means falsely thin—or slender, in English. Why, your bones show far less than mine do. Oh, Hero, I'm so afraid of you!"

I had the dress on me now, so I felt more at ease. I sat down on a stump to draw on my stockings.

"Don't be," I said dryly; "I can never harm you."

"Yes, you can," she said. "You see, Hero, I need Michael. I know you love him, but you don't need him. You're strong by yourself. I—I'm not. . . ."

I saw, suddenly, astonishingly, that she was crying. Pity is my weakest point. I got up and took her in my arms. She cradled her bright head against my shoulder and wept. It was the most amazing thing that had ever happened. Me, Hero Farnsworth, plain Hero Farnsworth, comforting this beautiful creature whom I'd always feared and hated. It was a wonderful, wonderful feeling. I felt warm and good all over.

"You don't understand," she whispered brokenly;

"you've—you've never had these—descents into utter darkness. . . ."

"Descents?" I said.

"Yes, yes! You go down and down and down, and it's
all black, Hero! Then suddenly, out of nowhere, you hear
your own voice speaking, saying terrible, beastly things!
You see your own face in the mirror, and it isn't your face
anymore—it—it's a devil's face, twisted, screaming! Oh,
Hero, I—"

"Yes, dear," I said. I was crying, too, by then; because
although I didn't understand her, I *knew* what she meant.
There is a vast difference between knowledge and compre-
hension. We know a great many things we don't understand.

"It—it started when I was a child," she said; "and it
got worse and worse, until even when I didn't go down—
into that blackness, Hero—it was easier for me to act the
same way. Then—Michael came, and brought me back. You
see why you mustn't take him away from me, Hero? Because I'd be lost without him, while you—"

I patted her bright head, like a mother comforting a
child.

"Don't worry, dear," I said. "I understand. . . ."

That day, despite the terror and pity Gillian MacAllister
had awakened in me, was the most enchanting of my life.
I swam and splashed with Michael. I ate a tremendous
lunch. I teased Greg about being so stiff. And I rearranged
the style of Gilly's hair, combing it in a way far more becoming to her. This was not deceit. I felt so sorry for her;
and, as she was now, I liked her very much.

I hated to see it end. But it was already getting dark,
and the boys were packing the things into the buggies,
when, suddenly, Gilly said:

"Oh, Michael, I want to see the moon come up!" Her voice was as wistful as a child's.

Greg looked at me.

"Let's leave these love birds," I said with forced gaiety. "They've been ever so good all day—and they deserve an hour or two's spooning."

Gilly whirled, and hugged me, hard.

"You are so sweet, Hero!" she said. "We won't be long. . . ."

The human mind is a curious thing. I've felt ever since that something inside me made me forget my bathing dress, which I had left drying on a tree. It was not deliberate, I swear; but all the same, one part of my mind forgot it with malice aforethought.

"Oh, Greg!" I cried. "I forgot my bathing dress!"

"They'll bring it," he said glumly.

"No they won't," I said. "They don't even know where it is."

With a weary sigh, Greg turned the horses about. We had already come four or five miles.

"I'm sorry, Greg," I said, when we reached the pine wood by the lake. "You wait right here. I'll only be two minutes."

I ran straight through the moonlit pines. Then, five yards from the lake's edge, I stopped, frozen.

Michael and Gillian were coming out of the lake. And— Michael hadn't a bathing suit on, either. The moonlight silvered their bodies. They were both such beautiful people. There, in that wash of silver, they looked like the gods my father used to read to me about in Greek mythology.

I could not move nor speak. But they had no eyes for me. A scant two yards from where I leaned, boneless and weak against a pine, they stopped and embraced, the droplets on their bodies like pearls, like diamonds.

"Oh, Michael," Gillian whispered, her voice the first movement of a fugue for flute and cello, "I—I want you to love me. Not like before. You see, I do remember that. . . . But tenderly— like I am, now. . . ."

I crept away from there. When I was far enough, I ran.

Greg stared at me.

"You don't have your bathing dress," he said.

"I know," I got out. "Oh, Greg, take me home! Take me home, please!"

And it is a measure, Jeff, of the quality of your brother that not once while I sobbed against his shoulder all the way home, nor ever thereafter, did he ask me to explain.

9

FREDERICH KLOVAC

Birmingham, April, 1895

The trouble was that I got back to Birmingham on their
wedding day. When I reached the house, the servants told
me that they were already at the church. I said: "They're
coming back here?"

"No," the butler said; "they purely ain't, Mister Fred.
Mr. MacAllister wanted to have a wedding supper 'n a
reception for 'em; but Miss Gilly wouldn't hear of it. 'Lowed
she done had enough of celebrating things ahead of time.
So they's heading straight for the station directly after the
ceremony, taking theyselves a train for New York. From
there, they's going to Europe. Lord knows when they'll be
coming back."

I stood there. One part of my mind said, Goddamnit,
Fred, let 'em go! That way you can double back to Selma,
and talk Heddy into—

But that was sentimentality. In this business, sentiment
leads to bankruptcy a little faster than it does in some others.
I'd been paid to find Heddy MacAllister. And now I'd

found her. Her present circumstances, and the effect they damned well were going to have upon that family, were no concerns of mine. I was a private dectective with a report to make to a client. The details of that report were unpleasant. But then, in my charming profession, they very nearly always are.

So I went to the church. I stood in the doorway, watching that poor devil Ames go through the motions. It was the damnedest thing: sort of like watching a man going about the preparations for suicide—joyfully. With a big fat, idiotic smile on his face.

So I waited until it was over. Until the bride had been kissed by all and sundry. Until they came dashing through the shower of old shoes and rice. I was going to touch her arm to detain her; but I didn't have to. She saw me. Stopped dead. Her blue eyes widened with the same pure joy that the Grand Inquisitor must have felt as he watched a heretic being prepared for a bath in boiling oil. As pure as that. And if you know human nature, Jeff, you'll know that's the purest joy there is.

"Fred!" she said. "You've found her! You've found Mother!"

"Yes, Miss Gilly—I mean Mrs. Ames," I said.

"Mrs. Ames!" she laughed. "Did you hear him, Michael? He called me Mrs. Ames! You're the first to say that, Fred. Anyhow—where is she?"

"In Selma," I said.

She stared at me.

"Why didn't you bring her back?" she said.

"I couldn't," I said.

She stared at me some more. Then she smiled. Damnit, I've seen everything at least twice. But a smile like that— hell, it wasn't any different from her ordinary smile. But somehow, I wanted to look around to see where all that

sleet was coming from. And what had happened to the sunlight at four o'clock in the afternoon.

"Then I will," she said.

I looked at Michael. At her father.

"Look, Mrs. Ames," I said, "maybe you and the happy
bridegroom had better go on about your honeymoon and
let Mr. MacAllister and me handle this—"

"I will not!" she laughed; "you men would only make
a mess of things. The honeymoon can wait. And so can
Michael—he's a patient old darling. . . . Father, you phone
the station and tell them that we won't be using those tickets
until the first of next week, say—"

"But, Gilly—" Michael protested.

"But, nothing, love!" she said; "you've got me. Don't
you think it would be ever so much nicer if we could sail
knowing that Father and Mother are back together again?"

She knew just how to hit him. Appeal to his better
nature. And he didn't have any other kind. Which was why
he was lost. A man without a crop with a peck or two of the
randiest grit possible in it, always is.

"Yes, darling," he said.

I kept on looking for a chance to get her off by herself
for a minute. Long enough to say, Look, Mrs. Ames, if you
have to, go down there yourself. But don't take either your
father or your husband with you, because—

But I didn't get that chance. I didn't because Gillian
knew I wanted to say something like that. And because she
didn't mean for me to say it. Not that it would have made
any difference. Not that anything anyone could say or do
would have made any difference to Gillian MacAllister.

Hindsight? Yes. Yes, of course. I didn't realize all that
so clearly at the time. All I did realize was that she scared
me somehow. Especially when she was gay and happy and
laughing. Because it was like listening to Messalina—or was

it Agrippina?—laughing as she watched her pet fighting fish
strip the flesh from the bones of a living slave.

It wasn't until they'd all gone upstairs to change into
street clothes, because Gillian insisted on our leaving for
Selma that very night, that it came to me how to do it. They
had left me downstairs; and Gillian had playfully ordered
me not to move. So I walked out of there—got into my rig
and drove down to Gilbert's Feed Store and asked Tom
Gilbert to let me use his phone. I called her. Flatly refused
to speak to anybody else. Sat there and waited 'til they put
her on. Then I told her—all of it. Said:

"So you see now, don't you, ma'am, why it's inadvisable
for either your father or your husband to go down there?"

She didn't answer me at first. And when she did, her
voice hadn't any expression to it at all. She said: "We're
quite ready now, Fred. All three of us. And the train leaves
at eight. Will you meet us at the station, please?"

So I took them there—to that house. Helped Gillian
execute her father's death sentence, though it took his body
another year to follow his heart. Helped send Heddy Mac-
Allister up to Byrce Hospital for the Insane in Tuscaloosa.
Definitely finished whatever illusion Michael Ames may
have had that his marriage could possibly have been successful or happy.

What happened? You mean I actually have to spell it
out for you? The oldest, most banal story in the world.
Heddy got tired of being hungry. Of serving as a govern-
ness for a family in Boston. As a companion to an elderly
invalid in New York. Of being a saleswoman in a Chicago
department store—all of which places I trailed her to, all
of which occupations I checked—and came back to Selma
in the company of one of her ex-lovers, a man in his seventies
now, whom she seems to have met by purest accident in

that Chicago emporium where he'd gone to buy a tie or something.

You see, Jeff, she was a genuinely feminine woman. A kitten made for cuddling. Warm-hearted, good, basically decent. Yes, yes! Decent. She was just tired. She wanted to quit. To hole up with that old duffer and hide from the world.

No, Gilly didn't make a scene. That, boy, was the quietest crucifixion that anybody ever saw.

She just turned to Mr. MacAllister who was standing there like a poleaxed steer, dead on his feet, needing only one little push to send him over, and said:

"You see, Father? A whore. First, last, and always—a whore."

And then, to Michael:

"Do—do you want to leave me, darling? I—I'll give you your freedom if you like. Because it must not be very pleasant to be married to the daughter of—*that*. . . ."

She could handle words. I think it was the way she pronounced the word *that*, printing those italics visibly on the air, that got to Heddy. Anyhow, the poor thing started to scream. And she went on screaming until the doctor came. He gave her a sedative. It had no effect at all though the doc swore it should have laid out a team of forty mules. She went right on screaming. For hours. Even after they'd put that straightjacket on her. You could still hear her when the padded wagon they carted her away in was five blocks from the house.

Then it was very quiet. All four of us sat there kind of helplessly—correction: except Gilly, who was never helpless—staring at that old, broken wreck of a lover boy. He was crying. Then Gillian stood up.

"Shall we go?" she said.

10

GEOFFRY LYNNE

Paris, 1895

I

Again, a note of caution. I could have edited this; softened certain aspects of it by interpreting it in the light of what I later came to know. But I didn't. To do that would have been cheating. For life moves in only one direction. And we cannot live it backward.

II

When the postman came, I was with Lisette on the terrace of my studio, looking out over the rooftops of Paris. My studio was only a few streets away from Sacre Coeur, on the very top of Montmartre, so all Paris lay at our feet. I had my arm around Lisette, who didn't have on any clothes, for three excellent reasons: one, she had been posing for me; two, it was quite warm that last week in June; and, three, Lisette detested wearing clothes anyhow. She had a marvelous figure and was in much demand among the painters of nudes. She was also a wonderful cook, and exceedingly talented in bed. We were, in the phraseology of Her Royal Majesty Victoria, Queen, by grace of God, of England, et cetera, living in sin. An activity which has much to recommend it. In fact, I do recommend it—wholeheartedly. Especially in Paris, in June, and with girls like Lisette.

"*Bonjour, m'sieur le facteur,*" Lisette said.

"*Bonjour, Lisette,*" the facteur said, and flopped into one of my cast-iron chairs. "*Mon dieu,* but my feet are killing me! Lisette, would you have the goodness to bring me a cup of coffee? Black—and with cognac in it—if m'sieur Lynne does not object."

"M'sieur Lynne does not object in the slightest," I said; "but, Lisette, cherie, don't you think you should put on *ta* robe?"

"*Mais non!*" the facteur cried indignantly; "what species of painter are you, M'sieur Lynne? To hide such beauty is a crime! Especially from me. After seeing my big cow with her hair in curl papers every morning, and the lard of her bulging from every crevice of her robe, looking at *votre* Lisette gives me great pleasure. Surely a free soul like you will not begrudge me such a simple thing—"

I reflected if there were anybody in all Montmartre who hadn't seen Lisette naked, it was only poor Pierre, the blind man who sold lottery tickets on the corner. And even he made up for it by the ritual of pinching Lisette where she sat every time she passed him. Which was a kindness on her part. Pierre was stone blind, and she could have escaped him easily enough. But every time he recognized her footsteps, he would sing out—in English, for my benefit:

"Ah, Lisette—a leetle peench, no, cherie?"

And she'd stand still and let him pinch her. So I didn't
feel that this little dwarf of a postman who weighed maybe
forty-five kilos soaking wet, and who was married to *sa
grosse vache,* his big cow as he called her, who weighed
surely one hundred kilos—roughly two hundred twenty
pounds in English measure—was doing any harm by feasting
his starved eyes on Lisette.

"Very well," I said; "forget thy robe, Lisette. Do not
habit thyself."

"Don't worry," Lisette said; "I wasn't going to. For,
after m'sieur le facteur has gone, we will go back to bed,
non?"

She was quite shameless. Which was one of the things
I loved her for.

The facteur sat there sipping his coffee and cognac.

"Do not believe you can hurry me this way, Lisette,"
he cackled; "I must rest my feet, and you and *m'sieur
l'Anglais* have all day and all night—"

"Mister the American," I corrected; "not Mister the English."

"But you talk like an English," the facteur said; "and,
in any event, it is the same. Ah, what a good thing is coffee
and cognac!"

"And spring, and love," Lisette added, and kissed me.

"Do not let me detain you," Mister the Postman said
with his wonderfully evil laugh. "The other bench is un-
occupied. Please to proceed, I pray you. Perhaps out of my
age and experience I can give you some pointers."

"*Voyeur!*" Lisette said; "*vicieux!*" By which she meant
he was a Peeping Tom and a dirty old man.

"Yes," the facteur sighed; "both, my dear. There are so
few pleasures left for the aged."

He finished his cognac and stood up. Walked to the
gate. Clapped a dramatic hand to his forehead.

"Ah, me! What a beastliness! What a sottishness! What a stupidity! I have forgotten why I have come. There are, *cher m'sieur*, two letters for you. One from the States United —written in a bold, masculine hand. The other, from Rome— lightly perfumed, and in a most delicate script. Art thou not jealous, Lisette?"

"No," Lisette yawned. "Rome is far away."

I stood there holding the letters. The first one was from Greg. But, although I know a great many people in Rome, the second letter wasn't from any of them. The handwriting was meaningless to me. I didn't remember ever having seen these beautifully formed letters before.

"Go on, read it," Lisette said. "Perhaps she will inspire you to feel romantic instead of fatigued. And of that, I shall profit."

I tore the letter open. Read:

"Dear Geoffry: It will be a surprise, I know, for you to hear from me. Greg gave me your address, in the mistaken belief that I was going to Paris. But I didn't. Instead I went to Rome, and here I am, comfortably installed in a little pensione on the Via Margutta—"

I stopped then, and turned the page to find her signature. I wanted to see what American girl I knew had so far taken leave of her senses as to settle down on the Via Margutta. I know Rome very well and Italians even better. The Via Margutta is Rome's left bank and Montmartre rolled into one, with a few particularly Italianate frills added for good measure. It is inhabited by the most ardent band of skirt chasers, bottom pinchers, and would-be seducers known to history. In short, it is no place for an American girl. Or, considered coldly, perhaps it is just the place. Depends upon the girl.

The letter was signed by Hero Farnsworth.

Dear Lord, I prayed, take care of that poor innocent—

that is if the devil even allows You into the Via Margutta,
which is purely his preserve!

I read on:

"Greg tells me you often come to Rome. The next
time you do, please look me up. It would be nice to
see a familiar face and hear a cheery word. Not that
I'm lonely. The proper word is besieged. Lord, Jeff,
what ever gave Romans their impression of English and
American women?"

"English and American women," I muttered, dryly.

"I have to keep my windows locked and barred
at night. And the things they say to me! Now that I'm
beginning to understand Italian quite well, I find some
of their remarks surprisingly beautiful and poetic, and
others unspeakably filthy. At any rate it is never dull.
I shall be here indefinitely. I'm studying Italian, trying
my hand at painting, having some voice lessons from
an old charlatan who swears that in two years I shall
be ready for La Scala. Write me when you can. Your
sincere friend, Hero."

Now what on earth made her go to Rome? I thought.
But when I opened my brother's letter, I found the answer
to that at once.

"I've given Hero Farnsworth your address [Greg
wrote]. Poor little thing, she simply couldn't stay here
and witness Michael's marriage to Gillian. So she fled.
I suggested that she go to Paris, where you could be
of some help to her, or at least keep a brotherly eye on
her, as heartbroken young women are apt to get themselves into some unsavory messes in foreign capitals—
but she seems to be bent on going to Rome for a while,
and from there to Athens. Influence of her father's
classicism, doubtless. . . .

"But speaking of Michael's and Gilly's nupitals,

they, or at least their honeymoon, was delayed by [This I will cut. In the previous chapter you've already learned what happened to poor Heddy—Geoffry Lynne.]

"So, Mr. MacAllister has been granted the divorce he doesn't want, and Gilly and Michael are on their way over there. Gilly insisted upon having your address. She says that they couldn't want a better guide to Paris, especially to the wicked parts of it, which, it seems, is precisely what she wants to see. They're sailing from New York on the tenth of this month, and should arrive in Paris by the twentieth. However, when they arrive, you'll know; because Gilly swears her first act after getting there will be to look you up. . . ."

"Lisette!" I called. "What is the date of today?"

"Don't know," she said yawningly, "the nineteenth, the twentieth, the twenty-first—something like that. With you, my old dearest, I lose all track of time."

"Where is the morning newspaper?" I demanded.

"Didn't come. The news vendor is drunk again."

"Oh, hell!" I said. "You hop right down to the kiosk and buy one this minute, Lisette!"

"All right," Lisette said, and started out.

"Not like that!" I howled. "Put some clothes on, dammit!"

"Oh," she laughed; "it is hot, and I am sleepy, so I forgot. Good thing you reminded me, or the agent of police would have tossed me into the salad basket for indecent exposure. *D'accord,* I will dress myself first."

It was a good thing that she did. Or at least that she got started. Because it wasn't the nineteenth, the twentieth, or the twenty-first. It was the twenty-third, and Michael and Gillian had been in Paris since the day before yesterday.

Lisette stuck her arms into the sleeves of a simple frock and came back out on the terrace. She turned around.

"Button me," she said.

Those buttons ran down the back of her frock from the collar to the hem, and there was nothing under that frock but Lisette. So I started modestly at the southern strategic end of it, got the buttons fastened to as high as the place where her knees bent, when that evil little bastard of a facteur let out his fiendish cackle:

"There they are," he cried.

I whirled, scarlet to the roots of my hair.

"Oh, Jeff!" Gillian's laugh was pure silver; "how charming! How perfectly, perfectly priceless!"

"Gilly, for God's sake," I said. "You could give a fellow a decent amount of warning." Then I saw Michael's face. For a moment I misunderstood. Michael had a reputation for being deucedly straightlaced.

"Now look, Michael," I got out. "I really am sorry, you know. This is damned awkward. Sorry to have shocked you."

"You didn't shock me, Jeff," Michael said softly. "I've become shockproof by now."

He put out his hand. I took it.

"You could introduce us to your bride," he said.

"Bride!" Gillian hooted. "Must you be quite so provincial, darling?"

"This," I said, "is Lisette, who, Michael, is not my bride, but something a great deal better: *ma 'tite amie;* my little friend. . . ."

"You mean," Gillian laughed, "*ta 'tite maitresse,* don't you, Jeff?"

I shrugged.

"Calling things by their right names is usually considered bad taste, Gilly," I said.

Gillian went up to Lisette, who had been listening to all this conversation in English a little sullenly.

"*Bonjour*, Lisette," she said. "*Je m'appelle* Gillian. *Je suis tres heureuse de vous connaître.* . . ."

I stared at her in astonishment. Her French was very nearly accentless. No, that was not true. It had an accent, all right; but a regional rather than a foreign one. Midi? I thought; Niçoise? Brêtagne? Then it hit me: Gillian, in one of her parents' vain attempts to tame her, had been sent for nearly five years to a convent school in Quebec. Her accent was Canadian.

"Equally, madame," Lisette said. "Now will you have the goodness to button me while Jeff talks to your so very beau husband?"

"Of course," Gillian laughed. "Turn around, *ma cherie!*"

Lisette turned, paying no attention to Michael's presence. Whereupon Gilly ran a slim hand over her back with an appreciation that was almost masculine.

"Look, Michael, darling," she said; "isn't she just too perfect?"

"Gilly, please!" Michael said; and there was real pain in his voice.

But I didn't know the reason for that pain. Not then.

They stayed in Paris three weeks. And in the middle of the second week, I found out. Michael Ames told me. Michael, like nearly every man of my times, would have died before discussing his marital problems with even his very best friend. And I wasn't his very best friend. Greg was. In fact, in those days, I didn't even like him. I thought he was an unmitigated ass. I was right. He was an unmitigated ass—in those days.

How he came to tell me is a story in itself. We, the three of us, were on the Left Bank, looking at an open-air exhibition some starving young painters were holding in front of a café on the Boulevard Raspail. That is, Michael and I were looking at the paintings. Gillian was looking at one of the painters. I knew him. His name was Leon Volkov, and he was a Serb or a Croat or a Czech or a Russian prince, depending upon which particular set of damned lies he happened to favor at the moment. He was clean-shaven, except for a mustache like those affected by Montenegran brigands. It was, without exaggeration, thirty centimeters from tip to tip. He belonged to that school who called themselves "Les Fauves," the Wild Beasts. I don't know about the rest of them, but the name suited Leon. He was a beast. A dirty beast, certainly; and doubtless more or less wild.

He looked back at Gillian, and the following conversation ensued between them:

Leon: "And this species of gutless wonder with you, who is he?"

Gilly: "My husband. He will buy something of yours, perhaps."

Leon: "But no. I don't sell my works to rich filth. But, thou, little species of a streetwalker, I am going to make you a present."

Gilly: "A present?"

Leon: "As you like. You can pay me for it with your pretty flesh."

Gilly (in a pleased tone): "You find truly that I have the aspect of a *poule?*"

[Note: *Poule*, chicken in English, is argot for prostitute. G. L.]

Leon: "Worse. You are a vicious, my little *garce. Les poules*, they have some excuses. At least they have hunger. . . ."

All the time this charming, elevating little conversation about les beaux arts was going on, Michael was standing in

front of the paintings, jotting down notes. About the paintings, I thought. I was wrong. Dead wrong.

For that night he showed up at my place—alone.

"Jeff," he said, "if Lisette will excuse you, I'd like for
you to come pub crawling with me. I want to talk to you.
In fact, I've got to."

"Okay," I said. "Lisette, *bebe*—sleep tight. See you in
the morning. . . ."

" 'Voir," Lisette yawned; "give me a kiss, *mon cher.*
Just a little kiss so it will not wake me up too much—or else
I shall have to go out and find someone to betray you
with. . . ."

I gave her the little kiss. Also a resounding whack on
her derriere.

"A sample," I grinned, "of what you'll get if you ever
even think like that again."

Lisette rubbed herself where she hurt.

"You're cruel," she said; " a brute. And a beast. Maybe
that's why I love you. 'Voir, *mon amour.* . . ."

Michael was staring at me in astonishment.

"You mean you can just up and leave her like that?"
he said.

I pointed at my painter's pantaloons of blue velours.

"*I* wear 'em," I said. "Come on."

We went into a nearby bistro.

"What'll you have have?" I said.

"I don't drink," Michael said, "but tonight—"

I turned to the garçon.

"Pernod," I said with malice aforethought. If he wanted
to start drinking, let him start with a bang.

He watched while the garçon (a shambling old wreck
of sixty-five; but waiters are always garçons, boys in France,
'til they die of old age) poured that lovely green poison in
the bottom of our glasses, then added water, which turned

it, to Michael's unveiled astonishment, into a kind of green-ish milk. He tasted it.

"It's good!" he said, and gulped the whole glass down.

You don't drink Pernod like that. Actually, the bloody stuff is a kind of absinthe. You sip it. Slowly and lovingly and with great respect. I started to tell him that; but I shut my trap. As I said before, I didn't like Michael Ames. He was looking around for the waiter.

"Gar-song!" he sang out in that American tourist French that gives me a gut ache and makes Frenchmen wince. *"On-core une!"*

The garçon brought him another one. He gulped that one down, too. Called for another.

"Easy, old boy," I said at last; "this stuff's ruddy explo-sive. . . ."

"Don't care," he said thickly. "Jeff—will you translate something for me?"

"Of course," I said.

He dragged out that notebook.

"Jeff," he said solemnly, blinking like an owl; "what does *'salauds riches'* mean?"

"Rich filth," I said.

Then it hit me. He hadn't been taking notes on those pictures at all!

He stared at his notes.

" *'Petite genre d'une putaine mignonne,'* " he muttered. " *'Tu me peux payer avec ton joli chair. . . .'* "

I stared at him. He was no fool. He had got the right parts, the essentials. Just as though he had understood. As he nearly had. His high school and college French had served him that well.

"Michael," I said, "you don't really want me to translate that conversation, do you?"

He brought his fist down on the zinc with a crash that upset my scarcely tasted glass.

"Yes!" he roared; "goddamnit, yes!"

"All right," I said, "you asked for it, old chap."

Then I told him. All of it. I have never been one to suffer fools gladly. And there was something in his eyes—a blank, hopeless misery that awoke a vein of cruelty in me. I have yet to meet a cuckold who did not richly deserve his fate. And Michael Ames was too bloody civilized.

It was difficult. There is no word in English for *garce*. God, how beautifully precise French is! No other word ever fitted Gilly better. I translated it as "strumpet." But that's not right; *garce* doesn't carry that idea of—well, unwashed sweatiness implicit in slut or strumpet which are as close as we can get to it. It is rather more elegant than our crude Anglo-Saxon, as Gallic expressions usually are. I could see Michael getting paler and paler, so I said mercilessly:

"So now you tell me, old boy: How many times has she been unfaithful to you by now?"

He didn't answer me. He looked around for the waiter. Called for another Pernod. Gulped that one down, too. Looked at me. Said:

"Ten times."

"Ye gods!" I said. "And you haven't broken her filthy neck?"

"No," he whispered. "You see, Jeff, I'm not sure. . . ."

"Why aren't you?" I said.

"I was seasick," he muttered; "and there was this Englishman. . . ."

I listened to it. But without pity. I don't suppose that those of us who were lucky enough to be born with all our male glands in their right places and working overtime, ever do really pity our less fortunate brothers.

He got seasick the first night out. Stayed seasick for

the entire ten days of the crossing. Which must have been just hilarious for his bride. Damned awkward to try to feel romantic about a type who is continually tossing his breakfast. And Gilly was—Gilly. She didn't waste even ten minutes' pity on her groaning spouse. She got dressed, and went blithely dancing with the Englishman. Came back at four o'clock in the morning with her hair mussed and her gown in some disarray.

Repeated that performance nightly, until the night before they docked at Le Havre. That night, she didn't come back to their stateroom at all.

So Michael did the worst possible thing he could have done. He got up and went looking for them. He didn't find them, of course. He was pounding on the Englishman's door when the night steward came to see what all the uproar was about.

"It's jolly late, sir!" the steward said.

"I don't give a damn!" Michael said; "open this door for me!"

"Sir," the steward said stiffly, "that's contrary to all regulations. I'm sorry, but I can't."

"Oh, cawn't you?" Michael snarled; "then I'll bash it in!"

"That, sir," the steward said icily, "is up to you. Your responsibility. I rather imagine you can afford to pay for the repairs. . . ."

Michael whirled, smashed in the glass case in which the fire ax reposed, getting a nasty cut for his pains. Lifted the ax—

"Oh, I say, sir!" the steward said.

Then they both saw the Englishman coming down the corridor.

"Ah!" he said; "Ames! Excitable chap, what? Looking for the little woman? By now she's safely abed and sound asleep."

He groped peacefully for his key.

And Michael caught the rich odor of Gillian's perfume. Raised that ax high.

"Sir!" the steward screamed.

The Englishman looked up. Saw that murderous blade lifted above his head. Waggled a solemn finger under Michael's nose.

"Shouldn't do that, if I were you, old chap," he said.

Then, very calmly, he opened the door, stepped inside; didn't even close it.

"Care for a nightcap, Ames?" he said.

And that was that. Too ruddy civilized. And an unmitigated ass. Both.

"Jeff," Michael whispered, pitifully, "what should I do?"

"Do?" I said dryly. "Enter into thy mother's womb and be born again."

"No," he said thickly, "thass no answer. What would you have done in my place?"

"Don't know," I said. "Can't even imagine. Because, being me, I could never be in your place—"

"Why?" he said.

"One, I should never have married Gilly," I said flatly. "Two, if I had, by now she'd be bringing me breakfast in bed, lighting my pipe, kneeling to put on my slippers—"

"Not Gilly," he said.

"Then she'd be dead," I told him.

"You—you don't know Gilly," he muttered. "I slapped her once—"

"Ha!" I said; "sterling heroism. Get a D.S.O. for it, old boy?"

"It was rotten of me," he said sadly.

"Wait," I said; "don't get me wrong, Michael. I've absolutely nothing against slapping women around when

they need it. Rather approve, in fact. The trouble is, you
didn't go far enough—"

He stared at me.

"Not far enough?" he said; "dear lord, Jeff!"

"Look, old boy," I said then; "I'm going to tell you a
story—a true story. It happened to me. I've been over here
five years now. Notice how well Lisette behaves toward me?
That's because of my reputation. Because of Ilona—"

"Ilona?" he said.

Then I told him. Like all writers, it's hard for me to
tell where truth leaves off and fancy begins; but essentially
the tale was true. Ilona was Hungarian. And a female of the
canine species. She was the type who went into shrieking
rages and wrecked a chap's flat. But she was blond and
beautiful in that way that only a Hungarian can be. I didn't
know what to do with her. She used to destroy me all night,
and then try to kill me with the kitchen knife in the morning.
And, while venomously accusing me of every little midinette
in Paris, she was betraying me all over Montparnasse. But
I wasn't Michael Ames. The moment I found out, I decided
to kill her.

"No," Pepe le vieux, that old bandit of an apache who
had appointed himself my mentor, told me, "that is not sage,
boy. The guillotine is sharp. Just beat the hell out of her."

I thought about that one.

"Thanks, I will," I said.

He smiled at me through his yellowed teeth. The
cigarette he never took out of his mouth clung to his lower
lip.

"Are you capable of beating a woman?" he said.

"Capable?" I howled; "why—"

"No, you aren't," he grinned. "You see, it must be done
scientifically. That is where Englishmen, Americans, and even
some Frenchmen fail. Either you don't beat them at all, or

you beat them only a little bit. *Seulement un petit peu,*" he repeated happily. "So, naturally, they are left with enough strength to go into a rage. To seek a divorce if you are married to them. Or to seek damages if you're not. Amounts to the same thing—"

"How should one beat them, Pepe?" I said.

"That depends on the woman. With Ilona, I'd recommend that you strip her, tie her to the bed post, and beat her with your belt—hitting her with the buckle end in order to draw blood. And, at least two hours. Beat her until you are tired. Then have a cigarette and beat her some more. After that, you should remark casually that you're going out to lunch, in order to renew your strength. Go out to lunch. Eat well. Drink hardy. Reflect upon the spectacle of Ilona in your rival's arms. Then come home and really beat her!"

"I—I couldn't do that!" I gasped.

"I thought not," Pepes said sadly. "So, for you *gentils-hommes anglaises,* I have a second proposal. You slap her face. Being Ilona, she flies at you. Then, in the heat of battle, you forget you're a *gentilhomme* and hit her with your fist. You should try seriously to break her jaw. Failing that, knocking out a few teeth should suffice. Once she is down, you kick her several times, enough to crack a rib or two. Then, if you don't propose to forgive her and take her back, you walk upon her face to destroy her looks—"

"Lord Jesus, Pepe!" I said.

"But if you do mean to take her back, break both her arms instead of kicking her ribs in and marching upon her features. Then she will crawl to you and embrace your boots. I guarantee it."

"And did you?" Michael whispered as I got to that part of my tale.

"Quite," I lied, because I did absolutely nothing of the

kind, and the whole thing ended messily and badly as real-
life stories always do. But my writer's instinct made me
change the ending to a more effective one. Besides, in order
to point a lesson with a tale, even the venerable saints have
lied. "I snapped her right arm over my knee like a stick of
firewood. That did it. Didn't have to break the left. Damndest thing you ever saw. She stopped moaning after a while.
Came crawling across the floor just as Pepe said she would.
Put her good arm around my legs, cried, kissed my feet,
sobbing:

"*Mon homme! Mon vrai, vrai homme. . . .*"

"And you think that if I—?"

I looked at him, with, as he afterward told me, naked
scorn in my eyes.

"No," I said, "you couldn't. You haven't got it in you."

"Then what do you propose?" he said miserably.

"That we go to that Croato-Serbo-Czecho-Russ' studio
and see if she's there. If she is, I'll beat the hell out of him
for you—"

Michael stood up. He swayed a little.

"What kind of cur dog do you think I am, Jeff?" he said.
"I can fight my own battles!"

"Can you?" I said; "then come on!"

She wasn't there. Only that portrait was. Leon was still
working on it, even by candlelight. My critical standards
are stern. I knew very well that I was the worst dauber in
all Paris. Besides, an English publisher had already picked
up my first novel by then, and was begging for more; which
helped me to judge even more fairly, since I was beginning
to realize where my own true talents lay. And, although
I hated Leon Volkov's bloody guts, because of, among other
things, Ilona, I saw one thing very clearly:

That nude study he had made of Gillian was a master-piece.

I could feel the sweat popping out on my forehead. It was that good. I forgot about Michael. I stood there staring at it, lost. It is very hard to explain why it was so good. Put it this way: Leon had put his lust down on canvas. You could feel it like a heat rising from that glowing, pearly skin. See it in the sheen on those parted, moistened lips; on the thrust and pucker of those matchless breasts; in (I later censored this line. Age does bring restraint. G. L.).

Then I heard Michael's sob. Turned to him. (Is it true that the presence of incipient masochism awakes the sadism latent in every man?) I said:

"Before? Or after? Ah, that is the question!"

Then weeping like a child, Michael fell upon Leon Volkov.

I didn't interfere. I stood there and watched Leon batter him to a bloody pulp. Then what little sense of shame I had left rose and smote me. I raised the huge porcelain wash-basin Leon never used and brought it crashing down on the wild beast's head. Then, thoughtfully, I stepped over his prostrate form, took out my clasp knife, and cut that portrait out of the frame. It wasn't dry, but I could paint well enough to repair the smears I made.

Only then did I help Michael up, got him out of here, found a hack, and took him back to the Grand Palais. I had to help him upstairs to his room, after explaining to the concierge that we had been set upon by footpads. The concierge was gravely concerned. For the reputation of the Grand Palais.

Anyhow, I got Michael to his room. Gillian leaped out of bed. She had on a nightgown that was a good deal more provocative than no gown at all would have been. In the glow of the gaslights, I saw again just what a master Leon

Volkov was. He had caught her, all right. To the last glisten-
ing pore. And I saw something else: why Michael would
never leave her. Why maybe even I wouldn't have, if I'd
been in his shoes.

"Why!" she whispered, "you've been fighting! You've
been fighting with—"

"Leon," I said dryly.

She smiled then, angelically.

"Who won?" she said.

"Well," I drawled, "I think maybe we'd better all get
out of town before somebody finds his body."

She came to Michael.

"You fought," she whispered. "Oh, darling, you fought
for me!"

Then she came up, and ground her mouth into his.
That, considering the fact that Volkov had pounded his lips
into a puffy mess, must have hurt like hell. Then she did
something else: caught his lower lip between her teeth, and
sunk them in, already moaning a little, deep in her throat.

"Cue for exit, Geoffry!" I said, and got out of there. But
neither of them were aware I was alive by then. And Michael
Ames would never leave Gillian, no matter what she did.

By the light of day, I stretched that canvas carefully
to touch up the few smears I'd made when I rolled it up.
Lisette came and stared over my shoulder.

"Animal!" she shrieked; "with this one you have couched
yourself or else you could not have painted this!"

"No," I said sadly," I did not couch myself with Gillian
of which I have not even envy, or paint this of which I have
very much envy, and even shame that I have not this talent.
Look at the signature, Lisette—"

"Ah!" she said; "ah, I am so happy, mon Jeff! But—
where did you get it from?"

"I stole it," I admitted cheerfully.

Then she shrieked again.

"Now what the devil?" I said.

"*Quel horreur!*" Lisette breathed; "the mirror, Jeff! Look in the mirror!"

I've seen some *trompe-d'oeil* in my time; but like that one, never. Looking at the portrait, you saw a beautiful, sensual woman, naked rather than nude. That bastard Volkov had painted droplets of moisture on that skin. I had the impression I could smell an oddly disquieting aroma of perfume and bitchy female. The woman was seated before a mirror. From it her reflection stared back at her. A perfect mirror image of that wonderfully lovely face.

Or was it? I bent closer, staring. The image floated before my sight; dissolved, re-formed. And a hag stared out at Gillian, white-haired, toothless, a wisp of hair on her chin, breasts like emptied sacks falling to her navel, skeletal arms of bone and greenish skin, in which putrefaction had already begun, although she lived.

I felt sick to my guts. Looked away. Looked back again. A smiling, girlish face stared out at Gillian from that mirror once again.

"He is—*un sorcier*, this man!" Lisette whispered.

And a genius, I thought. God help me if I've killed him; for, if I have, I've murdered the greatest painter since Michelangelo.

I hadn't, of course. That skull was too thick to crack. Leon Volkov lived.

And never painted anything else worth a casual damn the rest of his life.

A week later, I, upon Michael's desperate urging, took, along with them, the Orient Express to Rome. While I was gone, Lisette married the *boulanger*. It seems he promised to let her sleep all day, and all the rich, crusty white bread she could eat. Which, come to think of it, was one of the finest declarations of love I've ever heard of.

I sent them the painting I'd stolen from Leon as a wedding present. That seemed to me an excellent piece of irony.

It was. A year later, the baker sold Gilly's portrait to a rich American, who fancied himself as a connoisseur, for a cool forty thousand francs.

And there were four francs to the dollar in those days.

11

Nel mezzo del cammin di nostra vita
Mi ritrovai per una selva oscura
Che la diritta via era smarrita. . . .

THE INFERNO   Canto I

HERO FARNSWORTH

Rome, July-August, 1895

Paris is silver gray. Venice is a pastry cook's dream in pastel icings set down upon a blue platter. But Rome—Rome is splendor. It is dark umbrella pines and tinkling fountains. Cold marble palaces and matchless churches. It is the greenish yellow glow behind all seven hills. It is magic—an exciting, enchanting place filled with beautiful, utterly vile young men like my Giulio.

For I was never deceived. I knew what Giulio was like from the first. But you, my friend, had to have the plot for *Episode in Florence* arranged for you. So I had to be sacrificed before the altar of your cold-blooded scribbler's vanity. So you didn't tell me you were bringing Michael and Gillian to Rome—no. You had to arrange your dramatic confrontation, sit back and watch my face, and take your notes. And I—I was most obliging.

I allowed myself to be driven into Giulio's arms.

I saw the two of you coming up the Spanish stairs.

148

Where was she? With il Principe Cesari in his houseboat on the Tiber? Or at his villa on the Via Pinciana enjoying one of those parties of his that were orgies in the classical sense? How do I know? I went to one with Giulio. (Yes, I shall call him that. The name you gave him in *Episode in Florence*. I have to call him something, and I'd prefer not to use his real one.) I stayed approximately three minutes. Long enough to be ushered into that anteroom where il Principe's maidservants were helping all the ladies to strip themselves naked. In another anteroom, I was given to understand, his valets were performing a like service for the men. Then we were to come out and dance with each other, like that. You see, il Principe was giving a Ball of Adam and Eve. The ladies laughed at me as I fled. And Giulio reproached me bitterly. It seems I had dimmed his social aspirations considerably; made, in fact, something of a laughing stock of him.

Tell me, Jeff, how did she meet that princely swine? You introduced them! Oh, Jeff!

[Let me interrupt Hero's narrative long enough to explain that one. I was beginning to feel damned sorry for Michael Ames. I still didn't like him; but I had been with them long enough to see that he did have certain qualities; was, in a word, worth saving. Besides, Michael was Greg's very best friend; and I have much more respect for Greg's judgment than I do for my own. So I decided to play *deus ex machina;* perform the necessary surgery to amputate Gillian out of Michael's life; and to bring him and Hero together. I was still young enough, fool enough, then, not to know that meddling in other people's lives is folly. Dangerous folly. So I introduced Gillian to Cesari, who was certainly one of the most wonderfully corrupt individuals I have ever encountered. His life reads like a case history

out of the *Psychopathia Sexualis,* except that I believe a
good many of his vices were orginal with him, because it
took his kind of imagination to think them up. And like most
people who have forgotten there ever was such a word as
decency, he was very charming. I, for instance, liked him a
great deal better than I did Michael Ames. I reasoned that
he would debauch Gillian, with her willing and devoted
cooperation, to an extent that not even an infatuated fool
like Michael could stand her any longer. I was wrong. De-
bauching Gillian just wasn't possible. That would have been
roughly equivalent to adding a qualifying adjective to words
like "perfect" and "unique." Because you can't qualify abso-
lutes. Nor corrupt corruption.—G.L.]

I see. You thought you were helping matters. Sweet of
you, Geoffry. But your methods were not nice; and the end
is invarably shaped by the means employed to attain it.
Where was I? Oh yes—

I saw the two of you coming up the Spanish stairs.
Michael didn't have on a hat, and every drop of that matchless luminosity which hovers above Rome like a benediction
gathered itself above his bright, blond head.

I wanted to run. But I couldn't. I was speechless and
paralyzed and blind. I hung there thinking: Oh damn you,
Jeff Lynne! Damn you, damn you, damn you! Because I
knew it was your doing, my beamish boy! It had to be.
Michael would never have dreamed of looking for me. He
didn't care enough.

Then he raised his face and met my eyes. And all my
terror left me, all my shame. . . . (Which, I'll have to admit,
had been considerably modified by then, anyhow. A girl
doesn't go around for weeks with a type like Giulio without
rapidly forgetting how to blush.) What took their place was
pity. Then—rage.

You've seen in the Louvre that painting of the martyr-dom of Saint— Oh, I can never remember which one! Se-bastian or Stephen. The one who has been pierced with dozens of arrows? You've seen it, and you don't remember either? No matter, my point is made: you have seen Michael's face, his eyes, as they appeared to me that morning on the Spanish stair.

I came running down them. Caught both his arms. Felt my lips swell, as I held in check my need to kiss him. Said:

"Oh, Michael! What on earth has happened to you?"

He smiled at me then, ruefully.

"That's simple, Hero. Very simple. I married Gillian," he said.

I spent the whole day with the two of you, remember? You kept trying to catch my eyes, find some way to take me aside, and say—what afterward you did say. That fiendish advice of yours I followed.

You're sorry? Don't be. The only thing wrong with that advice of yours was that I didn't know how to carry it out—then. Though it wouldn't have worked in any event. Your theory was quite correct; only Michael was too hurt by then, too beaten, for any thing to have worked—anything at all.

I blessed you for the way you left us to ourselves after that. We wandered all over Rome, hand in hand like chil-dren. One day, in the gardens of the Villa Borghese, we ran into Giulio, who felt his Latin pride obliged him to make a jealous scene. Pure theater; but embarrassing. I was des-perately assuring him that Michael was only an old, old friend when I saw that Michael wasn't even listening to it, was looking past Giulio and me as though we were not there. And I saw how hopeless it was. How utterly hopeless. Giulio saw it, too; saw that Michael gave less than a damn about him, or about me. He was hurt, too, then; genuinely hurt. He slunk off like a whipped cur without another word.

I turned to Michael.

"Tell me about it," I said.

And he did. Slowly at first. Haltingly. Then in a torrent of words. That Englishman on the liner coming over. That wild painter in Paris. And now Prince Cesari. It was dreadful, Jeff. There is nothing worse—nothing in all the world. I sat there on a bench under a tree in the gardens of the Villa Borghese and endured it. Supported listening to the man I loved baring his very soul, hearing the pain vibrating like violin notes through his every word, occasionally even crashing through like cymbals. But that was not the worst of it. The worst of it was that despite it all, despite his suffering, despite the utter degradation, the unspeakable contempt she had heaped upon him, I could see he loved her still—and with all his heart.

He didn't know where she was. She had simply walked out of the hotel with the remark:

"I'll be back in a few days. Amuse yourself if you can, my sweet. Perhaps—who knows?—little Hero will prove cooperative."

He didn't tell me that last sentence, then. That last sentence which helped spoil your plan. He only told me that in nineteen five or six. He was too much a gentleman. A nearly extinct species, Jeff—like dodo birds. And as helpless as dodo birds, as well.

So I made up my mind to find her for him. To bring her back to him. Or to kill her if she wouldn't come. As it turned out, I did neither.

Hot as it was, I guessed they'd be on that houseboat on the Tiber. I was right. The steward helped me aboard. I'd filled out a bit by then, so I suppose he thought I was another of il Principe's favorites. Besides, his highness wasn't choicy; a man whose partners included all shapes, sizes, and colors couldn't be expected to be concerned about a woman's looks.

The steward probably thought my odd ugliness would interest him.

She was there, all right.

"The American blonde?" the steward said. *"Questa donna si bella?* Follow me, *per piacere. . . ."*

They were sitting under the awnings in the stern, having breakfast. At five o'clock in the afternoon. Because they'd just got up. She had on a robe that was as transparent as window glass.

"Gilly," I whispered.

"Hero!" she laughed; "dear, dear little Hero! Come join us. Would you like some champagne?"

That was what they were having for breakfast. Champagne. And caviar. And breast of pigeon under glass.

"Gilly!" I said again, idiotically. The words I needed wouldn't come.

"Int'resting," the Prince lisped; "the ingenue type, what? Refreshing. I say, my dear, could you arrange to stay overnight?"

I turned on my heel. Ran. Head down like an idiot, sobbing. Behind me I could hear them laughing.

That was when I decided to follow the advice you gave me. Only, you should have realized I didn't know how. I should have experimented with Giulio before, instead of after.

I invited Michael up to my little flat. Prepared supper for him. That supper he didn't eat. But he did drink the wine—a dreadful lot of wine. And I sat there looking at him, and getting more and more nervous and frightened and, well—rather pleasantly excited, too. Only, even at twenty-two, I was both innocent and a fool. Later, I should have known how to go about it—as I proved when the occasion arose. I should have said, "Excuse me, Michael, for a moment. It's so hot I think I'll slip into something more comfortable." Then I should have gone into my bedroom, leaving the door ajar and with my full-length mirror strategically placed so that he could see me undressing. Come out again in a negligee as transparent as Gillian's. Stretched out languidly on the divan. Told him to come sit beside me.

I did none of those things. I sat there like a wooden Indian before a cigar store. He was restless, bored. Finally, he got up, saying:

"I guess I'd better be going, Hero—"

Then I said it. With no preparation. Without his having touched me, or I, him. Blurted it out like a little girl making a recitation at a church supper, very fast, running the words together:

"Don't go Michael stay here with me tonight all night please don't go. . . ."

He stared at me as though he thought I was crazy. He was right. I was.

"What are you trying to say, Hero?" he said.

"That you mustn't go that I love you that I want you to love me—"

"But I do love you," he said gently.

"You don't understand!" I shrieked. "I want you to stay here I want you to love me I want you to—to go to bed with me!"

You have never seen a man more cruelly shocked in all your life. And I couldn't blame him. Remember that was 1895. Victoria was still on the throne. And, beyond all consideration of any particular epoch or its mores, the fact still remains that it is far, far worse to say a thing like that than it is to do it. There are some human activities that are linked with silence, that are tactile, visual, even olfactory; but never audible, never to be put into words. To kiss, to cling, to let one's fingers stray, to touch, to join, to gaze imploringly into each other's eyes—all this, Jeff; but to say it? Never.

Later, Michael told me that what he meant was he did not want my pity, could not accept what seemed to him my sacrifice of self in order to comfort him. He simply did not believe I was afire with need of him; and he was right: I wasn't. Again, it was a means, not an end. I was going to use my body to win him—fatal error! Love, especially carnal love, must ever be an end in itself. Later, he told me all that. But not then. Then he said:

"No, Hero."

And left me there.

I sat there like a stunned beast, for hours after he had gone. I did not even cry. I felt physically dirty. I stripped. Got into my tub. Scrubbed myself until my skin reddened, roughened. Got out feeling filthier than ever, feeling the slimy ooze of my shame clinging to my hopelessly befouled soul.

I stood there before my mirror looking at my body. I had a very good body—even Gilly admitted that. And it came to me that the only way to exorcise my degradation was by another act more shameful still; to stop the anguished, silent cries of my hurt pride, was to kill that pride altogether. I flung a frock over my head.

And went to Giulio's flat.

I don't have to tell you about it. You knew. When I found a copy of the unexpurgated edition of *Episode in Florence* at a bookstall on the quais of Paris two years later, I bought it at once. Took it home and read it all. When I got to that passage— that celebrated passage that cost your British publisher a fine and a jail sentence, and earned you a *succès du scandale* all over Europe, I cried and damned you for the monster that you are and ended up by penciling out the name of Phyllis Brownley, your heroine, and writing in mine, instead.

Like that, it reads better. Listen:

"Where was the beauty of it, the mystery, the magic?
Here were two people, all too palatably naked, making
haste to climb into a narrow bed. The woman (I) could be
seen in one of those mirrors that Giulio (practiced sybarite)
had all over the doors and walls of his bedroom. She (I)
was naked. This was not the nudity of paintings, of statues,
of art; this was nakedness. Flesh so damnably living flesh,
roughened and pimpled with cold, bare to his greedy eyes
that searched it from head to toe, lingering longest over
those parts that were darkened with hair; (not soft-plumed,
spiral-feathered, night-petaled, nor any other of those eva-
sions of unacceptable fact that poetic fancy can supply: just
retaining in places the pelt of the apish ancestors) flesh that
could shiver and sweat, give off its not unpleasent (I'm told)
faint smell of the female in season even respond—betraying
unaccountably my (leave this coward's game of false detach-
ment! This is I who am doing this thing; making this ritual
sacrifice of honor, principle, self) inward shrinking, my
bone-deep repugnance, passing even beyond betrayal (un-
accountable or not) into eagerness, into participation, under
Giulio's expert (let me admit that, at least, give him his
small credit for his small accomplishment) caresses, entering
upon this limb-entwined, silent struggle, flesh sweatglued to
flesh, mouth breaking on frenzied mouth—
     And this nakedness was mine. Mine this faithless flesh,
this perfidious blood that were browbeating my cringing
mind (which saw and knew and understood all, made no
excuses, rejecting even the dishonest pretense of love, of
fondness, of even liking) into ignominious surrender, dragging even the inner me (Who am I? This screaming jangle
of nerves? This panting, too willing, even too eager body?)
into this ugly now-begun grind of flesh, this mingling of

sweats, breath judder, even this (oh I am lost!) teeth
locked, throat locked, bitchthing moaning; this (oh lost!)
final, shattering (too soon, too soon, and I have reached it
first!) explosion of animal ecstasy in which neither mind nor
heart have part. . . .

That sound, that sound, that hideous reverberation was,
I sensed, the still ringing echoes of a cry. A scream. But who
had screamed? (Who, out of the mortal anguish of intolerable pleasure-pain?) Who but good little, chaste little, pure
little, Hero Farnsworth? Who but I, I, I!"

And yet, Jeff, as accurate as that is, it is not quite right.
It remains a man's interpretations of a woman's feelings.
It does not take into account our matchless feminine talent
for self-deception. I felt, at the beginning, just as your
Phyllis in *Episode* is made to feel in that passage. But Giulio
was neither a brute nor a fool. He gave me wine to drink.
Played the guitar and sang to me. Lulled me into a state of
very nearly calm acceptance, in which—and this is so easy
for a woman, Jeff—the whole thing became both beautiful
and right.

Why else would I have kept it up? For I did go to his
flat that one night only; continued to go every night for
weeks. And I shall be forever grateful to Giulio; he gave me
for that space a stretch of very nearly perfect happiness.
Knowing women as he did, he understood that I, even less
than most, could support sensuality unadorned. So he added
romance to it in heaping measure: We walked hand and
hand up the Spanish stairs. We tossed coins into the Trevi
Fountain. We watched the sunset wash the seven hills in
splendor. Then, when I was warmed by beauty, softened by
tenderness, lulled by the *dolce far niente* of his voice, only
then would he begin with his lips and hands to make me
want him. And I would go eagerly to his room, lend him

my body, make full use of his (warm, sun-browned, his mouth tasting of figs, of wine), and for that little time live —as I had never lived before.

I was not even aware that Michael had left Rome with Gillian. It was not until that accidental encounter with you, while you were spying upon my sweet folly, that I found out that they were gone. I didn't care. I wafted through my fool's paradise upon invisible wings, surrounded by light, by love, by music, my feet dancing to notes that were not there—

Until that morning that death came into that room and lay between us. Or rather death's corruption, grave mold, and the smell of decay. He asked me quite matter-of-factly, even gaily, to buy him a suit. He had assumed from the beginning that I was too intelligent to believe that my pitiful charms, my tiresome ardors were sufficient compensation for his wonderfully expert services. He obviously saw nothing wrong in whoring; and that male whoredom seemed to me somehow more degrading than female, had I expressed my thought, would have struck him as quaint.

But I did not express it. I bought him the required suit. I took a sardonic delight in having it made by the best tailor in Rome, and of the finest materials—for is not the servant worthy of his hire? I went with him to the fittings. He was, I think, relieved when I pleaded fatigue, and visited his rooms no more. When the suit was done, I took my pretty, cheap revenge: I bade him farewell, and told him why. That I just couldn't stomach the type of man who was for sale. I expected him to be crushed, humiliated, hurt. But he was the noblest Roman of all that race grown old in sin. He shrugged, smiled, said:

"Ma, signorina, there are always plenty of lonely English and American women in Rome. Some of them have found me worth more than the price of a suit. Tell me, signorina, if you can: Just what is wrong with your man?"

I left Rome, went to Venice, watched the pigeons circling in the blue sky above the Piazza di San Marco; listened to the bronze Mori striking the endless hours atop their tower. I did not throw myself into the Grand, or any of the smaller canals. And I did not contract a romantic lung fever, or die of a broken heart. One doesn't, you know. A pity. For death is no tragedy. Life is. The dead don't cry.

And after that?

After that, I went to Greece. Visited all the places my father had told me about. Lived in Athens an entire month, restless and bored, damning you and Michael and Giulio in my heart. Because, Jeff, as Rodney Farnsworth's widow I had known nothing, felt nothing. But now, because of your satanic scheming, Michael's worthlessness, and Giulio's inhuman skill, I was left—with a body that writhed upon my lonely bed at night and would not let me sleep.

I took a tour of Spain with almost conscious malice. It came to naught. Spaniards like women with flesh on their bones. I crossed the Pyrenees into France, early in the spring of 1897. Settled down on the Côte d'Azur. Where—dear, dear Jeff, how proud I was of that!—I shortly became notorious.

He was a businessman. He owned a chain of hotels. He was fifty-five years old. He had no idea that I had any money at all. And he was everything that a middle-aged, upper-class Frenchman can be; gentle, paternal, worldly wise, discreet, delicate, attentive. The kind of a man who *always* notices the dress a girl has on, and compliments her upon it. He was genuinely astonished that I didn't like my own looks. The only time I ever saw him truly angry was when I let my coiffeur, Andre, change the style of my hair.

He bought a villa in the hills above Cannes for me, installed me in it. I laughed myself to sleep the first night at the delicious thought of being probably the first kept woman in history who was very nearly a millionaire in her own right. It was a very pleasant, lazy, peaceful life that lasted nearly two years. Raoul did not visit me too often. He had, of course, a wife and several children.

Only I am a woman. I met this young painter. A year younger than I. Who was so little interested in money that I once saw him refuse to sell a painting at any price whatsoever to a would-be client who was not the type he wanted to have it.

What happened? The usual. Raoul found out. Tried to buy Jean off—the very worst tactics in the world. They almost came to blows. Over me, Jeff, over me!

Which, of course, was precisely what I needed. I had, finally, and at long, long last, been made to feel wanted, needed, loved. And by two men, both of whom were quite, quite something though in vastly different ways. I could go back home now. I was ready to face Gillian MacAllister. Ready to take Michael from her, and certain that I could.

I suppose, by Birmingham's standards, I had become a thoroughly immoral woman. But I didn't care. In this world, one has to be hell's mistress to become one's own. And I was my own mistress now—entirely so.

The only trouble was that I returned too late. For it wasn't until the fall of 1899 that I got back to Birmingham.

12

MICHAEL AMES

Birmingham, 1899

I

When I came to the house, Tim Nelson was in the garden, cutting back the hedges. He had insisted upon serving as gardener as well as chauffeur, boasting of his green thumb—and, I must admit, with justice. I had never seen the Mac-Allister gardens look as well as they did now.

I stopped there, swaying a little, because I'd already put away half a pint of bourbon with my lunch, having discovered by then that the kind of life I had to lead now became more bearable when it was kept a little blurred, its edges fuzzy, and said to Tim:

"Nice job, Tim. It looks great."

"Thank you, sir!" Tim said; "I try to do my best."

"It shows," I said grandly. "By the way, have you seen Mrs. Ames?"

"No, sir," Tim said, a little sadly; "I'd say she's upstairs, sir."

I went upstairs.

I entered Gillian's bedroom, and found her lying there, holding that fancy, gilt-edged Bible of hers in her hands. She wasn't reading it. In fact she didn't even have it open. That didn't surprise me. Gilly didn't read the Bible. She seldom read anything.

"What's that for?" I said; "displaying your piety, Gilly?"

"No," she laughed. "I like it. World's dirtiest book. Jezebel, for instance. The Song of Solomon. All those laws in Deuteronomy about whom a woman shouldn't lie with—not to mention those two dear girls who got their own father drunk and—"

"Oh, hell," I said.

"Amen," she said; then: "Why don't you get out of here, and finish that bender you're halfway on?"

"Thanks," I said; "I will."

And did.

That next morning, I reached out my hand to take the bottle from the night table beside my bed. But when my fingers closed over the neck of it, they shook so that the bottle slipped from them. Crashed to the floor. Broke. So it looked like I wasn't going to have any breakfast that morning. My usual breakfast: bourbon, with water for a chaser. My usual lunch, too. And my supper.

So now I was cold sober. I tried to remember the last time I had been cold sober. I couldn't. Too far back. Sometime in 1897. Oh, yes; the morning they read Henry Mac-Allister's will. Damnedest document you ever heard of, Jeff. Left me twenty-five per cent of MacAllister Iron & Steel stock; the other seventy-five per cent going, of course, to Gilly. I was to have full control of the management, and was to be paid a magnificent salary; but Gillian was to remain owner. Further, if I died, or—significant phrase, Jeff—left her, that twenty-five per cent was to revert to her dainty hands. Strings, all right. Old Henry knew his daughter. Figured that no man on earth would stay with Gilly, unless he was damned well tied down.

Only, he'd never heard about creatures like me. Didn't realize that I had a sickness in me, an addiction for which there was no apparent cure. That I craved my narcotic. Had to have it; would crawl on my belly through the mire for my poison, my destruction, my torment: Gillian.

We had separate rooms, now. But sometimes, still, she'd come to me. When she hadn't been able to meet Bart Byrce; or when he'd proved disappointing; or because, simply, she needed me to keep the foundry going and was willing to aportion me her small meaningless donations from time to time to prevent my breaking down altogether.

And how greatful I was, Jeff! How groveling, belly-down, cur-on-the-floor wriggling grateful. For that. For nothing.

Besides, I had a kind of a hold on her again since Bart threw her over for the second time. You didn't know about that? Naturally, you didn't. That was about two weeks after we got back from our communistic honeymoon—you know: share your money and your wife with everybody. Gilly didn't waste any time. In two weeks she had Bart in such a state that he asked Dorothy for a divorce despite the fact that she was in the last stages of her second pregnancy. Gilly asked me for one at the same time, kindly offering to keep me on as manager. I agreed at once, figuring that if she divorced me, and I got the hell out, went north to Pittsburgh, I'd get over her finally, and be saved. But Dot was stubborner. They already had a baby girl, you know. And she was drawing for an inside straight: If the new baby was a boy, Bart would never leave her. His pride of clan wouldn't let him. Besides, he had a guilty conscience about the whole thing, anyhow: Dorothy was one damned fine wife.

So Dot drew for a straight and pulled a royal flush. Twins. Both boys. And dear Gilly came home from one of those rides she was always taking and climbed into bed with me. It was almost like old times. Like our honeymoon in New York before we took that goddamned steamship. Good. Fine. Great. Wonderful. So much so that I investigated. Result? A quotation with some variation in the wording, depending upon who was repeating it, but essentially the same. Seems he had shouted it loud enough for half the town to hear:

"Marry you? I want Dot back! She's as good as gold; and there're my kids! Are you crazy, Gilly? I wouldn't marry you if you were the last woman on earth! You— you're a monster!"

So, scratch Bart's name from the list—for a while. After that, those trips. New York for clothes. Saratoga, New Orleans. People used to keep track of how often her absences coincided with Bart's. Damned often. But then again, just as often they didn't. They didn't know my Gilly. They were laboring under the romantic misapprehension that a woman who was betraying her husband was necessarily in love with her paramour, and would normally be faithful to him, at least. To repeat: they just didn't know Gillian.

But to get back to that morning in question: the morning I didn't have any breakfast. I was lying there staring at the ceiling when Tim Nelson came into my room—as usual without knocking. He made a great show of being fond of me; but around Gilly, he was goddamned near uxorious. I don't know why: Tim is the one human male I'm absolutely sure that she couldn't stand. She always used to say: "Ugh! The deacon makes me sick past the point of nausea!"

Yes, I said the deacon. It seems that Tim had some right to the title. He was a deacon of some splinter Protestant sect who called themselves Adventurers for Christ, or something like that. Definitely on the lunatic fringe as far as religious groups go. There was some talk about outlawing them, which was enough to make three quarters of England spring to their defense. The sacred cows, you know: freedom of speech, freedom of worship; and "I loathe and despise every word you're saying; but I'd give my life to defend your right to say it. . . ." Anglo-Saxon conception of fair play and all that sort of thing. . . .

You're perfectly right, Jeff: It doesn't make sense that Gilly kept a man she despised on as a chauffeur. And there was more: It was she who hired Tim; who insisted upon our bringing him with us to the States. Yes, I thought about that; it's the obvious supposition. But now you tell me, Jeff: What kind of a hold could Tim have had on her that would have bothered Gillian in the slightest? That he drove her to keep rendezvous with her lovers? That might be grounds for blackmail in somebody else; but when did Gilly ever trouble to really conceal her affairs from me? Oh no, that pay-up-or-I'll-tell-your-husband business simply doesn't apply. Gilly would have laughed at him if he tried that, would have said: "Tell Michael? Go right ahead, Deacon! I'm afraid you'll be disappointed though—dear Michael already knows. . . ."

Where was I? Oh yes, that particular morning Tim came tiptoeing into my room like the oily little shadow he was.

"You're awake, sir?" he said.

"Yes, Tim; why?" I said.

"There's trouble out at the Warrior Mine," Tim said.

"Mr. Riker's on the phone downstairs. He wants to talk to you, sir. Says it's ruddy serious. . . ."

I got up. Or tried to. My head fell off and rolled across the floor. I had the impression that Tim retrieved it and handed it back to me. The next thing I knew, he had un-corked a leather flask and poured me out a hooker calcu-lated to floor an ox. I took the glass between both my hands and got it to my mouth. I didn't spill much. It burned go-ing down. Like fire. Like lovely, lovely fire. My head stopped spinning counterclockwise, and spun clockwise, screwing itself back onto my neck. I sat up. Things leaped into focus. I could see Tim peering at me with an anxious grin.

"All right now, sir?" he said.

"Yes," I quipped. "Tophole! Ripping! Oh jolly, quite!" Then I went downstairs to the phone.

"Son," Bill Riker's tired old voice came over to me, "there's been a firedamp explosion in number nine. Seventy-eight workers trapped down there. All but two of 'em's convict niggers; but—"

"But they're human beings," I said, "I'll be right out, old-timer!"

I turned to Tim.

"Call both foundries," I said, "and the rolling mill. Tell 'em to shut down, load every man onto the coal train, and head for the Warrior Field. With picks and shovels. And dynamite. I'll be down in a minute, so get going, Tim!"

He looked at me, then he shrugged.

I knew what he was thinking. You can't shut down a foundry without at least a week to ten days' notice. Or else you'll be caught with tons of expensive steel in the fur-naces, becoming almost a dead loss. Nor a mill. The heat-treating furnaces used in tempering iron and steel have to be brought up to heat over a period of ten to twenty hours, held at that heat from forty-eight to seventy-two, then

backed down just as slowly. Shut 'em off and all that lovely
tool steel cracks just like a hot plate put into cold water.

So what I was ordering was that we kiss off a dead loss
of one hundred and fifty thousand dollars to save the lives of
seventy-six Negro convicts. They were farmed out to us by
the state, which was another of the ten thousand dodges
Abe Lincoln never thought of, by which the South maintains
slavery to this day.

You're surprised that I accepted the fiendish system of
renting black convicts from the state to do the work too
dangerous, too dirty, too inevitably fatal for us to be able
to get white men to do it? I didn't accept it, Jeff. I was
minority stockholder, and outvoted two to one by—my
wife. So we had our blacks, complete with guards armed
with double-barreled shotguns and mule skinners' whips.
And the only satisfaction I could take from the whole thing
was the fact that two of those sadistic bastards were caught
down there, too.

Tim drove me to the field in the car. Even in those days
our gas buggy ran like a watch. Tim kept it like that. He
was one damned fine mechanic.

But the minute I got there, I saw one thing: the train
which ran directly between the mine and the foundry
carrying the tons and tons of coal needed to keep the furnaces going, hadn't come. Nor the workers I'd called out
to help save those poor devils. I got on the phone and
found out why:

Gillian had been listening on the upstairs extension.
When I left the house, she called the foundry and counter-
manded my orders. Seventy-six niggers were seventy-six
niggers; but one hundred fifty thousand dollars was—

The price of my liberation, though I didn't know that,
then. I organized what few men we had, and started to dig.
They weren't very far down. The Warrior is a shallow seam.

I know—I know, Jeff!—that if I had had twenty more men I could have reached them in time, could have saved them. But I didn't have those twenty more men. They were back in the foundry saving Gilly's hundred fifty thousand. Which would buy how many high-fashion dresses? How many trips here, there, and yonder? How many lovers?

I swung a pick with the rest. Rad Waters, who is the foreman of the Negro miners—the hired ones, I mean, not the convicts—worked at my side. He was crying. I said: "What ails you, Rad?"

"My boy's down there, Marse Michael," he said. "He got in trouble with the law. Give th' sheriff some sass 'n drew six months. Got to git him out, suh—got to!"

"We will, Rad," I said.

We kept on digging. I was dog sick, down there in that heat, with nothing on my stomach but Scotch whisky. But I kept on working, until I heard Rad say:

"Lawd God, suh—yore han's!"

I looked down at them. By the light of the miner's lantern on my cap I could see they were covered with blood. From the blisters that had formed, and then broken, and the skin under that which had broken, too. I said: "It's nothing, Rad." And went on working.

Half an hour later, I fainted.

Rad brought me up. I had a glass of milk, a sandwich. Went down again.

We reached them just before morning. The Warrior seam is not very deep. We got to them all right. But they were dead.

I saw Rad lift his son in his arms and start toward the lift. Just a big black man holding a big black boy in his arms, and crying. I went up the lift with them. I was crying, too.

"Don't, suh," Rad whispered, "You done your bes'. God in glory couldn't of done mo'. . . ."

But had I? What claim had I now to justice, decency, simple manhood? My blistered, bloody hands? Ha! I who had hung up that phone saying wearily, "All right, we'll do the best we can with what we have. . . ."

Jeff, Jeff! I'd swear that God forgives evildoers; but those who would do right, but acquiesce in evil, never! The criminal has the excuse of his passion, his greed, his very wickedness, if you will; but what excuse has a decent man who equates the value of his presumably immortal soul with a little infrequent carnal play?

If I had pistoled those seventy-eight blacks, mowed them down with a Gattling gun, I should have had the pride of a big and terrible deed. But to say, "All right, Gilly, yes Gilly, to be sure Gilly, darling, I won't throw away a hundred fifty thousand to save a pack of niggers. . . ." and to let them die like that, down there in the choking dark— Dear God, Jeff! Dear God, dear God!

I got out of there. I had Tim drop me off at the nearest saloon. I meant to get filthy, rotten, stinking drunk; but I couldn't. Because my cure was working in me already. I was coming to the recognition of a thing I couldn't formulate, couldn't shape, couldn't say—not then. I had reached bedrock. As far down as I could go. There was only one way for me to go now: up.

When I came out of the saloon, and started home, we happened to pass Rodney Farnsworth's house. And I saw that the lights were on. I reached over and whacked Tim on the shoulder.

He pulled up on the brake handle. I got down.

"Don't wait for me," I said.

Buleah Land opened the door for me. That same Buleah who had been Gillian's nurse; but who had been sacked with all the rest of the blacks when we came back from London. I'd heard about Eliza's and Anxious' truly tragic deaths; but that Hero had hired Buleah to replace them seemed to me incredible.

Incidentally, Jeff, when you finish this one, that's another mystery you might look into. There're a good many things connected with the way Hero's house servants died that surely would have caused a long-drawn-out police investigation had they been white. You see, boy, our new European house servants were much too high-toned to be put to such heavy tasks as spring cleaning. So every spring, Gilly would have the Negroes in to really clean. Eliza and Anxious helped out in the spring of ninety-eight, working along with Buleah. And a week later, they were both dead.

Of food poisoning. At a church supper. And dear Buleah was the head of the committee of sisters who prepared the repast. Of course, four or five other people got mildly sick, but only Eliza and Anxious died.

Our colored community was mightily upset. There were whispers that Eliza and Buleah had quarreled violently while working in my house. Over what? Nobody knows.

But I wouldn't put it past her, Jeff. I've often wondered how much of Gillian is due to Buleah? Is due to the one black woman I know who is black all the way through, right down to the heart?

"Mister Michael!" she grinned. "I jes' nacherly do declare!"

I said: "Miss Hero's here?"

Then I heard her voice:

"Michael!" she said, and came out of another room. She had on a negligee designed, I think, for seduction. Her black hair was loose. It hung about her shoulders. And under that billow of cobwebs and moon mist, her body was—a flame, moving in smoke. I stared at her.

"Good God!" I said.

She looked at me and her nostrils flared a little in what I didn't know then was—disgust.

"Won't you sit down, Michael?" she said. "In fact, I think you'd better before you fall down. Buleah! Go put some coffee on. Make it strong and black. . . ."

"Hero—I—I'm sorry," I got out.

"For what?" she said crisply. And I saw that everything about her had changed. She had always been lovely in a strange, exotic way; but now she was—regal. Fine-drawn, brittle, absolutely mistress of herself. And so goddamned beautiful that my very guts ached with wanting her.

I was dirty as a pig. Covered with coal dust. I stank. And my breath was one long reek of liquor.

"Hero—" I blurted, "Hero—"

"What?" she said; and leaning over, took a long Russian cigarette from the sandalwood box on the table. Lit it, let the smoke trail negligently from her fine nostrils. "What, Michael?" she said again; but I couldn't answer her; I was mourning the Hero I had known and lost. The Hero who was dead.

She looked at me in silence. Buleah brought the coffee. I drank it. Then I said, "I'm leaving Gillian, Hero."

"Are you?" she said. "Why?"

"Why?" I echoed. "But you know why! I told you—all the reasons—in Rome—"

"That was," she said gravely, "four years ago. And you've lived with those reasons ever since. No reason why you can't go on living with them, Michael."

"Things—get to be too much," I muttered. "Hero—"

"Yes, Michael—" she sighed, with the weary patience of one listening to an idiot—or a drunkard.

"Come with me!" I said.

She put that cigarette down. Ground it out with slow deliberation in an alabaster bowl.

"No, Michael," she said.

"Why not?" I whispered.

She smiled.

"I once asked you to come with me, remember?" she said. "And not very far. Only a few paces—to my bed. And you refused."

"You're getting even?" I said.

"No. I'm not—petty, Michael. It's just that I'm not your kind of a woman. I don't know how to make a man suffer. And I haven't Gilly's talent for making you crawl on your belly and grovel and whimper. So—no. No, thanks, Michael. You're not what I want now. And, I'm afraid, you never were. . . ."

"What do you want, Hero?" I said.

"Something," she said quietly, "very simple, and not even very rare: a man."

I got up then. She stood up as well.

"Where will you go?" she said pleasantly.

"North, maybe. New York perhaps," I said; "what difference does it make? Since anywhere I go, I'll probably drink myself to death!"

"So?" she smiled; "it seems you've made a good start."

Then she put out her hand to me.

"Good-by, Michael," she said.

"Good-by, Hero," I murmured; but I wouldn't take her hand.

"So bitter against me?" she said. "Can't we shake hands and part as friends?"

"It's not that," I said; "I'm afraid my hands are a mess."

She reached down and caught my fingers, lifting my

hand toward the light. There was no skin left on the palm
of it, no skin at all.

"Michael!" she cried; "what happened to your hands?"

"Ask Rad when he comes home," I said. Rad was Buleah's latest husband. "He'll tell you."

Then I turned. Left her there.

Went out into the dark.

HERO FARNSWORTH

Birmingham, 1899

II

I sat there a long time after Michael had gone. I felt a
little sick, both at remembering how he had looked, dirty,
drunken, quavering; and at the way I'd treated him. Yet
I had been right. Michael—the Michael I'd spent my life
worshiping had been reduced out of manhood into this. It
was a thing to cry over. But not a thing to live with.

Then I heard Rad's footsteps in the kitchen. I got up
and put a robe over my negligee. I hadn't minded Michael's
seeing me very nearly naked; but, although I have no prejudices, Rad was quite another thing. I was about to go
into the kitchen, when I heard Buleah shriek:

"Po' Baby! Mah po' po' Baby! Daid! Lawd Jesus! Kilt!"

I knew she was talking about that no good boy of Rad's.
He wasn't hers as well, because Rad had had him by his
first wife. I supposed some policeman had shot him; he was
an impertinent boy. And impertinence in a black boy in
Birmingham, Alabama, is one hundred per cent fatal. I
stepped into the kitchen. Rad was crying, the slow, still

tears penciling his black face. I felt sorry for him. Buleah is a witch; but Rad is one of nature's noblemen.

"Rad—what happened?" I said.

"Th' mine, Miss Hero," he said dully; "there was a 'splosion. Marse Michael called for help. Tol' 'em to shet down the foundries 'n come; but Miss Gilly, she—she wouldn't let 'em come. So they's daid. Mah boy 'n seventy-seven mo'."

"She wouldn't let them come?" I whispered.

"No'm. 'N she own them foundries. Aw right Marse Michael runs 'em; but he jes' works for her. Po' feller, I ain't never seen a white man take on so over colored folks dying, or try to do mo'n he done. . . ."

His hands, I thought; his hands!

"What did he do?" I said, my voice already rising above the beating of my heart.

"First man down. In all that dirt 'n heat 'n smoke. Diggin' like a wild man. Worked 'til his hands was all blood—'til he fainted 'n I had to carry him out. Rested a spell 'n come back. Worked on 'til we found 'em. But 'twere too late then—they was—gone. . . ."

Rad looked at me, his dark eyes somber.

"Tell you one thing, Miss Hero," he said; "Marse Michael ain't very strong; but if there ever was a man, it's him!"

I was already gone by then, running toward the phone.

And by that fiendishly perfect working of my own private law of chance: that unpleasant things always happen by accident; pleasant things, never—Gillian herself answered it. But I simply didn't care.

"Hello, Gilly," I said. "Will you put Michael on?"

"Hero!" she said; "how nice you called! I'd heard you were back. Michael? I can't hear, dear. He's not at home. I'd rather imagined he was with you. . . ."

"Well, he's not," I said flatly. "When he comes in, will

you ask him to call me—no matter how late it is? It's dreadfully important, Gillian."

"You know," she drawled, "for some reason you sound just like you're trying to steal my husband. . . ."

"I am," I said. "Will you have him call me?"

"Of course, dear. Bye now," Gillian said.

MICHAEL AMES

1899

III

But I didn't call Hero; because I didn't go home at all. I slept on a couch in my office at the foundry. I often did that. I shaved, because I kept a set of razors there, too. I put the razors in their case, and the case in my pocket. I suppose, subconsciously, that I was taking them to cut my throat with, when the time for that came. As it would. I knew that very well.

Because I had lost everything, now. My pride, my self-respect had long since been gone. But I could have gained them back again, had it not been for Hero's icy contempt. All these years, like a complacent, smug, fatuous ass, I had held her in reserve, thinking that one day I'd be over Gillian, one day I'd drag up a little guts, courage, manhood from somewhere—and there Hero'd be, like patient Griselda, or Penelope, waiting still.

And now that mental crutch had been kicked out from under me, too. I was alone, more alone than any human being can bear to be, stumbling blindly through a night without stars, calling upon the empty void, upon that ter-

rible, eyeless, faceless nothing we call God, and give a bride
and a child to, to come and save me.

Not knowing that a man's salvation is always within
himself; that, and the sown dragon's teeth of his own destruction. He can will either; but first, he must believe.

I went to the bank to draw money for my journey north.
But Gilly, who didn't believe the sun rose before two
o'clock in the afternoon, had this morning—surely because
of Hero's call—reached the bank at nine, the minute it
opened. All our accounts were joint accounts—another proof
of servitude, Jeff. And they told me, with that half-veiled,
pitying contempt of men who are heads of their houses for
one who isn't, that I had no money in the bank, not one
red copper.

I stumbled out of there. Started walking. Kept on walking until I had left Birmingham behind me, trudging
through the golden Indian summer, mile after mile. I had
ten dollars in my pocket. Enough to keep me eating for
twenty days or a month. Or enough to keep me reasonably
drunk for ten or twelve days. That was the choice before
me. Do you even need to ask which I took?

I learned to beg. To steal. To ride the rods along with
another filthy, drunken sot who called himself Horsefaced
Hank. Occasionally, we even worked when there was no
other way to get the money for a half pint. At times we
were sober enough to think about eating; then we'd go
into town, pilfer a fruit stand, raid—yes, Jeff, even that—
garbage pails. We were both bearded, filthy, louse-infested.
If you'd put either of us in a closed room with a billygoat,
the goat would have come out begging for air.

We were holed up in hobo jungle somewhere in Mary-
land, or Virginia. Pete's place, we called it, because the absolute ruler of that squatter's camp, with its rows of shanties
made of packing boxes and roofed with flattened tin cans,

was a black-browed giant named Pete. Every day he beat
somebody up. For no reason, for the hell of it, to show who
was boss. Hank and I kept out of his way. He could have
murdered both of us together with one hand tied behind
his back, and we knew it.

All that time, I know now, I was groping for something:
a key, a golden key to unlock the riddle of man's fate, to
explain to myself the why of things. Why is one man
valiant, another craven? For what, in a man's life, does
unmerited suffering serve? I was, in my booze-fuddled way,
getting close to some answers: and one of them was that suffering is *never* undeserved. It seems to us so because we try
to fasten our puny, illogical morality upon the universe, just
as we created God in our own unlovely image. But if we rise
to the morality of the cosmos we don't suffer, Jeff; for then
we're kings! That morality? Absolute courage, cruelty, will.
Intelligence like a blade of ice cutting through to the heart
of things. For there are only two unpardonable sins, for
which the penalty is sure: weakness and stupidity. The
rest is nonsense. All the crimes invented by the lowing herd
of human cattle in defense or property, caste, and sexual
jealousy, have nothing to do with man's fate at all. We
impute to coincidences results whose cause lies elsewhere.
He is good and he prospers, we say; he is evil and he suffers,
or he will suffer, when a just and judging God gets around
to considering his case. What utter rubbish! What syllogisms
pure and simple! Do you think the cosmos knows or cares
what we mean by good or bad?

A bottle, a packing case, the stars above one's head.
Materials for philosophy, Jeff; for, through them, I discovered the basic flaw of my existence: the guilt of the victim;
the sin of suffering.

I'm crazy? Perhaps. But for the guiltless to accept undeserved punishment involves them in guilt. Because it is

to accept directly the dominance of evil. Martyrdom, Jeff, is always stupid; and sometimes criminal. The best, the noblest in man should be defended fang and claw. And modesty be damned! In terms of human values, I was worth more than Gillian; setting my individuality aside, removing this from personal issues; for a man who has something, however little, to contribute to humanity's slow march toward the broad uplands of the spirit, to submit to the moral vandalism, the sick destructiveness of the Gillians of this world is truly, Jeff, a crime.

How did I arrive at all this? I'll tell you. There was a night when Hank and I had a particularly handsome windfall—handouts enough to make a belly-filling mulligan stew. And a girl crawled out of the underbrush. A scrawny, starved kitten of a girl, maybe seventeen years old. We shared our stew with her. She was scared to death at first, but when she saw that neither Hank nor I were inclined to make her pay for her meal in the way she probably expected us to, she relaxed. Told us her story. The usual: Got in trouble with a boy, had a stillborn infant out of wedlock, couldn't stand the anger of her parents or the contempt of her fellows, so. . . . That completely banal tale of completely banal suffering. We made the properly sympathetic noises; told her to get some sleep; looked up—and Pete was there.

"That's for me!" he roared. "Ain't had myself a piece o' young tail in so damn' long—"

Hank got up. Got out of there, running hard.

I got up, too.

"Now look, Pete," I whined, "she's only a kid, only a baby and—"

He shoved me aside and started for the girl.

I knew I couldn't win, Jeff. I knew he'd fairly murder me. But I knew something else: that the groveling had to stop; the belly-wallowing; that I had retreated as far as I could. One more backward step and I'd have to use my razors, cure the cancer of my existence by extirpating it. I very suddenly wasn't afraid any more. Pete would kill me, but better that way, fighting for something, defending something, than by my own coward's hand. Dying was nothing; a match blown out by the gusty laughter of the mindless void we deify. Life, with this one more thing, this one more knuckling under, this one more capitulation, was the terrible, the terrifying thing.

So I waded into him, snarling over my shoulder for her to go.

His first blow unhinged my jaw. His second sent me down. But I came up again—how many times? Again and again, until after I couldn't see him any more; after my mouth was filled with blood. After I had stopped hurting, gone numb; both eyes closed; my nose broken; my body one long bruise. Then he tired of his sport; set me up with his left, crossed with his right, and the sky fell in on my head.

Funny thing, I wasn't entirely out, even then. I retained hearing, a vague blur of sight. Which cleared; and I saw the skinny pipestems of her legs standing almost above me. She hadn't run. She hadn't even wanted to.

He dragged her into my packing case and took her, there. And I lay there and heard it: the brief scuffle; the shriek of pain; then the beast snorting, the pounding, and then—contrapuntally, Jeff, my maiden in distress, panting, moaning, urging him on in the filthiest collection of obscene exhortations that have ever assaulted human ears. I was too weak, to sick, too battered to get up. I lay there, clawing the earth and laughing, tears of blood streaking the dirt on my hash of a face, laughing.

At the way it never lets go of you. At how when you

play it straight, it crosses you. How between man and cockroach, the cockroach has the advantage: Being unable to think, it can suffer only one kind of pain.

"Honey—" Pete bassed; "how's about another round?"

"All right, Pete," she said; "but couldn't you move that there feller away from there? I plumb don't like him watching us. . . ."

Pete got up. Came over to where I lay. Kicked me tentatively in the ribs. Just hard enough to bend them double, not break them.

"Git up!" he said; "you gawddamn' Peeping Tom, git up!"

I tried. But I couldn't. I pushed myself halfway up, fell back.

"Oh hell," Pete said, "reckon I'll have to drag him off—"

The girl laughed then, clearly, gaily.

"Puny lil' feller, ain't he?" she said.

My description, my obituary, my epitaph. Michael Ames, that puny little fellow, with his puny little soul.

I made it to the Bowery finally. Settled down there in one of those refuges for the hopeless. Learned to cadge drinks with the best of them. Floated time away on a red tide; drowned thought, retreated out of life into a cozy dream womb where nothing was real or hurt or made you cry.

Only I kept coming back. There were mornings when I lay there with my tongue tasting like the furry pelt of the vilest animal on earth, my fingers stuffed into my ears to drown the thunderous galloping of a housefly across the

ceiling, and identity came crawling over me, saying: You're
Michael Ames, remember? You've a couple of degrees
from Carnegie Tech. You're a first-class technician. What the
hell are you doing here?

And my answer: Dying. Inch by inch. The way cowards
always do.

HERO FARNSWORTH

1900

IV

I was seeing your brother Greg again by then. It was, after
all, the intelligent thing to do. I was twenty-six years old
now, positively ancient by Birmingham's standards. Time
I got married again, settled down into respectability. Buleah had spread the story of my smoking cigarettes all over
town; but I baffled the gossips by living the life of a nun.
It was—difficult at first; but I got used to it.

I'll be frank with you, Jeff; I wasn't in love with Greg.
I wasn't in love with anybody. But marriage for love is a
recent invention in man's history. There are better reasons.
To unite two kingdoms, join two estates—or even, as in my
case, that Greg was so wonderfully kind and undemanding.
I knew I'd grow accustomed to him, become fond of him,
finally, even love him in a calm and placid way.

I'd have my moments of nostalgia for the *feu d' artifice*
that exploded in my heart whenever Michael—the old
Michael, not the cringing wreck I'd seen last—was near me.

But in time, like all things of mortal clay, I should forget, forget—

When, finally, Greg asked me, I said:

"Greg, I'm not sure. I think I could come to love you, though hardly as much as you deserve. But I—I'd like to see Michael again. I was dreadfully unfair to him. He came to me in his suffering, in his need, after having performed an act of real bravery, of heroism even, and I scorned him. I'd like to know if I'm really over him, Greg, before—"

"You're forgetting one thing, Hero," Greg said.

"What thing, Greg?" I whispered.

"Michael is married. And to a woman who will never, never let him go."

I suppressed my smile. Greg is morality's self. I couldn't tell him that I gave less than a damn about Gillian's legally freeing Michael or not; that if I found that I loved him still; society and all its conventions could simply go hang. Deliberately I took out one of my cigarettes.

"Give me a light, Greg," I said.

Poor boy! His hand shook as he lit my cigarette for me. Watching the way I inhaled so expertly, the hurt in his eyes was very deep. So I decided, womanlike, to hurt him even more. We can't help that, you know, Jeff; it's the way we're made.

"Greg, my smoking shocks you, doesn't it?" I said.

"Yes," he said softly; "yes, Hero, it does."

"Haven't you ever thought that it is, perhaps, an indication that I'm not the kind of girl you think I am?" I said.

"No," he said stoutly. "A show of sophistication, letting people know you've been to Europe; that you're not small-town any more. But you're still my Hero. Still sweet, gentle, pure—"

I threw back my head and laughed aloud.

"Why do you laugh?" he said.

"At that word—pure," I said.

"Hero!" he said, "You don't mean that you—"

"Have had lovers? Yes, Greg."

"I don't believe you!" he shouted. "You're just torment-ing me. I don't—"

I leaned forward then, caught his face between my hands. Held him like that imprisoned, while inch by inch, I brought my mouth up to his. Fitted it to him, with dia-bolical care. Kissed him the way Giulio had taught me to kiss, taking all the time in the world about it, rotating my head on the column of my neck, clinging my mouth to his, soft and parted, adhesion of scalding underflesh, probing tongue tip's devilish play. . . .

I turned him loose. One second more, I am convinced, and he would have fainted. The great drops of perspiration on his forehead glistened under the gaslights. He dragged out a handkerchief and mopped them away.

"Oh, my God!" he whispered.

I took out another cigarette, lit it myself. The meek may one day inherit the earth, but it is the bitches who own it, now.

"Now, do you believe me?" I said.

But he didn't answer that. Instead, he asked me another question.

"Was Michael Ames among them?" he said.

His voice made me shiver. You have never believed he killed Gillian, I know. You don't believe him capable of it. But you didn't hear his voice speaking to me, putting that question, that night.

"No," I said. "Worse luck!"

He got up, then. Stood there looking at me. Then he said a strange thing. So out of context that it wasn't until the next morning that I realized what he meant.

"You'd better hire Klovac," he said.

So I hired Fred Klovac. Sent him looking for Michael. Told him what Michael had said about going to the Bowery, drinking himself to death. So Fred went there first. Found Michael within three days. Sent me the wire I'd asked him to. I got aboard a train. Went to New York. But I didn't see Michael.

Because, you see, he saw me first.

MICHAEL AMES

1900

V

God, yes! I saw her coming down the street on Fred's arm, and I dived into the nearest doorway. They passed right by me. I could have reached out my hand and touched her. And her face was again the face of the Hero I knew. The girl I loved. The one I was going to go on loving now until the day I died.

I was so shaken that the walls of my throat stuck together from wanting a drink so bad. I'd cadged a few nickels, dimes, even quarters that morning. I crossed the street into the saloon.

"A shot, Big John," I whined; "gimme a shot—"

"Lemme see the color of your money, Ames," he said.

I spilled all that loose change out across the bar. He gathered it in. Put a half pint in front of me. I gazed at it, delirious with joy. I hadn't realized I'd begged that much money. I reached out, poured myself a shot. Raised it to my lips. And saw Hero's face staring at me reproachfully out of the flyspecked mirror above the bar. I realized almost at once it was an hallucination, a rather more pleasant version of the snakes, lizards, and pink elephants of celebrated ill fame. But, very slowly, I put that glass down, untouched. Sat there staring at it for the better part of an hour, hearing the music in my heart playing: You can! You can! You can!

I picked up my bottle and walked out of there. I carried that bottle with me to the freight yards. I still had it with me when I got to Pittsburgh. And it was still untouched. But I smashed it against the pillar of the sign that read: PITTSBURGH CITY LIMITS.

Sort of a christening, you might say. Or a launching. Into life again.

13

NOTE: Reading these chapters over, I am struck with wonder that I let my narrators get so far afield, that I did not jerk them back to a consideration of the essential: some information that would save my brother's life. Yet I did not, for two reasons: I had a shrewd suspicion that this was the way to go at it; let them rush pell mell all over the landscape, enjoying the healing catharsis of talking it out, and I should be much more likely to arrive at the vital clue. Because I knew enough to realize I didn't know where that clue lay, either in place or time. A long-ago, far-off, forgotten occurrence can trigger a powder train of events which may lead to—murder. Rome, Paris, Pittsburgh, New York, Birmingham—who could say where, or what moment the spark was lit? For instance, in the last chapter, Hero gave me a most important clue. I ignored it as female vaporing. A few pages hence, she will give you another. Perhaps you'll prove a better sleuth than I. The second reason I did not check them is obvious: I am a writer. Confront

186

me with a tale of grief, laughter, tears, and life's eternal irony—and I am lost. I'll confess that, listening to this duet of Hero and Michael's, there were times that I forgot poor Greg entirely. All the world loves a lover, they say. I am no exception to the rule. Except that too much sweetness cloys me; but a tale as bittersweet as this, for me is the surest narcotic in the world.—Geoffry Lynne.

MICHAEL AMES

Pittsburgh, 1900-1901

Nineteen hundred was a good year. Most of the plants were hiring. So I got a job right away at Schuler Iron & Steel Works, a few miles outside the city. Schuler Iron wasn't big, which was precisely why I chose to apply there. In most of Pittsburgh's gigantic mills, a man got lost, became a number, a face known to three or four companions on his shift at best. But I had seen Hero. I'd quit hitting the bottle. And I made then and there a pledge to Hero, to myself, to all the world who had seen me down: I was going to end up *owning* Schuler Steel. Remember that in 1900 I was exactly twenty-eight years old. Men have started later than that, and gone far.

To illustrate, at Schuler, the plant manager did the hiring. You know how long I could have worked at Bethlehem, say, before getting a chance to talk to the plant manager? Twenty years. Maybe more.

"Vot can you do, poy?" he said. His name was Martin Muenster. He was a Bavarian, like Franz Schuler, himself. Before coming to the States, he had worked at Krupp.

"Anything," I said.

"Get oudt of mine sight!" he roared; "we dun't vant

poys what can do anything! We vant poys what can do something!"

"Wait a minute, Mr. Muenster," I said; "when I say I can do anything, I mean just that, sir! As far as iron and steel are concerned, I can. I can puddle, pour, run a crane, cap a wild one, tend furnace, draw slag, play a bessemer like a pipe organ. Furthermore, I can run a spectrographic analysis; do torsion, fracture, and impact testing; test for hardness, and heat-treat any given batch of steel to its maximum capacity."

He sat there staring at me.

"A college poy, *nein?*" he said. "Vun of dese Tech school scientists, *nicht wahr?*"

"Yes," I admitted, thinking I'd lost my chance, knowing that old ironmakers hate technicians worse than sin and death.

"So, I put you on de break-off gang!" he said triumphantly. "Away from der heat. 'Cause, next to a furnace, you faint, sure. Now git oudt of mein sight, college poy! You come to work tomorrow at eight sharp!"

Right then, I could have killed him. Every job has its distinctions of rank; among steel men, the break-off gang is the lowest of the low. I didn't want to work there. I wanted to work under a man like Iron John Kolowoski, who—in spite of working in a small plant like Schuler, out, it was said, of loyalty to Franz Schuler, himself—was a legend throughout the industry, the damnedest furnace man in all Pittsburgh. Even in my Tech school days I'd heard of him. Your number one furnace tenders are the aristocrats, begoggled gods, hurling authentic thunderbolts, pouring liquid sunlight, striding into hell's teeth unafraid. But the break-off gang—up in a sand-covered loft, breaking off the gates and risers with sledge hammers—

You don't understand what I'm talking about? Lord

God, Jeff, you were born in a steelmaking family! All right, all right— I'll explain it to you. When any object whatsoever is made of iron or steel, nine times out of ten it is cast. Which mean they make a mold of black sand to the shape they want the casting to have, and fill up that mold with molten iron. Now when it cools, you have the thing you wanted to make, but first you have to break the mold from around it, and get rid of the two extra pieces every casting has: the gate and the riser. The gate is the hole through which the molden metal was poured; and the riser is the vent on the other end through which it overflows, letting the pourer know the damned thing's full. So it cools. But when you break it out of the mold, there are these two rods sticking up with a funnel-shaped knob of frozen steel on top of them, that have nothing to do with the workings of the piece you've made. So you have to break them off with a sledge hammer. It's hard work, but it's not murderous the way furnace tending is.

As I said, I could have killed the old kraut. But I should have been grateful to him. He saved my life. I had been drinking for years. I was suffering from semistarvation, because drunks just don't eat. My hands shook so I couldn't drink a glass of water without spilling half of it down the front of me. If old Muenster had put me on a furnace, I'd have been dead within six months. To work in that heat in my weakened state and then go out into the snow to take the trolley car to my lodgings would have been asking for pneumonia.

I don't know how I managed those first few days. I could hardly lift my sledge hammer. I could see my foreman watching me.

"You'll have to do better than that, Ames," he said, "if you want us to keep you on."

"Look Tim," I told him. "You ever been out of work?"

"Yes," he said, "why?"

I jerked up my shirt, showed him my ribs.

"Know what it is to—starve?" I said.

Tim Murphy was a decent man.

"Maybe I'd better find you an easier job," he said; "had it rough, haven't you, boy?"

"Yes," I said; "but I don't want an easier job. Next week, after I get paid, and can start to eat, you'll see the difference."

"Holy mother!" he said; "you mean you still aren't eating, boy?"

"You know any place in Pittsburgh where they give grub away, Tim?" I said.

He put his hand in his pocket. Came out with a ten-dollar bill.

"Here," he said; "you pay me back when you can afford it."

Which was one of the reasons, three years later, I made him plant manager. The other reasons made more sense. He knew steelmaking backwards, and he had no prejudices against adopting modern methods.

But that summer and fall of 1900; the winter of 1900-1901; that spring were—how can I say it, Jeff? My rebirth. My time of healing. Strange. It started with my body. I used to come home to my dingy room and fall into bed, too bone-weary to even undress. Two weeks of that, and I found I could undress, even take a bath before turning in. I ate like a horse. I began to put on weight. Three months on the break-off gang, swinging a nine-pound sledge hammer twelve hours a day, and I went into a store to buy a cheap but decent suit. I told them my old size and they looked at me as though I were crazy. When they brought it, I saw why. The pants fitted me perfectly except that they were too big in the waist. But I couldn't even get into the jacket. My shoulders and my arms would have burst the sleeves.

And there is a connection between the body and the soul it houses, Jeff. Generally speaking, you don't find a pack rat's soul in the body of a lion. And I was a lion now, roped all over with muscle that I even had sense enough to be proud of. Another thing: To the man able to give her the bout of fornication she craves, the bitch goddess fortune has a way of being kind. Accidents, coincidences, chance— you serious writers have to rule them out, because your intelligent readers won't believe a man's life can be shaped by fortitudinous hazard. In one way they're right—a stroke of luck changes nothing—except for the man who's poised on tiptoe waiting for it. Except for the battered fighter coming up with the count of nine still ringing in his ears, but grinning through the blood and sweat, because he has seen his opponent's fatal flaw.

They'd poured a wild heat. A complicated casting. New kind of a pump for a big city's waterworks. And it went wild on them. Wild. Yes, Jeff, a wild heat, you traitor to the house of Lynne; by definition a heat with trapped gas in the molden metal, bubbling like a witch's brew and getting set to blow that casting, the mold, and everybody within twenty-five yards to unholy hell.

"Cap it!" Iron John Kolowoski roared.

But nobody was going to get near enough to that man-made volcano to cap it. It was going to let go any minute now; and anybody who tried to cap it was going to be dead. Messily dead. Showered to death with molten steel. Which, boy, is far from a cozy way to die.

I put my hammer down. Swung myself over the rail of the break-off loft. Dropped to the cooling floor where the molds were traveling on their little train, spouting fire and rattling in their guts like a giant with a bellyache. I got

to the man who was supposed to cap it, blow it off, chill it—
the term depended upon where you worked; each plant had
its private slang, then. Grabbed that pot of aluminum and
magneseum dust from his hands. Started toward that tower-
ing mold that was rumbling like Etna.

"Goggles, you fool!" Iron John barked, and handed me
his own.

"Thanks!" I said, and put them on. The world dimmed
out, became a purple hell of shadows and white fire. I ran
in, straight in, feeling that heat grow solid, become a wall
I banged into, crashed through, dragging flame into my
lungs, my skin blistering yards away from it; my hair, because I, as a member of the break-off gang, wore no pro-
tective cap, already afire; my clothes smoking; the smell of
my own skin as it puffed and peeled, stinking in my nostrils,
along with all the other smells, fluor spar, manganese, tung-
sten—hot iron! Hot iron, Jeff! When I got to that mold,
dancing now from the internal pressures building up in it,
rumbling, belching, getting ready to go, I was laughing.
Laughing from pure delight, like a child!

I jumped up on the train, dumped that powder into
the gate and riser spouts, threw myself down, my feet already running before they hit floor, sprinting back toward
the others, heard that roar—and a pillar of fire taller than
the one that God set before the children of Israel stood up
and licked the iron beams seventy feet above the floor. I'd
capped it. Poured in those inflammable powders that made
the gases go up in a tongue of flame. Blown it off, chilled
it, capped it, by God!

It, and maybe my life.

I put down the empty can. Handed Iron John his goggles. Started back toward the break-off loft.

"No," Iron John growled. "You're staying here, boy.
I'm sending this yellow bastard up there to take your place.

A man oughtn't to be wasted on the break-off floor. Go get him a cap, Jim. Gloves. Pair o' goggles. Tell me: What's your name, boy?"

"Michael," I said; "Michael Ames, sir."

"All right, Mike," he said; "I'm sending you over to Number Three with Jim. Third helper. And you get third helper's pay from right now. You learn fast and you'll get promoted. I'll see to that."

"Thank you, Mr. Kolowoski," I said.

Third helpers got ten dollars more a week than break-off men. But it wasn't that, Jeff. No, it was something else that made me so damned happy that I could have choked. He'd called me Mike. For me—the opened door, the pass-word, the ticket of admission into the world of—men. Do you realize what it is to have been named Michael, and never, in all your life, to have anyone even think of calling you Mike? To have that goddamned much wrong with you?

A week later he stopped at Number Three furnace to check up on me.

"How's the boy doing, Jim?" he said.

"Just you watch," Jim told him.

I was puddling the heat then, with the big paddle. Then, seeing it needed it, I threw a little fluor spar in. Watched through my goggles the color of that shimmering mass.

"Ready to pour, Jim!" I said.

"Stations!" Jim growled, which was his way of telling us to take our places. Nick and I picked up the iron rods with the pointed tips. Jim stood by, watching Ivan, the Number One tender, spin the wheel so that the furnace tilted, aiming the black pouring spout dead at us. Then Nick signaled to the hooker, and he made wigwags to the crane operator, who brought his big Vulcan rumbling toward us with the ladle swinging beneath it, red-hot and glowing, because they'd been shooting flaming gas jets into it for twelve hours now to get it hot enough so the molten steel wouldn't crack it all to hell when it hit it. It's like pouring boiling water into a cold glass, Jeff; the principle is exactly the same.

The crane hooker talked that ladle down with sign language, until the operator up there on his sky-high seat had swung that red-hot ladle directly under the spout. Then we went in, like lancers to the attack, thrusting those iron rods into the pouring spout to break through the plug of fire clay that was holding the molten metal back. Nick thrust first, drew back, then I, staggering the blows. Or it should have been like that. But knowing Iron John was watching me, I thrust all the way home.

You've seen it, Jeff. To an iron man it's the most beautiful thing in the world. That first white trickle, that gush, that roar, that arc of pure whiteness, so goddamned white, Jeff, that there is nothing to compare it with except itself, the whiteness of white heat, arcing the dark, rumbling, bellowing, making thunder, splashing into the ladle, spilling over, some drops of it, onto the floor, and dancing there like stars.

Only this time Ivan slopped it. He was having woman trouble and his mind was not on his work. I jumped two yards back or else I'd been cased in steel.

"Goddamnit!" I roared at him; "don't you know how to pour?"

He eased back on the wheel.

"You do it, college boy!" he sneered.

I was already up there. I spun that wheel like a sailor, making a blur of the spokes. Kicked one lever forward; eased back on another; spun one more spoke—and that white arc cut the dark in half, bending itself into the exact middle of the ladle—the way it should be done.

"You just lost him, Jim," Iron John said. "He goes on Number One, with me."

I wasn't tired when I got home now. I'd change into my glad rags; steelworkers' high fashion, boy; hunky style! —and go join the others at the bar. Have myself four or five shots and quit. That's how cured I was. Walking through the snow, I swaggered a little, proud of those shoulders, proud of the strength in me. Proud even to be accepted as an equal by a gang of horny-handed roughnecks, most of whom couldn't read or write their names. My peers, my fellows, my brothers. Men. Because Hero was wrong. Real maleness is not simple, and it is rare. The higher up the social scale you go, the more complicated it gets, and the rarer; until, when you reach a certain level—Bart Byrce's, say; mine—the level I'd abdicated—it's just about nonexistent.

No, I wasn't tired. I went out with the others.

And met Anna Hell.

Anna was Ivan Petrokov's woman. Not his wife, because she had a husband. A cripple named Georg Hell. Incidentally, I don't suppose I need to tell you that Hell means clear or bright and hasn't anything to do with hell as in English. Georg had been the biggest, strongest man in the rolling mill. But one day a sheet of plate they were rolling jumped the roller bed, and took off both his legs. So now he rode about in a gocart, selling pencils and shoelaces. Schuler gave him a small pension and was roundly damned throughout the industry for doing it. Set a bad precedent, those steel barons thought.

I didn't know poor Georg was Anna's husband. But I doubt I should have acted any differently had I known. Because, just looking at her, it was as if somebody sank a puddler's glove—they're armored with steel wire, you know

—into my middle and twisted my guts. No, she wasn't pretty. She wasn't even good-looking. She was big. Deep-breasted. Heavy-hipped. Female. And I wanted her. I stood there looking at her, and the way I wanted her was a happiness in me. A big, fine, uncomplicated feeling. With the last faint drop of falsity gone from it. Because, you see, Jeff, I didn't want to hold her hand and quote poetry to her. Nor go walking with her in the moonlight. I wanted very simply and peacefully and happily to throw her down, rip the clothes off her and take her, right there on the barroom floor. For me, a damned fine feeling. I was happy with it. Proved something: that I had left the world of children, idiots, and romantics far, far behind.

Ivan saw me looking at her.

"What the hell do you think you're looking at, Mike?" he said.

"Don't think," I said; "I know. At her."

"Okay," Ivan said. "You've looked enough. Gonna close your glimmers for you—right now!"

They called him Ivan the Terrible. But I didn't care about that. That happiness that was in me all the time now, stayed with me. I knew I was going to take him apart. Because I knew I could. Because I wasn't afraid anymore. Because I was over being yellow, just like I was over being a drunk.

He started for me with his hands spread wide like claws. I stood there waiting until he was close enough. Then I tried to lift his head clear off his neck with a right hook. Damned near succeeded. He went down, taking two tables and six chairs with him. Came up, roaring. We stood toe to toe and slugged it out. There was no art to it, nor any science. We made hash out of each other's faces. We knocked each other down, got up, and went on pounding.

Funny thing, Jeff, I knew I was going to win. I knew it.

Because I'd grown a new set of guts by then; or my old ones had been plated with steel. And it was that kind of a fight. Each of us was too big, too rock-hard for the other to put down and out. So it had to go to the one who wouldn't quit. And I didn't even know how to spell that word anymore.

I could feel him weakening now. So I swarmed all over him. Sent him down backwards across the bar. He admitted defeat then, in a curious way: He reached up, snatched a bottle, smashed it in half and started for my face with the jagged neck. I backed away from him, fell over a pile of broken chairs, went down. He screamed like a panther, coming in. But I got my feet up, caught him under the chin with both hobnailed boots, and sent him flying. He went through the plate-glass window into the snow outside. He didn't get up after that. He couldn't.

I took Anna by the arm.

"C'mon," I said.

I took her to my place. And that was good. Very good, fine, the best. At least up until then. Because I'd never really had a woman before. Gillian? You can't call Gilly a woman, Jeff. What's that French word you're so fond of? *Une vicieuse.* Right. Making of love a sadistic orgy. Frills, quirks, near perversions. Anything but this big, fine, simple uncomplicated love-making. Because she wasn't capable of it. That required a woman like Anna, who liked it. Who wasn't ashamed, not even secretly. Who thought it was great. Who had a real talent for, and a respectful appreciation of, the bed.

So after that Anna wasn't Ivan's woman any more. She was mine. And nobody was even starting to dispute that fact. They'd seen what I had done to Ivan. To the victor, Jeff, damned well belongs the spoils!

I was well now. My soul may have been a mass of scar tissue, but that armored it. Besides, with this happy feeling inside me, everything I put my hands on went right. The doors kept opening. The road spun out, smooth and flat ahead.

They got this big order from one of the biggest manufacturers of sporting goods in the East: castings for hunting knives. An advance order for a thousand. And, if the knives came up to specifications, all Schuler Iron & Steel could make.

Old Muenster started in to make knives, the same way he made everything else: by guess and by gosh. Only he'd never made knives before—and they're damned tricky. On the inside, they have to have a soft, woody steel, to give them flexibility, and on the outside they have to be as hard as diamonds, which makes them damned near as brittle. The two things are contradictory, because they call for two completely different kinds of steel in one solid object. So you have to case-harden them. You start out by making them out of a soft, tough, flexible steel. Then you pack them in a canister full of charcoal and bring the whole business up to 1,650 degrees Fahrenheit. You hold them there for seventy-two hours. By that time the charcoal has penetrated three or four millimeters into the steel, making the outer surface a hard, brittle, carbon steel alloy, while the middle retains its flexibility. Then you cool them, slowly. Bring them back up to cherry-red heat, quench them in a bath of cold oil, and that's it.

So now you know how to make knives and you still don't give a damn? All right. But, Jeff, if it hadn't been for those knives, I'd still be a Number One furnace tender in Schuler Iron & Steel Works in Pittsburgh. Old Muenster figured rightly that knives called for a nickel-chrome alloy. Only both those elements are hardeners. Muenster, making up his alloys by guesswork, put in too much, and those blades came out as brittle as crystalware.

The whole place was in an uproar, everybody blaming everybody else. I just stood there, pouring my heats, and grinning to myself. Because I knew my time had come. That night I put on my one good suit, tailor-made and cut to an English pattern. I brushed what was left of my hair over that bald place where the heat had destroyed even the roots. Put on a gray Homburg I'd bought; slipped into my new Chesterfield coat, picked up my gloves.

"Where're you going, Mike?" Anna said suspiciously.

"Out," I told her, and went.

I took a hack to Schuler's mansion. The butler was damned respectful, so I knew I looked all right. I handed him my card—the cards I'd had printed two months before. "Michael Ames, B.S., M.S., Technical Consultant. Chemical and Physical Analysis. Special testing. Heat-treat problems solved."

I didn't have to wait any time at all. Franz Schuler was in trouble and he knew it. But he wasn't alone. His daughter Hilda was with him. She should have been called Brünnehilde. Six foot tall, a real Norse goddess out of the *Götterdammerung*. Damned good-looking. Even pretty—if one hundred sixty pounds and six feet of woman can be called pretty. And if you like 'em big. I don't.

"Sit down, my boy," Franz Schuler said.

I told him the truth. That I was only a Number One furnace man at his foundry, but that I could solve the problem of the knives. That I had the training to do it, and could prove that, too. Only I hoped he wouldn't make me waste time sending for diplomas, certificates, references. That could wait. What couldn't wait were those knives.

"What do you propose, Ames?" Franz Schuler said.

"That you give me one of those little tool rooms in the

rolling mill for about a week. Advance me a thousand dollars to buy some stuff with—"

"A thousand dollars!" he roared.

"Then lend it to me," I said. "If my scheme doesn't work, you can take it out of my pay a little every week."

He stared at me.

"How do I know you just won't run off with the thousand?" he said.

"You don't," I said, "except that I don't think I even look like a fool. A thousand is cigar money to what you're going to be paying me a year from now. . . ."

Then Hilda got into the act.

"Give him the thousand, Father," she said in her soft, deep voice; "or else I will!"

I put double locks on that tool-room door. Sent a telegram to Detroit. Three days later I had a batch of those knives the Finns of upper Michigan make. And the Finns made the best damned knives in the world. I ground two of those blades down into round, pencil-shaped rods. Mounted those rods as the electrodes of a Telsa coil circuit—I know you don't understand, Jeff, and to hell with it! You don't even have to—jammed enough voltage through them to make the arc, bled the light of that arc through a glass prism, so that it made its own special rainbow. I read those colors until I was sure what was in those blades. Every element has its own wavelength and hence its own special color, Jeff; it's that simple. Then I went to my retorts, breakers, Bunsen burners. I ran one chemical analysis after another—all quantitative because I already knew *what* was there from the spectrograph; now I only needed to find out how much. I didn't go home for five days. I slept on my workbench, lived off black coffee brewed over a Bunsen burner, and the sandwiches they brought me.

Then, when I was sure, I went back to the foundry. I mixed that heat myself, or they would have sabotaged it sure. I wouldn't let anybody touch it. Old Muenster was openly scornful. Kept muttering: Gott tamned college poy!" The rest of them were skeptical. Except Tim Murphy, who said:

"Ever hear Mike say he could do a thing and then fail to do it? I'll put my money against any man's that he'll pull this one, too!"

He got quite a few takers. Mr. Schuler came to the foundry himself. Hilda came with him. And the tension started building up. You can't make steel fast. I brought that batch up to heat as slow and sweet as you please. Held it there. Poured it myself. Got out of the foundry with those knives once they'd cooled. Took them to the heat-treat plant. Nursed that heat-treat furnace like a mother worrying over a sick child. Seventy-two hours without leaving it. Slept on a couch beside it. Rigged up a dry cell gizmo that would ring an alarm if the temperature fell more than ten degrees. Supervised the opening of that can of charcoal and knives. The reheat. The quenching. Ground ten of those blades myself. Honed them. Stropped them like razors.

Then I telephoned the biggest barbershop in town to send a man out to the plant. I waited 'til Schuler got there. Schuler, and Hilda. By then I was calling her, cynically, my short cut. All I had to do was to marry all that woman and I'd be the next owner of Schuler Steel—inside of a year. Then, with all of them watching me, I put my ten finished knives on a table. Told Hilda to take her pick. Took the knife she'd selected. Laid a ten-penny nail on an anvil. Put the blade on that nail. Hit it with a hammer. It sheared that spike in half. Then I put a silver dollar on a block of wood. Lifted that knife, drove it down, point first, stabbing. It went through the coin with ease.

I turned to the barber, handed him that same knife.

"Pierre," I said grandly, "a shave, if you please! But with *this* blade. . . ."

It wasn't the best shave I've ever had. But it wasn't the worst, either.

Tim Murphy went the rounds collecting his bets, his face split with an enormous grin.

Mr. Schuler looked at me, with at least two kinds of speculation in his eyes. He said:

"Tomorrow's Sunday, Mike. Will you spend it in the country with Hilda and me? You and I have an awful lot of talking to do, my boy. . . ."

That same night, for the first time, I wrote Hero. I could now. I'd made it. I put my soul into that letter, Jeff. I told her I had nothing to offer her; but that I wanted her to know I had made it. That I was cured. On my way up again. And that I owed it all to her. Which was the truth. Maybe even less than the truth.

I was so wrapped up in that letter that I didn't even notice Anna wasn't there. I got up, went outside to mail it. Put it in the box, started home again. Then I heard those cries. Saw the crowds running toward the slag dump, heard the shouts: "Georg—Anna! He's trying to kill her!"

It wasn't far—about two hundred yards. I got there with the first of them.

The slag dump train was puffing up that track, loaded down with those cradle cars that could be tilted over sidewise, letting the molten slag, the waste of steelmaking, spill like lava down the slope.

Then I saw what the shouting was about. Georg Hell was on the track in his gocart. He had his arms around Anna. Big as she was, strong as she was, she couldn't get away from him.

Anna had left him long ago. Six months after he had become useless to her in the only way she wanted a man to be useful, she had left him for the first of that long line of lovers who had preceded Ivan. Who had preceded—me. And big Georg Hell, reduced to rather less than half a man, had sat there alone and brooded.

I started up the cool side of the dump. Raced toward them from one direction. The train came on slowly, blowing its whistle, from the other direction. Two or three other men followed me. Among them, Ivan. I don't suppose they were in any real danger. The engineer could see them. And the train was barely moving, crawling along under its burden of glowing slag that was reddening the sky above it.

But when Ivan and I were both almost close enough to grab Georg's arm, he suddenly rolled his huge, truncated bulk out of the cart, dragging Anna with him. The two of them went down the incline, still locked together, rolling. Anna screamed, shrilly. The sound of it confused the engineer. He reached for the whistle cord, pulled instead the signal to the dumping crew. And one by one those cradle cars went over, spewing out that thick, syrupy ooze of liquid fire, cascading down, lighting up the slope, blasting the night back, bloodying the sky.

I hesitated barely half a second; but Ivan, not even that long. He went running, sliding, leaping down that slope on a long diagonal calculated to bring him to the place where Georg and Anna struggled before that slag hit them. He was right. He'd get there before the slag. Maybe half a second before. In time to go with them. To die in that way which is high on my list of bad ways to die.

So knowing there was no chance at all to save Georg and Anna, I went for that fool Ivan. I raced along the tracks until I was above him. Then I went straight down, hoping I wouldn't put my foot in a hole or fall flat, or that the heat already there wouldn't burn through my shoes. I got to him, all right. Pulled him down with a flying tackle that must have looked good from above because the others let out a yell. He whirled, lifted his big fist, pounded me in the face. I gave it to him low in the belly. We rolled farther down that slope, still pounding each other. But at an angle away from that slag.

Then we heard Anna scream. She'd been screaming before, but that was different. What we heard now were the tissues of her throat ripping as that scream tore through. Heard mortal agony slashing the night apart like a blade. Heard Georg's voice join hers, his cries deep, gut-deep, bestial; but rising up the scale until they almost matched hers.

They didn't scream very long. Two minutes, three— just long enough for anybody who heard it to feel it in his guts forever.

I looked at Ivan, then. He was crying. I helped him up, put an arm across his shoulders, and the two of us went up the slope of the slag dump, like that, together.

14

HERO FARNSWORTH
Birmingham, 1901

I

When Michael's letter came, I was in the midst of a furious argument with Greg. Oh, yes, he had come back to me by then, after staying away nearly six months during which time, it seems, he was trying to reconcile himself to the fact that he was in love with a fallen woman. I should have sent him packing, but I couldn't. I was too lonely. I had suitors enough, God knows; but even after I'd ruthlessly weeded out the fortune hunters, I was still lonely; because the two or three fine, upstanding Birminghamers who now sought my hand bored me to tears. I'd been spoiled. By Jean, by Raoul —even by Giulio. By men who considered courtship one of the fine arts, and practiced it as such. But these were men who needed a wife in a hurry to give them the sons they had to have to leave the foundry to.

And Greg, whom I'd always considered a benign and smiling marble statue, turned out to be considerably less of a bore than the others. For one thing, I was genuinely fond of Greg. For another, his very real suffering over the fact that I had been unfaithful to him, had betrayed him—I swear, Jeff, that's precisely the way he thought of it!—was somehow touching.

So he had come back, stiffly. Standing at attention like a soldier, he'd ripped out:

"All right, Hero, you've won. I've come back, because I couldn't stay away. Will you marry me, please?"

I wanted to laugh so badly that my throat hurt. Instead, I took his hand and said:

"Sit down, Greg."

He sat down. Hat and gloves on his knees, his back like a ramrod, his eyes wild.

"Put down your hat and gloves, Greg."

He put them down.

"Now kiss me like you mean it," I said.

He kissed me. And he did mean it. I could feel pure anguish trembling on his mouth.

"Very well," I said; "I will marry you, Greg; but upon two or three conditions."

"Any conditions, Hero," he said; "any conditions at all!"

"My conditions are," I said, "that you never mention my lurid past; that you forget I'm a scarlet woman; and that you hereby agree that the first time you sink into this infantile jealousy and start accusing me of someone, I have a perfect right to leave you, or—" I added wickedly, "make your accusations true!"

"Hero!" His voice trembled, saying my name.

"Do you agree, Greg?" I said.

He was shocked to the core of his soul. Completely horrified. But he truly loved me.

"All right," he groaned. "God help me, but—all right. . . ."

But there was something about your brother, Jeff, that made me want to torment him. He was such a perfect stuffed shirt! I dragged out all the theories that I didn't really believe in: that conventional morality was for the stupid; that free souls should be allowed to enjoy free love; that a woman not only ought to have the right but should actually be encouraged to have as much fun as a man does before marriage; and that her fidelity afterward should be conditioned upon her husband's ability to keep her happy and contented, both in bed and out of it.

That was what we were arguing about when Michael's letter came.

I recognized the handwriting at once. Tore it open and read it without so much as a by-your-leave to Greg. I know my face changed. Worse, before I had read it all, I was crying.

I realized that Greg was staring at me, his eyes filled with concern. Wordlessly, I passed Michael's letter over to him. It was the kind of letter I could show to anybody; and Greg was, or was supposed to be, Michael's best friend.

He read it. Looked up.

"I'm glad," he said simply; "I'm very glad. I knew she couldn't keep Michael down. . . ."

I went right on crying.

"But—but, Hero!" Greg said. "Why on earth—"

I stood up. Slipped that marvelous star sapphire he'd given me—I was born in September, you know, so sapphire is my birthstone—off my finger. Handed it to Greg.

He sat there, staring at it.

"I'm going to him, Gregory," I said.

Greg shot to his feet.

"But, Hero!" he said. "Don't you realize Michael is married to Gillian? I happen to know she'll never give him a divorce! So what do you—"

I smiled then, through my tears.

"You're forgetting something, Greg," I said. "I'm a bad woman. A bad, bad, ba-a-a-d woman! And I don't care!"

"Hero!" Greg's voice had tears in it then; "you can't! You simply can't—"

"Oh, can't I?" I said. "Just you wait and see!"

Then I turned and raced down the hall to my bedroom and started to pack my things.

MICHAEL AMES

Pittsburgh, 1901

II

That Sunday in the country was great. Franz Schuler wasn't nearly as pigheaded as most Dutchmen are. Besides, I'd won my point already. I didn't have to go into the long arguments I'd used to convince Henry MacAllister of the efficacy of scientific steelmaking. Schuler had an educated German's profound respect for science; but I did have to fight with him a little over the cost.

"It can't be done so cheaply, sir," I told him; "but in the long run, you'll find the cost is a relative thing—"

"Relative!" he said. "God in heaven, Michael! You're asking me to spend between ten and twelve thousand dollars a month!"

"A conservative estimate," I said calmly; "it could go to twenty."

"Great balls of fire!" he roared; "why—"

"Pin money," I said. "Look, Mr. Schuler, the trouble is you're thinking in terms of Schuler Iron & Steel as it is now, not as it's going to be even a year from now; and certainly not the giant it will be in five. Those costs won't increase—

or, at most, very little. While your profits will. And at such a rate that your operating expenses, including my laboratory, will be much smaller in proportion than they are now."

He looked at me shrewdly.

"How much smaller?" he said.

"I estimate that I can cut them in half," I said. "But that's not the point. You make a comfortable living from your plant now, sir. Your personal earnings are, I'd think, about one hundred thousand dollars a year. . . ."

His little blue eyes opened wide. I'd called it to the penny and I knew it. But he wouldn't admit it.

"Upon what do you base that assumption, Michael?" he said.

"Sir, I was almost born in a foundry," I told him; "and if I seemed to be prying, I'm sorry. The matter doesn't interest me from that angle. My own interest is, frankly, selfish. I'm damned tired of being poor. So, if I have to show you how to make five million a year in order to make one million myself, I'm quite willing to do that. What I am a little unwilling to do is to spend too much time arguing about it. I'm quite sure that among the smaller plants there must be some interested in a chance to grow big enough to survive before Carnegie and Morgan snap them all up. . . ."

For the first time during the morning, Hilda spoke up.

"Father, that makes sense!" she said.

"It does," Franz Schuler said slowly. "And your salary, Michael?"

"The same salary I'm getting now," I said, "for the next twelve months. Then, if I haven't made you at least one million dollars clear profits, you can fire me. Or you can keep me on, paying me whatever you think your increased profits —because I guarantee you a substantial increase in any event —are worth."

"And if you make me that million?" Franz Schuler said.

"A one-third partnership in Schuler Steel," I answered him.

He stared at me. A long time. A very long time.

"Take it, Father!" Hilda cried.

"Look, girl," Franz Schuler said, "those are mighty high stakes! I don't know—"

"Well, I do!" Hilda said crisply. "For Michael to play for those kind of stakes means he's awfully confident he can do it. And, if he can, we'll all profit. I, for one, should like very much to be a millionaire, Father. And you don't lose control. You've already given me a third; but between us, we hold two thirds, so—"

"That's just the point," Schuler said. "How do I know you won't vote with Michael, and against me, daughter mine? He's a fine-looking young fellow and—"

"Oh, Father!" Hilda wailed; but her face was like a peony. I don't suppose there ever is any way to separate business from biology. I started thinking then, Jeff, thinking hard. Searching for an out, to save my hide the day they found out I was already married. But the idea didn't come to me, then. It wasn't until much later that I thought of it.

"Look, sir," I said; "put it this way: Over what, in the name of everything unholy, could a conflict of interests arise? You make me a partner and our interests become identical. The only thing that could get your dander up would be a policy I proposed that might lose money; but, as a partner, I can only lose money for you by losing it for myself as well, so I don't see—"

"I know you don't," Mr. Schuler said. "For instance, a conflict could come up over your pushing an idea that you honestly believed was going to make us a pot of money, but which I, out of a hell of a lot longer experience than you've had, son, might be damned sure was going to lose us our shirts. Then, if you two young people got together against the old fogy—"

I smiled.

"That chance you'll just have to take, sir!" I said.

He smiled, too, then.

"Spoken like a man," he said. "Done! Here's my hand on it."

"Oh, Father!" Hilda said, and kissed him.

"There are some advantages to fatherhood," I said.

So she kissed me, too; right there in front of him. On the cheek, of course, and lightly; but I was getting in beyond my depths, and fast.

That night, when I got home, I found Ivan Petrokov waiting for me. Up in my rooms. My landlady had let him in.

"Look, Ivan," I said; "I don't feel like fighting tonight—"

"Me neither," he said. "Fact is, I came to thank you for saving my life, Mike. Anna was—a great girl; but she wasn't worth getting roasted alive over. . . ."

He put out his hand. I took it.

"Thanks, Mike," he said.

"Sit down," I said; "I've got a bottle somewhere about."

He sat.

"Mike," he said, "how'd you learn so damned much about steel?"

I started to tell him, then it hit me. Ivan was damned good-looking. He looked like a Cossack. Probably because his ancestors were. And he was getting interested in this scientific business; truly interested. My brain raced. Night school—some pointers from me; a promotion to my assistant; some good tailoring; more pointers from me about speech, manners, behavior, and—anyhow, he liked 'em big!

"Did you finish high school, Ivan?" I said.

"Yes," he said proudly; "got good grades, too. Damned good for a Russki bastard like me—"

I sat down. Drew up my chair until it was facing his. "Ivan, you listen to me—" I said.

The next two weeks flew by. I was busy, happy. First of all, I moved to cleaner, better lodgings in a more respectable neighborhood. Then I pitched in: setting up my lab, getting it rolling. Helping Ivan with his night school homework during lunch hour—he was doing fine, his head filled with visions of success. I came home dog-tired, but too happy to sleep. I wrote a new letter to Hero every night. As it turned out, she got only one of them. Because by the time the others got there, she was gone.

I came home that second Friday night to find my new landlady looking at me with mighty suspicious eyes.

"Tell me one thing, Mr. Ames," she said. "You married?"

I stared at her. There is one rule that never fails: When it doubt, tell the truth.

"Yes, I am," I said. "Why?"

"Never mind why," she snapped; "answer me two more questions: Where, and on what date did you wed?"

"Birmingham, Alabama, April 20, 1895," I rattled off; "but why the living hell—?"

She smiled then, if that grimace her vinegary old mouth made could be called a smile.

"Yer wife's upstairs," she said; waiting for you. I told her to show me the license, and she asked me if I'd ever carried mine around with me when I went traveling. She had me there. Nobody does, I reckon. So I asked her the date and place of her wedding and she rattled 'em off, just like you did. Warned her that if you didn't say the exact same thing, I wasn't going to let you go up. I run a respectable house, Mr. Ames!"

I didn't half hear her. I was too sick. I felt like throwing

up. Now! I thought; now of all times! Oh goddamn Gilly to
deep blue hell, I—

I went up those stairs.

[NOTE: There are, of course, two versions of this: Michael's and Hero's. I prefer Hero's. Michael, being a gentleman, was understandably reticent about certain details. But
Hero was, as she always insisted, truly a pagan, with all a
pagan's frank delight in sensuous things. Michael, Greg, and
and everyone who knew her, believed that her sojourn
abroad changed her. It did *not*. It simply burst the artificial
bonds that her early environment had imposed upon her, and
set free the warm and vibrant nymph who was always there.
One word of caution to those readers who will find her
frankness shocking: remember that she was talking to me,
privately and alone; to a kindred soul, who, she knew, believed along with her that life is to be lived, its joys to be
tasted; and that halo, wings, harp, and seat upon a cloud
were damned poor compensation for the wine unsipped and
the lips unpressed below!—G.L.]

HERO FARNSWORTH

Pittsburgh, 1901

III

When he opened the door and saw me sitting there, I thought
he was going to faint. He came through that door with an
expression of pure disgust on his face that startled me until
I remembered that he'd naturally be expecting Gillian,

after all the lies I'd told. Then it changed. He put out a hand
to steady himself, big and strong as he was then.

"Hero!" he whispered. And I—did I launch into my carefully rehearsed speeches, begging his forgiveness for having
doubted him, tell him that I loved him and was his forever
more? I did not!

"Oh, Michael, you've gotten bald!" I wailed.

He raised a hand in a pathetic gesture, pushing what
was left of that bright blond hair I'd so loved, across to cover
his pink scalp.

"It—it burned off," he said, lamely; "it might grow back,
the doctors say. . . ."

Then he came into that room. And, for the first time, I
saw what he was like, now. He'd always been tall; but it
had been a pine-tree tallness, before. Now he was an oak.
I've seen shoulders like those on Negro furnace tenders down
home; but on a white man, never. I hadn't realized that a
man could be trapezoidal, all bulk and spread and rippling
muscle in one place, then slanting down to a waist that was
nearly nothing, in the other. And that a human being could
have biceps as big around as Michael's were now.

The way he looked had a strange effect on me. Now
just you wait a minute, Geoffry Lynne! And wipe that knowing smile right off your face! As you well know, men and
women are vastly different animals. Men are visual. Let
a gust of wind lift a skirt and show a pair of dainty ankles,
and men are off, the bit between their teeth, running wild.
But women are tactile. We've got to be petted and caressed
a good long time before we even begin to get interested that
way. We may like a man, even love him, as I loved Michael,
with all our hearts; but we have to be kissed and teased into
wanting him—which is a good thing. What a mess the world
would be in if we gave one look and started panting the way
you men do!

No, that wasn't the effect it had on me, Jeff. I didn't hurl myself into his arms with an animal-like snarl and start to devour him with kisses. I stood there, and I started to tremble. I was suddenly both frightened and shy, like a sixteen-year-old at her first high school prom. I opened my mouth to say—what? But no words came out; no words at all. I had the maddening feeling that I was going to start to cry in another minute. I was right. I was going to. In fact, I did.

I hung there with those idiotic tears flooding my cheeks and my lips quivering so that I could feel the motion like a thing apart from me, thinking all the time how lord awful I must look to him, because crying makes a mess of my face in short order, until he came to me and took me in his arms.

He said, rather sharply:

"What ails you, Hero?"

I didn't even dare kiss him. I hid my face in the hollow of his throat. Sobbed:

"Don't you know what ails me, Michael? Oh, why must you always back me into corners! Why must you shame me? Force me to play the brazen hussy—and say it like in Rome?"

He stood there looking down at me. His eyes were very peaceful.

"Are you sure, Hero?" he said.

"Sure," I stormed, "of what? That I want you? To the point that I hurt! That I need you? To the extent that I'm not entirely sane, and haven't been in years! That I love you? Oh, Michael!"

"But," he said slowly, stubbornly, "I've nothing to offer you; I'm not even free and—"

"Oh Lord!" I shrieked. "Michael Ames, if you don't take me in your arms and—and love me right now this instant I'm going to hit you with something hard!"

"Well, I never!" Michael's landlady said from outside the doorway, completely unable to contain herself.

I sprang to the door, jerked it open. She almost fell into the room. I stared at her pityingly.

"You mean you've never?" I said wonderingly. "Not—ever? You poor, poor thing!"

She whirled then; fled down those stairs as though the devil were after her. I fell into Michael's arms, laughing, laughing—

Then, all of a sudden, it was quiet in that room.

Michael picked me up bodily, as though I didn't weigh anything at all; but then I almost spoiled it, because I shocked him once again. Seeing him bending to blow out the lamp, I said:

"No, Michael. Leave it on. I—I want to see you!"

And it was magic, Jeff.

We lay there, kissing long and quietly before our hands began their quick, tentative exploration of one another, before society's imposed encumbrances were thrown off, and we lay naked with our love. I thought suddenly, bitterly about Giulio; but this was not Giulio; these morning-star eyes did not harden into greedy wanting, but softened into awe, into wonder, into tenderness. And nothing about it was the same, nothing at all. Instead we were like temple dancers praising the Most High with our body's rhythms, all light, all grace, all slow, sweet, undulant joining, there in the lamplight with sighing and delight worshiping each other and love with our body's melting into and encompassing one another in ever quickening measure, so that the end was no unwilling cry torn out in anguished pleasure-pain, but bells plunged in space, chimes silvering the night with the sound of our mutual, together-reached joy. . . .

By the time the sun crawled up over the eastern rim of the world, we got around to talking.

"I'll go down to Birmingham," Michael said grimly; "have it out with her. Demand that she divorce me—"

"Oh, don't be silly, darling!" I said.

"Silly?" he said gruffly; "I don't see anything silly about it. I love you. I want to marry you, I—"

I laid a finger over his mouth.

"That first part's all right," I said; "that part about your loving me, I mean. But the second's superfluous, immaterial and irrelevant. What's being married or not got to do with love?"

He stared at me with that expression of pained shock that he could have borrowed from Greg. Men are at least ten times more conventional than women—especially when they're in love.

"Hero, listen to me! We can't—"

"Go on living in sin? Why not? Actually, beyond the fact that I find it utterly delightful, especially with you, it is practically the only thing we can do, Michael, darling. You don't seriously imagine that Gilly will give you up so that you can marry me?"

"She gave me up a long time ago," he said.

"She abandoned you. Quite a different thing. But I *know* women, which is why, perhaps, I like men so much. Let her hear, think, or imagine that another female is seriously interested in you, and she'll come after you so damned fast it'll make your head swim."

"You're probably right, Hero," he said gloomily.

"Not probably; perfectly. Mind if I have a cigarette, love?"

"Not at all, fallen woman," he quipped. "In fact, I'll have one myself."

"Oh, Michael, don't tell me you smoke, too, now?"

"Yep," he said cheerfully, "I smoke, drink—mildly, and sleep with women who aren't my wife. . . ."

"Women!" I said in mock jealousy. "Who are the others?"

"Well," he said, "there're Mary Jane, Martha Lee, Susie, Lillian, Anna—"

His face tightened when he said Anna. I knew that he had let slip the name of a real one; and, for all my pretenses toward modernity, freedom, liberality, that knowledge was a kind of a death. I got up, walking in my nakedness with that tension-taut stride that Raoul used to call tigerish; opened my handbag slowly, slowly, took out the cigarettes. Lit one for me, another for him. Crossed to where he lay, supine and content; put the cigarette in his mouth. Lay down beside him. Blew smoke rings at the ceiling. Said:

"Now, tell me about—Anna."

He stared at me.

"Are all women witches?" he said.

"Yes," I said; "only you spell it with a 'b.' Now, about Anna?"

"Please, Hero," he said, "I'd rather not." There was real pain in his voice.

"Why not?" I said.

"Because she's dead," he said softly. "Because I may even have caused her death; or at least contributed to it. And because, frankly, Hero, it's none of your goddamned business—since Anna belongs to that period in my life when I wasn't what you wanted; when you didn't consider me one of those simple and not even very rare creatures—a man. So, forget Anna, will you?"

"Consider her forgotten, darling," I said a little breathlessly. He heard my voice tremble. Looked up and saw those stupid tears I couldn't hide.

"Lord, Hero, I'm sorry!" he began; but I bent and stopped his mouth with mine.

"Don't be, love," I said; "I deserved that. Let's get back to the subject at hand. Marrying me is out for the moment. It simply isn't worth all the trouble, since you've got me, anyhow. And besides, you can't afford the time now. You've got to make Mr. Schuler a millionaire. After which, you marry Hilda, and he deeds you over the plant as a wedding present. Then I show up, and loudly accuse you of bigamy. Exit Hilda. Enter me. And then—"

"Oh, Lord!" Michael said.

"Have you any better ideas?" I said.

"No," he said; "right now, I can't think."

"Well, I can," I said brightly; "and this time I'm serious, Michael. First I'm going to buy us a house—"

"Hero!" he said; "do you think I'd accept—"

"Yes," I said flatly, "because if you don't, I'm going to hit you over the head with something hard. I know, I know— you're a great big strong steelworking man and you can't live upon a woman's bounty. All right. But we've known each other all our lives. If you needed the money to buy a house would you be ashamed to accept the money from me, knowing perfectly well that you were going to pay it back?"

"Well," he said, "if you put it that way—"

"I do put it that way," I said; "and the interest's six per cent, compounded semi-annually!"

"Done!" he laughed; "Hero F. Shylock!"

"So I'm going to buy us a house somewhere near Pittsburgh. Where would you suggest?"

"Laurel Gardens," Michael said.

"Good. Laurel Gardens it is. Then I'm going to buy us a gas buggy. ."

"No," Michael said; "an electric. Gas buggies don't work."

"An electric so you can come home to me every night. And we're going to live in sweet sin and be very, very happy until you're on your feet. Then, after we're all set, you can divorce Gilly and marry me—if you still want to by then. First things first, my boy!"

And that's the way it worked out, Jeff. We bought our little love nest, as the yellow journals call them, and lived in delighted sin. Michael commuted to work in the electric, charging its batteries every night. It was a dream existence. I prayed nightly to Eros and Aphrodite to keep it that way forever. Vain prayer! Those two are notoriously fickle. And there are other gods. Such as Hera—Juno, if you will—the patroness of conventionality, the protector of outraged wives; the mother goddess of all big, horsy girls—

Like Hilda.

15

BULEAH LAND

Birmingham, 1902

I

I was coming back from the 'ployment agency when I seen
your brother, Mister Greg. He was standing out in front of
the house looking at it. 'Course it was all shuttered 'n barred,
jes' like Miss Hero told us to do when she left. Me'n Rad
was living in the little 'partment up over the stable where
the coachman 'n his family used to live in the days when
folks still kept a coach 'n four. The bank paid us right along
to take care of the place jes' like Miss Hero told 'em to. So
I didn't rightly need no job nohows, only, sitting there looking at Rad, I was purely gitting on my own nerves.

"Howdy, Mr. Greg," I says.

"Buleah!" he says, like was kind of startled-like. "Why
—hello. Any news from your mistress yet?"

"No suh," I says; "but then Europe's a mighty long
ways off."

"Europe?" he says in a funny kind of a way. And right
then 'n there I was certain sure. I hadn't been able to make
out all their talk that day afore she left so sudden-like. But

221

nothing in what I did hear would of made a body believe
Miss Hero was even thinking 'bout going abroad ag'in. So
I says to myself, I says: Europe, my foot! She's a-gone
wherever 'tis Mr. Michael's at!

"Yessuh," I says, playing nigger dumb; "ain't that there
where's Pittsburgh's at, suh?"

He looked at me like I'd done slapped him in the mouth.

"Pittsburgh!" he says. "Lord God!"

Then he turns around and starts off. But here come
that there rattlety-bangity noise 'n that there gas buggy of
Miss Gilly's come flying around the corner with that there
little sawed-off English feller a-driving it—and Miss Gilly
a sittin' there in the back seat looking as pretty as you
please. 'N she picks up that there rubber tube 'n says something in it, and the shofur hauls back on that brass handle
on the side they uses to stop them things 'stead o' reins.
Me? I wasn't even fixin' to go in the house, then!

"Greg!" Miss Gilly says; "how nice! Locking the stable
door? Ah, no—rather inelegant way of putting it, what?
Observing the nest after the bird has flown?"

"Something like that, Gilly," Mr. Greg says. He talked
real stiff. Funny thing, he was the only young feller I knowed
of what wasn't just crazy 'bout mah baby. . . . What's that,
Mr. Jeff? How come I was so fond of her after she done
put me out? Oh, that didn't make no nevermind! She was
jes' play-acting, a-wanting to be elegant. 'N all them nice-
looking white folks in they pretty uniforms was a heap tonier
than a passel o' niggers. Ain't I got no race pride? Nawsuh,
Mr. Jeff, nary a bit. Reckon I knows us cullud folks too
damn well. . . .

"Greg," Miss Gilly says then, "I'm going to pry. Please
forgive me, but I do have good reasons for asking you about
a thing which shouldn't concern me. One of those reasons

is that it does concern me, in ways you cannot possibly know. . . ."

"All right," Mr. Greg says, stiffer'n ever. "Only I reserve the right not to answer you, Gilly, if I feel I shouldn't."

"Greg," Miss Gilly says, "she—she broke your engagement, didn't she?"

"Yes," Mr. Greg says.

"Might I ask—why?" Miss Gilly says.

"You might," Mr. Greg says, dry-like; "but I won't tell you."

"Sorry," Miss Gilly says. "Greg—where is she?"

"Europe," he says. "England, France. I don't know. I haven't heard from her."

"England," Miss Gilly says then, quiet-like; "for I have."

"Then why'd you ask me?" Mr. Greg says.

"Greg," Miss Gilly says, "is—is Michael with her?"

"Why should you care?" Mr. Greg says.

"I don't," Miss Gilly says, "but I'd like to know. I hope he is, and that they're happy."

"Generous of you," Mr. Greg says.

"Is he, Greg?"

"If she's in England, no."

"Why not?"

"Because Michael's in Pittsburgh, working for Schuler Steel. Making quite a go of it. They seem to value him highly."

"Greg, you don't seem to believe she's in England. I have the letter right here. English stamps, post mark, hotel stationery—"

"Ha!" I says.

Miss Gilly turned around and looked at me.

"What the devil do you mean by that, Buleah?" she says.

"Nothing, Miss Gilly," I says.

"Oh yes, you did!" she says. "I know how your evil mind works, because mine works the same way. It should. You taught me to think like you, you no-good witch!"

"Gilly!" Mr. Greg says.

"Sorry, Greg," Miss Gilly says; "but I can't stand her. I'll admit my language is hardly ladylike; but that's another thing my childhood nurse taught me. All right, Buleah; out with it: What does that 'Ha!' mean?"

"Nothing, Miss Gilly," I says; "I was just remembering—"

"Remembering what?"

"That Mister Jeff is over there in England, ain't he? 'N him 'n Miss Hero's mighty good friends—"

"Ha!" Miss Gilly laughs, sarcastic-like. "Hero would never throw Greg over for Jeff! Even she is not that big a fool!"

"Ain't a-saying that, Miss Gilly," I says; "all I'm a-saying is that Mr. Jeff wouldn't rightly mind doing her a favor. I 'members when I was married to that there preacher man Reverend Forbes. Had me a mighty powerful yen for Rad. So I tells the good reverend I has to go to Montgomery where's I'se got a sister. 'N I lights out for Tuscaloosa, instead, with that sweet devil Rad. Puts the nicest, lovingest, wifiest letters in a envelope 'n mails 'em to my sister Eva in Montgomery, with a note for her to mail 'em back to Birmingham—"

"That's a lie!" Mr. Greg says; "you can't read or write!"

"Oh yes, she can," Miss Gilly says, "and very well, too. Buleah, you're a witch. And I'll never forgive you for corrupting me, ruining my childhood. But there is one advantage to having a dirty mind, isn't there? That it's so often right!"

Then she turns to Mr. Greg.

"As for you, Greg darling," she says, "thank you so very much!"

"For what?" he says.

"For the address," Miss Gilly says. "You may drive me home, now, Deac—I mean, Tim. . . ."

"Wait!" Mr. Greg calls out; "Gilly, you wouldn't!"

"I wouldn't what?" she says.

"Go up there; torment him; torment—"

"Her?" Miss Gilly says, soft 'n sweet, kind of; "why, of course not, Greg, dear. In fact, I wish them every happiness. Home, Tim, please!"

MICHAEL AMES

Pittsburgh, 1902

II

I sat in my office, looking at Fred Klovac. He was frowning. His conscience was bothering him. I knew that, because he'd just told me so.

"It's like this, Mr. Ames," he explained earnestly; "every profession has its ethics. Now, for a private detective, one of the main points of professional ethics is to give the client the full and truthful report he or she is paying for."

"She," I said dryly.

"All right, sir—she. Your wife. She wants to know where you are, what you're doing, and if you're living alone."

"And you know the answers to all those questions, I suppose?" I said.

"Yes sir. Only there are answers and answers. The real answers to those questions wouldn't be very acceptable to my client, Mr. Ames."

"On the contrary," I said. "She'd be delighted to discover that I'm living in sin with a woman whose reputation has always been considered spotless—"

"And remains so, for my money," Fred Klovac said. "No, sir. You misunderstand me. In this rotten job of mine, I get to see all kinds of things. Took me a long time to realize that the rules make no sense half the time. No; make that three quarters—"

"What do you mean, Fred?" I said.

"Just this, sir. I could go back and report: Your husband, ma'am, is working for Schuler Steel as head of the quality control department. He is one-third partner in the business, and is already considered a wealthy man. Miss Hilda Schuler, daughter of the owner, is head over heels in love with him. But she is unlikely to get very far, ma'am, because Mr. Ames is living in adultery with Mrs. Hero Farnsworth, widow of the late Rodney Farnsworth. And all that would be true; and yet every implication that she, or even most folks, would put upon it would be a goddamned lie!"

"More light and less heat, Fred," I said.

"Sir, do you know what Miss Gillian has been doing all these years? Wait—I don't mean to tell you, because that *would* be a violation of ethics. I just want to know if you know."

"Yes, Fred," I said; "I know."

"That's just it!" he burst out; "I come up here and find you, a sober, hard-working man, living a perfectly decent life with the woman you love, and who loves you. All you haven't got is a certain little piece of engraved paper—or rather two: the bill of divorcement, and the marriage license. Your crime consists of ignoring some arbitrary rules of church and state, because the means of fufilling them lies in hands that damned sure wouldn't grant 'em to you. You're doing no harm, and hurting nobody. Yet I, in behalf of a woman who is guilty of everything in the books, and some variations she thought up herself, am supposed to dig up enough to enable her to crucify you—"

"There's just one point on which your ethics are damned shaky, Fred," I said quietly.

"What's that, sir?" Fred said.

"When a job looks too dirty, you don't have to take it. Morally, you have not only a right, but the duty, to refuse."

He sat there staring at me. In his life, he'd been hungry a few times too often. And that proposition I'd just handed him is damned rough for a man with the memory of hunger still in him.

He dropped his gaze. Raised it again.

"You're right, sir," he said; "I—I never thought of it that way. Reckon I'm in the wrong profession for a man with a conscience—because nearly every job we're given is too dirty for a decent man to take. I suppose I'd better get out, try learning something new—"

"You should," I said.

"But, sir—about Miss Gillian. What should I do? What would you like me to tell her?"

"The truth," I said.

"But sir! She'll ruin you. Old Schuler is strict; and—and his daughter has hopes. She'll—"

"Let her," I said.

He stared at me wonderingly.

"She can't ruin me, Fred," I said softly; "nobody can ruin a man except himself. She can strike; but for me to fall, the softness, the rottenness have to be there. And I don't believe they are any more. Let her do her damndest, boy. This time it's she who's going to be surprised."

As soon as Fred left my office, I put on my hat, climbed into the electric and drove downtown. I could have done what I was planning to do by telephone; but I didn't want even the girls at central listening in. I parked the car outside of Spiers, Murray, Goldstein and O'Hara, Brokers— and went in. Will O'Hara and Abe Goldstein both greeted me. They were playing pinochle as usual, and arguing, also as usual.

"Mike!" O'Hara grinned; "how's the fair-haired boy of Schuler Steel?"

"You mean bald-headed, don't you?" I said.

"Ah, you scientists can't keep your hair," Abe grinned; "all those ideas stewing away cook the roots—"

"All right, all right," I said; "but this is business, boys. Couldn't we go inside where we can talk?"

We went inside. Talked.

"So," I said to Abe, "you're sure that when Schuler reorganized four years ago he sold enough common stock on the open market to make a voting block heavier than the common and preferred he and his daughter hold?"

"Yes," Abe said soberly, "especially when piled up on that one-third interest you've already got."

"Can you get it?" I said. "In one hell of a hurry? All of it?"

They both stared at me.

"Yes," Will O'Hara said. "Schuler hasn't declared any dividends in years—though, with your help, looks like he's going to be able to. But the stockholders don't know that yet, so they aren't clinging to his paper."

"How long will it take you to get it?"

"About a week," Abe said; "but it'll cost you more than a million, boy. Can you swing the cash?"

"Yes," I said. In fact I could write my check for that much by then.

"Then it's yours," Abe said. "Mike—"

"Yes, Abe?" I said.

"Franz Schuler's a nice man. His daughter and mine are great friends. So—go easy on 'em, won't you, boy?"

"Wait a minute!" I exploded; "I don't mean to ease the Schulers out, Abe! I don't play that kind of dirty poker. I'm just feathering my nest to make sure they don't ease *me* out, boy."

"Why should they?" Abe said. "Franz dotes on you, and Hilda—"

"That just might be the reason," I said. "Personal and private, Abe. I just want to make sure they'll have to think twice before doing something hasty. Get me that stock, boy."

HERO FARNSWORTH

Pittsburgh, 1902

III

Michael had warned me that there was going to be trouble. But even he wasn't sure what form it was going to take. I had my own pet theory about the matter. Since nobody knew Gillian in Pittsburgh, I was willing to bet she was going to stage a confrontation; you know, the weeping, young, pale blonde wife, her face scrubbed until it shone; the simple, even somewhat dowdy dress; the swimming eyes; the sobs of: "Oh Michael, darling, how could you do this to me?" I underestimated her. She was far more subtle than that.

So, when the doorbell rang at eleven o'clock at night, after we were already in bed, I wouldn't let Michael get up to answer it. You see, we only had a couple of day girls,

Jeff. I thought it wiser, under the circumstances, not to have the servants sleep in.

"No," I said; "I'll answer it, darling. It's me she wants to see, anyhow."

"Hero," Michael said, "I don't think it's Gilly. I don't believe she'd—"

"But I do," I said flatly; "I believe she'd do anything, Michael, anything at all."

I slipped into my robe. Picked up a cigarette. Lit it.

"Baby," Michael said, "don't you think that cigarette is overdoing things a trifle?"

"No," I said; "I want to blow smoke in her eyes."

Then I went to the door.

But it wasn't Gillian. It was Hilda Schuler, and her father.

I recognized them at once from Michael's description; but I had to pretend I hadn't.

"Yes?" I said quietly. "What may I do for you?"

We had electricity by then. I'd switched the porch lights on, and they could see me clearly.

"Is this," Hilda said icily, "Mr. Michael Ames' residence?"

It was clear from her tone that she'd come to see a brazen hussy, and I had no intention of disappointing her. I raised the cigarette to my mouth; inhaled deeply, let the smoke trail blue streamers from my nostrils.

"No," I said; "why?"

"Oh," she spluttered, "I am sorry! We've made a mistake. You will forgive us, won't you? Come, Father—"

"Wait a minute!" Franz Schuler said. "Young woman, would you mind telling us where Mr. Ames lives—that is, if you know?"

"Not at all," I said; "and I do know. As a matter of fact, he lives here."

"Oh!" Hilda gasped; "but you said—"

"That this was not his residence. It isn't. It's mine. And, since, whatever your mission, it would be rude of me to keep you standing there, won't you come in, please?"

They came in. I could see them staring at the furniture, curtains, drapes. I only hoped that they had taste enough to appreciate how exquisitely that house was furnished.

They sat down, heavily. They were literally paralyzed with embarrassment. I wasn't. Not at all. But I most certainly wasn't going to make things any easier for them.

"Perhaps," I said calmly, "you'd like a cup of tea? Of course the servants have gone home; but it will only take me a minute—"

"No, thank you," Hilda said.

I smiled; said:

"I must confess I'm a little mystified by your visit, especially at this hour. If it's Michael you want to see, I'll call him; though, frankly, I'd rather not. The poor boy's dreadfully tired."

"No," Hilda said; "don't call him."

"Then?" I said.

"Young woman," Franz Schuler said heavily, "yesterday we received a letter from—"

"A Mrs. Gillian MacAllister Ames, of Birmingham, Alabama," I supplied. "Please continue, sir."

"So you know her?" Hilda said.

"Too well, unfortunately," I said; "but we're interrupting your father, Miss Schuler."

"And you know me too!"

"Of course. Michael's rather good at discriptions. He said you looked like a Norse goddess. You do."

"Young woman," Franz Schuler said, "I want to know only one thing: Is the information contained in Mrs. Ames' letter— true?"

"I don't know," I said; "since I have no idea what information is contained in that letter—"

"All right!" he snapped. "I won't stand on ceremony! Is this Mrs. Ames legally Michael's wife?"

"Yes," I said.

"And you—?"

"And I'm not," I said quietly. "Yes, again. And now, Mr. Schuler, I'll ask you one: What concern of *yours* is all this?"

"Well, I never!" Hilda gasped.

"Just one minute, Miss Schuler!" I said sharply. "You and your father, both complete strangers to me, came to my house at eleven o'clock at night. I received you courteously, invited you in. Then the two of you proceeded to pose me questions, the answers to which, quite frankly, are absolutely none of your business. I think I am within my rights both legally and morally to ask you just why you're prying into my private life?"

"Morally!" Hilda snorted. "Ha!"

"Shut up, Hilda!" Franz Schuler said. "You're quite right, Miss—"

"Farnsworth, Hero Farnsworth. And it's Mrs., not Miss."

"Oh!" Hilda said. "So you have a husband, too, who—"

"Is not Michael," I said. "Yes, Miss Schuler. Or rather, I had. Unfortunately, he's dead."

"Mrs. Farnsworth," Franz Schuler went on, "you're quite right. Your private life is your own concern. But, as a partner in Schuler Iron & Steel, Michael's isn't, quite. The reputation, the probity of a great industrial concern, is the reputation, the probity of those who run it. And let this be noised abroad—"

"Mr. Schuler," I said, "will you kindly inform me who is going to do the noising? Certainly not I."

"My child," Franz Schuler said, "things like this can't

be hidden. And whatever the motives that impelled you into this unfortunate mode of life—"

"Unfortunate?" I said. "What's unfortunate about it? Michael and I are very happy."

"Yes," Michael's deep, rich voice came from behind me; "very happy indeed, Mr. Schuler. So Gillian wrote you? I rather expected she would. It's just like her. But no matter. I most certainly do not propose to defend our manner of living, because it doesn't need any defense; or apologize for a thing of which I'm not ashamed. If an apology is due anyone, it is due Hero, for a deuced intolerable invasion of her privacy, as well as for a series of rather veiled insults. But again, no matter. On her behalf, I waive the apologies, knowing that she doesn't need them."

I half-turned, put both my hands on the arm he had resting against the back of my chair, and laid my cheek against his hand. I thought Hilda was going to faint. But my gesture wasn't brazenness, it was pride. Michael had always been so—so gentle. And so helpless. The way he was handling himself now was enough to make my heart chant hosannas.

Hilda stood up, her blue eyes blazing. That is, if blue eyes can blaze. They don't really. Rather, they glitter like the eyes of the forest beasts you Nordics actually are, Jeff.

"Father, I've heard enough!" she said. "Will you please come on!"

"Hilda," Michael said evenly, "you're in my house. Must I ask you to remember that fact? That, and a few others. The house you live in now, is it the same one you lived in when I first came to Schuler Steel? Even the neighborhood is different, isn't it, my dear? And your father has recently become, I'm told, a member of the Manufacturers' Club and the Pittsburgh Chamber of Commerce. You're not a child. By now you must know that everything in this world of ours has its price. And I've paid your price, the price of both of you, many times over. Sufficiently, it seems to me, for you to at least consider leaving me alone to live as regularly or as irregularly as I please."

"Michael!" Franz Schuler thundered. "You go too far!"

"Do I?" Michael said softly; "I think you'll find, sir, that I'm prepared to go even farther. Good night, sir. Good night, Hilda. A very good night to you both."

When they had gone, I swung around his neck, kissing him, kissing him.

"Oh, Michael," I said, "I am so proud of you!"

MICHAEL AMES

Pittsburgh, 1902

IV

The next day, of course, Franz Schuler called me to his office. His face was sick with worry.

"Sit down, my boy," he said.

I sat.

"Michael," he groaned, "you've put me in one hell of a position. Frankly, considering all you've done for Schuler Steel, as you were ungracious enough to remind me last night, I'd be inclined to overlook—the irregular way you're living. But—"

"Hilda," I said; "that's it, isn't it, sir?"

"Yes," he said. "I'm afraid she's allowed herself to grow rather a bit too fond of you, Michael. And—"

" 'Hell hath no fury like a woman scorned,' " I said bluntly. "All right. But you'd better see that she contains that fury, sir. Certainly to the extent that not one word about

Hero ever reaches the public. If it does, I should be forced, regretfully, to take drastic measures."

He bristled, then.

"Are you threatening me, Michael?" he said.

"No. Warning you, sir," I said. "There's a difference. Threats are often empty. But my warning is not."

"I see," he said. "You're banking on that one-third interest. To show you whom you're dealing with, Michael, I want your resignation on this desk within an hour, together with a stipulation of the price you'll take for that stock."

I smiled.

"Fair enough," I said; "but I'll make you a counter-proposition: your resignation on my desk, and a stipulation of the price you'll take for yours and Hilda's stock. Believe me, I'll pay what you ask, and throw in a vacation in Europe for you both, with all expenses paid."

He stared at me.

"Have you gone mad?" he said.

"Hardly," I said. "I'll play this one, cards face up on the table. Here's the phone. You call the brokerage house of Spiers, Murray, Goldstein & O'Hara, and ask them who owns that hundred fifty thousand shares of common you dropped back in 1897. Then you might consider, on the basis of the quite accurate information they'll give you, who is in a position to fire whom."

When he put down that phone, there was death in his eyes. He kept whispering, "My God! My God! Ruined! Lost control of my own company—ruined!"

I took one of his fragrant Havanas out of the box on his desk. Offered him one. His hands shook, taking it.

"Now," I said peacefully, "to show you whom you're dealing with, I wouldn't accept your resignation if you offered it, sir. And you're very far from being ruined. This plant remains Schuler Steel. You stay boss. I will take your orders quite cheerfully, just as before. And one day, I may resign. In my own good time, and for my own good reasons. In the meantime, we go on as partners; and, I hope, as friends—with the unwritten, gentlemen's agreement that my private life is my own, and that its unconventionality is not to become public knowledge, either through you or through your daughter. Fair enough, Franz?"

He sat there, staring at me.

"Michael," he said, "I—I thought she was a wonderful girl, last night. And the lengths you've gone to in order to protect her confirms me in that belief. Agreed. Not one word will be let slip by either Hilda or me. But, son, why can't you arrange to marry her? The law of Alabama permits divorces, I believe."

"Yes," I said, "the law does; but, sir, there are other obstacles besides the law. For you to understand my predicament, I'd have to tell you half my history, and defame my —wife, completely. That the defamation would be entirely true does not remove the fact that no man with any pretense to being a gentleman can blacken a woman's character to defend his own. Think what you like of me, sir. But consider this one thing: If you were to go to Birmingham, you could go from house to house, cover the entire city, and you'd be unable to find one person who wouldn't take his solemn oath upon Hero Farnsworth's goodness, sweetness, and— her chastity. What she has risked, and goes on risking for my sake, leaves me awed and humbled. You wonder that I staked my last red copper to defend her? I'd do more than that, Franz; I'd stake my life."

"I see," he said; "but it's going to be rough explaining all this to Hilda."

"Then let me explain it to her," I said, "I'm sure I can put it in such a way she'll understand—"

And I had learned all kinds of dirty fighting by then,

Jeff. To the extent of having the electric break down on a country road, where I'd driven Hilda, and having Ivan come to the rescue, dressed to kill, in a spanking new rig, about an hour after the mishap, thus giving me time enough to reduce Hilda to helpless tears. This, without telling her anything beyond the very broadest outlines: that I had been thrown out of a minority partnership, reduced to destitution, ruined. And that, I gave her to understand without actually saying it, my wife was involved in my ruination, that she had stubbornly refused me a divorce while just as stubbornly refusing a reconciliation; that Hero, my angel and my salvation, had found me in the gutter, restored me to self-respect, thrown away everything: her high place in the world, the life she could have had, even her reputation for my sake, et cetera, et cetera, et cetera. I honestly don't think you could have done it better, and you're a professional at spinning yarns.

So I had Ivan drive her home, while I waited for a set of freshly charged batteries to be sent out, since all I had done was to exceed the electric's cruising range of twenty-five miles. I figured that I had smoothed Ivan down enough by then, polished him sufficiently, for him to make reasonably effective use of a broken heart, and twenty-five long, lovely miles.

I was right. They were married in the spring of 1903.

HERO FARNSWORTH

Pittsburgh, 1903-1906

V

Yes, Michael was right. It was love at first sight. Hilda fell in love with Ivan, and Ivan fell in love with five million dollars. Of course, the fact that a great big strapping girl like Hilda came along with all that money had its influence, too. So, when, less than three months after the wedding, Mr. Schuler died, as industrial magnates nearly always do of a quite unexpected heart attack, it was Ivan, not Michael, who inherited the business.

But Michael really didn't care. You see, by then, Schuler Steel was doomed; and *because* Michael had pushed it so high up the ladder; all his success had done was to put us in a vulnerable position. You see, Jeff, when in 1901, J. P. Morgan paid Andrew Carnegie three hundred million dollars for his steel empire, to make sure there wouldn't be annoying competition, Mr. Morgan also bought up all of the smaller independent plants he could get his hands on. Those who wouldn't sell he ruined by the simple method of shutting off their supplies of raw materials, and having his agents in Wall Street spread rumors that such and such a stock was going to fall. But Schuler Steel and a few others escaped that, because, Michael says, they were too small in 1901 to interest Morgan, and because he needed them as window dressing in case the government charged him with holding an absolute monopoly over steel.

But, by 1903, Schuler had grown so big and was doing so much business that it was attracting the Steel Trust's notice. Shortly after Franz Schuler's death, Abe Goldstein called Michael and warned him that well-dressed characters had been dropping into his office, asking questions about Schuler stock outstanding. Only there wasn't any stock outstanding. Michael held sixty per cent of it, and Hilda and Ivan the other forty.

Michael was worried. And so—when he explained it to me—was I. You know how they operate, Jeff: by corporate raiding—by buying enough of a company's stock on the market to give them voting control. Or, if they can't buy control, you wake up one morning to find yourself with a filing cabinet full of orders, and not one pound of ore or one lump of coal to fill those orders with.

So Michael did the only thing to do. He called in Ivan and Hilda and told them he was going to dump his stock, giving the Trust a chance to buy it, and advised them to sell, too, warning them they'd be ruined if they didn't. They argued like the dickens, offered to buy Michael out at any figure he cared to name, so that they could retain control. But Michael finally lost his temper, and shouted at them:

"You think you can lick one billion dollars, you damned fools? That's what you're up against. The Steel Trust wants this plant. They'll buy it, because that's quicker. But they'll ruin you inside of a year and get it for nothing if you force them to."

They agreed then, fortunately for them. Then Michael proved that if he'd been interested in only making money, he could have taken his place along with Hill, Harriman, or Morgan himself. He didn't rush to sell. Instead he sent off letters to the railroad interests, especially the Rockefellers and the Harrimans, pointing out to them the advantage of owning a modern, well-equipped plant in Pittsburgh, capable of producing a respectable amount of rails for their lines. That advantage was nil, as Michael well knew, because

Mr. Rockefeller had already sold his Minnesota ore fields
to Morgan, and anybody who didn't own his own raw
materials was at Morgan's mercy. But Michael was sure
they'd make him a offer, because he'd been watching them
operate for years, now. A steel mill in Pittsburgh didn't
have to be worth anything. The mere fact that they owned
one, in the very heart of Morgan's territory, could, when
let slip at the right time and place, start a wave of panic
selling in U.S. Steel paper that would cost old J. Pierpont
a pretty penny. In other words, as Michael explained it,
Schuler Steel, cleverly manipulated, would acquire a "nuisance value" of more than twice its actual worth.

They made an offer, just as Michael had predicted.
They offered Michael ten million dollars for Schuler Steel.
Then Michael called Mr. Schwab, the president of United
States Steel, and asked for a luncheon appointment. Charley
Schwab roared at his secretary so loud that Michael could
hear him over the phone:

"Just who the hell does this fellow Ames think he is?"

So when the secretary turned back to the phone and
began, "Mr. Schwab is very sorry, but—" Michael cut him off.

"Tell Mr. Schwab," he said, "that this fellow Ames thinks
he's the fellow who has an offer from Harriman and Rockefeller to buy his plant, sight unseen, on his desk, right now.
In fact, you tell Mr. Schwab he's sure of it!"

Then he hung up. What's more, he put on his hat and
went for a ride. By the time he got home, I was nearly out
of my mind. They had been calling every ten minutes for
three hours. How they got that number I'll never know,
because it wasn't even listed. I asked Michael that. He
smiled at me and said:

"Baby, J. P. Morgan could get the angel Gabriel's telephone number if he wanted it."

Then he took the phone.

"Yes?" he said. "Why yes, I could meet Mr. Schwab for supper tonight. Not at all. Thank you very much."

When he came home that night, we had a personal fortune of twelve million dollars, sixty per cent of the twenty Michael had sold Schuler Steel for. And in cash, Jeff. Michael had answered Mr. Schwab's offer to buy the plant with an issue of U. S. Steel stock in our names, with a remark that somehow got out, and was repeated even in the *Wall Street Journal*:

"Why don't you offer us the Atlantic Ocean, Mr. Schwab? That's the only thing I know that has more water in it than Morgan's stock. . . ."

And to prove how right he was, Jeff, in an investigation in 1908, the House Ways and Means Committee proved that $726,846,000 of U.S. Steel's stock was in excess of visible property value, which was Congress' polite way of saying they were pure water.

They kept Ivan on to run the plant. Offered Michael the management of a group of others. But Michael wanted no part of that. Instead, he bought a building that had belonged to one of the smaller plants gone bankrupt under the pressure of the times, and set up a full-scale testing laboratory. He sought out young metallurgists from the campuses of the greatest universities in the land. Very soon he was offering a service that U.S. Steel could neither buy nor put of business, a service which they, themselves, had to use.

So now they were no longer asking "Who the devil does that fellow Ames think he is?" They were inviting us to banquets, making Michael a member of the board of several of the concerns embraced by the Trust. Oh, yes, Jeff, among the lesser lights, we could very well hold up our heads. And when you consider that in Pittsburgh, the greater lights were those several families who could honestly count a personal fortune of one hundred million dollars by that year of our Lord, 1906; if you had to be lesser, Pittsburgh was the place to be lesser in.

Only Michael kept getting more and more restless. I didn't know why, but I could guess. In Pittsburgh, he had made it; but in Birmingham, he was still the poor devil Gilly MacAllister had hung antlers of every conceivable size, shape, and variety upon, the man she'd driven to drink, thrown out of her life like a discarded shoe. In Birmingham, the fortune Michael had made would have put him among the lofty few. In Birmingham—

"Go to Birmingham, then!" I screamed at him, after hearing him say it for the twelfth time in half an hour. "Gilly will take you back, now! Your shoulders will intrigue her, and—"

"Don't be unnecessarily idiotic, Hero," he said. "Do you know why I really want to go?"

"Beyond the fact that you're tired of me, no," I said. It was hot, and the wrong time of month, and I felt unusually bitchy.

He lifted my chin with his hand.

"Because I want a son," he said. "Our son."

I started to cry then in good earnest.

"But you can have a son!" I stormed; "you've been preventing it all these years for stupid reasons—"

"Hardly stupid," he said. "The fact that I can safeguard his future financially isn't enough. There remains the moral question, Hero. One doesn't deliberately wish bastardy on a child. I won't. I want him to look up to me, be proud of me, to love and respect his mother. None of which he'd do, after he found out. And he would find out, the world being what it is—"

I subsided into the sniffles.

"What do you plan to do?" I said.

"Buy into several plants, so we can go back home. I miss Birmingham."

"So do I," I admitted.

"Then, when I have the standing I need," he said flatly, "I'm going to crack down on Gilly."

"How?" I said.

"I'm going to divorce *her*," he said. "By now, she's gotten careless. I'm going to slap an adultery charge on her, and make it stick. Ungallant; but effective methods often are."

"Oh, Michael, you should have done that years ago!" I said.

"I know. But it requires leaving you, which is why I didn't—"

"Leave me!" I gasped. "Michael, you wouldn't!"

"For a little while," he said; "I'll come back every six months or so—"

"Six months!" I screamed. "Michael, I'll die!"

"No, you won't, Hero," he said; "just you wait and see—"

And I didn't, though there were times I thought I was going to, and other times when I wished I had.

16

MICHAEL AMES

Birmingham, 1906

I got back to Birmingham in good time. Things were beginning to slow down by then; that creeping paralysis which was to culminate in the Panic of 1907 was already making itself felt. For a man bent on buying, it was the best possible time to arrive. I didn't rush. I checked in at a downtown hotel. Drifted around, listening. Made it my invariable custom to have lunch at the Manufacturers' Club. The things I heard there convinced me that I could pick up holdings in Anniston, Bessemer, Gadsden, and Birmingham, itself, for less than what it had cost to build them. That I had even brought too much money with me, because I'd been thinking in terms of what I wanted to buy would have cost me in Pittsburgh. I drove all over town until I'd found exactly what I wanted: four one-furnace plants, almost side by side, that were cutting their own throats by engaging in a murderous price war. A little farther off, there was a rolling mill with equipment for rod and wire work. I went to a

244

couple of brokers and walked out holding in my hands most
of the outstanding paper on those little plants.

Then I paid a few quiet calls. They were, Jeff, pathet-
ically eager to sell. The handwriting was on the wall by then.
Tennessee Coal & Iron, itself, was in trouble. The rumors
—quite correct, it proved—that United States Steel was
planning to move into Birmingham in full force frightened
them. They knew they couldn't compete. So they sold. I
didn't think I was going to be able to compete, either, then.
All I meant to do was to put together a unit that would be
big enough to be a thorn in U.S. Steel's side, when they did
come in—to have a nuisance value great enough to force
them to pay me my price for it, which price was damned
sure going to include an executive vice-presidency in whatever corporation they formed in Alabama—and for life.

I bought those four plants, the rolling mill, and a pipe
plant, for a total price of just over five million dollars. I spent
a half million more on the properties that separated them;
laying track so that an interplant railroad system connected
them all. In the largest of the four plants I saw there was
space enough for a bessemer alongside the open hearth. I
wired Tim in Pittsburgh. A day later the parts for my bessemer were on the way south.

All this took me about a month. In that time, I had
seen neither hair nor hide of Gillian. Nor, for that matter,
of Greg. I had been too busy putting together my minor-
league empire. I had seen quite a few men I knew from
before. Without exception, they hardly bothered to speak
to me. One of them inquired testily of the doorman, "What
the devil is that chap Ames doing in the Manufacturers'
Club, anyhow?"

But, if I thought I was going to be able to keep secret
the biggest single operation in Alabama's industrial history
until U.S. Steel dwarfed it by paying $35,317,632.64—I have

always loved that that extra sixty-four cents in that quotation!—for the Tennessee Coal & Iron Company that very
next year, I was dead wrong, Jeff. I was having lunch at the
club, when the doorman came in, bowed respectfully, and
told me that the gentlemen of the press were fairly besieg-
ing him outside. He didn't want to disturb me, but if I'd
tell him if and when I'd be willing to talk to them—

I saw the others staring at me. And I'd had a bellyful
of their cold-shouldering.

"Now," I said; "I'll talk to them, now. . . ."

I forgot to mention, Jeff, that one of my first acts on
reaching Birmingham was to renew my membership in the
club. So I could admit those reporters if I wanted to. I was
a full-fledged member, with all a member's privileges. The
reporters came in. There was Griffiths of the *Age Herald;*
Thomas of the Birmingham *News,* which didn't surprise
me. But the measure of the splash I'd made was the fact
that Wilkes of the Montgomery *Advertiser* was there, too,
with a photographer, camera, flashpan, and all.

Out of the corner of my eye, I could see that not a
man in the club dining room was eating any more. As the
reporters clustered around me, firing questions, they sat
there glaring. I parried the questions nimbly, admitting
that I'd bought the properties, telling them that I was con-
solidating them into a workable unit; saying, Yes, at least
one bessemer blower was on its way; yes, I planned to add
more; no, I shouldn't like to say the price I'd paid for what
was going to be called Consolidated Steel. . . .

The photographer fired off his magnesium powder,
sending the smoke drifting against the ceiling. Then, as
they turned to go, Wilkes asked me the question that turned
Birmingham, Alabama, upside down.

"You are, of course, acting for a holding company,
aren't you, Mr. Ames?"

I smiled at him.

"No," I said; "I am acting for myself."

He stared at me.

"Mr. Ames," he said, his voice rising in honest astonishment so that those at the nearest tables heard him clearly, "you mean to tell me that you've bought twenty million dollars' worth of steel properties out of your own pocket?"

I thought about that one for a fraction of a second. He hadn't asked me if I'd paid twenty millions for those plants. He had simply made a rather conservative estimate of what they were actually worth, put together and tied down into an efficient unit. So I answered him quite truthfully:

"With, Mr. Wilkes, the reservation that the valuation of twenty millions is *your* estimate, and should be indicated as such in your story, the answer is yes. I bought those holdings out of my own funds. There will be no partners, nor any stock issue floated. I mean to maintain full control."

"Thank you, sir!" Wilkes cried; then: "Brother, what a scoop!" Then they all rushed out of there.

It was comical, Jeff. And a little sad. All you could hear was the scrape of chairs being pushed back, as all those who had heard it, and after them, all the rest, as the word flew all over the dining room, came trooping over to my table like sheep to voice their congratulations, offer me their hands. I could afford to be gracious, then; so I casually announced that the members of the Birmingham Manufacturers' Club and their good wives were invited to be my guests at a banquet to be held at the town's largest hotel, tomorrow night. By then, I knew those papers would have hit the streets. In a way, I was giving Gilly fair warning of what she was going to be up against. But I had forgotten one thing: Gilly, too, was a wife of a member of the Manufacturers' Club. Because as far as the world was concerned, she was still—mine.

I left all the arrangements in the capable hands of the hotel's staff. That is one of the good things about money, Jeff: it relieves you of so many minor annoyances. Call me a Philistine if you will; but life is ever so much more pleasant when you can say: "Hang the expense! I want it done this way, at this time, and at this place. Use your own judgment and don't bother me about the details. . . ."

I didn't go to the club for lunch that day. I knew that I wouldn't be able to eat in peace. After the first ten calls that morning, I sent a bellhop out to buy the papers. After I read them, I ordered that all calls were to be politely but firmly refused. For reporters are frustrated novelists, Jeff. Those stories were out of Hans Christian Andersen, Grimm, and Horatio Alger. I had paid variously twenty-five, thirty-five, and fifty millions for those plants. Sources worthy of credence put my personal fortune at between eighty and one hundred million dollars. I was on the board of directors of X, Y, and Z plants in Pittsburgh—this part was quite correct; I suppose they wired the Pittsburgh papers for the information— I was owner and director of highly respected testing laboratory, whose services were in constant demand by the giants of the steel industry. . . .

Then, of course, they had to cap it, chill it, blow it off: I moved in the very highest social circles of Pittsburgh. My good wife and I had no longer than a month ago been among those present at a soirée at the Laurel Gardens Country Club, given by Mr. and Mrs. Charles Schwab; and Mr. and Mrs. Corey. . . .

I guess all those millions had gone to their heads, boy; because it surely never occurred to them to check what everybody in Birmingham must have known: that Mrs. Michael Ames, née Gillian MacAllister, had never been in Pittsburgh, Pennsylvania, in all her life. And that a month ago she had given a little soirée of her own which the local press had dutifully reported.

I was quite literally sick. I had handed Gillian the weapon she needed. And the scandal was going to be a big one. I was thinking it all out: how I could get a wire off to Hero telling her to get the hell out of Pittsburgh for a while without that wire going through the local telegraph offices whose employees, I knew damned well, sometimes sold information to reporters in order to pad their meager salaries. I'd have to drive out to Anniston or Bessemer, and send it from there. . . .

Then, when I calmed down, it came to me that Gillian had learned nothing from the papers that she didn't know already, that she very probably wouldn't strike at all. Because, if she'd wanted to, she had years in which to do so, years during which Fred Klovac's report rested in her hands. That she had tried to wreck me meant nothing. She had failed, and had surely known that her trick of using Hilda Schuler hadn't worked. Yet, thereafter, she hadn't done anything. Why? Obviously because it suited her purpose not to.

I smiled, thinking that. Because it was only Gilly whom I had to fear. With half Birmingham quaking in its boots because of the financial disaster looming on the horizon, nobody was going to offend a man with the eighty million dollars the newspapers said I had.

Then, just as I was dressing to go out, the bellboy knocked at my door. He had a tray covered with visiting cards: all the poor devils who wanted to seek advice, borrow money, or—so sad a thing is human nature, Jeff—merely boast that they'd "had a little chat with Ames this morning, and he says—"

I glanced at those cards idly. But one of them stopped me cold. It was your brother Greg's.

I stood there looking at it. Hero had told me the story of that broken engagement. And Greg, reading the papers that morning, had surely been struck by the item about my exalted social life. Greg is my friend, a veritable prince, Jeff, with nothing ugly, base, or mean in his make-up. He hadn't come to borrow money or to congratulate me. He'd probably come to tell me what an unmitigated bastard I'd turned out to be.

"Send Mr. Lynne up," I said. "Tell the others I'm tied up for today. . . ."

Greg stood there looking at me. Took my proffered hand. Sat down, at my request. Still looking at me.

"Well, Greg?" I said.

He handed me the clipping. That clipping.

"So?" I said.

"I'd like to know," he said heavily," if this particular Mrs. Ames is—Hero—still?"

"Still?" I said.

He looked at me a long time; a very long time. Then he said it, his voice very quiet:

"If you ever desert her, I'll kill you, Michael."

I smiled.

"Even breaking into the insane asylumn to do it?" I said.

"Even breaking into hell. But why—the asylumn, Michael?"

"Because that's where I'd be if I deserted Hero," I said. "That, to me, would be the only conceivable reason: that I'd gone out of my mind completely. Funny. The papers were full of eulogies of my great fortune. Only they don't know that my only real fortune weighs one hundred five pounds and has jet black hair. . . ."

He stood up then; put his big hand on my shoulder.

"You mean that, don't you, Michael?" he said.

"Why the hell else do you think I'm here?" I told him; "to buy steel mills?"

"So," he whispered, "you're going to ask Gilly—"

"I," I said, "am not going to ask Gilly one goddamned thing. She's going to offer me that divorce, boy; just you wait!"

His eyes, then, were the bleakest things I've ever seen.

"I see you still don't know Gillian," he said.

I knew what Birmingham was expecting, so I dressed the part. Diamond studs on my dress shirt, each of them nearly the size of a ten-cent piece. Diamond cuff links the size of pigeon eggs. A formal evening suit of heavy black silk, which was a thing they'd never seen before. One ring on my finger, but with a locomotive's headlamp of a stone sure to blind anyone who looked at it too hard. Vulgar ostentation, Jeff! That was the ticket: the more vulgar, the better. I knew my town, knew better than to indulge in subtleties. I had ordered enough champagne to float a Cunard liner, every exotic French dish the hotel's chef had ever heard of, and a few new ones he had dredged up by telephoning every other chef in town; their lists exhausted, he'd slapped French names on local dishes. Hush puppies became, so help me, *Roulade de petits chiens silencieux!* Tone, boy, tone!

I came down early to greet my guests. Bart Byrce and Dorothy were among the first to arrive. Bart shook hands with me sullenly; but Dot was plainly delighted with the way I looked. She leaned over and whispered in my ear:

"She'll take you back now, Michael! And what's more, from the looks of those shoulders, you'll keep her worn out enough to leave my Bart alone!"

Then, when everyone had taken his place at the table,

I noticed something: the maître d' had put place cards for each guest, having I suppose, got the list from the secretary of the club. And two chairs were empty: one a considerable distance away from mine; but the other, at my side. I picked up that place card, read: "Mrs. Michael Ames."

There were the usual noises of a feast: glass clatter, laughter, the clank of silver, the hubbub of voices, even the lilt of the soft dinner music I'd ordered played. Then, abruptly, it all died.

As Gillian came through the archway on your brother's arm. . . .

I thought then that she made Greg bring her because his spotless reputation made him the obvious choice; but I wonder, now. There was something about his looks, the fact that he refused to meet my eyes, that— Yes, you're right. It's nonsense. Greg fairly hated her.

The gown she had on, I was told afterward, was new. Dot Byrce swears that Gillian put seven seamstresses to work on it in the sewing room one hour after she'd read those papers. If she did, it was worth the effort. It was of coral velvet, with a filmy top that Dot called a fichu of turquoise-blue chiffon. It had a black velvet bow looping her tiny waist, pinned to the back of that gown with a spray of diamonds, and then falling almost to the hem of the skirt. The skirt was embroidered with what looked like precious stones; and the hem of it was trimmed with ermine. Who else would have thought of that, Jeff—to drag ermine across a ballroom floor!

Greg led her up to me. Bowed silently, and left her there. Went and took his seat.

I smiled. Put out my hand to her.

"Well, Gilly?" I said.

"Oh, Michael! How perfectly stunning you've become!" she said, and leaning forward, kissed my mouth.

Everybody laughed gaily. There was a patter of hand-claps. The waiter held Gillian's chair for her, and she sat down, blushing prettily, like a child.

The banquet went off swimmingly. I was eulogized by several speakers, called upon to reply. I made my talk as brief as possible, expressed my faith in Birmingham's future; concluded with the hope that we would all march forward together, now that very concretely I had gotten into step. I received much more applause than my dull remarks warranted. Gilly managed one last handclap even after the others had done.

When I sat down again, she slipped her hands through my arms, turned up to me that face of sweet innocence she had inherited from poor Heddy, along with, perhaps, its invulnerability to vice, crime, and the passing of the years, and said in a tone of perfect, wifely pride:

"You were splendid, darling! I am *so* proud of you!"

Astonishing? What about Gillian wasn't astonishing, Jeff? She was thirty-one years old, and she looked about twenty-two. If there were a form of sensuality within those broad limits which we call normalcy in which she had not indulged—as well, I suspected, as having occasionally strayed outside them, her appreciation of Lisette's beauty was far too keen, it seemed to me—I'm sure I don't know what it was. And yet, she had not the slightest hint of that look of a jaded *poule* one would have expected her to have by then. She had grown a trifle heavier; but *embonpoint* was far from frowned upon in those days. Looking at her, I saw a sweet, soft, stunningly beautiful woman whom any man would have been proud to acknowledge as his wife. It was—frightening, Jeff.

After it was all over, the last of the guests having reluctantly gone home. I looked around for Greg to entrust

Gillian once more to his care. He was gone. I checked with the doorman to make sure.

"Yes sir, Mr. Ames," he said, "Mr. Lynne left half an hour ago."

Gillian pouted a little when I told her that. But not for the reason that I thought.

"Oh, Michael," she said, "how dense you are at times! Of course he's gone. I told him I'd be going home with you. . . ."

I stared at her, trying to read what there was behind those candid blue eyes—so softly, sweetly glowing. I felt cold all over, because I knew one thing very surely: Gillian is always sweetest when she's figuring out just how to rake up hell's bottom pit.

"Very well," I said; "I'll see you home."

The doorman called a cab. On the way out to the MacAllister mansion—to that museum of horrors where every degradation possible to a man lay enshrined in my memory—she didn't talk at all. She simply sat very close to me, letting her head rest on my shoulder. I put one arm around her lightly, first because, physically, it's damned uncomfortable to sit next to a woman who is leaning her head against you unless you do put your arm around her; and second, upon the same principle that a man who doesn't dare have an occasional shot of whisky isn't really cured of drunkenness. So, like that, we came up to the house.

I helped her down, lifted my hat, said:

"Good night, Gillian."

"Oh, Michael!" she wailed. "Are you going to be difficult?"

"Depends upon what you mean by difficult," I said.

"I want you to come in," she whispered; "sit and chat with me for a while. I won't insist upon your resuming your husbandly duties—though, from the way you look now, I confess I am intrigued. For old times' sake, Michael, I—I'm so lonely. . . ."

"Lonely?" I said. "Now really, Gillian!"

"Yes," she said; and her voice went high, tight, trembling on the brink of tears. "So very lonely, Michael. I—I have no one who belongs to me. You can chide me for my sins if you like, darling; but they've carried their own punishment: that there's no one I can chat with over coffee in the morning, no one who I'm sure will always be there. Besides, I'm afraid—so dreadfully afraid! Are you so lacking in pity that you couldn't—"

"I don't lack pity," I said dryly; "but then neither do I lack judgment. Maybe you'd better begin by telling me what you're so dreadfully afraid of."

"I don't know!" she wailed; and her eyes were the perfect counterfeit of terror. "All I know is what I'm afraid *for!*"

"All right," I said wearily; "I'll rise to your bait, Gilly. What are you afraid for?"

She let her voice sink to a low, intense whisper. Pitilessly, my mind supplied the stage directions: Scene, a foggy night; a gust of wind blows through the open window bringing a wisp of fog in with it; G. downstage center, shudders, turns away, faces the audience, says: "My life!"

I had all I could do to keep from laughing aloud. And, as you know, Jeff, Gilly's powers of perception bordered on the supernatural.

"You don't believe me," she said. It was a statement, not a question. And no one else on earth, I am prepared to swear, could have put such utter hopelessness into that simple phrase.

"Frankly, no," I said. "Why should I? And even if I did, what difference would it make? Do you honestly believe that if I *knew* you were going to be killed tonight, I'd lift a hand to save you?"

She stared at me; and her lips curled into a smile. A pitiful, trembling smile.

"Yes, Michael," she said gently, "I do honestly believe you'd lift a hand to save me. In fact, I know you would."

She had me there. She knew me much too well.

"All right," I said; "I'd try to save you; granted. But don't depend upon my overdeveloped sense of compassion. I know when and where to apply it. Certainly you have no need of it. An actress of your talent never does."

"Actress!" she said; and the tears were there, hot and bright and sudden in her eyes. "I am not acting now, Michael! Please, please—won't you do this little thing?"

"What little thing?" I said.

"Come in with me. Talk to me. That's all. That's all, I promise you!"

"All right," I said wearily; and turned to the hackie. "Come back for me in about an hour," I said.

She looked at me reproachfully.

"Couldn't you have told him to come back tomorrow? An hour is so little time," she said.

It was too little time, Jeff. I have spent some enchanting hours in my life; but I don't think anything has ever equaled the fascination of that one. Yes, fascination is the word. I sat there, trying to find a flaw in her reasoning, trying to reassure myself that I and all the rest of the world were real, solid, living beings; that prick us, and we bleed; kill us, and we die; trying to convince myself that these fens, bogs, and marshlands of the spirit wherein Gilly dwelt had no existence outside of her weird, warped mind. Only I could not do it, quite. She made her world too real.

For instance, when she posed gambit number one:

(When will a woman bent upon seduction find a new one, Jeff?) "Relax, Michael, dearest. Take off your tie, and your jacket. Your shoes, too. There must be a pair of your slippers somewhere about. Meantime, I'll slip into something comfortable. . . ." I thought: Aha! A filmy negligee that will conceal almost nothing, and seem all the more provocative for what it does conceal. Gilly, you disappoint me; I'd thought you subtler than that. . . .

Aloud, I said: "My slippers? Or, at any rate, someone's slippers. . . ."

She turned and looked at me, and the hurt in her eyes was, I swear, Jeff, genuine.

"Michael," she said quietly, "the only slippers in this house are yours. And the only man who has ever entered my bedroom, occupied my bed is—you."

I looked at her; gave her back the perfect answer, which was another question:

"And the only man whose bed you've occupied, Gilly?"

But she had an answer for that one, too.

"In a way—yes," she said.

"In a way!" I laughed.

"Yes, Michael. In a way. Because the girl who did those awful things—wasn't I. She—was Buleah's child. Now make yourself comfy, darling. I'll be right back. . . ."

So there I was, Jeff, left with that one. Buleah's child! What the devil did she mean by that? All right, Buleah Land had been her nurse since babyhood. And from what you've told me, it appears that that black witch was an even more unsavory character than we knew. But—her child? Did Gilly mean that—no. Impossible. Buleah is a pure Negress, or damn near it. And even if Henry MacAllister had— The child would have been mulatto, clearly. For a mixed-blood child to be born white, its mother must be quadroon or octoroon, never black. I went over all that, ridiculous as it seems to me now. Because that was not what Gilly meant. No—what she meant was quite another thing.

She came back, finally. And she didn't have on a filmy negligee. She had on a quilted housecoat, somewhat the worse for wear. Her face was clean and shining, every trace of cosmetics scrubbed away. She'd brushed her hair straight back, tied a ribbon around it, and let it fall straight down her back. I have seen Gilly look tempting, sensual, provocative; but—God, how she knew me!—never so winsome, sweet, appealing as now.

She curled up like a kitten in the big chair opposite me; said, in her clear, childish voice:

"Do you mind if I have a cigarette, Michael? That's Hero's fault, you know! Buleah told me that she smoked like some European women do, so I just had to try it. I'm afraid I've formed the habit—"

"No," I said; "smoke if you like, Gillian."

She took a cigarette out of the box on the table. I lit it for her; took out a cigar and lit it for myself.

"Oh, Michael," she said reproachfully, "you never used to smoke!"

"Well, I do now," I said.

She sat there looking at me: Little Bopeep. Little Girl Lost, curled up in a big chair, staring at this great big, ugly, bald man out of eyes both frightened and shy.

"Now—about this business of your being afraid for your life?" I said.

She didn't answer me. Instead, she put out her hand. In it was a sheet of blue stationery. I opened it. The usual thing, Jeff: Letters cut from a newspaper and pasted together to form words. I don't remember what it said exactly. Part of it was a Biblical quotation, that verse about the Strange Woman whose lips drippeth honey, but whose feet lead down to destruction. The rest was gibberish, incoherent threats that the punishment for her sins was at hand. The whole thing was signed with a crude drawing of a flaming sword. . . .

Just a minute, Jeff; I'm awfully sorry, but I don't want you to build your hopes up. Don't you realize that if I'd considered this a clue I'd have told you about it long before now? No, boy, this was another piece of Gilly's trickery— only, I was oddly sorry to see, she was losing her verve. Because that notepaper was her own special blue stationery she'd brought back from London—its like simply doesn't exist in the States; and the flaming sword was drawn in that violet ink she always used.

I folded it, slipped it into my pocket. Afterward, on my way home, I threw it away. I wish I hadn't now, because I can see the idea still troubles you. So, let me call your attention to another thing, even though it means getting ahead of myself: In the entire rest of the night, she never even so much as mentioned it again. Was that the behavior of a woman who really believes her life in danger?

"Don't worry, Gilly," I said; "I'll take care of this. . . ."

She relaxed completely. Thinking she had me hooked again, I guessed.

"By the way," she said, "how is dear Hero?"

"Very well, thank you," I said.

"Michael, do you—do you love her so very much?"

I stood up.

"Good night, Gilly," I said.

She sprang from that chair, caught my arms.

"Oh, no!" she cried. "Don't go, Michael! I'll be good, I promise you!"

I sat back down. I suppose the reason I did was that remark about Buleah's child tormented me. I had to get to the bottom of it, had to know—

"Thank you," she whispered. "To get away from dangerous subjects, let's talk business. Michael, will you take back your quarter interest, please?"

"No," I said.

"Michael, I need your help! The business is going to the devil. Bart and Greg both have helped me all they could, but they're occupied with their own plants, and—"

"So am I occupied with my own plant, Gilly," I said. "Which, though you may not have noticed it, is bigger than either Lynne Steel or Byrce & Company. As big as both of them put together."

"Oh, Michael!" she wailed.

"But," I said, "in spite of that, I will help you out—for old times' sake. In memory of the year we were engaged, and our honeymoon in New York. In forgetfulness of all the rest; because the rest doesn't matter, now."

"You," she whispered, "are as sweet as ever. I—I wish you'd let me kiss you; but I can see you don't want me to—"

She was that perceptive.

"No, I don't," I said flatly. "Gilly—"

"Yes, dearest?"

"What did you mean about your being Buleah's child?"

She looked at me in honest wonder.

"Did I say that?" she said.

"Yes," I said dryly.

"Then I don't know what I meant," she said; "I—I sometimes say things that don't make sense, Michael. . . ."

"And do you *do* things that don't make sense to you, either?" I said.

"Yes," she said sadly. "I often do—or rather Buleah's child often does—"

"There!" I said. "You've said it again! 'Or rather Buleah's child often does—' What the devil do you mean by that, Gillian?"

"I—I don't know!" she wailed, her eyes wide and frightened. "It just came out like—"

I bent forward and took her hands, gripping them hard. "You—you're hurting me, Michael!" she said.

"You do know, don't you?" I said harshly. "You're lying to me, Gilly! What is this business about Buleah's child?"

She turned her face sidewise, away from my gaze. Her whole body shook in a gale of weeping. But I was merciless.

"What does it mean, Gillian?" I said.

"She—she is the other—me," she whispered. "The one who does awful, awful things. Who hates men, really—and tries to hurt them all she can. Who hates me, Michael! Who strikes at me by destroying everything and everyone I love. Like she destroyed Mother. Killed my father. Tried to wreck you—and almost succeeded. Sometimes—for weeks, months, half a year—she isn't here. Then one night she will rise up out of me, leaving me lying on the bed— I swear it, Michael! —how often has Buleah's child looked back and waved good-by to that inert, unconscious me sleeping there—and gone out to offer her body to some panting swine, proud of the fact that she could always leave the strongest of them broken and helpless before she was through—"

I was staring at her, hearing the utter ring of conviction in her tone.

"Which is why, Michael, you have no right to scorn me. I've always loved you, respected you, wanted you forever, I have never been unfaithful to you. That was—Buleah's child. . . ."

"Gilly," I said patiently, "why do you call her Buleah's child?"

"I don't know," she said simply. "I think it is because when I was small, when I was eleven or twelve years old, say, Buleah created her in me. How—I don't know. I was, Father told me, dreadfully sick for a year, about that time.

During that year, I started to keep my diary. But the things I wrote made no sense at all. Even the handwriting is different. I can't remember what I meant to say when I was awake. But sometimes, in dreams, I do remember. And every time that happens, I wake up screaming. Yet, the minute I am awake, it's gone. Funny. I've kept that diary ever since, Michael. One day, if you should come back to me for keeps, I'll show it to you. You can tell, just from the handwriting, which parts of it Buleah's child wrote, and which parts, I. My parts are rather dull. Schoolgirlish, full dreams—and since you've gone, one long lament about how I miss you, how I long for you to come back. But, Buleah's child! Nothing but a list of her conquests over men. Sometimes in such nauseating detail that I scratched them out, all those, 'Then I did this and he did thats!' I—I hate her, Michael! But she is stronger than I—"

"Making," I said dryly, "bigamy an even poorer bet in your case than it usually is."

"Yes," she said; "you're right there, Michael. Listen, darling; I—I have a suggestion to make. Please hear me out and don't get angry. You've become overnight one of the biggest men in Birmingham. And you know there is no more conventional town on earth. That's why, I think—you ought to stay here. . . . Michael, please! You can have a separate bedroom if you like, go and come as you desire; only the appearence of things will be better, then. In public, we will be a devoted couple; in private, I will stay as far away from you as you want me to—"

"But not," I said, "as far away as *you* want, Gilly?"

"No," she said simply; "because if I did what *I* wanted, I'd be in your arms right now."

I was tempted, Jeff. Goddamned tempted. Such sweet vengeance, boy! To show her who it would be who would cry quits, this time! Who'd leave her sprawling, helpless, unable to move, as she so often had left me. Then, when her eyes were already widening, glowing with anticipated triumph, I stood up.

"Thanks, Gilly," I said peacefully; "but no. You see, I don't care what Birmingham thinks. If necessary, I can buy Birmingham and order it to shut up. So, no thank you. Wouldn't do to put such a weapon into Buleah's child's hands, now would it?"

"A—weapon?" Gillian said.

"Yes, a weapon. Tell me, Gilly, how many nights could I sleep here before Hero received a letter telling her that the man for whom she's sacrificed everything has deserted her, has gone back to—his wife?"

I picked up my hat. Smiled at her. Said:

"And it would be most interesting to see whose hand penned those lines: Buleah's child's—or yours. . . ."

Then I went out into the street to where my poor cabbie still waited, bowed over the reins, fast asleep. I was surprised to see it was already dawn.

17

MICHAEL AMES

Birmingham, 1906–1907

II

It was about this time that I had the stroke of luck that put me beyond the Steel Trust's tenacles. Byrce and Company, hard pressed, decided to sell some of its ore fields, and a coal mine. But, times being what they were, they found no takers. I waited, very calmly, knowing that Bart would have to come to me.

Meantime, I took an entire floor in one of the new buildings whose promoters had had the misfortune to complete just before the depression came. Part of that floor I turned into offices; the rest into an apartment furnished with a degree of luxury that made it the talk of Birmingham. And with malice aforethought, I hired new caretakers to watch over Hero's house, and took Rad and Buleah Waters to work for me.

Part of it was curiosity: I wanted to find out what, if anything, had happened to Gillian in her childhood to make her what she was. Even to see if she could be cured. But the rest was malice. I reasoned that a talkative witch like

Buleah would let something slip—something I could use
as a lever to pry my freedom out of Gillian. For that, too,
I was prepared to wait.

And since it did not matter where I waited, I left the
address of my brokers with the secretary of the Manufacturers' Club and took a train to Pittsburgh.

We—Hero and I—had a second honeymoon. I told her
everything, even of Gilly's attempt to win me back, and her
explanation of her perversity. Hero listened to me with
grave and troubled eyes; then, instead of laughing Gilly's
excuses to scorn, said:

"She may be right, Michael. I've had that feeling about
her before: that she's not one person, but two. Remember
that picnic? The one where she forgot her bathing dress
on purpose, and you so obligingly took off yours?"

I stared at her.

"Who told you that?" I said.

"Nobody," she smiled. "I saw you. Even then you
were very fine, Michael—though you looked more like
Apollo than like Hercules, then. That was one of the various
occasions upon which you broke my heart. Anyhow, I hope
you won't again—"

"I won't what again?" I said.

"Break my heart," she whispered. "Because it would
be very bad now, Michael. Before, my love for you was
impressionistic, even abstract; but now it's concrete. Real.
Too real. I feel the weight and power of you even when
you aren't there. The imprint of your body lies forever
along all my flesh, like a slow tingle, like a warmth, a glow.
Sometimes, when I'm alone—and even when I'm not—I
raise incredulous fingers to my mouth to trace the heat, the
bruise, the arrogant sweetness of your kisses there. I'm
walking in a crowd, on a shopping trip, say—and, as often
happens now, Michael, someone says your name: 'Ames?

Damned miracle worker, that boy!' Or something like that. And I stand there like a fool, unable to force my idiotic feet to take another step; or to drag the breath that has fled back into my lungs; or quiet the awful thunder of my heart! Yes, yes, like that! Thrusting my head aside so they won't see my cry, ask questions, offer help—help to the helpless, Michael! Pity for one destroyed by joy—by fear—"

"Fear?" I said. But instead of answering me, she seized both my hands, bent to them, covering them with anguished kisses, bathing them with her tears.

"Hero!" I got out, "you mustn't—"

But she turned her head sidewise, so that it rested in my open palms like a flower in a granite cup, and whispered brokenly:

"Yes, fear. That one day you will leave me—and I shall lose my mind. . . ."

I laughed. It was damned shaky laughter.

"You precious little idiot," I said. "What makes you think that anything, anything whatsoever could make—"

She straightened up, staring at me. And what was in her eyes was very bad to see. Very bad. The worst. Something like—terror.

"You leave me?" she said. "I don't think. I know. Gillian could."

"Oh, Hero, for God's sake," I said.

"Because she's not quite human," Hero said. "She has a woman's body; but she hasn't any soul. To look into her eyes is to look into—vacancy, Michael. At least at times. At other times it is to look into the fires of hell."

"But I," I said quietly, "am attracted neither by soullessness nor by the fires of hell. I don't even know why you put it as a matter of choice, when I have no choice at all. There aren't any other women. My responses have become so conditioned, so specialized, that I don't really see

another face. And even if I could, there is no other face
like yours. I've tried for years now, to describe you to myself, catch your elusive quality in words. I can't. The
similes don't come. Your eyes are your own eyes, big, dark,
and with that tiny slant to them. And your mouth is—just
your mouth, which is enough as perfection always is. I
suppose I am too fleshly to be a poet. I remember the taste
of your skin at all the places that I kiss; the dusk rose and
honey smell of you. I bear memory in my finger tips,
Braille-coded with your taut resilience from head to toe.
And one thing more, little Hero: I was not born until the
hour you came into my life, until I moved out of death and
entered into the wonderful, trembling warmth of you. So
why then do you fear what I cannot even call to mind?"

She came up then, her head already curving sidewise
to meet my mouth. Which disposed of the question of
Gillian for that night. And for many nights to come.

I went back to Birmingham a month later. And Bart
Byrce came to see me. Bart is a decent sort. He could
hardly look me in the face. I poured him a drink. Watched
him down it. Said:

"Well, Bart?"

"I hate like hell to come to you, Michael—" he began.

"Why?" I said.

"Because—because—" he spluttered. "Oh, Christ!"

"You mean," I said dryly, "because of your relations
with Gillian? Forget it. That has no importance at all."

He stared at me.

"Damned if I can understand you, Michael!" he said.

"I know. And that's not important either. You see,
Bart, I have no especial need to be liked, appreciated, or
understood. . . ."

He went on looking at me.

"How about—respected, Michael?" he said.

"That I can manage for myself," I said peacefully. "Now sit down. We're here to talk business. So let's keep personal matters out of it."

"Can we?" he said doggedly; "is that possible?"

I took a cigar out of the box on the table. Offered him one. We lit up, sat there facing each other through a screen of smoke.

"For me, it is," I said; "but I can see your point. Let me dispose of it, Bart, once and for all, so we can get down to business. Your relations with Gillian, past, present, and future, don't interest me at all. As humiliating as the idea may seem, you as a person meant nothing to Gilly, and less than that to me. So if you have any romantic notion that I am going to use the weight of industry to crush a hated rival, forget it. I am neither a child nor a fool. I don't see the point of setting wheels in motion to revenge myself upon one of the various implements that Gilly used. Rather like burning the stick employed to beat one instead of striking at the hand that dealt the blows, from my point of view. Besides, the whole idea of vengeance is damned primitive, Bart. Getting even never, in all of history, either righted a wrong, or healed a wound. . . ."

"You," he said, "have sure got one hell of a funny way of thinking, Michael!"

"Funny?" I said. "I call it—civilized. Gillian Mac-Allister is a woman who passed through my life, causing me, admittedly, a certain amount of pain. But she's out of my life now, and the pain went with her. So, Bart, I haven't the slightest intention of taking advantage of the straits you're in at the moment. I offer you seven hundred and fifty thousand dollars for that ore field; and two hundred thousand for the coal mine adjacent to it. You know the quality and capacity of them both, so you know my offer is fair."

He looked at me.

"Make it a million for them both, Mike?" he said.

"Done," I said, without hesitation. "You've brought the deeds with you?"

"Yes," he said.

I pulled the bell cord. Rad came in. He was rather splendid in his butler's uniform.

"Rad," I said, "hop across the street to the club and ask the doorman if he can't get two of the gentlemen there to come up here. Tell him I need them as witnesses to close a deal."

"Yassuh," Rad said.

And naturally, the next day, that story was all over Birmingham, too.

With exaggerations.

As soon as Gillian heard it, she called me.

"Michael!" her voice came over the wire, bearing with it its burden of fear; "is it true that you've bought Bart out? That—that you're planning to ruin him?"

I should have known that interpretation was going to be placed upon it.

"No," I said, "it's not, Gilly—not either one."

"But everyone's saying—"

"I know. The facts are that I bought a minor holding of theirs that they wanted to sell, and offered to me. Nothing more. Now you tell me, Gilly: Why on earth should I want to ruin Bart? What has he ever done to me?"

"Oh!" she said blankly. "Why—why, nothing, of course. Stupid of me to have listened to gossip. 'Bye now. Call me sometime, won't you?"

I spent the rest of 1906 getting underway. I personally interviewed every man I hired. Beyond their professional qualifications, I asked each of them some questions that shocked them to the core: How did they feel about management? Did they think that steelworkers as a class were oppressed? What suggestions had they to remedy matters?

Most of them didn't dare answer those questions.

"Speak out!" I told them; "I want the truth!"

"That might be so, Mr. Ames," they answered ruefully; "but we *need* your jobs!"

I held out my hands to them so that they could see the calluses, the burn scars. It was a little theatrical, Jeff, but effective.

"You see these hands?" I said. "You know how a man gets hands like these?"

"Yep!" they growled. "Puddling iron!"

"And pouring," I said; "and working a drop forge, and taking his share of steam scalds from the cooling spray on the rollers of a rolling mill. From capping wild heats. From getting splashed when he lances the plug out of a pouring spout. Goddamnit, men! You think I'm capable of slaving and starving my own kind?"

"No!" they roared. "We're with you, Mr. Ames!"

Then they told me. The truth, Jeff. That they hated management's guts—and with good reason. That steelworkers as a class were the most oppressed workers on earth. That two or three things would go a long way toward remdying matters: safer working conditions, fewer hours, and a hell of a lot better pay.

After that I talked to them one by one, taking down their names, addresses, and job experience. I couldn't hire them all. Many of them didn't know enough—and not a few were so broken in health by then that the risk of hiring them would have been too great.

Afterward, I got all those whom I'd chosen—those who knew their jobs and were not quite dead on their feet

—together in the rolling mill and put it to them straight:

"All right," I said, "here are my conditions: Ten hours a day instead of twelve. Pay two dollars a day above any plant in Birmingham. Two weeks paid vacation every year. A pension fund for which I will dock each one of you one dollar a week, but will match each dollar with one of my own. If you work overtime, you get paid overtime. If you're hurt on the job, the plant pays your doctor and/or hospital bill. Half pay will be continued during the entire time you're laid up because of any injury caused by an on-the-job accident. I'm also setting up a sickness insurance to take care of you if you can't work for a spell because of illnesses. This insurance will cover your wives and children as well, with special attention to maternity cases. It's not compulsory; but I hope you'll have sense enough to join it. Cost, twenty-five cents a week. . . ."

Listening to it, they were stunned. Some of them were emboldened.

"And the union?" they growled.

"If you like," I said. "But I think you'll find you won't need a union to make demands; because you'll be working for me. I worked my way up from your ranks, and I know what you're up against. Any time you've a grievance you just march right into my office and tell me about it. I've given standing orders that nobody's to stop you. . . ."

"Plant guards, Mr. Ames?" a diehard shouted. "Pinks?"

"Plant guards to be elected by you, from your own ranks," I said; "and for only two weeks' duty. I've found that men get too damned fond of authority mighty fast. And if I catch a goddamned Pinkerton agent on my grounds, I'll throw him off personally and bodily!"

"Even if we strike?" one of them said.

"If you strike, you strike," I said flatly. "But what the hell are you going to be striking *for*, since I'm granting you from the outset all the things you've been walking out over, and been clubbed back to work without getting, for years?"

"Damned if that ain't the truth!" they said wonderingly; then: "Three cheers for Mr. Ames!"

They gave those cheers right lustily.

And you know what happened next, Jeff? What I might have expected, if I had thought about it. I was expelled from the Manufacturers' Club by a vote of better than ninety-seven per cent of the membership. Called, in the public press, a damned radical and a traitor to my class. The telephone calls stopped; the invitations. I was outcast number one in Birmingham again.

But within a year, I made them stop and think. You know what 1907 was like. A panic year. Banks closing. Men lined up before the soup kitchens in every big city in the land. Yet, incredible as it seems, last year, 1907, I *made* money. For one thing, I lived that whole year in a Pullman car, going from one place to another, dredging up orders, no matter how small. For another, my operating expenses —which all Birmingham was sitting back confidently waiting to see ruin me—turned out to be lower than theirs. Why? I paid higher wages, threw in all kinds of benefits; but received in return some things that were absolutely priceless: the loyalty, devotion, and even the love of my workers.

Intangibles? The hell they were! Because nobody was spoiling heats for me. They worked two hours less a day than in any other plant. But they did nearly twice as much work in those ten hours than their jaded, disgruntled, undernourished brothers in Byrce Steel or even in T.C. & I. did in twelve. My losses from absenteeism, from breakdowns, from scrapped heats were damned near zero. Which more than made up for my higher wages.

That was the year that Morgan bought Tennessee Coal

and Iron. And the year I beat even them. I was the only person in all Birmingham who dared offer a lot of armor steel to the government in competition with T. C. & I. I went up to Aberdeen myself. And came back with an order which guaranteed me a full schedule throughout last year and this. In open competition, my steel proved indisputably superior to theirs.

But everybody else was in trouble. Bad trouble. The money Morgan poured into Birmingham stabilized things a bit by the beginning of this year. Most of the plants, by January, had enough orders to keep open 'til things pick up again. But their profits were going to be damned slim. Much slimmer than they liked. So one and all, early in the spring, they decided to cut wages. To cut those wages a man couldn't eat from, couldn't feed his family with. They were that short-sighted, that blind. So, to give them something else to think about; I raised wages a whole dollar a day more at Consolidated Steel.

For a time, there, Jeff, my life was in danger. I received threatening telephone calls, anonymous notes with crude skulls and crossbones drawn on them; all the childish paraphernalia of hysterics; of men who have nothing inside of them, no spiritual resources, nothing to hold them up but artificial backbones made of sweatshop gold. I had, in all of Birmingham, but one friend—or rather one supporter, and he was somewhat of an embarrassment to me. Who? Why, Tim Nelson, Gilly's chauffeur. Tim always tried to give the impression of being a strait-laced character, which was why Gilly kept on calling him the Deacon behind his back. More than once he'd hinted to me that he was on my side, that he didn't approve of his mistress' actions. So, during all that rough time, he discreetly shadowed me, acting, I afterward learned, as my bodyguard.

"I'm not too big, sir," he told me when I asked him about it; "but I'm a handy chap with weapons. I've had to be. Led a rough life, you know."

I realize his loyalty to me seems excessive to you. It struck me the same way until I remembered something: Tim had reason to be grateful to me. He'd established a reputation for piety all over Birmingham, when the actual fact is he just can't leave women alone. And I'd stumbled upon him in the throes of a tremendous romance with that plump, untidy brunette who works in MacGilvray's Tavern. I walked in there one evening and caught them holding hands across the bar. He begged me not to mention it to anyone, and I gave him my word. After he saw I'd scrupulously kept it, his gratitude was touching.

Anyhow, I ignored all the threats. I had planned to go up to Pittsburgh; but I knew they'd interpret a journey, now, as flight. So I wrote Hero why I couldn't come.

And she—she came to me.

Which, of course, was purest folly. I sent her packing once again. But not before we had an hour together, in the country, in a wood, under the benevolent stars. An hour that was shattering; miraculous. Like nothing ever before. I lay there beside her, looking at her face in awe, in wonder, until it came to me that she wasn't breathing. I shook her, slapped her face, crushed her to me in a perfect agony of fear.

Heard a sob tear loose in her throat. Released her, saw her eyes flutter open, close again.

"Hero!" I said.

She opened her eyes, smiled at me. Raised a trembling hand. Stroked my face.

"Hero!" I said gruffly, but she heard the tears in my voice.

"Don't cry, Michael," she whispered. "I—I died. For a

time—I died. But I—I've come back now. I suppose that—
that a feeling like that was more than I could bear. . . ."

Then she smiled up at me, her dark eyes clear again,
full of light, and love, and mischief.

"Michael—" she said.

"Yes, Hero?" I muttered; for I was shaking still.

"If you ever do decide to kill me," she whispered, "do
it that way, please!"

And I didn't recall then, nor did the events of the next
few days permit me to remember that I had taken none
of the usual precautions, none at all.

I had advised Gillian not to cut wages at MacAllister
Steel. She listened to my reasoning with big-eyed wonder,
murmuring: "You're right, darling. . . . You're perfectly
right! But then you always are. . . ." And went back to her
office, immediately thereafter, and cut them straight to hell.

I found out about the strike in a funny way. Wilkinson
and Jacobs, who were the union representatives in my
plant, came into my office, hats in hand, and with badly
troubled eyes.

"Listen, Mr. Ames," Jacob groaned, "we're going to
strike—"

"The devil you say!" I said. "What for?"

"It's like this, sir," Wilkinson said. "We don't have no
grievances, nary a single one. But we got to strike in sym-
pathy for the others—at least for one day. Else they'll call
us scabs and—"

"I see," I said. "You know this tomfoolery is going to
cost me a mint of money? With all the heats we've got
cooking now— When is it set for?"

"Next week," they said.

Then I grinned.

"What do you say we work a few swing shifts around the clock and get everything poured?" I said. "You can put your strike off a day or two, can't you? Get all those heats cleaned away, and I'll strike, too. Hell, we'll celebrate it with a picnic out at the lake. Barbecue half a dozen pigs and—"

They were staring at me in a mighty strange way.

"What ails you two?" I said.

"Nothing, Mr. Ames," Wilkinson grinned; "but a feller is plumb got to look at you twice to make sure you's real!"

So, when it hit, I was out at the lake, playing baseball with the boys. I had eaten so much I could hardly move, because every worker's wife and damned near all their daughters had baked something special for me. I was truly happy. I suppose I have a real Southerner's paternalistic instincts. But the sight did my heart good: my people; the men big, robust, strong, showing by every gesture that they always got enough to eat; and perhaps even because of so simple a thing as that, had recovered their self-respect; the women in their bright calicoes, most of them running to plumpness, an unheard-of thing in a steelworker's wife; the children fat, laughing, happy, crawling all over me when I sat down to rest.

Which was the only thing that made me sad. I sat there holding Jacob's youngest, thinking: If there were only some way, some way. . . .

Then a shadow passed between me and the sun. And looking up, I saw Greg sitting there on his horse. He had a revolver in his belt; and his face, his face—

"What is it, Greg?" I said.

"Gilly—" he whispered. "She's—"

I got up. He climbed down. We walked a little way off from the others.

"Gilly's what?" I said.

"She's been kidnapped," Greg said. "Big John Klovac shoved a gun into her back and used her as a shield to—"

"Wait 'til I get my buggy," I said. "Tie your mount behind it. You ride with me. You can tell me on the way. . . ."

It was soon told. The strike had turned ugly. Governor Comer called out the National Guard. And, as always, in the Land of the Free, the Home of the Brave, men had been killed because they objected to—hunger. Because they believed a working stiff had some pretenses toward dignity; some of the elementary rights of human beings.

And, as I should have expected, one of the sorest spots was MacAllister. The fighting there had been particularly intense. There had been three deaths. True to form, Gillian had ordered Tim Nelson to drive her out to see the fun. Had sat there in the car, watching with undisguised pleasure men being clubbed with gun butts, bayonetted, shot down.

Then the Guardsmen had formed for one last charge; and Big John Klovac, Fred's older brother, had jammed a pistol into Gilly's back, forced her to order Tim to drive away from there. They'd found the car in the foothills of that wild, mountainous country north of Birmingham. Tim lay beside it, trussed up like a hog and bleeding from a savage blow. The next day, all the papers lauded his heroic defense of his mistress.

But Gillian was in the absolute power of a man crazed by rage and grief. A man who'd seen fellow workers killed before his eyes. And nobody knew whether she was still alive.

Except me, Jeff. I knew she was. Because life just

doesn't hand out easy, perfect solutions to a man's problems on a silver platter. The person I felt sorry for was Big John.

BIG JOHN KLOVAC
State Prison, 1908

II

Well, it was like this, Mr. Lynne: you take the worst working conditions anybody ever heard of, in the worst damn' plant in the state. Then you multiply 'em by ten, and you come close to what working for MacAllister Steel was like. While the old man and Bill Riker were still alive, it was bearable. You see, they'd puddled iron up around Pittsburgh, themselves. They didn't make it no bed of roses, 'cause they figured that what they'd stood up to as youngsters oughtn't be too much for us. Only they never figured that what with the railroads, and new bridges, and even boats being made out of steel now, they was calling on us for a lot heavier production than they ever met. Still, it wasn't meanness; it was just short-sighted, maybe.

Then, for a while, when young Ames come in, things got to be a lot better. That boy always understood that you could catch a heap more flies with honey than with vinegar. He was a great one for coming around to our furnaces and talking to us. I remember one time he plunked down right next to me when I was having lunch. I was eating one of them torpedo sandwiches—a yard of bread with salami, sardines, onions, olives, and every other thing Silvetti had left over in his hash house. "Lord, that smells good, Big John," says he. So I handed it to him, and he tore off a hunk and stuck it in his mouth. Reckon that's why Consolidated is right up there on top. Treat us working stiffs like folks, and we'll damn near die for you.

But she wrecked him. She's the kind what can't stand seeing a man happy. The kind what just has to stick her claws in, come out with her little gelding knife and—

Anyhow, she brought convict labor in. Not much—just enough to use it as a threat in case we ever got the notion of striking. Hired the damnedest bunch of plug uglies as plant guards you ever did see. Mr. Ames wasn't even around to see that. She'd already chased him away by then. Even after she'd turned him into a stinking drunk, he was too much man to stomach the way she murdered them poor niggers.

The strike? Goddamnit, Mr. Lynne, we was starving! Tell you a funny thing, though: them big fellers who got so mad at Mr. Ames was right, in a way. I don't think we'd of ever got riled enough to really strike if it hadn't been for them Consolidated workers rubbing it in: "Look at us— ten hours a day! Hell, Mack, I just bought my kid a safety bike. Saving up to send the lil' bugger to college. Gonna make a steel control engineer out of him just like Mr. Ames. . . ." And the women: "Why sure, Nell, it's a new dress. My Jim don't work at no slave shop like MacAllister. No, sir. Works for Mr. Ames, who treats him like a white man. Comes by his furnace, stops 'n chats, a-saying, "How's it going, Jim? Tell you one thing, boy; can't nobody pour a heat like you!"

Jesus, Mr. Lynne! You see how it was? Us in rags and starving, working from can to can't. Twelve hours some days, fourteen others and nary a cent more for them extra two! Listening to them Consolidated boys and their women got us wild. They'd got plain uppity. Damnedest fight I ever did see was when one of our boys said to Jake Jacobs: "Now look a here, Jake; Michael Ames plumb ain't Jesus

Christ, you know!" 'N Jake waded right into him—'cause
by then there wasn't a man at Consolidated who was rightly
sure Mr. Ames *wasn't* the good Lord. . . .

So, afore we struck, we tried to get even with that
Consolidated crowd by making them go out, too—token
walkout, to demonstrate solidarity. Knew they'd felt like
skunks if they didn't. But the night before the thing was
called, Wilkinson drops by with a grin wider'n a boilerplate
on his phiz, and says:

"We's striking all right, Big John! Whole plant. Told
Mr. Ames what you boys said 'n he says: 'Hell, I'll strike,
too. Let's shut up shop 'n have ourselves a picnic out at
the lake. . . .' "

So we was mean mad thinking about that, Mr. Jeff.
Them Consolidated bastards demonstrating solidarity by
going off on a picnic with their boss! A man can put up with
a hell of a lot when he ain't sure that what he wants, the
kind of life he's dreaming of, is actually possible. But there
was that Consolidated bunch living that life, eating high
off the hog, and bragging about it!

So we struck. Thinking maybe this time we had a
chance. Thinking that the kind of ideas Mr. Ames was prov-
ing could work had maybe sunk in a little. We should of
known better. The Byrces got on the phone and called the
Governor's office. And the third day of the strike, the National Guard was there. Funny—heard that at your mill
your brother wouldn't let 'em in. Kept 'em patrolling outside
while he dickered with his crew. Settled for a ten per cent
raise, and closed the strike with nobody getting clubbed or
kilt. Bless him, I say—even if he did try to shoot me. . . .

How come? I'm getting to that. Just you let me explain
it to you my way, one thing at a time. Anyhow, settling
things peaceful just wasn't Miss Gilly's way. No, sir! I
could see her sitting there in that there flossy gas buggy of

hers while the Guardsmen and her own hired thugs was making hash out of us. And when a Guardsman put a bayonet clear through Til Hocher's belly, I seen her throw back her head, heard her laugh. Like a kid with a new toy, Mr. Jeff!

I couldn't take that. Til was like my own brother. No, more'n that. Him'n me was closer than Fred and me ever was. So I smashed my way through 'em with a puddling iron. Got to that car; put the revolver I'd taken from one of them Pinks whose head I'd bashed in, against that scrawny little English bastid's neck, told him to git moving, fast. I know they say it was her I threatened, but they lied. He got moving, all right. She sat back looking at me with a smile on her face. A smile, Mr. Jeff! She wasn't even starting to get scared. I kept little limey pouring it on 'til we was out of town, headed for the hills. She drawled out, kind of slow:

"Where're you taking us, Big John?"

"To hell, Miss Gilly!" I said.

When I saw a likely spot, I made him stop the car. That was when he made the fool mistake of rushing me. I could of gunned him down, but I thought better of it. So far I didn't have a killing on my hands they could prove. So I just knocked him flat, tied him up with the tow rope of the car, and left him there.

I hit for the hills, dragging her along. I didn't let her stop to rest. I just kept dragging her to where it was darker and wilder and the thorn bushes ripped and tore us both all to hell. Then, 'long about nightfall, we come to that little cabin. I broke into it easy enough. She smiled when she came in. Like it wasn't the first time. Reckon it wasn't, at that; because, at my trial, there was a mighty heap of talk about Mr. Barton Byrce's hunting lodge. The damned place was stocked. Canned goods, hardtack, whisky. A rack of

guns, ammunition. A couch that was a sight too big and
soft to have been put there for no lonely hunter to rest his
weary bones alone.

I made a fire in the fireplace. But I wasn't thinking
about making no supper when I had a woman along to
make it for me. All right, Pa brung me to this country when
I was just a kid; but in some ways I'm old country, still.
Woman was made to wait on man, is the way I figger it.
So I told her that. She stood there looking at me a long,
long time, Mr. Jeff. Then she says:

"Listen, you Polack bastard, I'll see you in hell before
I'll fix a crumb for you!"

So I give her the back of my hand across the mouth.
She went down in a heap, then she come up like a wildcat,
raking for my eyes. I caught both her hands in my left and
held her off at arm's length. Then I started slapping her
back and forth across the face with my right and kept it
up 'til I was tired. When I turned her loose she sort of
crumpled up like a paper sack and lay there on the floor
a-moaning.

Oh hell, I thought to myself, reckon I'll have to fix my
own grub after all. . . .

That was when I made the mistake of turning my back
on her. Good thing I got ears. I heard the scrape she made
when she started up. I turned and there she was with that
big hunting knife in her hands. I picked up a stick of firewood and give it to her across the forearm, hard enough
to make her let go of that knife; but not hard enough to
break the bone. I kicked that blade out of her reach. Then
I unfastened my belt, took it off. She didn't move or run.
She just crouched there staring at me and her eyes went
smoky.

Reckon that was the first real beating she'd ever had.
But she was stubborn. Wouldn't scream at first. So I gave

it to her for her poor ma up there in Tuscaloosa, for her
poor pa in his lonely grave; for Mr. Michael who she'd
damned nigh wrecked; for them seventy-seven niggers; for
Til Hocher and the others lying there in front of the mill
gates like sacks o' meal somebody'd let the meal out of and
daubed in red. Until she was screaming all right. Until
she'd hit a note like the plant whistle at knocking-off time.
Then I quit.

"Git up, you bitch," I said, "and fix my goddamned
supper!"

And she did. Heated me some soup. Opened a tin of
frankfurters. Heated them, too. Put out her hand to take
one for herself; but I figured I hadn't learned her enough
yet. So I whacked her across the fingers with the blade of my
knife, flat side, of course, so it wouldn't cut her.

"Where I come from," I told her, "when a man gits
through he feeds his scraps to his chickens, pigs, and—
women. In that order. So just you sit there 'n wait!"

She sat there and watched me eat. Her eyes were like a
cat's. They kind of picked up the light from every which
way. She was a mess by then: her face swollen, a little
trickle of blood dried in the corner of her mouth. And if
she really wanted to be a tiger cat, she could be, now, for
God knows I'd give her stripes enough.

I stood up, yawned. "Now you kin eat," I said.

But she didn't. Instead, she got up from where she sat
and came to me. Put up her hands and let 'em hook around
my neck. Said, real soft and kind of purring-like: "You brute!
You filthy Polack brute!" Then she come up all at once and
caught my bottom lip between her teeth, hung on like a
fyce dog, worrying it, digging her fingernails into my back
like cat claws, and a snarling through them teeth she had
set all the way through my lip:

"Beast! Beast! Beast!"

I pushed her down on that rough board floor and took her then and there, just like she wanted me to. That couch wasn't a yard away, but I knew what kind she was by then: the kind you have to beat. The kind what likes the feel of splinters in their hides.

I tried to take her apart. Damned near did, too. Made her beg me. Made her call it quits. Afterwards she told me it was the first time that any man ever had.

Which is why, Mr. Lynne, it took 'em five days to catch us. We knew better than to stay there. No, we had to keep moving, throw 'em off our track. That little girl knew them woods like the palm of her hand. I asked her how come she knew 'em so well, and she laughed and said:

"You think this is the first time I've hidden out up here with a man?"

Even after they brought up the bloodhounds. She showed me that trick of soaking our shoes in kerosene from the cabin. Them dogs sniffed that and run off howling. We'd packed grub from the cabin; I had one of Mr. Byrce's best guns and lots of ammunition. You'd of thought a woman'd be half dead come night, after beating through the brush all day. But not her! She could march all day, and still have enough left in her to damn nigh kill a man all night. We led 'em a merry chase 'til it looked like they'd give up. Then we come back to that cabin and tried to pound the rest of them boards loose from the floor. Which was what give 'em time enough to surround us. I was laying there next to her, resting a bit, when somebody sung out:

"Come on out, Big John! With your hands in the air! We've got you covered!"

I lifted my head, sneaked a peek out that window. There was about fifty of 'em with rifles. Dogs, too. If I'd of started shooting, I wouldn't of lasted five minutes.

"All right," I said real peaceful-like, which was just the way she'd left me feeling; "I'm coming out. . . ."

I got up and marched through that door, my hands in the air. But she shot pass me like greased chain lightning, for all the way her clothes was tore up she wasn't rightly decent.

"Kill him!" she yells. "Oh, Michael, kill him! He—he raped me!"

That was when your brother, Mr. Greg, lifted up his gun and shot at me. He would of got me, too, if Mr. Michael hadn't knocked his arm aside. . . .

Yep, I know. You thought it was Mr. Byrce who tried to shoot me. Funny, it even got in the papers that way. But it was Mr. Greg all right. He purely went wild. . . .

"No, Greg," Mr. Michael says to him, "Gilly just isn't worth killing anybody over. . . ."

But I had ducked back inside by then. Unslung that Winchester, and laid it over the sill. Pointed at—her. I knew I wasn't going to come out of that alive; but I was going to have the satisfaction of putting a ball through that bitch's gut before I went. Only I never figured on there being a man in this world like Mr. Michael.

"Big John," he said, soft and pleasant-like, "I'm coming in there to have a word with you. Without a gun. See?" And he throwed his Colt automatic on the ground. Started walking toward the door.

"Don't be a damn' fool, Michael!" Mr. Bart Byrce yelled at him. And your brother, Mr. Greg, sings out:

"Michael, for God's sake!"

But he kept right on. Like a man walking up the church aisle to take Holy Communion. As safe as that, too; because my finger was paralyzed on that trigger. I couldn't of pulled it for the life of me.

He come into the cabin. Took a cigar out of his pocket,

handed it to me. Lit it for me. Stuck another one in his jaw; lit that one, too. Then he said, just as peaceful:

"About this rape business, John; did you?"

I give it to him straight.

"Mr. Michael," I said, "I'm gonna tell you the truth, 'cause I don't think you care, no more. I didn't, but only 'cause I never had to. You honestly think anything in pants would of ever needed to do anything else but maybe fight her off? Hell, sir, the first time that little girl fell out of her cradle, she landed on her back!"

"I see," he kind of sighed. "Look, John, you give up peacefully, and I'll see you get a fair trial. You've my word. I suppose my boys have convinced you that my word is worth something, haven't they?"

"Yes, sir," I said; and handed him that Winchester, butt first. He took it, left it dangling, pointing at the ground.

"Aim it at me, sir!" I begged him. "It'll look better that way! Them fellers are gonna think you ain't man enough to defend your wife. . . ."

He smiled, then.

"Big John," he said, "you know when a man is grown? Not when they give him the vote. The day he stops giving a tinker's damn what anybody thinks about anything. Besides, I haven't a wife. Now come on!"

We walked out of there, like that, together, him with that rifle still pointed at the ground. The others jumped for me, roughing me up, reaching for the handcuffs, 'til Mr. Michael said:

"Stop it! Leave him alone. And don't put those damned cuffs on him. He won't run."

"How the hell do you know that, Michael?" Mr. Bart Byrce kind of snarled.

Mr. Michael looked at him.

"Because he's given me his word," he said.

They were all set to railroad me. Brought me to trial
inside a week, which was the first time in the history of the
state of Alabama that a white man's case was up before the
court so fast. There was some lynch talk, too; but it didn't
get far. Too many fellers in town who just couldn't figure
how raping Miss Gilly was possible, knowing her like they
did. Besides, Mr. Michael put a stop to it with a paid announcement: "As the presumably injured party, I place my
faith in the impartial justice of Alabama's courts. And it
seems to me that men less vitally interested than I could do
the same."

My trial was a wonder. Them reporters came from all
over the state, and even from up North to cover it. That
young district attorney was out for blood. Demanded hanging. Would of got my neck stretched too, wasn't for Mr.
Michael. He brung her into court. Sat beside her, talking
to her, and his face was mighty stern. So when they called
her to the stand, she said:

"I—I was hysterical. Mr. Klovac committed no offense—
against my decency. What I meant to say was that he—he
kidnapped me. Don't know why I used that word—rape—"

And try as he would, that young D.A. couldn't break her
down. Every time she'd sort of hesitate, Mr. Michael would
look at her and she'd buck right up again.

"So I drew—life. Mr. Michael has been to see the governor twice, trying to git it reduced. But old Comer ain't
even thinking about doing nothing for no working stiff. . . .

What's that? Why yes, Mr. Jeff; I'm sure it was your
brother who fired that gun.

18

MICHAEL AMES

Birmingham, 1908

I

That autumn night, I came home from the plant late; it was
nearly eleven o'clock when I got home. I was dog tired, and
a little sick. For the Klovac case had set me back a long, long
way. If Gilly had ever dreamed of divorcing me, she knew
better now. I was sure she'd long since given up all hopes
of getting Bart Byrce to leave Dorothy for her sake; and I
think she realized how strict Greg's code of morals was.
Because I'm sure that she had her eye on Greg. She wasn't
in love with him. Gilly, in all her life, never loved anyone
but Gilly; but Greg was still single; and women like Gillian
need a façade of respectability. Besides, she had actually
come to respect me by then. The way I stood her down,
forced her to tell at least part of the truth about Big John,
had taught her a thing or two.

How'd I do it? I'm not sure I know, really. Naturally,
Fred Klovac helped. After all the dirty jobs he'd done for
Gilly, her cute caper in trying to get his brother hanged
abruptly adjusted his concept of professional ethics into
closer conformity with reality. He turned over to me enough

proof to get seventeen divorces and maybe even hang Gilly to boot. There was only one catch: she still had in her possession that damnably convincing evidence against Hero and me that Fred had gathered for her earlier. You know what the law says about *both* parties being guilty? No divorce, ever. That way I'd really be stuck, Jeff. . . .

Anyhow, the hold Fred had given me over Gillian was enough to save Big John's life. She realized I was capable of making her shame public in order to do that, even if she wrecked me afterward in retaliation. She knew human life is sacred to me. And while she rather liked people gossiping and speculating about her, it seemed she didn't want them *knowing*. . . . Funny. I guess she did have some faint vestige of a sense of shame left, after all, or—

Or what? Jeff, I'd rather not finish that thought. I've sent you flying up too many blind alleys now. Yes—you're right. How can you know they're blind until you've explored them? And a man's life is at stake. All right. Let me put a preamble onto what I started to say: Gilly, in all the time I knew her, never gave the slightest indication of even knowing what feminine modesty and personal shame meant. If there ever was a human being who truly didn't give a damn for God, the devil, the law, and the prophets, not to mention such paltry things as the conventions of society and public opinion, it was she! When, out of pure desperation, I threatened to use the information about her Fred had given me, if she didn't retract her murderous lies, her patently false accusation against Big John, I was literally astounded when she gave in. I expected her to tell me to use it and be damned!

So, that "or." A guess, Jeff. A vague feeling. Pure speculation. Since Gilly was completely unashamed of anything she did, might she not have given in because she thought Fred knew or had told me something that put either her freedom or her life in danger? Those are two things she'd go to any lengths to protect. Since she loved only one human in this world of sin, herself, those were her vulnerable points. And, knowing Gilly, can we assume that her exquisitely diabolical mind would remain content with mere sexual peccadilloes? Any damned woman can commit adultery; but Gilly just might have wanted to find her proper niche alongside of Lucrezia Borgia or Catherine di Medici. If I were you, I'd check with Fred to see if there were anything in that part of her past we didn't know that could have stretched her dainty neck, or put her behind bars. . . .

Yes, you're right again. If Fred had had any such information, he would have volunteered it at once, seeing that Big John was in as serious danger then as Greg is now. I grant you that. But I'm going to make one more suggestion, and then quit playing detective: What if there *were* something that Fred didn't know, but that Gilly thought he did? You see the possibilities there, don't you? Good. . . . It could be a lead at that, couldn't it?

Anyhow, I was worried, Jeff. The last two letters from Hero had seemed—depressed, out of sorts. She wrote that she didn't feel at all well, that she had nightmares, premonitions of disaster. She complained of sleeping badly, and of feeling sick when she woke up. I wrote back, advising her to see Dr. Berger. But I was more worried about what Gillian would do next, for I already knew what she had on her mind. After the trial, she said to me:

"Michael, don't you think that if we'd had a baby, things might have been different? I'd have settled down to being a good wife and mother, and—"

"Oh, hell!" I'd said.

"I should have," she insisted stubbornly. "Michael, you have an awful lot of money now, haven't you?"

"Enough," I said grimly.

"You know," she said in that odd, grave, little girl's voice that is absolutely the most shocking thing about her when you really know her—that obscene assumption of innocence that isn't really pretense—that is, I'd swear, Jeff, for her a matter of stepping through a door into another part of her being, "we could leave here forever. Go live far, far away. Out in California, or even the Philippines. Where nobody knows me, knows how bad I've been. We could start over. I'd give you a flock of babies. I'd be ever so good, Michael! You'd never have cause to complain—"

"Wherever you go, Gilly," I said, "you take yourself with you. And people don't change. Not ever."

"But I shouldn't have to change," she said sweetly. "All I'd have to do is to kill—her—"

"Kill who?" I said.

"That other me. The one Buleah put inside me while I was sick. I even think I know how. . . ."

"How?" I said.

"Go to Buleah. Force her to—to take her away. Tell her I'll take my book to the police if she doesn't, and—"

"What book?" I said.

"Oh, never you mind!" she said gaily; then to herself, "It might work—at that!"

So, that night, when I came home and found Gilly in my flat, I was more disgusted than surprised.

"Who the devil let you in?" I said.

"Buleah, of course," Gilly said. "Give me a light, darling."

I lit her cigarette. I don't like seeing women smoke, even though I tolerate Hero's doing it. But, of course, I was prejudiced against everything that Gilly did. She had on a white summer frock that was wonderfully becoming. A trace of rouge on her lips and cheeks, which, pale as she naturally was, she needed. She was wearing, besides, her starry-eyed look, her expression of sweet innocence that always disgusted me.

"Come sit beside me, darling," she said.

"Hell no!" I said. "Will you be so kind as to go home where you belong, Gilly?"

"But I am where I belong," she said reproachfully. "A wife's place is at her husband's side. . . ."

"What wife?" I said, "I don't see any. All I see is everybody's woman. You want me to make you a list?"

"No," she said sadly. "Why won't you believe that wasn't me? That was—"

"Oh, hell," I said again.

She pulled the bell cord. Buleah appeared, grinning her evil grin. I've often thought that there was no one on earth worse than Gillian; but I was wrong. Buleah was.

"Fix us some tea, Buleah," Gillian said.

"Right away, honey lamb!" Buleah said.

She came back with that tea too fast. As though it were already made. I was frankly suspicious. I sipped it. It had an oddly sweet-sickish taste.

"Buleah," I said; "what the hell have you put in this tea?"

"Nuthin', Mr. Michael! Hit's jes' a new kind. They calls it Chinee green tea. . . ."

"I don't believe you!" I snapped; but Gillian took my cup out of my hand and drank the tea down.

"Now," she said a little sadly, "you can stop thinking that Buleah and I are trying to poison you or something."

"All right," I said; "but it does taste odd as hell. . . ."

"That's because it's green," Gillian said, and poured me another cup. Took one herself. Sat there sipping it and gazing at me—waiting.

It didn't put me out. That wasn't the way it worked. A

tongue of fire coiled in my belly, licked hungrily up my throat. I reached up, tore my collar open.

"What's the matter, Michael, darling?" Gillian said.

"As if you didn't know!" I howled. I stood up. The room wheeled about my head in slow and stately circles. The fire tongs turned into serpents and crawled off across the floor. Faces appeared at all the windows, distorted, horrible, gibbering. I reached out to pull the bell cord, but it hissed at me, its tongue forked, its eyes lambent, its scaly body coiling, coiling. . . .

Fire appeared at my feet; pooled; leaped ceilingward, searing. The heat was more intense than that of a bessemer from half a yard away. Sweat popped out of me in rivers. I tore at my clothes, which were suffocating me. I had the feeling that somebody was helping me out of them. I was right. Somebody was.

My eyes cleared momentarily. I saw Gillian stepping out of a little pile of silk on the floor like a Botticelli Venus—as lovely as that, as goddamned achingly lovely. Then the wild delirium set in again; but I was never out, Jeff, never unconscious. I knew, I knew what was going on; I was simply powerless to stop it.

Have you ever been made love to by a woman? Wait a minute, don't stare at me like that! I didn't ask you if you'd made love to a woman, or had made love with a woman. My wording was precise: Have you ever been made love to *by* a woman? No, of course not. I can assure you it is absolutely the damnedest thing. They'd fed me some kind of nerve poison; and one, evidently, from the lack of effect it had upon her, that Gilly was immune to from long use. I retained sensation, but lost control. My limbs would not obey me. They slumbered there, inert; but alive and tingling with feeling, while dear Gilly amused herself thoroughly, used me in sort of living necrophilia that entered into and explored the meaning of horror to the last screaming nerve end.

When I woke up in the morning with a tongue coated with green pond scum, a belly full of brass carpet tacks, slightly tarnished; a legion of inch-high fiends driving stakes into my skull, I turned over, and found Gilly lying at my side, as enchanting as something by one of the Pre-Raphaelites, sleeping so softly, sweetly, dewy with innocence, warm and replete with accomplished love.

I got up from there. Reeled to the bathroom and threw up. When I came back, she said:

"Poor Michael!"

"Gilly," I said, "what was in that tea?"

"Don't know," she smiled. "That's Buleah's secret. She's a witch, you know."

"The world," I groaned, "is full of witches. All right, get up from there!"

She gazed at me wonderingly.

"Get up?" she said. "Why, Michael? Oh, I know! You'd rather we lived at the house than here?"

Now it was my turn to stare.

"Got it all figured, haven't you?" I said. "You feed me gris-gris in my tea, climb into the hay with me; and that, to you, constitutes a reconciliation. But, Gilly, you oversimplify things. The point is, Gilly, dearest, that I don't want you. That I am in love with Hero. In love with a woman. You might look the word up in the dictionary. No, don't. You still wouldn't understand."

You know what an actress she was, Jeff. Well, she was something more—a director, too; for she knew how and when to stage her own scenes. She started to cry—soundlessly. Letting the great tears spill silently down her face. Not one word of argument or reproach. She just got up from that couch, still crying, got dressed, without ever interrupting the slow rhythmic flow of her tears. Put on her hat. Came over to where I sat, wrapped grumpily in my robe, like Caesar in his toga. Bent and kissed my mouth, her lips tear-wet and salt, but vibrant with a tenderness, a longing, that I'd stake my life were real.

Real, but not to be depended upon. Because that fiendish temper of hers was just as real. That vicious streak. That bone-deep cruelty. Gillian, at will, could be an angel or a witch.

What she couldn't be was—human.

I fired Buleah that same day. Somewhat reluctantly, Rad quit. I suppose he was as much under Buleah's spell as I'd been under Gillian's.

Two weeks later, to the very hour, Hero arrived.

I came home from the plant to find her in my flat, just as Gillian had been. Seated on that damnable couch. And I—quite frankly, Jeff, was almost equally annoyed.

"Hero, for God's sake!" I said. "Can't you get it through your head that you shouldn't come to Birmingham at all while I'm here? And above all, not to my flat? You'll ruin everything! Gillian doesn't want to give me the divorce. So the only way is to catch her out; but if you give her a weapon for a counterattack like this one—"

She sat there listening to me, her dark eyes luminous, glowing. When she spoke, her voice was slow, slumberous, magic.

"I'm afraid I've already ruined everything, Michael," she said.

Her tone caught me. It vibrated with suppressed joy, like a chord held, held. . . . I came to her. She stood up, slipped into my arms. Arched her head back to meet my kiss. I could feel her trembling.

"What ails you, Hero?" I said.

"Nothing," she laughed tremulously; "nothing at all. It's just that in seven and a half months you're going to be a father. But whether in or out of wedlock, I really cannot say. . . ."

"Hero!" I got out. Then I really kissed her. She pushed me away at last, saying: "You'll have to be more gentle now, darling. I really am quite delicate. . . ."

"Lord God!" I said, and picked her up. Carried her into my bedroom, laid her down on the bed; fretted over her worriedly, asking her if there were anything she wanted, anything I could get her.

She looked at me gravely, but pure mischief lay in those almond-shaped eyes.

"Yes," she said wistfully; "I'd like a dill pickle, Michael —with whipped cream on it."

I stood there staring at her, until I saw her smile. Then we laughed together, joyously; and life was suddenly very warm and sure and complete.

"I'll open the house," she said, "and you can sneak in the back way every night. I'll hire only day girls; but in the meantime, you—you'd better work on Gilly, Michael. Or else we'll have to start all over again somewhere else. Where nobody knows us."

"All right," I said grimly; "I'll have it out with her tomorrow!"

I went up to the MacAllister mansion at eleven o'clock in the morning, knowing from sad experience that Gilly has never even fluttered an eyelid before that hour. Oddly, when Jacqueline, Gilly's personal maid, admitted me, I could see she was scared to death.

"Oh, M'sieur Ames!" she said; "I am so frightened!

Madame, she is so very seek! This morning we thought she
was going to die!"

"Go see if she's up to seeing me," I said.

"That, yes! We 'ave been calling your office all morning at her request; but you were not there. Nor at your flat.
Madame kept saying, 'Michael! I must see Michael! Oh,
find him for me!' "

"All right," I said dryly; "you've found me. Now let's
see what the Sarah Bernhardt death scene was all about.
Lead on, Jackie!"

But she really did look like hell. And Buleah, of all
people, was with her, applying compresses to her forehead.
That black witch looked up at me with what she probably
thought was a roguish smile.

"Menfolks!" she cackled. "Ain't you 'shamed of yourself, Mister Michael!"

"What the devil are you talking about, Buleah?" I said.

But Gillian raised her head, then.

"Leave us, Buleah," she said with quiet dignity; "I'd
like to talk to my husband, alone. . . ."

As soon as Buleah had gone, I struck.

"Look, Gilly," I said, "I want a divorce. And I want it
now. What you're doing is unfair to me, unfair to Hero,
even unfair to yourself. Whether you want to believe it or
not, the possibility of a reconciliation between us just doesn't
exist. Nothing you could say or do would make me even
consider it."

She looked at me, her blue eyes very soft and grave and
tender.

"Nothing, Michael?" she said. "Not even that—your
son—should have his father?"

The blow was physical. It smashed into my gut like a
trip hammer. How the devil did she find out? I wondered:

Hero only got here last night, and— Then the second bl⟨
smashed home. A drop forge with a hundred thousa⟨
pounds behind it. She wasn't talking about Hero! She w⟨
talking about herself!

I hung there, whitening to my lips.

"Sit down, Michael," she said gently. "I've heard th⟨
young fathers often do faint at the news; but I never ⟨
pected you to."

I sat, clawing deep for reason. Thinking: It's a lie! Sh⟨
not! She wants to get me hooked, make me throw off He⟨
and then— I leaned forward, staring at her, seeing h⟨
greenish tint, her deathly pallor; all the evidences of—

Oh God! I groaned; she is! She really is! Both of th⟨
at once. Goddamnit, that's overdoing virility!

"Michael," she said reproachfully, "don't look at ⟨
like that. I'd thought you'd be happy at the news, inste⟨
of—"

"But I am!" I said, a little blade of icy joy stabbi⟨
home at what I'd just remembered: "deliriously, Gilly! A⟨
the little bastard's real father is going to be even happ⟨
when you tell him; that is, if you even know who he is."

She looked at me, her eyes wonderfully misty with ⟨
tears.

"I do know, Michael," she whispered. "*You* are!"

"Of course," I laughed; "easier that way, isn't it, G⟨
darling? You've got that engraved paper with my name ⟨
it—that quite meaningless paper you've so hopelessly ⟨
fouled. But let me point out one thing to you, my deare⟨
You came to my flat. You had Buleah prepare one of ⟨
swamproot aphrodisiacs. You played your little game. Wh⟨
Because you couldn't wait any longer. Because you'd alrea⟨
learned that your dewy charms interested me little, a⟨
tempted me not at all. Because you'd despaired of getti⟨
me into your bed within a time limit that would enable y⟨
to say: 'Oh, Michael, it came a week—or two—or a mont⟨

early; but that often happens, dearest, particularly with the first one.' You had to go to that extreme, Gillian, knowing that you were very probably pregnant; and not knowing by whom: Bart or Big John or any of a dozen others whom I don't know—"

"Michael!" she wept. "How can you think a thing like that? How can you?"

"How could I think anything else, knowing you?" I said dryly. "No, Gilly, not even this way. I'll never come back to you. I wouldn't, even if this child were mine. So you might as well have the decency to grant me a divorce."

She shook her head.

"No, Michael," she said quietly. "If my son cannot have his father's love and guidance, he will be at least born in legal wedlock, and bear his father's name."

She had me, and she knew it. In cases of this kind, if there is the faintest shadow of a doubt, the courts give the benefit of it to the woman. Which, while chivalrous, is often hardly just.

And she had me in another way, as well: How on earth was I going to explain to Hero that we'd have to leave Birmingham now, sell my new-built empire—surely at a thunderous loss; give up all our plans? For if Hero ever found out about that episode with Gilly in my flat, it would be her I'd lose. I knew that very well. Listen to it, Jeff: Gilly drugged me. While I was out of my head, she climbed into my bed. And because of that, she's got some basis for her claims. God in heaven, boy! Who'd believe a tale like that? It doesn't even sound right to *me,* and I *know* it happened. As a writer, you ought to know there's nothing more implausible than the truth.

I stood up then, turned to go, so she tried another tack.

"Wait, Michael!" she said. "All right. A lot of your accusations are—true. I'll admit that. You're much too clever,

now, for me to try to fool you. But it's your very cleverness
that is making you fool yourself. . . ."

"I'm listening," I said grimly.

"Your—your line of reasoning is correct," she whispered,
"except that having taken off from the wrong premises, every
part of it comes out wrong. Listen to me, Michael! If I
were an ingenue, you'd have a good bit more justification
for your theory. But does it fit me, darling? Your portrait of
the erring young wife, panic-stricken at the consequences of
her sins, clumsily trying to shift the burden upon the shoulders of an already estranged husband is—well, a little ridiculous, applied to me. According to your contention, I've been
sinning for years. So, pray tell me, Michael, why should
I have been so miraculously fortunate as not to have gotten
caught before now?"

"Damned if I know," I said.

"Buleah taught me many things," she said quietly;
"among them, how to protect myself that way. So I did
trick you, darling. But not to make you a scapegoat. Because I truly want you back now. And since you won't credit
any romantic reasons—although they exist, although one of
the most vital reasons is that the man you are now excites
me, intrigues me past endurance, in a way the boy you were
before never did—I'll give you some of the hard, cynical ones
you seem to desire: I'm thirty-three years old. My reputation
is such that I can never hope to win another husband, should
I divorce you. I don't like living alone. I need a man. And
I'm dreadfully tired of this childish game of amorous musical
chairs! I finally and truly want one good man for keeps.
Last of all, Michael, like it or not, this child is yours! With
all the rest, I took precautions. With you, deliberately, I did
not. And that's the truth!"

I stood up.

"Perhaps," I said, "your precautions failed, as precautions often do. Or, more certainly, Gillian, you had neither

the time nor the means, when Big John Klovac dragged you into the woods. So my doubt remains. And even if it didn't, my answer would be the same. No, Gillian. Not ever!"

Then I turned and left her there.

I didn't tell Hero anything but that Gillian had flatly refused. Which was a mistake. Then I went to my office and spent the whole day making tentative plans to see if there were any way to liquidate my holdings in Birmingham without taking a crushing loss.

There wasn't. Fortunately I still had my testing laboratory in Pittsburgh; and enough cash left for us to live quite comfortably for a good many years. The loss would just have to be faced, with whatever equanimity I was capable of. And, though I didn't know it, Jeff, I damned well was going to need equanimity by freight-car loads.

Because, very shortly, I had a hell of a lot more to think about than that. For when I got to her house that night, I found Hero packing—to leave me.

HERO FARNSWORTH

Birmingham, 1908

II

I was packing to leave. But what Michael doesn't know is how close he came to finding me bent over the bathtub with my throat cut from ear to ear. I had even stropped and honed one of poor Rod's razors to do it with. I took an absolutely fiendish delight in imagining how Michael's face was going to look when he turned me over and my head lolled back, showing that dreadful, dreadful gash—

But then I thought about that formless lump of cells growing inside me. Who hadn't asked for life. Whom I was condemning along with me. My life was my own to end; but my child's? Even—Michael's child's? I went all soft on the inside then, Jeff, seeing him—a chubby blond cherub in my arms; seeing his first toddling steps, watching him growing tall, becoming more and more his father's image every day. Women are like that—sentimental fools! I could kill myself; in the process, even kill my own child. But it was Michael's child I could not kill. Hair-splitting? Perhaps. But the distinction was important to me. It always is to a woman in love.

I had, of course, brooded over Michael's announcement that Gillian was flatly refusing to divorce him; that, what was worse, he had been unable to get any conclusive evidence against her. So, womanlike, I decided I could do better; that, being female, having my just share of bitch and bitters in me, I'd know how to handle Gilly far better than Michael had. So I got dressed, went to see her.

She was in bed, looking pale and sick.

"Gilly," I said, "what on earth's the matter with you?"

She smiled. It was a very sweet smile, Jeff—almost maternal.

"Let's not talk about what's wrong with me just yet, Hero dearest," she said; "it's been so long since we've had a friendly chat that I shouldn't want to spoil it."

"There's a connection," I said, "between your health and the friendliness of our chat?"

"Yes," she said; then: "Oh, Hero, you look perfectly stunning! Every time I see you, you seem to be getting younger. How old are you, anyhow? I know you're a little older than I am—"

"Not quite two years," I said dryly; "I'll be thirty-five in September."

"You certainly don't look it!" she began; "why—"

"Gilly," I said flatly, "why won't you give Michael a divorce?"

She looked at me sadly.

"Hero," she said, "why won't you give me my husband back?"

"After all that you've done to him, you think that you deserve him?" I said.

"No," she said; "I'm not fit to tie his shoelaces; but I—I need him, Hero—"

"And you think I don't?"

"I don't know whether you do or not," she said; "but I know *I* do!"

I leaned forward, putting my hand on her arm.

"Gilly," I said, "I've seen you, when you wanted to, behave as sweetly, as decently, as any woman born. And I don't quite believe in that Jekyll-Hyde business of yours. Michael loves me. With me, he'll be happy—"

"With you, he has been happy," she corrected me.

"All right, he has been happy with me," I said. "He is a good man, who's had more than his share of suffering. Whatever your intentions are right now, you'd drag him down again. Besides, there's another reason why you must give him up, Gilly; the very best of all reasons."

"And that is?" she said, her eyes softly glowing.

"I'm going to bear his child," I said.

She looked at me a long, slow time before she began to laugh. But when she did begin, her laughter was whole-hearted, pure, breaking in crystalline peal after peal against the ceiling.

"How priceless!" she almost wept; "how perfectly, perfectly priceless!"

"I don't see anything funny about it," I snapped. "In fact, if you don't relent, it can be tragic."

She shook her head then, dashing the tears of laughter from her eyes.

"No, dear. Life is never tragic. Life is at best—a farce; at worst, a tragicomedy. Dear, dear Michael! Had to prove what a virile specimen of masculinity he is now, didn't he? So how does he do it? Very, very convincingly, I must admit: by getting both his women pregnant at the same time!"

I couldn't move. A hand reached in with iron fingers and squeezed my heart into a bloody pulp. My breath stopped. Down deep inside me, something started screaming.

"You—you lie!" I breathed.

"You think so, Hero, dearest?" she said. "You believe I've been in bed for the last two weeks unable to keep even water on my stomach—for my own amusement?"

"Then—then it's not Michael's!" I said; "it couldn't be!" She smiled.

"Still so trusting, Hero?" she said. "I'll tell you what: You go ask Michael. He'll tell you whether it can be his or not. There's one quaint fact about him I'm sure you know: Michael never lies. . . ."

I stood up then, death in me.

"Incidentally," Gillian said pleasantly, "I really should thank you, dear. You've taught him a lot. He was never better than mediocre before; but now he's quite talented. Hidden depths, haven't you? Tell me, Hero, where did you acquire all those charming little vices? In Rome?"

I quit the field then. And my retreat wasn't orderly. It was a rout.

When Michael came home and found me packing, he didn't say anything. I didn't say anything either. I just went on packing, hopelessly spotting all my silks with tears. I slammed my valise shut, wisps of cloth sticking out from every angle. Tried to pick it up. It was much too heavy. I stood there jerking at it like a fool.

"Here," he said; "let me. That's a sure recipe for a mis-carriage. . . ."

"I don't care!" I screamed at him. "And you don't either! What do you want a child of mine for since you've got Gilly's? All nice and legal! Not a b-bastard like—"

He took my wrists, held me powerless.

"I do care," he said gravely. "The only two humans under heaven I do care about are you and our son—"

I collapsed against him, sobbing.

"It couldn't be yours, could it, Michael?" I implored him. "She lied, didn't she? Oh, Michael, please say she lied!"

"No," he said just as gravely; "it could be mine. About that, she didn't lie."

I let my knees go limp then, slumped until he was hold-ing me up by the wrists. He turned me loose, let me crumple to the floor. I don't know where or how, but he'd learned an awful lot about women by then.

I lay there crying like an idiot child. All I could see of him was his shoes.

"Michael!" I stormed; "how could you? Tell me, how could you?"

"Easily enough," he said calmly; "the difficulty would have been not to. You know Gilly. Say I was tired, say I was drunk, say, even, if you like, I was tempted beyond my strength. There are excuses, Hero; very real excuses; but I shan't give them. For any way they're put, excuses demean a man."

"Ohhh, Michael!" I wailed.

"All this is damned pointless," he said then; "and it's getting tiresome. I slept with a woman I don't love. Like most men, I've slept with a good many women I didn't love. So now the one I do thinks that sufficient excuse to leave me—"

"It is!" I shrilled, sitting up; "because it wasn't just any woman! It was Gillian, Michael, Gillian!"

He was smiling at me with a complacency that infuriated me. Because, by then, he knew I wasn't going to leave him. The worst of it was that I knew it, too. But, like all the weak, I had to argue. Ever notice that the strong, the sure, never do? Michael was right: excuses are a symptom of weakness. Arguing is another. The valiant, the whole of heart, the complete, never do either. They give commands, and take action. Most of the time, Jeff, anything which has to be justified, can't be.

"So, I *am* going to leave you!" I screamed. "I am! You've no excuse at all! Tell me what excuse could you have? Tell me, Michael!"

"None," he said; "but you aren't going to leave me, baby. If you try to walk out of that door, I'll smack the living daylights out of you, which is the only treatment that female idiots understand. Now get up from there. You heard me, get up!"

I got up. Wonderingly.

"Come here," Michael said.

I came.

He took me in his arms.

"Michael!" I wept.

"Shut up," Michael said. And kissed me.

And that—at least about ten minutes later—was that.

"Don't unpack your things," Michael told me. "We'll go down to Mobile and lie on the beach in the sun for a few days. Do us both good. You're as nervous as a sick cat; and I'm damned tired. We'll leave tomorrow night, after I've had time to get the plant tied down. . . ."

I kissed him. I was so relieved that I didn't have to leave him after all, that with no reasons at all the only thing I could do was to stay, that I was wildly happy.

"All right, darling," I said.

MICHAEL AMES

1908

III

I was on my way to the plant when I ran into Greg. He looked like pure, undiluted hell. A little knot of muscle above his jaw kept jerking. I couldn't keep my eyes off it.

"What ails you, boy?" I said.

"Michael," he said, "have you seen Gilly? Do you know—?"

"That she's with child?" I said. "Yes, Greg. The question before the house is—whose?"

"The—it—it's not yours, Michael?" he whispered. "You —you're sure?"

"As shooting," I said cheerfully. "But why the devil are you so upset about it?"

"Because of something that I think," he muttered; "something that I almost know—a thing so goddamned rotten that—"

"Would it help anything for me to know it?" I said quietly; "I mean could I pry a divorce out of Gilly with it?"

"No," he said; "no, Michael. It wouldn't help anything at all. . . ."

"Then keep it, boy," I said.

We came back from Mobile after a week, bronzed by the sun and feeling great. I took Hero straight home. Stayed there myself. Dozens of people saw us pass. But I no longer cared. That farce of separate residences served for nothing.

Gillian would never relent. Hero and I would have to get out of Birmingham, make our lives elsewhere, that was all. That evening I went to the Manufacturers' Club, alone. They'd readmitted me, you know, when they saw the results of my labor policy proved during that strike. I stayed until about eleven o'clock. Started home. Passed Gilly's house at eleven thirty-five.

The exact instant that the murderer was battering out her brains.

Which, of course, I did not know, or I should have stopped, tried to save her. I had reached peace of soul enough even for that by then. What was unfortunate was the fact that I passed no one, had no single witness to my whereabouts from the time I left the club until I reached the Farnsworth house.

And that, for the police, was enough. I'd be staring the gallows in the face right now if it weren't for Greg.

Who didn't do it, Jeff. Who's lying to protect someone. To protect—whom?

GEOFFRY LYNNE

Birmingham, 1908

IV

Interview with Fred Klovac

Fred looked at me and rubbed his lean jaw speculatively.

"No," he said. "No, Mr. Lynne. Beyond the fact that adultery is itself a crime in a good many states, I don't know of anything she's ever done that would put her within reach of the law."

I sat back, studying how to word that next question. That damnably vague question that could well be vital.

"Fred," I said, "have you ever had the feeling— Oh, goddamnit!—I don't know how to put this. . . ."

"Try," he said earnestly.

"All right. Have you ever had the feeling that Mrs. Ames believed you knew more about her affairs than you actually do?"

"Yes," he said promptly; "on more than one occasion she hinted about something that happened in London as though she were trying to find out how much I knew. For instance, she'd say—I'm not quoting, Mr. Lynne; I don't remember it that clearly because, since she knew I've never been in England, I thought she was acting a little crazy— anyhow, she'd say something like: 'Reminds me of the dreadful time in London; but then you know all about that, don't you?' And, each time, I'd say: 'No, Miss Gilly, I've never been in England, remember?' And she'd say: 'Oh, that's right! Stupid of me.' And let the subject drop."

I sat there, my mind working like millstones, grinding, grinding.

"Well," I said finally, "she might have believed some-body told you—"

"Yes, but who? The only people who might have known about her stay in London were Mr. Michael, who was away in Pittsburgh when she asked me that; those English house servants who she knew never talked to me; and you, sir. But then, you hadn't come back."

"Fred," I almost implored him, "think, man! There must have been some occasion when she hinted or implied that some specific person told you—"

His eyes were blank. He sighed.

"There probably was," he said; "only I don't remember it. Didn't seem important, I guess. Miss Gilly was more than

a little crazy, to my way of thinking; so I didn't really pay
too much attention to her idle chatter. And yet—"

"And yet, what?" I said.

"There *was* something. I know there was something!
Only—it's like the words to a song you used to know. You
hear the tune, and they're trembling on the tip of your
tongue; but they just won't come. You ever have that
feeling?"

"Yes," I said; "but it sure doesn't help. Can't you
remember, Fred?"

His face showed the intense effort he made. But his
eyes remained blank.

"No," he sighed. "Let me sleep on it, Mr. Lynne. If it
ever does come to me, I'll let you know."

That was when I got my brainstorm.

"Fred," I said, "how would you like to visit London?"

He stared at me.

"At my expense," I went on. "Enjoy yourself, if you
like—while talking to the employees of the hotels where
Gillian Ames stayed while she was there. Tracing hackies
who drove her about. Checking with the police or Scotland
Yard to see if she were ever booked for anything. And,
more specifically: if she ever did anything to anyone over
there which would make him want to kill her. . . ."

Excitement leaped in his eyes.

"Done, sir!" he said.

"Good," I said; "I'll get a list of the places they stopped
from Mr. Ames. That'll give you a lead. And anything you
find out, no matter how slight, you cable me. Hang the
expense. There's a train leaving for New York at midnight.
I want you on it. And on the first tub sailing for England
after you get off that train. So get going, now!"

"Yes, sir!" Fred Klovac said.

19

GEOFFRY LYNNE

Birmingham, 1908

What do I know now? Too much. And all of it designed
to pull that noose tight around Greg's neck.

Item: The relationship between Greg and Gillian was
much closer than I thought. Sufficiently close for him to
have tried to kill Big John Klovac for her sake.

Item: The fact that no one had ever seen him enter
Gillian's house except to escort her somewhere meant
nothing. Greg was a bachelor; lived alone. And Gillian was
not above visiting her men.

Item: The friendship between my brother and Michael
had been shaken to its core by their rivalry over Hero.
Could not Greg have said: "You beat my dog; I kick your
cat!"? Conceived of himself as taking vengeance upon
Michael by—

Dear God! This is no way to stop a hanging. There
must be something else—something I've overlooked, have
not yet found. . . .

I went through that pile of foolscap again, page by

311

page. Here and there I had penciled in a cross, beside words, passages, that had seemed to me significant then. And each time I had been wrong, each time in light of subsequent events, that significance had faded out, disappeared. I picked up an eraser and rubbed those crosses out one by one, starting at the very beginning of my notes, eliminating them as I checked to see if they meant anything, if they could possibly mean anything. But as I neared the end of all that pile of paper, reached the borderline of pure despair, having accumulated a history that was very largely Hero's, Michael's, with Gillian as villain of the piece, and poor Greg hovering ineffectually in the wings, my eraser poised above two marks, just two. I let it fall, and did not efface them from the page.

And yet, it seemed to me, they had nothing to do with Greg at all. I had placed them out of idle curiosity as things I would come back to, after my quest was finished, as pieces of psychological exotica worth looking into later, for themselves. One of them was the expression "Buleah's Child," which Gillian used to refer to her *Doppelgänger*, her poltergeist; and the other—

I almost cried aloud. For I had interviewed everyone directly connected with Gillian MacAllister's history. Everyone except the most important person of all: Gillian, herself. An obvious impossibility, since she was dead; since her death was the cause of my beginning this in the first place. And now, I was going to repair that omission: I was going to interview Gillian MacAllister Ames, listen to her very voice, speaking far off and faint, from the eternal shades.

How? Very, very simply, without crossing the Styx or adventuring in Hades. Because I had placed that last remaining cross beside these words: "I was, Father told me, dreadfully sick for a year about that time. During that year,

I started to keep my diary. . . ." And [the italics are mine] *"Funny, I've kept it up ever since*, Michael. One day, if you should ever come back to me for keeps, I'll show it to you. . . ." Then, farther along: "Go to Bulaeh. Force her to remove her. Tell her I'll take my book to the police if she doesn't and—"

That book. That diary. That autobiography of Gillian MacAllister and of—that other being who dwelt in her whom she called—Buleah's child. That journal that might show me the way, point a finger at the guilty, lift the noose from—

I put on a pair of tennis shoes, picked up my electric torch, armed myself with a stout walking stick, and went down the stairs.

All of Gilly's servants had gone by then. Which reminded me of another omission: I had interviewed only Jacqueline, Gillian's personal maid; and left the others alone, figuring that their activities had precluded their knowing anything of any real value about Gilly's affairs at firsthand.

Yet, I was not to have the advantage of searching an empty, unguarded house. For Buleah Land, that fat, black gravedigger of human hopes remained. She and poor Rad were taking care of the MacAllister mansion by order of the court (I suppose the judges felt them reliable because of the excellent fashion they had managed Hero's residence in her absence) until such time as a will could be found and probated. If not, out of the eternal laughter of the ribald gods, the final result of Gillian's stubborn refusal to divorce Michael Ames was going to be that he, as her legal husband, in the total absence of any other surviving kindred, would inherit MacAllister Steel and his late wife's house. That he, if he wanted to, could bring the woman for whom Gillian had perhaps even lost her life in her efforts to balk, home to that house as his bride.

Needless to say, Buleah's presence complicated things. Because there was something in that book that had given Gillian a hold over her. Something that was a threat to Buleah's freedom, even—her life. So, I couldn't ring the doorbell, walk in, say, "Hello, Buleah! Miss Gilly's diary, if you please. I know quite well you have it."

Actually, I didn't believe she had it. I thought Gilly had hidden it too well for her to find it, even if she'd ransacked the house.

I walked all the way over there, and by a roundabout route. I wanted no cabby remembering my face. I climbed the ivy-covered iron fence in back of the house, shinnied up the back porch columns, gained the roof. The window was down, and locked. But I have written half a hundred shilling shockers about the activities of cunning sleuths. I turned the big signet ring on my finger, scraped the solitaire across the pane, once, twice, thrice, four times, making deep rectangular cuts into the glass. Spread my handkerchief wide over the pane, pushed hard—and a neat rectangle fell inside the room, landing on the cushion of a chair with the faintest tinkling sound.

I stood there in astonishment. It had actually worked —this trick I'd employed a dozen times in my fantastic yarns. You could cut a pane of glass with a diamond ring; you actually could! I pushed my hand through, found the catch, released it, pushed up the sash, stepped into that room. I stood there, trying to orient myself. I had not been in the MacAllister mansion in years, or upstairs in it since my childhood.

The servants' quarters were downstairs in the basement so I wasn't afraid of running into Buleah or into Rad. But I hadn't the faintest idea which room was Gillian's—nor, for that matter, was I sure she'd have the diary hidden there. Nothing to do but search. I opened doors. Flashed in my torch. Withdrew. When I came to Gilly's room, I recognized it at once. There was photo on the dresser, of Michael in younger days. The room was almost oppressively feminine. The odor of Gillian's perfume lingered in it still. I flashed the torch around it—saw that stain on the rug just beyond the fireplace, the place where she had died. I shivered, looking at it. And my heart sank to my boot tops. Because Greg had said at the trial:

"I struck her down, with all my force. I don't know whether the blow I gave her killed her or the impact of her head striking the andiron. Anyhow, I knelt beside her, felt her pulse. There was none. I couldn't see her breathe. So I—I got out of there."

Oh God! I thought, could it be that he was telling the truth after all? Was I going to have to stand by helpless and watch my brother die?

No. By heaven and hell, no! The diary remained. And it must contain some answer, some clue. . . .

I wasted two full hours opening drawers—drawers which clearly showed the signs of prior search, sticking hatpins into pillows, cushions, mattresses, pressing the carved woodwork in search of the hidden catch that would send the ghostly panel sliding back, reveal—

Nothing. There were no hidden panels. And either Buleah had already found and destroyed that journal, or—

Or Gilly's mind had existed on a level superior to that of a hack writer of poor detective tales. I sat down then and tried to think. What it required was the subtlety of a Wilkie Collins or a Poe. Because Gillian's perverse mentality would naturally operate something like—*The Moonstone? The Lady in White?* No. Collins had lacked her gift for mockery.

But Poe? Like, like—I was already rising from my chair, my eyes agleam with hope—"The Purloined Letter"!

Leave the damned thing in plain sight! Casually disguised, so that a searcher looking for a thing that anyone in his right mind would have buried in the bowels of the earth, would pass right over it!

A book then, stuck among all her other books on that shelf? No. It was not there—and Buleah's greasy fingerprints had marred them all. Or—dear God—where else?

I turned, saw a handsome, hand-tooled, gilt-edged holy Bible lying on the night table beside her bed. One of those Bibles which could be fastened shut. She had done that, all right. Fastened the catch; locked it. How well she knew the Southern Negro mind! And Buleah, witch or not, had left it untouched and had not dared to break that catch; had not, perhaps, believed that even Gillian would desecrate the Word of God.

If she even thought about all that. If she did anything more than mutter: "Hmmm, th' Good Book . . ." and left it there.

But I, knowing Gillian, found a Bible at her bedside as odd as holy water at a witches' Sabbath. I had never in all my life seen any evidence of interest in religion on Gilly's part. Not even the interest of an atheist or an agnostic. Her lack of concern for things spiritual was so complete that, discussing the matter later, both Michael and I agreed that neither of us had ever heard her so much as even mention them.

So I picked up the Bible. It was unusually light. It should have been. Those heavy silk paper pages had been cut through with a razor to make a hollow box. And in it reposed—Gillian's diary.

I took it out, flashed the torch over the pages—and a thick, black hand reached over my shoulder and snatched it from my grasp.

"Thank you, Mister Jeff!" Buleah chuckled softly;

"thank you mighty kindly. I been looking all over for this here book!"

"Buleah!" I said. "Give me that book!"

"Nawsuh, Mister Jeff! An' don' come no closer, please. Please, Mister Jeff! This here's a razor I'se got in my hand. And it's mighty sharp, suh, I tell you. You's a nice young feller, Mister Jeff. You'n Mister Greg, bof. So don't come no closer, I'm a-beggin' you, suh. I sho Lawd don' want nothin' bad to happen to you lak what happened to Liza 'n Anxious. . . ."

"So," I whispered, "it wasn't ptomaine poisoning! You—you killed them, too! Just like you—you killed Gillian!"

"I didn't kill mah baby, Mister Jeff," Buleah said reproachfully. "That nosy Liza found out too much 'n tol' Anxious. So busy gabbin' they didn't notice what they was eatin'. No wonder that there po'k soured on they stummicks."

"Buleah," I said softly, "what did you hit her with? Why did you kill her?"

"I didn't!" she screamed at me; then: "Fo' Gawd, I didn't, Mister Jeff! She was mah baby, don't you understand! I birthed her! She was mah own flesh 'n blood!"

"Buleah," I said, "you lie. Gilly was Heddy MacAllister's child. Born in this house with a doctor and two nurses attending. And crazy as you are, you black witch, you can't really believe that a child who looked like Gillian ever came from something black as you!"

She stared at me, her eyes blank. Then grief filled them. Real grief.

"She were mine," she whispered. "All right, Miz Heddy birthed her sweet lil' body; but her sperrit were mine. 'Cause I called it back, Mr. Jeff, back from the grave 'n put it there. Couldn't let my po' Lillian lie there in the dark. That's how come I give Miz Heddy that there name for her, only she got it wrong. 'Twere Lillian, not Gillian. But I

couldn't let mah baby lie there with her sweet lil' throat
cut in the moldering grave—you understands that, don't
you, Mister Jeff? So you understands I had to, suh? And
that she was mah baby what 'longed to me'n not nobody
else? Daid! Lawd Gawd, daid! Daid two times—kilt twicet!
First time a damnfool nigger crazy jealous cut mah baby's
throat with he razor, him! Second time some fool white
man horny wild, a beatin' in her haid! Lawd, whut I done?
Whut I done done so bad you takes away mah baby twicet?"

"You," I said, "are as mad as a hatter. Give me that
book!"

"Nawsuh, Mister Jeff," she said patiently. "Body whut
gits this here off'n me is got to kill me first. And mighty
sorry as I'd be to hafta, man what tries it gonna git cut up
sumpin awful!"

I have led a checkered life. And in my wanderings, I've
found myself in tighter scrapes than this. I feinted suddenly;
and as she brought that razor whistling toward my face, I
met it with my cane, like a fencer, so hard that not even
all that fat could protect her arm. I heard the bones go.
The razor clattered to the floor. And big as she was, Buleah
whirled, already running hard. I pounded after her, even
dashed ahead to block her entrance to the curving staircase.
She ran past it, caught at a rope I hadn't even seen, and
one of those swinging ladders came down from the ceiling
of the hall. She squirmed up it. I was just behind her, I
even caught her arm, but she was sweating so I could not
keep my grip. Then she was out the little trapdoor and onto
the roof. Onto that widow's walk from which there was
no escape.

I came toward her, step, by step.

"The book, Buleah!" I whispered. I could see her eyes.
In the blackness of her face they were coals of yellow fire.
"The book!" I roared.

Then she sprang. I threw myself sidewise or all that
bulk would have crushed me. She went past the place I had
been an instant before, like a black avalanche, hit that iron
rail, tottered there, her huge arms flailing, while under her
weight it gave, it gave—

And she trailed that long, long tearing shriek down
eighty feet of empty air to smother it against the dark bosom
of the earth, her mother.

When I got there, poor Rad was kneeling beside her
and crying.

"Kilt herself, Mister Jeff!" he croaked. "Swore she was
a-goin' to! 'Lowed that 'fore she'd let the white folks string
her up, she'd—"

"String her up for what, Rad?" I said.

"Don't know, suh! Sumpin in that there book o' Miss
Gilly's. . . ." He bent to pick her up.

"Don't move her, Rad!" I said sharply. "You go phone
the police, first. They've got to see her just as she fell. Or
else they might think that another murder's been done. I'll
wait here. You go call them."

While he was gone, I searched for the book. Found it
under a rosebush five yards away. Stuck it in my pocket.
Waited nervously for the police. I had been away too long.
Perhaps I've always been away from Alabama in my heart.
I had forgotten that I was still a white man, and that this
wasn't anything but a big black dead nigger woman. They
asked me a few questions. I could see they didn't even give
a damn about my answers. They probably figured I'd killed
her for my own good reasons. Which didn't matter. She had
the wrong color hide for it to matter.

I said: "I was passing by. She jumped or fell from up
there. I don't know why—"

Then I came home and read Gillian MacAllister's diary.

I flipped it open. And my eye fell upon these words, scrawled in her difficult, angular script:

The fools! Cannot they see I am an Empress born out of my times—such a one as would have had the right, returning wearied from the hunt, to order slain the first three serfs she met, and refresh her hands and feet in their warm blood?

And I knew I was going to have my task cut out for me. The first of it was gibberish:

Sick. Day night. Night day. Sick. Buleah. Medicine. So bitter the medicine. Fire. Fire and snakes. Coiling. Faces against the window pane.

The script was childish. Written long ago, clearly when she was feverish, delirious, even. But there was something familiar about those words. I turned the page.

Bitter the medicine like fire going down all around my feet the fire leaping up. Clothes smothering me. Take them off! Faces at the window seeing me naked. Nice. Nice naked. Bitter the medicine. Snakes coiling.

"Lord God!" I said aloud. "The stuff she put in Michael's tea!"

I read on.

Down. Down into darkness. Into the pit, screaming. Whirling. No help. No help. Mother! Hit Mother! Hit her! Claw out her eyes! Kill her! Kill—kill—kill. . . .

I shook my head. This damned thing wasn't going to help at all. I read on, pages of this gibberish which I didn't dare to skip, until startlingly, I came upon this:

I am quite all right, now, I have been in my right mind for several days. I poured the bitter medicine into the potted plant. It has killed the plant. I think Buleah knows. That's why she doesn't give me the medicine any more. She doesn't dare. She's afraid I remember. She's right—I do remember.

Mad, I thought, even at twelve she was already mad. . . .

Then pages of childish nonsense; but quite normal non-sense. Remarks about how handsome Michael Ames had become. A line: That Jeff Lynne is the world's biggest fool! But Greg is nice, I think . . ." Afterward, abruptly:

It happened! Now I can do it, myself! Buleah wasn't even here! Nobody gave me the bitter medicine, but I went down just the same! Into the pit into the black black black black night no stars no moon all fire all fire even the fire black no light no light at all and it all came back to me how she took me to that place that horrible place where men chased naked black and yellow women up and down the stairs thinking I was sleeping because Buleah had given me that stuff to make me sleep only it didn't work nothing works any more.

"My God!" I whispered, half aloud. Then I turned the page.

She took me to that place to the house called Lou's because she had to get the money to buy that stuff she used to put into her veins with a big safety pin sticking holes in herself like that and rubbing that stuff into them into her blood. But what happened wasn't her fault. She didn't know that horrible horrible man was going to try to abuse me would have abused me if Big Lou herself hadn't caught him and stopped him and the next day when we met him in the street Buleah tried to cut him to pieces right in front of a half dozen people. Because of what he said and what he'd tried to do to me.

My God, I thought, no wonder Buleah was afraid of being lynched if this book got out!

Reading the diary made a pattern. There were long

periods of sanity, then those delirious pages of gibberish. Or was it gibberish? For instance:

The body is the temple of the soul. But can two souls live in the narrow confines of my flesh? The answer is: Yes. Two souls do live in me. One of them is I, myself. But the other is—Buleah's child. A yellow nigger wench. A wanton. I even know where Buleah got her from. I followed her one night. Down to the nigger cemetery. Earth from a grave. From that grave, her child's grave, her yellow child's grave. Her child whose father was a white man— Who? Buleah's child, dead of a razor stroke at sixteen. Black men are jealous, too.

Earth from that grave. Little blue flies that feed on dead things, their bodies crushed. Roots. Leaves of certain plants. The juice of—hellebore, witches' bane, mandrake root? Of these is the bitter medicine made? Reincarnation of the child she loved. A body needed to house that vagrant soul. A body available. Helpless and at hand. My body.

I put down that book. I had to. I wanted to keep my own sanity. But I picked it up again. I had to go on. Had to find something, anything, to save poor Greg.

At sixteen, the first clearly sexual references. I don't know the boy, whom she identifies only as K. From her description, he sounds foreign. One of the steelworker's children, doubtless.

There is an obscure passage here which would indicate that Heddy found out. Packed her off to Canada again. Strange how little she mentions her stay in Quebec, in that convent school, every summer between her thirteenth and her eighteenth year. A phrase or two in French, that's all. Probably because nothing happened there.

But, from there on, the diary becomes a manual of

pornography—except that it retains, curiously, a certain
naïveté, a deep, unreached, and perhaps unreachable innocence. . . . There are no further passages I can quote
until her marriage to Michael. She seems completely un-
aware that her language is unprintable, and the things she
discusses so calmly, nauseous. And here, too, a certain
megalomania. Here for the first time she speaks of any
attempt to thwart her desires as *lèse-majesté*. Here that
reference I have already quoted in which she speaks of
herself as an empress born out of her times.

Then, her adult life. Nothing here I didn't already
know. She had been Bart Byrce's mistress since she was
seventeen. She didn't mention names, referring to Bart by
an oddly written "B." When, after her break-up with Bart,
she started having her affair with Michael, she refers to
him by a letter, too; but not, as I had expected, an "M";
rather, a lower-case "u" written backwards, with the tail
of it on the wrong side—*µ*. Notice that point well. It turned
out to be of crucial importance.

The marriage and honeymoon. Michael's picture of
them was rather accurate, except that both he and I sadly
underestimated little Gilly. She lists, beside the wild beast
painter, the seagoing Englishman, and il Principe Cesari,
seven additional lovers, all initialed, who are happily lost
to history and reappear no more. In Rome, too, this cryptic
note:

"A girl. C's idea. No fun. Didn't like it." So I had to
absolve her of Lesbianism. Thank God there was something
I could absolve her of!

Then: London. I read this part with such attention
that I ached all over from the tension tightening my every
fiber. But it was incomprehensible. Gibberish? No. Too
orderly, too patterned to be gibberish. A code, maybe.
There was one man to whom she referred again and again,

using a symbol like a fat letter "O" lying on its side with
a verticle line drawn through it, thus: Φ, followed by the
arabic numeral 2. She speaks of her adventures with him,
using the words "danger" and "excitement." Then, abruptly
Φ2 vanishes from the diary to be replaced by the man
indicated by the drawing of a triangle. That she feared
and loathed this man was very clear. What is not clear is
why. A phrase: "Oh, damn Δ anyhow! I'll never be able to
get rid of him; not even when we go back." In another
place, she spells out the entire word for which the triangle
stood; thus: "Will somebody please deliver me from Διακονος
and his foolish flaming sword?"

But, after their return to the States, for many, many
pages, she mentions Triangle no more.

I read on doggedly, all through the weary night.

She mentioned Michael's drunkenness. She seemed to
pity him. I turned the page. I didn't dare skip so much as
a line. But it was dreadful labor. Finally, toward the end,
I had my reward. For Gilly devoted one entire exultant
page to a description of how she seduced my brother Greg!

Just as I had thought. Because of Hero. Because of his
jealousy, his despair. He, who had everything to offer Hero,
had to stand by and watch her hurl herself into the arms
of a man who had nothing to offer her but shame. Greg
seems to have felt in some obscure way that he was reveng-
ing himself upon Michael. Gilly made gay mock of his naïve
unawareness of how many other partners there were simul-
taneously sharing her bountiful favors in her polyandric
scheme of life.

And then, at long last, the answer. The answer that
did me no good at all, because I didn't know who she meant.
She wrote:

Triangle [she used, of course, the symbol, not the
word] is getting troublesome again. I'm afraid. I'm

really afraid now. Because, when he finds out what he's
so proud of isn't true, he'll—— [The dash is hers; she
seemed to fear to even write her thought.] And he is
capable of it! He is! All right, they acquitted him in
London; but they didn't know she couldn't read or
write. . . ."

Then it hit me: I didn't have to probe who the murderer
was! All I had to do was to cast a strong doubt on Greg's
guilt. And I had more than enough to do that now. Because
Triangle wasn't Greg. For Greg, clearly identifiable from
her mocking remarks, she'd used a symbol like a lower-case
"y." And there was something else, something not in the
diary itself, that kept tugging at the edges of my brain.
I picked up a transcript of the trial that Judge Rollins had
graciously allowed me to make. Flipped through it, and
almost shouted for joy.

For it was there. The lever I needed to pry open the
door to Greg's cell and set him free. Not the solution to the
mystery, but a strong and convincing doubt. Strong enough
to win a stay. Maybe even a retrial. To win time. Time to
find Triangle. To slip that noose around his neck where it
belonged.

I went to bed. Slept two blissful hours. Got up, took
a bath. Shaved. Put on fresh clothes. Ate a hearty breakfast.
Then I set out—

For Police Headquarters.

GEOFFRY LYNNE

1908, Conclusion

"Now look, Mr. Lynne," Chief Watson said, "I know this diary proves she was scared spitless, that this here Triangle fellow was aiming to kill her; but your brother *confessed!*"

I said: "Chief, we've been missing the boat right along. Both of us, for different reasons—I, because I thought Greg was lying to protect somebody; you, because you thought he was telling the truth. You were closer to it than I. He was telling the truth, by his lights. But what neither one of us ever considered was the possibility that he thought he was telling the truth, but was mistaken."

"How's that?" Chief Watson said.

"Look," I told him; "Judge Rollins let me take a transcript of the trial. And in all the cross-examination, only one discrepancy turned up. Here it is, right here. I'll read it to you:

> DISTRICT ATTORNEY: Then, having struck Mrs. Ames down in a fit of rage, you seized her by the throat, strangled her, banging her head repeatedly against that andiron all the time?
>
> GREGORY LYNNE: I did not! I struck her just once! When

I saw how still she was, I bent to see whether she was still alive.

DISTRICT ATTORNEY: Your Honor and Gentlemen of the Jury, I refer again to the official photographs of the body which have already been submitted and marked. Sergeant Leichester, will you please be so kind as to pass these photographs to the Jury?—Very well, gentlemen, I'm sure you can see Mrs. Ames was throttled by powerful hands, as well as having been beaten savagely. Mr. Lynne, Mr. Lynne, you mean to say you struck her only once?

GREGORY LYNNE: That's right, sir!

"So?" Chief Watson said.

"Good God, Chief! It's as plain as the nose on your face! Greg had confessed. He was and is resigned to dying for what he conceives to be his crime. In the end, the D.A. convinced the jury he was lying. But does a man who has confessed, who all along has made not the slightest effort to even reduce the charge to manslaughter, suddenly, for no reason at all, begin to quibble about the details of the killing?"

Chief Watson was nobody's fool. He looked at me with troubled eyes.

"You've got a point there," he said. "So you think—"

"That someone else came into that room, found her lying there stunned, and finished her off! And I'm betting it was this fellow she calls Triangle!"

"Well," the chief said, "if you knew who he was, we could bring him in for questioning."

"I don't," I said; "but maybe Greg does. Let's go down to the jail and ask him."

"All right," Chief Watson said. "I'll bring Hendricks along to take down what he says."

The turnkey admitted us to Greg's cell. He stared at the three of us rather sullenly.

" 'Lo, Greg," I said. "You stupid ass!"

"What are you talking about?" he said listlessly.

"You, stupid ass!" I said. "Listen. I'm going to read you something."

I took out Gilly's diary. Read her exultant account of his seduction. Went on reading her deadly mockery of my poor brother's naïveté. Her listing of her simultaneous lovers.

"All right," Greg said wearily, "I slept with her. Though I don't know why you have to shame her memory before Hendricks and the chief. I was a fool. So all right. So she's dead—and in peace, while I—"

"Have yet to die for a killing you didn't do," I said.

"What do you mean?" he said harshly. "I killed Gilly, all right!"

"Why?" I said.

"That's my business," he said sullenly; "and it's going to die with me. . . ."

"No, it isn't," I said. "Because it isn't your business any longer. You went to Gilly to have it out with her, because you had found out she was trying to force Michael to leave Hero and to come back to her by using the baby you thought you'd fathered."

Greg's eyes opened very wide then.

"How—how'd you find all that out, Jeff?" he said. "Her diary?"

"Yes. In part. But let's get on with it. When you got there, she taunted you with the fact that the little bundle from heaven she was expecting wasn't even yours. That it was sired by either Big John Klovac or the man called Triangle."

"Triangle," he said. "She didn't say—"

"Oh, yes, she did," I said. "But no matter. In your rage, you hit her, knocked her down. The back of her head hit the andiron of the fireplace. You knelt, couldn't hear her breathe. So, in a panic, you got out of there. Isn't that right?"

"Yes," he said. "What about it?"

"This about it! Did you take her by the throat? Strangle her so hard that you left purple bruises in her flesh? Bang her head repeatedly against the andiron?"

"I did not! I don't know why the D.A. had to tell all those lies. I'd already confessed, and—"

"Greg," I said softly, "they weren't lies."

"But I tell you—" His eyes were very wide and dark suddenly, searching my face. "Jeff," he croaked, "you don't mean—"

"You never got a look at those photos the D.A. was showing the jury, did you? Your bright boy of a lawyer never even thought to demand the simple right of having you see them. Or else you'd have seen those finger marks on her throat, seen what a mess the back of her head was beaten into. And then the dim possibility exists that it might have dawned upon even that quarter wit you've got that you didn't kill her after all!"

"Jeff!" he breathed, his eyes sick with pain. "That door had a spring latch on it. I—I thought I heard her move, groan. I tried to get back in, but I couldn't. Then I heard footsteps on the service stairway."

"What kind of footsteps?" Chief Watson said.

"Light. Like a little, catlike fellow—or even a girl. So I got out of there. But don't you see, I must have killed her! Nobody could have entered that room unless—"

"She recovered from that love tap you gave her, got up and let her murderer in," I said dryly; "which is just what happened. Unless you've suddenly remembered that you did strangle her, after all; that you banged her head again and again against the—"

"No," Greg said stoutly, "I did not!"

"Greg," I said, "who is Triangle?"

"Damned if I know," he said.

"You must! Because he did it! He had to! He probably overheard your conversation and thought that she—"

"Let me see that book," Greg said.

I passed it over.

"Hmmm," he said; "Mu—that's Michael."

"What did you say?" I said.

"Mu—for Michael. The Greek letter mu. Here it is right here."

"So," I said, "when she put down what looked like a "y" for you, it was actually a gamma she was writing, wasn't it?"

"Yes," Greg said.

"But she had to write a 'C' for Prince Cesari, because there's no such letter in Greek. A triangle is delta, isn't it? Corresponding to our letter 'D'?"

"Yes," Greg said.

"But," I said, "there wasn't anybody in her life named David or Dalton or Daryl or—"

Greg went on reading the diary. Suddenly he looked up.

"Why," he said, "she tells what that delta stands for. Here it is, right here!"

And he pointed to that strange word followed by the symbol of the flaming sword.

"That," I groaned, "is so much Greek to me!"

"Exactly," Greg laughed. "I remember old Professor Giles saying you were the worst student he ever had. Look, Jeff: Delta, iota, alpha, kappa, omicron, nu, omicron, sigma —don't you get it?"

"Hell no!" I said.

"Me neither," Chief Watson said.

"All right," Greg said; "using the English equivalents, D, i, a, k, o, n, o, s. *Diakonos,* meaning a servant, or in the religious sense a servant of the people, hence a minister. That's where we got our word 'deacon' from—"

"Now aren't we erudite," I began sarcastically; then I stopped short. "What—did—you—say?" I breathed.

"I said that *diakonos* was the Greek root from which we derived the word—"

"Deacon!" I roared. "What Gilly always called—Tim Nelson!"

"Have him picked up right now, Hendricks," Chief Watson said.

"No!" I got out. "For God's sake, Chief, no! Not now, not yet—"

"Why not?" the Chief said.

"Because," I said, almost choking in my haste to make them see, "we haven't a thing on him that we can make stick. And he's so damned sure of himself he hasn't even left town. Chief, for God's love—don't tip our hands yet!"

Chief Watson stared at me. So did Greg and Hendricks. I don't blame them. I must have sounded like a blithering idiot.

"Oh, what a fool I've been!" I groaned; "what a fool!"

"I grant you that," Greg said dryly; "but what about, this time?"

"Michael told me! Positively identified Tim as the deacon of a lunatic sect called Christ's Avengers! Only Michael got it wrong. He said Adventurers. That's what threw me off—"

"There *is* a point to all this?" Greg said.

"Yes, boy!" I shouted, pounding him on the back; "a point that's going to save your life! Let me out of here!"

"Where're you going?" Chief Watson said.

"To send a cable," I said, and rushed through the opened door.

I took Fred Klovac's answer to my cable down to Montgomery and showed it to Governor Comer.

"Hmmmn," he said. "So Mrs. Ames' chauffeur, Nelson,

was tried for the murder of his unfaithful wife. Acquitted because no positive identification of the long deceased corpse could be made. The murderer was clever enough to remove her teeth, which, apart from the fingerprints—lost, in this case, by decomposition—are the only positive means of identifying a cadaver. No clothes marks, corpse was nude. Hmmn—Nelson produced in court letters sent him from Australia by his wife admitting to have fled there with her lover, thus indicating she was still alive at the time of the trial. But your man Klovac has conclusively proved that Mrs. Nelson was illiterate, and somewhat half-witted to boot. Very well, Mr. Lynne. You've gathered evidence that Tim Nelson can be presumed to have been guilty of murder —in England. So now you tell me, sir: Just what the hellfire has this to do with your brother's confessed murder of Mrs. Ames?"

"Everything!" I said. "Governor, if you'll just be patient—"

His smile was frosty.

"Before I'll be guilty of furthering a miscarriage of justice," he said, "I'll be as patient as you please."

Then I told him. All of it. How in my researches into the ways of criminals for my *Black Cat* series of mystery tales, I'd stumbled onto the tail end of Tim Nelson's trial, while waiting to hear a much more sensational case. It had bored me. I had scarcely even paid attention, which was why, although I remembered having seen Tim's face before, I couldn't remember when or where. But later the papers had been full of the doings of those madmen, Christ's Avengers. They were agitating to make prostitution a capital crime! To have whoring punished by death. And though I'd read their leader's name was Nelson, I'd never associated him with that mousy little man acquitted of the charge of murdering his wife!

But now, it made a pattern: A small, unattractive man,

with overactive sexual desires, embittered by being often
rebuffed by the women he so ardently lusts after, is betrayed
by the one woman who has accepted him. He murders her,
but that is not enough. He must war on all unfaithful wives,
all unchaste women everywhere to satisfy the madness
seething in him. And for such a man, what victim was more
made to order than:

Gillian?

"So," I concluded, "he blackmailed her into bringing
him to the States as her chauffeur. Into—I'm sure of this,
sir—submitting to his advances; into—"

"How?" the Governor said.

"I don't know!" I said. "I have Klovac investigating that
angle now. What I am sure of is that a reasonable doubt
of my brother's guilt exists!"

"If so," Governor Comer said, "you haven't established
it, Mr. Lynne. In fact, you've given me no legal grounds by
which Nelson's arrest could even be ordered. Now, if the
English authorities were to request our holding him for
extradition, we might be able to trick or sweat a confession
out of him. And that's what I'd suggest to you; get Klovac
to present his evidence to the authorities there. There's no
statute of limitations on murder in any country in the world.
Once the British government asks us to hold him, we can
pick him up. . . ."

"Then you won't even order a stay of execution?" I
whispered.

"You've twelve days still left. A man can work wonders
in twelve days if he really buckles down to it," the Governor
said.

I fired off a cable to Fred that same night. Two days
later I had my answer. The British wouldn't order Tim's
arrest. A quirk in their law: the principle of double jeopardy.
Tim had been tried once for the murder of his wife. And,

under an old, old principle, a man's life couldn't be put in jeopardy twice for the same offense, even though it were established later that justice had miscarried.

I almost lost my mind. I had ten days! Ten days before Greg was to be hanged. And, knowing him innocent, I was going to have to let him die!

Then it came to me. That one slim chance. Or maybe, those two slim chances. I called Dr. Conner long distance.

"So I'm going to send this chap up to you," I said, "on the pretext that you need a chauffeur—"

"For my tin Lizzie?" he laughed. "Why, Jeff—"

"For your grand aunt's baby carriage if necessary," I howled. "Doc, this boy is a homicidal maniac—only I can't prove it, yet. You keep him there under observation until I do! Will you do that much for me? It's my only chance to clear Greg—"

"Of course, Jeff," Doc Conner said.

Then I put that question to him. That vital question.

"Why, no, Jeff," he said. "Nurse Meadows has never come back to us. Why?"

"Never mind why!" I shouted. "Give me her address!"

"Hold on there, boy," he said pleasantly. "I'll have to look it up. Where are you? At home? Very well. I'll call you back in half an hour."

He did.

Thirty minutes later I was talking to Tim Nelson. Tim rose nobly to my bait.

"Why, to be sure, sir!" he said. "I'd be delighted to work for Dr. Conner. Perhaps he could help me with Tilly Meadows over again. When does he want me to come?"

"Tonight, if you can," I said. "The matter is—urgent, Tim. And—please don't quote me, old chap, but I think there's more to it than merely chauffeuring. Why, he even asked me to buy a ticket for you. Here it is. And that means —big things, Tim. . . ."

His little eyes widened.

"You think so, sir?" he said.

"I'm sure of it. You make quite an impression on people, Timothy. Quiet but competent. A chap to be trusted, what? I'm sure that the doctor has some secret, confidential mission in mind for you. . . ."

Nothing is more certain than the vanity of small men. Tim almost grabbed that ticket from my hand.

"I'm off, sir!" he said happily. "Just as soon as I throw a few duds in the old bag, what? And, Mr. Lynne—"

"Yes, Tim?"

"Thank you, sir! Thank you from the bottom of my heart!"

You poor bastard, I thought, and got out of there.

Another thirty minutes and I was aboard a train, bound for—Mobile.

Josiah Meadows had a long and sorrowful face; but there was an iron shape of determination about his jaw. His wife, Mathilda, for whom their daughter, Nurse Tilly Meadows, had been named, was a little, round, fluttery woman, who reminded me of a partridge.

But they were both certain sure of one thing: Tilly Meadows had not been home since Christmas of last year. And she hadn't written them a line since October 2.

"Fact is," Josiah growled, "I got so worried, I wrote Dr. Brandt! And he writ back she's resigned. He thought she'd come home to us. As if she dared!"

"Why doesn't she dare?" I said.

"She done fell in love," Josiah said. "Now falling in love's all right, but when it's with a critter what no sensible girl ought to even think about getting hitched to, that, mister, is another matter!"

"There—there's something wrong with the man?" I said.

"Well, I wouldn't say that, exactly. He's a foreigner.

English, he says. But he ain't got two nickels to rub together. Chauffeurs for some rich woman up there in Birmingham. Now for a registered nurse like my Til, that's stooping mighty low. . . ."

"Do you know his name?" I whispered.

"Yes sir," Mathilda Meadows piped. "Name o' Nelson. Tim Nelson. Says he's a widower—"

"He is," I said soberly. "But you're right about one thing, Mr. Meadows. He's not suitable for your daughter. Look, if I run across her, I'll—"

I heard, with a crawling sense of shame, my voice running on, making those fake, empty promises. Because even then I knew how Tilly Meadows would be found, and what she'd look like when we found her.

Before leaving Mobile, I sent a long telegram to Dr. Conners asking him to check at the Tuscaloosa railroad station to see if the clerk remembered where Nurse Meadows had bought a ticket to. When I got back home, I already had my reply. Just as I had guessed: She had bought a one-way rail fare. To Birmingham.

Next, I went to MacGilvray's Tavern where Michael had seen Tim holding hands with the waitress. The minute I came in, I saw a change had been made. The girl behind the counter wasn't a fat, untidy brunette; she was a trim, pert, starched and spotless blonde.

I didn't question her. Waitresses automatically assume you're getting fresh. I talked to MacGilvray himself.

"What business is it of yours, Bud?" he growled.

"My name's not Bud," I said; "and it damned well is my business. For your information, *Bud*, I happen to know that the guy she used to be sweet on is a homicidal maniac. Now, would you mind telling me when you've seen her last?"

"Judas!" he whispered. "Last time I seen Mary, was walking out that door with him—eight, nine months ago.

Lord God, mister, you don't think—"

"Unfortunately, I do," I said. "You got any idea where he used to take her when he took her out?"

The blonde spoke up then.

"Down on Lover's Lane," she said. "Tried to take me down there too, once; but I wouldn't go. Didn't like his eyes. And, mister—"

"Yes, baby?" I said, tiredly.

"You ought to talk to the girls at Tiger Lil's. They come in here sometimes, when they're wore out from pounding the pavement."

"What about them?" I said sharply.

"Four, five of them have upped and vanished. They—they think he's kind of crazy. But they don't know for sure 'cause all the ones who had anything to do with him ain't never come back from the rides he took 'em on. . . ."

"You tell me one thing, baby," I said. "Why'd the last three or four of them go out with him after the first one didn't come back?"

"Well," the blonde said, "he was fairly rolling in dough, mister. Always dressed to kill—"

So, I thought, it figures. Gilly's money, which she had to give him, for the same reason she had to give him herself. . . .

"And he told them," the waitress went on, "that his sister had fallen into that kind of a life. And ever since she died, he'd devoted his time and a part of his immense fortune to setting poor girls like them in a decent trade once more. He—was so sweet 'n gentle-spoken. If it hadn't been for them wild eyes o' his, maybe I'd of—"

I turned to the bartender.

"Mac," I said, "have you got a phone?"

But it wasn't that easy. It wasn't until the morning of the day before Greg was to swing that we found those bodies.

They weren't down on Lover's Lane. They were in the last place we'd ever thought of looking for them: in the garden of the MacAllister mansion. Then I remembered that Michael had mentioned, casually, in passing, this business about Tim's insisting upon serving as gardener as well, about his boasting of his green thumb. It was green, all right; because there weren't just six or seven of them. There were twelve.

Nurse Meadows we identified by her white uniform— or what was left of it. Mary Lenox, the waitress, by her gold teeth. But the rest were going to take too much time; and I couldn't wait. Chief Watson and I took the express to Montgomery.

It was midnight when we got there, six hours before Greg was to die. But I'll give Governor Comer credit: when we told his secretary our errand over the phone, the Governor received us even at that hour.

He listened to my story. Turned to Chief Watson.

"Chief," he said, "as a public official, you vouch for Mr. Lynne's story?"

"Absolutely, sir," Chief Watson said, "Heck, Governor, I was there when they was dug up!"

The Governor smiled. As a politician, he must have been relieved at not having to hang so prominent a citizen as my brother Greg. . . .

"You win," he said. "Chief, tell my secretary to get Birmingham on the phone."

Even after that, I played it smart. The Chief and I went up to Tuscaloosa. Stopped at the local police headquarters for reinforcements. Drove out to Byrce Hospital.

Then, as I had requested, they waited outside, their ears cocked, and let me enter Tim's room alone.

"Tim," I said, "you're one hell of a deacon, aren't you?"

He stared at me. But he didn't say anything.

"A traitor to Christ's Avengers," I went on. "Took your

solemn oath to have no more to do with women; now look at you!"

"I say, sir," he said solicitously. "Don't you think you'd better lie down?"

"No, Tim," I said; "I've got the goods on you all right. I've just had a talk with Mary Lennox, and she says—"

His eyes were on me. I could see them start to glitter.

"That you're guilty of her," I went on, smoothly. "Furthermore, Tilly Meadows says the same thing and—"

"Sir!" he said. "You *are* daft, you know! Neither of them could have—"

"Nor Grace Knox?" I pressed home mercilessly. "Nor Sue Schneider? Sally DuBois? Mildred Harris? Phoebe Holt? Or—"

He took a step toward me, his eyes flaming.

"Did you," he said almost pleasantly, "also see Mrs. Ames when you made that trip to hell, Mr. Lynne? She was there, too, wasn't she—queening it over all the rest of the dead strumpets I killed? You've found out. Went digging around my garden, didn't you? Wondered why my flowers grew so big and bright. Best fertilizer on earth, that! All the jolly dead trollops! Dead and in hell, where they belong!"

"Yes," I said. "You've called it, Tim."

"But you don't imagine I'm going to let you get out of here alive, do you?" he snarled. "You don't think you'll have the pleasure of seeing me kick and choke in your lout of a brother's place? Oh, no, Mr. Geoffry Lynne, gentleman, so-called—as if you ruddy Yanks could ever be! You're getting yours, now!"

Then he jumped me. In two seconds I knew I was fighting for my life. I'd never imagined so small a man could be so strong. Not even a maniac. If Chief Watson and the others hadn't come into that room when they did, I shouldn't be among those present, now.

EPILOGUE

A Summing Up

I was sitting on the porch of Hero's house with Michael and Greg. Hero was not with us. She was lying down, inside. Heddy MacAllister was taking care of her. Oh, yes, they'd let Heddy out. She was quite all right now. Even happy. With her share of the MacAllister money—Henry had left some bequests to charity; and Gillian hadn't bothered to make a will, thinking, characteristically, that she was going to live forever, I suppose—she'd bought a smart dress shop in Atlanta, Georgia, which was far enough away. Nobody knew her there, or had heard about her past. The only reason she was still in town was that she had waited to attend Michael's wedding.

Which had taken place that morning, in Anniston, with Greg and me for witnesses. I think the justice of the peace was a trifle shocked. When you looked at Hero closely, now, you could tell.

"Jeff," Michael said, "just what are you going to do now?"

"I'm going back to France," I said. "Had a letter from Lisette two weeks ago. Seems the poor baker dropped dead from overwork. Should have expected that. Keeping a whole *quartier* supplied with bread is hot, back-breaking work; and being married to Lisette—well, the same adjectives apply. She's afraid I won't like her anymore since she's gotten *trop grosse*—she weighs sixty-seven kilos now. But I don't mind. That will make her a little less restless. Guess I'll make it legal this time. I'm getting a bit old for adventuring. . . ."

"We wanted you to stay for the christening," Michael said.

"Sorry," I said; "that's still too far off. If I don't get to Paris soon, Lisette will have found herself another *boulanger*. Draft Greg. He'll make a fine godpappy. . . ."

"Tell me, Jeff," Michael said, "just why did Gilly insist upon bringing Tim Nelson back with us? Even by then she must have known what he was like. . . ."

"She did," I said; "and he's the one man on her list she wanted no part of. She loathed him; but—"

"She got into bed with him, just the same," Michael said. I was surprised at the lingering pain in his voice.

"Only because she had to," I told him. "For the same reason she had to keep him on as chauffeur, bring him back to the States. Because he was blackmailing her. And he wasn't content with just money. He demanded her snowy flesh as well. . . ."

"Blackmailing her?" Michael said. "Gilly? I'd have said that was impossible!"

"Yet, he was," I said; "and by the methods you, yourself, suggested to me, sometime ago: her fear of losing her freedom; and, in this case, her life. You see, Michael, on one of her pub-crawling expeditions, Gilly stumbled upon Phil Linton, the best cat burglar in London. That was who the Greek letter phi—you know, a fat 'O' cut through with a vertical bar, and followed by the number two for second-story man—indicated in her diary. I knew Phil. Quite a character. Small, wiry, handsome as a matinee idol. So, as the price of the usual kind of excitement she provided him, she got him to take her along on a few of his jewelry raids. For kicks. Dressed in black tights and mask. Anyhow, she slowed him down, being a woman, and not knowing the tricks of the trade. So they got caught. And somebody opened fire. A policeman was killed—"

I paused.

"You don't have to spell it out for me," Michael said wearily. "I know London. Policemen don't carry guns unless their assignment is considered very risky. Cornering a second-story man would not be so considered. No professional burglar would have been idiot enough to carry a gun, knowing, as a pro would have, the difference between the penalties for armed robbery and plain burglary. What caliber were the slugs?"

"Twenty-two," I said. "The gun was never found. . . ."

"Naturally," Michael said; "it's upstairs in my safe right now."

"Nor did the police have much to go on. Her hair was covered. Her eyes were masked. That she was female was evident from the merest glimpse of that skin-tight black outfit she had on, with nothing under it. Seems to have bemused the bobbies no end. So she got away—"

"Back to our hotel?" Michael said.

"No; with the police after her, she didn't dare. Nor could she risk going back to Phil's flat to change back into her clothes. It seems she hid in an alley until Tim drove up a certain street as she had told him to—"

"You mean he was in on it, too?" Michael said.

"Of course not! Tim Nelson wasn't a part of the plot except in so far as she had duped him. And, as I said before, she didn't have time to change back into street clothes, arriving in that skin-tight sheath, thus arousing both Tim's suspicious and his all too easily aroused desires. So he was free to press his advantage. He took her to his cottage in the country that very night. . . ."

Michael shuddered a little.

"And to keep her in line," he said sadly, "Tim would send her those threatening notes pasted on her own blue stationery, with that flaming sword of his drawn in her own violet ink. . . . I threw you off there, Jeff. Since it never occurred to me that the murderer was an inmate of the house and had access to her things—"

"No," I said; "you didn't, Michael. Your guess was probably right. Frankly, I haven't even checked that point. But in all his long career, Tim Nelson never did anything either that stupid or that childish. What reason would he have had to send her threatening notes, when he could threaten her verbally all he pleased as he drove her about? No—that was one of Gilly's tricks, all right; and, I submit, coming from her, it was anything but stupid. She didn't dare accuse Tim openly; but she gave you good enough clues then and there to hang him, had you acted—"

"Only I didn't act," Michael sighed; then: "I suppose that Klovac dug up all this information for you?"

"Yes," I said. "Fred's an ace. He's still apologizing for not remembering that it was only after Gilly came upon him having an idle chat with Tim—about the weather, that she started trying to find out how much he knew about her London escapades. If he had remembered that, he swears he could have solved the case for me, months ago. . . ."

Michael looked at me.

"Jeff," he said, "if Tim was only interested in—that— why'd he kill her? Sure way to spoil his fun, it seems to me."

I didn't suppose that Michael really cared anymore,

so I told him. Tim had been laboring under the delighted misapprehension that he was the father of Gilly's unborn child. With all the contenders there were for that dubious honor, the whole thing had degenerated into a low comedy turn, from my point of view. And his motive for killing Gillian MacAllister was another thing I put down in my notebook of basic plot ideas, along with all the cheap, petty, mean, idle, silly, stupid, senseless reasons for which people do ninety-seven per cent of everything they do.

It was snobbery.

Snobbery, by God! He was frightfully proud that he was in a position to perform services above and beyond the call of duty for madame. He also took good care of two of the downstairs maids, who had survived because he was afraid they'd be too quickly missed. He had also hugged to his bosom a warm delight at the ironic vengeance he was taking upon the world of his betters, the world that daily scorned and humilated him.

I knew all that because he told me himself, talking frankly and freely, when I went to visit him in jail.

"'Is little tyke, y'know, was going to be brought up like a blinking lord! No matter that 'e'd 'ave to carry another man's name. Served the ruddy toff jolly well right, it did!"

But thinking it over, he had gotten frightened. Had brooded over the fact that no little bugger of his could possibly look enough like Michael to fool the world. Had decided to get the money from Gillian to finance a trip home to England. Had, finally, and fatally, arrived in time to hear Gillian's quarrel with Greg, hear her say:

"Noble of you, Greg. Only the child's not yours, either. Its father is—"

Then she had dropped her voice, so he could not hear the name.

He had heard Greg shout: "Goddamn you, you shameless witch, take that!" Heard the blow. The thud as Gilly fell. Heard, too, a moment or two later, Greg's trembling footsteps going down the stairs.

He'd tiptoed to the door, called softly:

"Madame—Mrs. Ames—open up, if you please. . . ."

And Gillian, recovering from that love tap Greg had given her, having no more than a scratch on her chin, and a rather nasty cut on the back of her head where she'd struck the andiron in falling, staggered to the door and let him in.

Tim had been solicitous at first. Had stanched the flow of blood with his handkerchief. Then she'd said, rather sharply:

"Oh, leave me be, Tim! What the devil did you come up here for anyhow?"

And he'd told her.

She'd laughed, said:

"You've nothing to fear, my friend. There's no danger of the brat's looking like you—none at all. You see, Tim, the baby actually is—my husband's. . . ."

He'd caught her by the shoulders then. Shook her, forgetting his painfully acquired diction in his rage, slipping back into his native cockney, snarling:

"You lie! 'E's mine! Th' blinkin' little tyke is mine, 'e is!"

She looked him straight in the face and said it, then; perhaps because subconsciously the death wish was already in her; because she must have realized what her life was going to be like from here on in, with Michael, or without him, the dull slow years stretching out ahead, her beauty fading; and every man's hand, and more especially every woman's, lifted against her through her fault, through her own fault, through her most grievous fault, so she said it, spat those words out venomously through set teeth:

"You low-bred cur! Don't you realize I'd die before giving birth to a whelp of yours?"

And died. Of those words. Of that monumentally ill-— or well-chosen phrase.

Michael looked at me.

"Poor Gilly," he said softly, "do you suppose there's any possible forgiveness for her—wherever she is?"

I started to bring him up sharp against all that adolescent cant he used to spout about the "eyeless, faceless void we deify." But then I saw his eyes.

"Have you forgiven her?" I asked him.

"Yes," he whispered.

"Then that is enough," I said.

Madrid, Spain   June 20th, 1960